The Nesting Dolls

a novel by

Cynthia Rogers Parks

Leigh Walker Books

Published by arrangement with
Leigh Walker Books
Atlanta, Georgia

10 9 8 7 6 5 4 3 2 1

ISBN 978-0-9832431-5-1

Acknowledgments

I am deeply grateful to my dear friends, Genny Marsden, Joan Ingraham, and Janice Hoover for their faithful reading of my manuscript in draft stages, and to my daughter, Angela Baldasare, the discerning, engaged reader of whom every writer dreams. Special thanks is also owed to Dr. Hanchao Lu, professor of Technology and Society at the Georgia Institute of Technology, for his help with the historical details and local geography of postwar Shanghai. Finally, my love and gratitude to my husband, Adrian Bowers, who is simply the engine that keeps me going.

The Nesting Dolls

Prologue

I will begin Olena's part of the story in the place where Maria left her. In that place where Maria would always remember her and where, long after they had parted, Maria would still persist in seeing her, imagining her mother moving through the shabby but comfortable rooms of their flat on Rue Joffre.

It was in this place after all, this dry and draftless two-bedroom flat in Shanghai's French Concession, where life had finally taken a better turn for all of them. If Olena Petrova had not exactly been happy here—not in the way she had been happy in carefree youth when hunger and want and fear were still the merest of abstractions—then here at least she had found a substitute. Here at least she had begun to have hope for her daughters.

I will wake Olena Petrova here, and to a most extraordinary day. Her day will begin miraculously. It will progress unusually. It will yield many surprises.

It is beyond my power to make all of those surprises pleasant ones. This is my story to flesh, but its bones are not mine, and much of the telling is beyond my control. I am bound by certain bald truths, and hampered by details of recorded history. I must be guided by the memories of the living and acknowledge the authority of the dead. I am constrained by dates certain in Maria's own diary and by the words of her own hand.

I cannot change the fact that even Olena's fair substitute, her hope, is already misplaced, and that soon she must learn it. There is only so much I can do. But I will do what I can.

I will wake her pleasantly. To an unusual day. I will wake her from a dream of her girlhood. A dream of walking in the early morning with her sister, Ana, in the gardens of the Rose Palace. In the dream she had felt the soft warmth of the early sunlight on her face. She had heard the twitter of birds and Ana's high, silvery laughter. She had seen clearly—the last remembered image—Ana's slender white hand reaching for a flower. The flower had been a rose, perfect and garnet red, two glistening round crystals of dew standing high on its velvet petals.

Part I.

Olena's Doll

21 August 1945

I know that Mama doesn't think about happiness anymore. Even for Katya and me she doesn't pray for happiness. She prays only that we will always have food to eat and a clean place to live and that we will be safe. Mama has lost too much to believe in being happy. But I do. I intend to be happy!

From the diary of Maria Petrova, translated from the French

Chapter I.

There were no roses in the Petrov apartment. No roses, as far as Olena knew, anywhere on Rue Joffre. This late in the year, almost September, there probably weren't roses to be had in all of Shanghai, unless in some florist's case. Yet the perfume of roses, definitely roses, had reached her even in sleep. On waking the fragrance was still in her nostrils and had come and gone all morning. The whispery sweet scent had wafted up from her cup of tea, in the motions of brushing her hair and drying her hands, from ordinary objects and with the most common of morning tasks.

She had dreamed of her childhood before. Not often in the last years, when it was rare enough even to sleep the night through, more common to lurch into wakefulness at some silent, predawn alarm, to rise then to pace and pray for her daughters, no trace or remnant of any dream at all left in her conscious mind. But there had been a time when she had dreamt of the old days often, and not all of those dreams had been pleasant. They might begin innocently enough. With some lovely vignette from the past—the two of them, perhaps, she and Ana, taking their morning lessons from Monsieur Pécaut, or picnicking beside the river. But it had been the nature of those dreams to turn dark. To bring other memories best forgotten and a lingering sadness to her day. This dream had been different, thoroughly pleasant, leaving her rested and calm. But rare as that was, it wasn't the miracle.

The miracle wasn't the dream, but the lingering, preternatural fragrance, this scent that somehow could drift across the very membrane of consciousness.

There had surely been roses, though she could not honestly now recall them, long ago in her family's gardens. And it was true that the Gubinov estate had been called by that name. There hadn't been a peasant in eight day's ride who hadn't known of the location, and inhabitants, of the Rose Palace. But it was the distinctive pink limestone, the façade of the manor house, which had given rise to the name. Certainly not flowers. Not roses.

And what of Ana? Dead these twenty-five years. What meaning was there in Ana's small young hand reaching for the flower? In the droplets—two of them—of dew?

The rose was the Blessed Virgin's flower. Its perfume could be a message from Our Lady herself. But how to put it all together? To understand what it meant, and why the message of the dream had been visited upon her in this way, and just now.

All of this Olena pondered as she dressed and put up her hair, moving to the tiny kitchen to make tea, sitting down only long enough only to sip a single cup and to chew a single bite, dry and tasteless, pulled from the heel of last night's bread. In moments she had stood again, rinsed her teacup and capped the samovar, breathing again the scent of roses rising from the charcoal. And then, abruptly, she sat down again at the little kitchen table.

Everything about this morning was odd. Not only had she slept well, and so late, awaking to the memory of the dream and the smell of the roses, but there was the remarkable fact of being alone at this hour in their rooms. Sergei and Maria had somehow managed to rise, breakfast, and dress without waking her, a thing so strange as to be nearly impossible, a thing so strange that she couldn't recall it ever happening before.

Certainly they were capable enough. Sergei ate almost nothing these days but what the hotel fed him and assumed the care himself of his ridiculous doorman's uniform. And Maria was already seventeen, a working woman herself now that the war had ended and the Americans had come. But these two had always needed her for something. To start the tea or cobble some breakfast or find clean linen to wash with. Sergei found it hard to hurry and would ask her after the hour three or more times in a morning, and Maria could mewl and hiss like a kitten if her hair went wrong or if she couldn't find a shoe or a stocking. But not today. Today they had gone about their business independently. Quiet as rabbits.

She could not quite make herself believe that this was the meaning of it. That the Holy Mother would send her a dream and the scent of her flower as a sign that Olena's own mothering, almost, was over. This morning, for the first time, she could see that it *would* end.

For Katya, safe now, and married, perhaps it was already done. And now Maria had reliable work and apparently could manage at least one morning all on her own.

Olena smiled to herself, thinking how this morning's calm contrasted with the frenzy of a typical morning not so long ago. Then she would have risen at dawn, bone weary from staying up late to plan for her own day's lessons after preparing their meal, then tutoring the girls, hearing their prayers and getting them off to bed. For some of that time they had shared rooms with the Kropotkins and those mornings had been a *cauchemar logistique*—a logistical nightmare of heating water for seven and allowing each their minutes in the bath, the children, and adults too, stumbling sleepily into one another while she scurried about, feeding and dressing the girls, washing their faces and grooming their hair, gathering their tablets and books and coats, getting them all out of the door just on time—or earlier, if there were no coins that day for a rickshaw or the tram.

She could scarcely remember now the mornings of those even earlier times. Before she had been given the teaching post at the French school, when she had still clerked in the shops, or labored, before that, in the canning factory, or earlier still when there was nothing but selling boiled water in the streets.

Those days certainly were now behind her. There were only three of them now in far better rooms than they had shared with the Kropotkins. She was the only one still to be off to the school in the mornings and now they were here, in the French Concession, where the school was close by.

Perhaps that *was* the meaning of the dream and the rose. A benediction from the Holy Mother because the tasks of her own mothering would soon be set aside.

But which were the two droplets, then? Maria and Katya, her daughters? Or Sergei and Maria, the two she still looked after? For surely she had mothered her husband, too. Not his person so much, but his fragile manly pride. It had suffered—it still suffered—so many terrible wounds. In her own heart she knew that, without her, Sergei might have given up. That he might have given in, as so many had done in those early years, to drunkenness and despair. Better soldiers than Sergei had lain down to their last sleep in the gutters or doorways of the narrow streets. To be carted off in the morning in frozen rigor, already embalmed by vodka.

If for nothing else he had needed her to confirm his own worth. To supply the constant reassurances that better times would come and that she didn't regret tying her life to his. Poor, brooding Sergei. No, he would always need her. And always in the same way.

A loud jangling ring came from the sitting room, instantly scattering her thoughts and causing her heart to make a small jump in her chest. Ah! The new telephone. The gift from their son-in-law which so delighted Maria but which Olena herself had not yet begun to appreciate. They had managed twenty-three years in the city without a telephone in the house. For her part, they could have managed twenty-three more.

Olena stood up and hurried to the telephone, less curious about her caller than she was eager to stop its noise.

"Mama? Are you there?" It was Katya's voice coming through the heavy black receiver, as clear as if she were standing only steps away.

"I'm here, kiska."

"Are you dressed yet, Mama? I was wondering if it was too soon to send the car."

Dressed? The car? What questions were these for Katya to be asking, so early and over the telephone?

And then she remembered. It was a banker's holiday and there were no classes today. It was foolishness, really, a holdover from before the war. The foreign banks had been closed in Shanghai for almost four years now. But for some reason the French school had still observed the holiday throughout the entire Japanese occupation. Some day she must remember to ask about it. But for now Katya's questions made sense, and Olena remembered their promise, made more than a week ago, that they would spend the holiday together. *What a very strange morning this was.*

"I'm dressed, Katya. You can send your car. But are you not coming yourself?"

"I'm thinking not, Mama. I've a few more things to do. The amah and I are making a special lunch for you. Do you mind it terribly? If I don't come, I mean?"

"Of course I don't mind, little goose. But don't fuss for my sake. It will be enough to have the visit."

"Oh, I *want* to fuss!" Katya cried. "I want you to be very impressed! Sidor is leaving now. He'll be there within the hour."

Olena said goodbye and placed the receiver carefully down in its cradle. There it was again. The drifting scent of roses as if borne on moving air. That was it then. Katya and Maria.

In the time while she waited Olena went about tidying the rooms and spreading the coverlets over their own bed and Maria's. In Maria's bedclothes she found the small tablet where Maria had been practicing at making the Oriental characters. Olena tossed it aside, noting a blotch of ink that had ruined the pillow casing. Maria's time could be better spent on something else. At the very least, if she must spoil a pillowcase, on improving her English stenography. The Americans hadn't hired her to write in Japanese. Or Chinese, if that's what this was. Maria said the characters were the same. But either one, why did it matter? The child was still stubbornly impractical. Completely without her sister's common sense.

In under half an hour there was a knock at the door and she opened it to old Sidor, who stood with his cap in his hand, bobbing his head in greeting. The big black roadster stood idling at the curb. Olena ran a hand over her hair and hurried to pluck up her handbag. At the wooden ikon hanging by the doorframe she quickly crossed herself and stepped out, pulling the door behind her and locking it with the key. If evil wished to enter, it would find its way. Still. One must take precautions.

Sidor held the door and Olena entered the car, settling herself comfortably in the spacious back seat. She had greeted Sidor in Russian and thought he had given her a mumbling reply, but she knew it was useless to try to engage the taciturn old man in real conversation. Perhaps he had found it difficult to communicate with his previous English employers. Perhaps they had taught him to keep silent. She leaned back into the unaccustomed luxury of the sedan's upholstery and looked out through the window as they pulled away. The September day was clear and warm, spring-like almost, though the trees in the French Concession were already losing their leaves. She felt herself strangely becoming a spectator, a new-eyed observer of the city she knew so well.

The city was the same, and yet distinctly different, some of its changes more sensed than visible. The streets, if that were possible, were more crowded than ever. Now that it was safe, refuges were pouring into the city from the outskirts where their villages and crops had been plundered or burned by the enemy. They would find food scarce in Shanghai, but at least there was the chance here of scavenging something. Something better—she had heard the stories—than the boiled bark of trees. The sidewalks were a living river of peasants flowing in both directions. They stepped over and between the tangled limbs of others sleeping on the pavement.

The Japanese soldiers were mostly gone. Most of them had been garrisoned, advised to keep a low profile for their own safety even though General Chiang had warned the citizenry not to show them hostility. There were still little clots of them to be seen, though, and still carrying arms, their drab uniforms now reduced to filth and tatters, their faces dull and expressionless as they looked out on the crowd. But for the most part the Japanese had disappeared, been whisked away and replaced by other soldiers—the Chinese in their own ragged yellow uniforms and straw sandals, the Americans, in their crisp starched khakis and good leather shoes. There were American jeeps everywhere in the traffic now and other new kinds of vehicles, too. A transport truck filled with standing American soldiers passed by the car and a roar of delight lifted from the sidewalk and followed it down the street.

Horns blared all around them and Sidor braked every few yards in the stuttering traffic, but he used his own horn only once, when a pedicab wheeled suddenly across their lane. Its furiously peddling driver flashed them a toothless grin. The city was the same and yet different. Vendors still hawked their wares at passersby. The old letter writer still squatted at the same corner. The tall, bearded Sikh policemen still blew their whistles in the snarl of traffic. But now there were signs everywhere above the shops congratulating the Allies and the Nationalists. Stores were advertising "Victory" sales and "Peace" brands. A portrait of General Chiang, three stories high, hung on a building above the street.

There was also something else—less visible, but still obvious, to one who knew the city well. There was a definite electricity in the streets today, and the pace of everything seemed, if not more hurried, at least more purposeful. As though the human river was now flowing *somewhere*, and *something*, possibly something good, would be reached at the end of it. The streets seemed imbued with a new energy, an inordinate gaiety. In doorways the shopkeepers stood smiling or laughing together happily in groups of two or three. A naked Chinese toddler waving a paper American flag ambled about unmolested, today annoying no one. Even the grunts and cries of the coolies, struggling as always with their overloaded carts and preposterous bundles sounded almost gleeful. The war was truly over. And whether or not anyone knew what that might mean for the future, the city was celebrating.

In the Central District on Honan Road they passed the Police Station, the American Club, and then the block-long building that had housed the Shanghai Municipal Council. In one of its offices, she surmised, her son-in-law, Grieg Waechter, was going about his morning's duties, oblivious to the fact that she and Sidor were passing in his own car, making their way to his house. How well it had gone for Katya after all! To have fallen in love with this handsome young German and to have her love returned.

Sergei didn't like the Germans. The Germans, he said, were enemies of Russia. But Katya's Grieg, like their own girls, had been born here in Shanghai. He knew almost nothing of Germany, or of Russia. Little of the Nazis or the Reds. He was only a young man but already a shrewd businessman and his position with the Council had provided him important connections. Those connections had meant a great deal to their household in the last years. Even in the early days of their courtship he had been able to procure coffee and sugar, even first grade flour. Sergei had grumbled, but he'd eaten the delicious white bread. He'd fallen completely silent when Grieg's connections had produced the house on Columbia Road.

The din of the city gradually diminished and the car picked up speed as they traveled on westward into the city's better suburbs where shops and the throng of pedestrians gave way to quiet streets and private single residences behind brick walls and iron gates. This was the part of the city with which she was least familiar, that until only recently had been as alien to all of them as an unexplored continent. Most of the fine homes here had been owned by Europeans, the bankers and business taipans who had once controlled Shanghai. Here and there she saw the red-lettered notices in Japanese characters still tacked on the doors. Maria, perhaps, could actually read them, but their meaning was clear to anyone. They proclaimed these homes the property of the Emperor. The former owners of these houses—if they had not been among the lucky ones to flee Shanghai in time—had probably been interned in the Japanese camps. For the first time in this unusual, miraculous morning Olena felt the tightening in her chest, her body's familiar response whenever she sensed danger to her offspring. The war was really over now. She had seen the truth of that all morning in the city's jubilation. Why then did she have this vague unease?

Long ago, as far back as the days of her girlhood in the Rose Palace, she had cared about the politics and principles of war. She had even, from a position of comfort and privilege, felt some secret sympathies for the soviet ideals and wondered if it were really true that only a great upheaval, a revolution, could bring about great progress. Alexander had freed the serfs, the Americans their slaves, and the world had not come to an end after all. But in Russia she had seen one war merge into another and the clarity of ideals completely obscured by violence, washed away by the tide of blood. And hadn't it been the same in Shanghai? It was all her children had ever known. National war. War in Europe. World War. One war was always superseded by another, today's politics becoming the *raison d'être,* the excuse, for tomorrow's bloodshed. None of the big ideas, the grand ideals, really even mattered.

Sergei thought they mattered. After all this time he still went to his little anti-communist meetings and fed off the worthless agitations brewed in *Slovo* or the other anti-Soviet newspapers. They held nothing but rumor and speculation and false hope. There would be no second *good* revolution to replace the one gone bad. And she knew they were never going home. But Sergei still looked to a new war for salvation and still mourned the outcome of an old one. After all these years he could still lapse into black depressions, groaning aloud and weeping like a child at what they said had been done to Nicholas and Alexandra, to the precious Tzaravitch and the other children. "Your heart is made of leather," he would tell her, when she would not help him to recall the name of some fallen soldier or refused to play his sad little games of reliving pointless victories.

Maybe so. Perhaps it was even turning to stone. She had felt only the barest twinge of pity for the English banker and his family whose house had been given to her son-in-law. She, who was the only one of them to know what it was like to have your home, your prized possessions, taken away, had felt almost nothing on Grieg's announcement that the house had been given to them. War was a game that men played. A game, it seemed, that men would ever play. If this turn in the game must benefit someone, why should it not be her Katya?

But there. That was the problem. The source of the tightening in her chest. It *was* a game. And the morning's drive had shown her that the rules had changed. Again. What might it mean to Katya? And to her handsome young husband.

They had come now finally to Columbia Road and the site of

Katya's house, and Olena crossed herself again as Sidor pulled through an open gate into the short drive between tall evergreen privets. She was suddenly terribly eager to see Katya, to take her hands and look into her face and see what there was to read there.

Katya, it seemed, was eager too. Olena had not followed Sidor more than a dozen steps to the garden-side door before it sprang open, and Katya fairly leaped at them, laughing and exuberant.

"Bienvenue!" Katya cried. And then, "Dabro pazhalavat!"

Olena accepted, and returned, her daughter's greetings and caresses. This was Katya's home and she should get to choose, but Olena was glad today that Katya had not strung on *Willkommen*—to signal that they would be conversing in German.

Katya was radiant. As beautiful, almost, as she had been a year ago on the day of her wedding. Today she wore a slim-fitting crepe dress, flared at the hem, which Olena had never seen before. But its lines and the brilliant blue were wonderfully flattering to her daughter's skin and her tall, willowy figure. Katya wrapped one arm around Olena's shoulders and practically carried her inside, kissing her twice en route on the top of her head as though Olena herself were the child. This was Sergei's daughter as surely as Maria was hers. Where Sergei and Katya were tall and strong and athletic, she and Maria were short and light-boned—toys almost next to these two.

It was cool inside the house, and so much dimmer than outdoors that Olena's eyes took a moment to adapt. It was quite a beautiful house, really. Cool and calm and tasteful. Its uncluttered mix of new and antique furniture, the paintings, imported porcelains and small exotic accessories, were as carefully considered and quietly understated as the English themselves, those who had taken centuries to pick and choose, to acquire and discard from their colonial plundering, reducing themselves at last to only what was simple and fine, beautifully made or exceedingly rare. This house, this particular boon from the

Japanese, had come not only lavishly furnished and with a fully larded pantry and wine cellar, but with two house coolies, an old Amah and a number one houseboy, in addition to Sidor who served as chauffeur and gardener. All together it represented a standard of living that no Petrov had ever imagined in Shanghai. A style of living that no one, other than Olena herself, had even imagined anywhere.

Katya led her into the house, propelling her through the large fragrant kitchen into the adjoining dining room where the table had been beautifully laid with china and crystal and where the old Amah was setting down a silver tureen of soup.

Olena waited until the amah had left the room, and then she lifted the lid to peek inside.

"Oroshka! I didn't know you could make it!" It looked wonderful. The classic Russian cold soup of vegetables, potatoes, eggs and ham, cooked with kvass.

"Oh, I couldn't!" Katya cried. "Until the amah and I practiced it three times. Grieg has had oroshka every night for a week!"

"Well, you've certainly succeeded in impressing me," Olena laughed.

The soup was delicious, a meal in itself, but Katya had also made a variety of canapés, delights like salted herring which Olena had not tasted in decades. By the time that the amah had brought coffee and dessert, a smooth creamy kisel made of berries, Olena was thoroughly satiated, as well as a little sleepy.

"It's wonderful, isn't it," said Katya, "about Maria's position? The torture you put us through has paid off well for her, at least."

Olena smiled. Katya was obviously referring to the language lessons that had been part of the girls' daily routine almost since their births. With Maria it had been almost effortless, her gift for tongues surpassing even Olena's own. But Katya had always resisted, preferring some rowdy game or the ease of lapsing into Russian, her father's language, and the language, for their father's sake, of their daily lives and their household. Katya had been a good student, too. Especially at mathematics. And not one to get into trouble with the teachers. But then, as now, Katya seemed a little envious of her sister's special gift.

"And not for you?" asked Olena. "Do you think we'd be here, now, groaning from this lovely lunch, if you knew only Russian?"

Katya laughed delightedly.

"No, I don't suppose we would! My German is still terrible, but it's better than Grieg's Russian. Without the torture of your lessons, Mama, I could never have seduced him."

"Hush!" said Olena, "I said nothing about seduction. I meant only that you two could not have conversed. That it would have been difficult to come to know one another and to . . ."

"Mama," said Katya, reaching across the table to lay her hand on Olena's. "I understand what you meant. And I shouldn't tease you. I know what you did for us. I know that you earned almost nothing at the school after our tuitions. I remember how you and Papa would squabble about it. If you'd left us alone, to run in the streets all day with the other children . . . well, I'm not really so ungrateful. I remember."

Olena thought back to the beginning of her strange day. To her own recollections of those other mornings, years ago.

"Really?" she asked. "What do you remember?"

"More than you think," said Katya, solemnly. "Maria and I have talked about it. How little there was. How you pretended, always, that *you* were never hungry. *You* were never cold. Papa was never afraid. We do remember, Mama. You must forgive us if we pretend to forget."

Katya's eyes were glistening now and Olena felt ashamed that she had asked such a question. This was not a door she'd meant to open. This was no conversation for a holiday.

"My memory, though," Katya said, suddenly bright again, "is not as good as Maria's! Maria seems to believe that she began life in the Rose Palace!"

Olena drew in a sharp breath. *The Rose Palace?* She had

really thought, she could almost have sworn, that she had shared little of those days with her children. They knew their Papa had been a soldier. They knew a good bit about the end of it. About the terrible flight from Vladivostok and the stop in Woosong and the awful voyage to Shanghai. They knew because Sergei spoke of it. Because he *would* still talk of it, if anyone would listen. But if she herself had ever traveled so far back in time, so much farther still in time, to burden her innocent children with memories, with visions, of that lost, long ago world, she could not remember it at all. It must have happened in a state of terrible weakness. A state of unconscionable selfishness.

She was afraid to ask Katya more and was thrashing about for a change in topic, about to tell her about this morning and the novelty of her father and sister stealing away so quietly and leaving her asleep, when Katya startled her by changing the subject herself.

"Eggers is dead," said Katya abruptly.

Olena was confused.

"Eggers? Who is Eggers?"

"The Englishman," Katya said. "Roland Eggers. The man who owns this house."

Olena said nothing, but she felt immediately the constriction in her chest.

"He died in the camp at Lunghwa," said Katya. "A heart attack apparently. And not long at all after the Japanese took them. After the Kempeitai came here, to the house, and took them. Eggers and his wife."

"And there was a child, too," she went on. "A boy of about twelve. His books and toys and things are still upstairs. He must be rather shy, I think. A collector of stamps."

Katya took a slow sip from her coffee cup.

"And how do you know?" Olena asked. "How did you learn all of this?"

"From Sidor," said Katya. "I have made him tell me

everything."

Olena leaned back in her chair. She wasn't really surprised. There had been something secretive, something deep and troubled about the old man from the very beginning.

"Sidor is one of us, Mama. He came from Russia in twenty-two. Out of Vladivostok, just ahead of the Red army. The same as you and Papa."

"But Mama," she went on. "Sidor is a Jew. The son of a watchmaker from Danilov. The Eggers were the only ones to know it, you see. Sidor was a quiet man. Without friends or family. He was content with them, and they with him, and they gave him the place over the garage and the care of the garden, and of driving and watching the boy."

Now Katya took a deep breath. Her eyes were filling and her voice had become low and raspy.

"When the soldiers came and asked who else was in the household, Madam Eggers told them no one. No one else. An old amah and a Chinese coolie boy. A deaf Russian, she said, who prays all day to Jesus but is otherwise worthless. They let her pack one suitcase, Sidor said. And took them all away on the truck."

"But because of what she said to them, Sidor thinks—what they put that day in their reports—he didn't have to go to the ghetto in Hongkew. Instead he has spent almost three years here, guarding this empty house, and stealing food for the others. Weeding this lawn and tending this garden and keeping the car in repair."

Olena sighed. She had heard stories like these before. Even in war there were still such people.

"But Katya, what of Madame Eggers? What about your house?"

"She's alive," Katya said. "But not well. She and the boy are with friends in the International Settlement. She's returning to England soon. She won't be wanting this house."

"But what will it mean? Will it be sold? Who does this house belong to now?"

"I don't know," Katya said. "It will take some time to sort it out. But I don't want it either, Mama. Unless it can be had honestly."

"But Katya, don't be foolish! If Madam Eggers doesn't want it. If it's already . . ."

"I won't argue with you, Mama. I've argued too much over it already with Grieg. And besides, it's more complicated than that. Remember that Grieg is a German citizen. Unless there's someone like Madam Eggers to protect us, but someone this time who would say that *we're J*ews, it may be us in the camps soon, Mama. Grieg and me."

Olena was about to laugh at the joke, poor though it was, that her daughter had made. But the look on Katya's face stopped her. Of course! It was all upside down now. The marriage that had been the key to her daughter's safety could well now imperil it. She could see this now and knew that she had already felt it this morning though she had been unable to place her anxiety, to understand why she could not share in the city's celebration.

So that was it after all. Not a blessing but a warning. She touched a linen napkin to her lips and, as if to confirm her understanding, the delicate fragrance of roses was there in its fabric, or was stirred from the motion of laying it down again by her plate, but reached her nonetheless and made her certain. Not a blessing, but a warning.

They had talked more, and for hours, moving first to the cool, well-ordered living room and then outside to the trim grounds and to the delight of Sidor's small gardens. They had parted quietly and affectionately, having reviewed the possibilities calmly and agreeing that it was much too soon to make conjectures. The war was over now and there must certainly be good in that. There would be time for decisions as events unfolded.

It was already dusk when she left, and on the drive home, Olena was nodding and somnolent, paying no attention at all to the sights that had flowed by her window this morning. Those same sights were now being illuminated by thousands of electric lights, the whole of Shanghai becoming a glittering neon spectacle. But her thoughts now were on something other than the city's vibrant night face, and she stared through the windows unseeing. In what seemed half the time that it had taken to accomplish this morning's trip they were there, in the tree-lined streets of the French settlement, at the curb before their own place in Avenue Joffre.

Sidor opened her door and stepped chivalrously aside. She got out of the car and moved in the direction of her doorway, taking only a step or two before she heard the soft, solid thunk of the car door closing behind her. But on hearing it, she turned round again, returning instead to him, the quiet old Jew, the Russian, her countryman, who had confided so much in her daughter. He still stood beside the car, as dull and impassive as he had always seemed to her and yet, knowing him as she did now, not dull at all, but complex and subtle and unspeakably dear. His face did not change when she lifted her hand, taking the curve of his cheek in her palm and looking sincerely into his eyes.

"*Spasiba*," she said. "*Thank you*." And then she stood on tiptoe to plant a light kiss on his cheek and waited for nothing before moving to her door, easily finding the key in her handbag and slipping inside their flat. She was tired. It had been an unusual day. And while she couldn't begin, tonight, to place its meaning on the day's bewildering continuum, that faint perfume, the delicate fragrance of toilet water she had encountered on Sidor's cheek, had reminded her, again, of roses.

20 September 1945

Now we can be sure about it. The great flare that so many saw in the southern sky. I did not see it myself, but I heard the birds. Every pigeon in Shanghai took flight, I think, and now we know what startled them.

I cannot make myself glad about the terrible bombs that fell on the Japanese homeland. The newspapers say there are so many dead there. Many more even than here last summer when Dr. Chu and so many others were killed in Hongkew. But surely this is the end of the bombs. Finally the war is over and the world can begin anew.

From the diary of Maria Petrova, translated from the French

Chapter II.

"It just stinks," Callahan was saying. "It stinks to high heaven!"

Callahan's pink Irish cheeks were a little brighter than usual, but, as usual, he was talking with his mouth full. Charlie Atwood hesitated for a moment before dropping his mess tray on the table across from Krebs, but it was already too late. Callahan was already looking up at him expectantly, his mouth half open, a white slurry of mashed potatoes riding on his tongue.

"What stinks, Callahan?" Charlie asked. He pulled out a chair and sat down, allowing himself a barely audible martyr's sigh.

"Their stinking point system stinks!" said Callahan. "Look at this!" Callahan pushed a folded copy of *The Stars and Stripes* across the table and then jabbed viciously with the corner of his fork at a small article just below the fold.

Charlie picked up the newspaper and used the edge of his little finger to clear the spot of mashed potatoes that Callahan's fork had left on the headline. DEMOB PLAN ANNOUNCED, the headline read, and from there the article proceeded to explain the War Department's discharge plan for male enlisted personnel. It was a pretty complicated system actually, with various credits being awarded for months in service, months spent overseas, combat awards, even parenthood. Apparently, the critical score for being considered eligible for discharge was an 85.

"Yeah?" said Charlie, pushing the paper back towards Callahan. "So what's your beef?"

"My beef!" Callahan exploded. "Are you kidding? I've been in one hellhole or another for a year and eight months. I'm still flying the hump as a PFC while the brass keep their behinds warm at headquarters. I haven't had a furlough or a rotation since I got to Kunming. Now I find out that I'm twenty points shy of doing my bit. The war may be over for you assholes, but it's just beginning for me!"

The table went quiet, everyone a little surprised by Callahan's intensity. Hugh Callahan was a chronic griper. The kind of guy who could rain on an Easter parade. But he was the best radio op in the outfit and a real stand-up if you ever needed a favor. This was strong, even for Callahan. And everyone knew he had a sick mother back in the States. Maybe his complaint was legitimate this time.

Joe Janowski, Callahan's bunkmate, and the only one who had always seemed immune to Callahan's brown-offs, broke the silence with a chuckle.

"Aw, come on, Mick," Janowski said. He reached up beside him to knuckle the top of Callahan's red head. "Don't get yourself so worked up. It says it's a *temporary* point system. And you know the Army. They'll fix it up. After they've broken it two or three more times."

Charlie laughed with the others and then bent to his meal. It was the familiar shit-on-a shingle again, the sinewy little gravy-soaked squares that most of them took for water buffalo. But this time they'd been given the potatoes instead of the endless rice.

The point system didn't really interest him. He hadn't even tried to do his own math yet. But he couldn't help feeling a little empathy for Callahan's anger. Probably, if his own duty record, his Tech Sergeant's stripes, and the combat hours he'd spent lying on his belly in the hot, claustrophobic, four square feet of a B25's tail gunner compartment wasn't good enough for Uncle Sam, he was going to be a little irritated, too. In his own case, though, it would be merely the principle of the thing. Because he wasn't ready to go back.

In the weeks since the War Department had finally declared V-J Day, the thought had been churning inside him, leaving him confused, and guilty. But now, just now, he realized that the churning was gone. Unlike Callahan, maybe all of them, he felt no restless eagerness to return to the States in general, or to Hazel Grove, Georgia, in particular. He didn't care about their plan for demobilization. Because he wasn't going home.

"It says here," said Hitch Morgan, who was now in possession of the passed-down copy of the newspaper, "that Emperor's combat stars count three points each for personnel who have been shot at and a half point for those who haven't."

Morgan dropped the paper and looked up, an expression of comic bewilderment on his face.

"How they gonna' figure *that*?" Morgan asked.

"There you go, Mick!" said Janowski, clapping Callahan hard on the back. "All we have to do is count the fuselage holes in the Linda Luck! Even if we divide by six, I bet there's enough for the whole *crew* to be outta' here!"

The laughter erupting from this one produced one theatrical, but at least two genuine incidences of choking. Charlie himself spewed a swallow of tea halfway across the table.

"You stupid Polack!" Callahan fairly shouted. "You're

reading the wrong article! That's the one about the *Japanese* point system. We don't *have* an emperor, remember? And even if we did, he wouldn't give you three points a bullet!"

Charlie pushed his tray away, giving up completely on his lunch, but surrendering, again, to the laughter. Half the mess hall seemed to have heard Callahan this time, and a few soldiers began lobbing wadded napkins and pieces of bread at Janowski. Janowski's face was now nearly as red as Callahan's, but, sportingly, he pushed back his chair, stood up from the table, and gave dramatic formal bows to all four corners of the mess hall. Callahan, looking happier than he ever did, stood up, too. Both of them retrieved their trays and began making their way to the exit amid whistles and catcalls and a light hail of flying food.

Morgan, grinning, watched them go and then slid his tray down next to Krebs, taking the seat that Callahan had abandoned.

"Those two!" said Morgan, "the Mick and the Polack. Sometimes I think they're just putting on an act, you know."

Charlie and Jack Krebs exchanged a quick glance across the table. Morgan, really, was the slow one.

"I think you may be right, Hitch," Charlie said. "You might just be on to something there."

Krebs tipped his chair slightly behind Morgan and crossed his eyes for Charlie's benefit. It was the Harpo Marx bit he did when words were just unnecessary. Charlie looked away quickly and pressed hard on his mouth with his napkin. Morgan was a good man. He was just really, *really* thick.

"That point system thing, though," Morgan said. "That thing's messed up. I'll be a hundred years old before I get out of China."

Now Krebs leveled his chair.

"My personal favorite," he said, "is the parenthood credit. Twelve points for each child under 18 years, up to a limit of three children."

"See, Atwood? " Krebs continued. "I told you that you

shoulda' knocked up your cheerleader. A set of twins would have put you almost a third of the way home!"

Morgan thought this was pretty funny, too, but fortunately Krebs had kept his voice down. Only one nosey parker, halfway down the long table, was still paying attention.

"She's not a cheerleader," Charlie said. "Like you didn't know."

Krebs was just playing with him, not really betraying any confidences. But it felt awfully close and Charlie didn't like it. Krebs knew everything about Bonnie Jo Richards. Everything. Charlie had read him every one of her letters, and Krebs had helped with some of the more poetic passages that Charlie had written to her. That was some good stuff they'd come up with together. But Krebs knew it for what it was. *Didn't he?*

Krebs, the mind reader, was smiling slyly at him across the table. He knew all right. The problem was that maybe Bonnie Jo didn't. Charlie couldn't remember everything he'd said in those letters. Whether he had, or hadn't, promised her anything outright. If he had, it had probably been that night after Danny Griffin had blown himself up on the airfield. After they'd finally gotten back from finishing Danny's job of loading the guns. And from cleaning Danny's brains off the Plexiglas hatch.

Everything had looked different that night. The war was going on forever and probably none of them were getting out alive. He knew he'd written pages to Bonnie Jo that night, his hands shaking like a leaf, even if he couldn't remember anything he'd said. But it didn't really matter now. Since the Japs had finally thrown in the towel, everything had changed. He hadn't written a word to Bonnie Jo since August.

Charlie reached for the small bowl of rice pudding on his rejected tray and drew it toward him. They always found a way to get the rice in. But this stuff was dry-sticky and barely sweetened. Nothing like Mother and Aunt Cassie made back home. He pushed the little bowl away again. If there was any single unchanging constant in the great China-Burma-India Theater of War, it had to be rice.

"I'm done," Charlie said. "Want a smoke?"

Krebs gathered up his tray and utensils and together they walked to the small window where Chu, the little one-eyed Chinese, was separating the dishes from silverware, from napkins, from food, raking all the plates into one giant bamboo bowl. The pile looked disgusting, but the leftover scraps from this one meal would feed a whole village tonight.

At the exit to the mess hall, Krebs had already stopped to check the latest additions to the big bulletin board. Here there was always a chaotic, thumb-tacked litter of reg changes, base announcements of upcoming movies, softball game schedules and table tennis tournaments. The bulletin board was also good for a few off-color GI jokes, some cartoons, and the occasional magazine pin-up that was just too fine not to share. Krebs was ogling a *Look* magazine photo of Lana Turner. Charlie had only begun to skim the clutter of papers when a yellow sheet with a thin-ruled black border caught his eye. U.N.R.R.A. CALL FOR PERSONNEL, the heading read.

"What's that?" asked Krebs, as Charlie pulled out the thumbtack and brought the notice down to eye level.

"It's a help wanted ad," said Charlie. "For something called the United Nations Relief and Rehabilitation Agency. They're looking for people to stay on in China."

"*Un-rah*," Krebs pronounced. "Yeah. I read something about it somewhere. They're supposed to help put the county back together. You know, *you breakee, we fixee*."

"Says here that they need personnel with expertise in road, river and rail transportation on the Chinese mainland."

Krebs laughed. "I don't think bombing and strafing that stuff counts as expertise, Atwood. And that's about all anybody around here knows about it!"

"I don't know," Charlie said. "It sounds like an office job to me. Says they need *clerical and administrative assistance in the distribution of food, clothing and medical supplies to war-devastated areas.*"

"Uh-oh," said Krebs. "You're not thinking what I *think* you're thinking . . ."

Charlie was already walking away, pushing through the mess hall door with the notice still in his hands. He could hear Krebs scurrying after him.

"Atwood! You're not serious. You're not really thinking about staying on?"

Charlie kept walking, heading for the hard-packed, butt-littered patch of ground around the splintery old picnic tables where the soldiers usually smoked their first cigarettes after a meal. In the beginning, when he'd first arrived at Kunming, the men had been allowed to smoke in the mess hall. But somebody, nurses probably, had complained, and "No smoking in the mess hall, please!" was now up with the regs on the bulletin board. Charlie sat down and reached into the breast pocket of his suntan shirt for a Lucky Strike. He placed the UNRRA notice on the table where he could see it.

Krebs had caught up and stood over him.

"You're not!" Krebs said. "You were kidding me, weren't you?"

Charlie didn't answer and finally Krebs sat down across from him and pulled out his own smoke. When he spoke again his voice was calmer, almost plaintive.

"But man, aren't you *sick* of this country? Haven't you had enough of this heat and the stinking monsoons? And the snakes and the rats and the leeches? Aren't you tired of jungle rot? Aren't you tired of . . . of *rice*?"

Charlie had to smile.

"Yeah. Sure. I'm sick of it. But we're talking Shanghai, Krebs. The HQ is going to be in Shanghai. The Paris of the East! The Whore of the Orient! That's what they call Shanghai. This is a *city*, man. With streets and big buildings. Bars! Restaurants where you can get a steak. Women in real dresses and high heels."

Krebs was silent for a few seconds. When he spoke again it was with the voice of a high school principal.

"It's the girl, isn't it? That Bonnie Jo back home."

Again Charlie didn't answer.

"You're killing me, man. I see it plain as day. You're scared she's got you!"

"Shut up, Krebs. You don't know what you're talking about."

Krebs scrambled up and circled the edge of the picnic table to stand directly at Charlie's side.

"Oh, I know what I'm talking about all right. You don't want to marry her, but you're scared to tell her. You're going to stay in fucking *China* because you're scared to tell a little cheerleader in Hazel Grove, Georgia, that you don't want to marry her!"

"She's not a cheerleader," Charlie said dismally. But Krebs was on a roll.

"You're *killing* me, man. Where are your balls? For that, you're going to hide out in *China*?"

"Listen, Krebs . . ." Charlie began. But Krebs interrupted him.

"Maybe China's not good enough. What about Africa? Maybe you should re-up for a whole different continent! I know a guy who's helping out the Brits in Egypt. She'd never even *find* you there!"

That was it. Charlie flicked his half-smoked Lucky into a high arc and stood up from the picnic table. But Krebs didn't step away. He was practically in Charlie's face.

"And what about you?" Charlie said angrily. "What's *your* big hurry? What have *you* got to go home to?"

A shadow of surprise, and pain, passed over Krebs' face. It was a lousy thing to have said and Charlie knew it immediately. Krebs was practically an orphan. He had been reared mostly by his grandmother, a chilly old lady named Nona who had given Krebs the basics apparently, but not a whole lot more. But Nona had passed away two days before Pearl Harbor and there had never seemed to be anybody else, at least not anybody that Krebs ever talked about. Krebs had lived vicariously through Charlie's letters, his family, and his romance with Bonnie Jo Richards throughout the entire eleven months they had bunked together. Krebs could never get enough of hearing about Hazel Grove. About Mother and Aunt Cassie and especially his sister, Abigail.

The truth was that he and Krebs had become pretty tight in these last few months. Especially since Danny Griffin had made them see that the dangers of this war weren't always in the air. They'd even talked about going into business together back in Hazel Grove after it was all over. That was *if* it were ever all over. They'd talked about starting a little magazine or an ad agency or something. Charlie was sort of artistic, and Krebs was a Shakespeare with words. But that had just been talk. Something to calm the jitters. Krebs knew that. *Didn't he?*

Krebs was still staring at him, that slack-jawed wounded expression on his face. Finally he dropped his own cigarette and crushed it underfoot. He did a slow about face and began walking away.

Charlie watched Krebs' receding back. A spark of belated insight suddenly caught, flared, and illumined everything. Krebs *didn't* know. He didn't know at all!

Krebs had swallowed every bit of it. Every dumb idea the two of them had come up with. He hadn't just swallowed it, he'd been *counting* on it. Actually, now that he thought about it, Charlie realized that the whole time these last few weeks, while his own stomach had been churning like crazy and his own head had felt like a swarm of bees had moved in to take over his thinking, Krebs had been as serene as a Buddhist monk. Well, sure! Because Krebs had been planning to go home to Hazel Grove himself. To become Charlie's business partner. Maybe the best man at his wedding. Maybe the one at Sunday dinners who never forgot to compliment the chicken or help with the dishes. Krebs had been counting on going home to *his* home town and *his* own family—to picking up with a life he'd never had for himself.

Charlie sat down again and pulled another cigarette from the pack. This was just great. Just *great!* Now he had Krebs on his back as well as Bonnie Jo.

Maybe Krebs was right about some of it. Bonnie Jo was a sweet girl. A looker by most standards, and respectable. Church-going and all that, even if her family was Methodist, something his mother could barely abide. A guy could do worse, for sure. But everything was different now. It just seemed too soon for marriage and kids. To settle down in Hazel Grove and work in a hardware store or something equally dull for the rest of his life. But Krebs had nailed that part. He knew Charlie'd never be able to explain that to Bonnie Jo. And that he didn't know if he had the stomach for disappointing all of them. Women could twist screws in you that you didn't even know you had. Odds were Bonnie Jo had already picked out a wedding dress. And his mother and Abby and Aunt Cassie had already seen her in it.

Charlie looked across the field at the crew of a C40 scrambling on the revetment. They were going about their business all right, but almost casually, as though whatever the mission was it wouldn't be a very big deal. There wasn't much coming out of the base lately and the few missions that had been called were entirely different from those of only a few weeks ago. Mostly taking out river mines and dropping leaflets and relief packages in the populated areas. The Linda Luck's last run—was that only a month ago?—had left her pretty much scrap metal, but at least she had ended her days with dignity. The crew had turned out to salute her as she'd been towed off the airfield, all of them knowing that her wheels were down for the last time and that their own little fraternity was finished, too. Clark was already gone, volunteering to pilot some press corps non-coms around

China and India to take pictures or something. Of the five of them remaining, only a couple of them had even been back in the air, subbing for other crew members who were sick. Or hung over. There wouldn't be much call for a tail-gunner anymore. The party was over. But what now?

Charlie picked up the UNRRA notice and studied it again. Krebs hadn't really even listened. But it didn't sound half bad. And the beauty part was that the work—the phrase was right there in the paragraph in the smaller type—was a *humanitarian* effort. Maybe there was a way, if he pitched it just right, that he could make it sound important. Not just important, but *Christian.* His mother was a sucker for the work of "foreign missions" as she called it. He could practically hear her, telling everybody in the congregation of the Hazel Grove First Baptist Church, that her son had been called by God to continue His work in China. She and Bonnie Jo and the Richards wouldn't just save face, they'd turn him into a martyr. A soldier now for Jesus Christ.

It was good. At least it *could* be good. But Krebs would have to be brought on board. Krebs could help him write to them. Once he understood that Hazel Grove would still be there. That this didn't really change anything. It just postponed their plans a little. To give them a little more time to see some of the world. Like Shanghai. The Paris of the East. The Whore of the Orient.

18 October 1945

The Americans are wonderfully confident, like the English, but their confidence is so masculine, so swaggering. Oh, they can be so loud sometimes! But these Americans laugh more than anyone else and it's gay to be around them. Tonight there was dinner and dancing with some of those who will work with the Agency. We took these Americans many places and at last to the Cathay before Papa had ended his night.

Papa is worried about me. About what he thinks the new position might mean. But it isn't like that. I went because Manny asked me and because I wanted to.

One of the Americans is very interesting.

From the diary of Maria Petrova, translated from the French

Chapter III.

Janowski had been right about the point system for demobilization. The War Department had already revised it, several times. The critical point score had now been reduced to 60, and the word was out that all two-year men, regardless of their duty records, would be home by March.

He and Krebs hadn't exactly explained any of that in the letters home. They'd composed both of the letters—the one to Mother and the one to Bonnie Jo—in only three evenings and done a pretty good job, Charlie thought. In the letter to Mother they'd put in enough references to the "lessons I've learned" and the "suffering I've seen over here" to make a good case for a crisis of conscience. Krebs's suggestion that he ask his mother to pray for him had been positively inspired, and then Krebs had added a postscript to Aunt Cassie, in his own handwriting, telling her that the stories he'd heard about her cooking had gotten him through the war. He couldn't wait, he'd said, to taste her legendary blackberry cobbler.

They were no fools. Certainly not Abby. But they couldn't know for sure how the war had changed him. He hadn't even gotten a handle on that himself. And at least he'd given them something to say to anybody who asked. *Tiu lien*, as the Chinese said. A way to save face.

The letter to Bonnie Jo had been the hardest. Krebs had insisted that he leave the hint of an open door. So it didn't sound like a "kiss-off," as Krebs had put it. Not a Dear John letter. But it had been kind of a short letter, more telling in its brevity than in their carefully considered words. Charlie was pretty sure that Bonnie Jo would get the idea, if she *had* bought a wedding dress, that it might be a good idea to return it to the store. They'd ended both letters by saying that he'd send an A.P.O. address from Shanghai as soon as possible. He hadn't written his sister.

Convincing Krebs to come along for the ride hadn't taken too much effort and signing up for UNRRA had been ridiculously easy. A couple of inquiries, the half-hearted formality of an interview, two signatures, and he and Krebs had been easily "loaned" to the new relief organization, their ranks and military status with the Army Air Force unchanged, except that they now they would have a new CO, the Base Command would now be Shanghai, and they could not muster out for at least twelve months. The other guys had even cracked a few jokes about how joining UNRRA could even turn out to be a shortcut. Point system aside, it was going to take a lot of doing to get the millions of American personnel who were still in China and India back home to the States. In their last weeks at Kunming they had helped out with transport and you had to figure the shipments would be going on a good while longer. Practically the whole 14th Air Force would be coming through Shanghai, sooner or later, for processing and discharge in Seattle.

Their own decision, made spur-of-the-moment in Hangkow, to hitch a ride into Shanghai on a mailer, had seemed a pretty good idea at the time. They would have no responsibilities on the journey up the Yangtze, and they'd arrive in Shanghai well ahead of the pack. But they'd been three days aboard the ship now and the novelty had worn off.

The maps they knew already by heart. Shanghai was fifty-four miles from the mouth of the Yangtze at the Pacific. That was forty miles up the Yangtze to where it joined the Woosung tributary and then another fourteen miles up the Woosung to Whangpoo harbor at Shanghai. But being on the river was quite a different thing from flying over it, and Krebs especially had become cranky and restless, mentioning more than once that it had been a damn *bad* decision. There had been nothing to see but rice paddies for two days along the muddy Yangtze, and while the last hour of plying the narrow Woosung, with its factories and warehouses passing on both sides of the ship, had at first been mildly interesting, they had leaned on the deck rail for some time now, bored and silent.

"Would you get a load of that!" said Krebs suddenly, as the river made a last hairpin turn and they caught their first glimpse of Shanghai.

"Didn't I tell you?" said Charlie, trying to sound matter-of-fact, but feeling his insides go weak with relief. Across the harbor, behind the loaded jetties and the bustling wharf, rose a majestic mile-long row of buildings. Skyscrapers, hotels and other enormously solid brick and glass and granite structures in a variety of classical, gothic, and western-style architectures glinted in the late afternoon sun, their thousands of windows returning fiery flares. It was a helluva of a skyline. And it looked about as Chinese as Manhattan.

For another half hour they took in real sights now, Krebs shouting and laughing as he pointed out some crazy local craft on the river, a tanker dipping a Norwegian flag, the remarkable number of American and British ships passing through the busy harbor. Charlie was glad to see him so excited and felt something within him, held coiled and tense in the weeks since Krebs had acquiesced to this adventure, began to slowly unwind and relax. From the looks of it, Shanghai wasn't going to be a disappointment, and the rest of it wouldn't be either. It was going to be great. It just had to be.

Their own ship, smaller than the bigger vessels forced to anchor far out from the shallow harbor, drew closer in to the city and was soon met by a small tender which took them to the customs jetty, a floating pontoon in a long row of others directly below the city's elegant skyline. The mailer's timing apparently had not coincided with the arrival of any big passenger steamers or other vessels to require the attention of the customs officials. The jetty was crowded with milling people, but the customs line was surprisingly short, and the clerk, glancing up quickly to take in not their faces but their uniforms, only pushed paper forms through the caged window for their signatures.

Together they stepped away from the customs window, dropped their duffels on the damp planks of the jetty, and looked around. The arrangements had been that an UNRRA official would meet them, but the wire had said nothing about who, or even precisely where. They could strike out on their own, of course, but Charlie wasn't quite ready to propose it. Krebs had lit a cigarette and Charlie was about to follow suit when he thought he heard his name being called. He stuffed the pack back down in his pocket and looked hopefully in the direction of the voice.

A stout but swarthily handsome middle-aged man holding an arm high in the air was pushing toward them through the throng. He broke free and approached them, smiling broadly, holding out his hand.

"Atwood?" he asked. "And Sergeant Krebs?" They exchanged handshakes.

"Welcome to Shanghai! I'm Emmanuel Rosario. Manny, for short."

"Glad to meet you, Manny." said Charlie, mildly surprised by the fluid, unaccented English. "*Rosario*? Is that Italian?"

"Portuguese, actually," said Manny. "But born in Hong Kong. I came here about ten years ago. But my family has been in China for generations. I'll be your UNRRA escort."

"Our escort!" Krebs said. "That's all right! We're not much used to getting escorted. Unless it's by a Zero."

Manny laughed. "Well, I'm not sure you *should* get used to it. But the plan is to give the first volunteers a little help getting acclimated. I was asked to meet you, show you around a bit, give you the unofficial orientation until we can put together an official one."

"The *first?*" said Krebs. He threw Charlie a look of exaggerated astonishment. "You mean *we're* the first?"

Manny had hoisted their duffels and was already leading them through the crowd.

"Practically,'" he said over his shoulder. "We've got about fifty recruits coming in from the states by air next week. And volunteer applications are starting to come in from all over. But we're still getting organized. The headquarters hasn't even been outfitted yet and so far we've got a clerical staff of exactly two."

Charlie and Krebs hurried after Manny who was leading them past the line of jetties up a low set of moist and slippery steps. They emerged into a narrow strip of green park space that separated the river from the street above.

"This used to be the towpath for the trackers." Manny explained. "The teams of coolies who once pulled the boats in with ropes."

Charlie hesitated a moment and looked back, trying to imagine those picturesque, if labor intensive, dockings of long ago.

"Well, it makes a nice front door now," said Krebs, and they hurried on after Manny, who was carrying both of their bags and seemed remarkably fit for a man in his fifties.

Following Manny's lead they timed a lull in the traffic and crossed the broad street. In another three hundred yards or so they entered a narrow alley and came upon an American jeep, parked at a precarious thirty-degree incline in front of a closed shop or service door. A young Chinese boy sat on the hood of the jeep, arms crossed and frowning. Manny heaved the bags into the back seat and reached into his pocket to extract a paper bill, which he offered to the boy. The boy stared for a long moment at the bill before taking it, giving Manny a blank look, and sliding off the jeep. He watched them sullenly as Krebs took the jeep's shotgun seat and Charlie clambered into the back. He still stared after them as they pulled away.

Manny shifted the jeep into gear and shook his head.

"You know," he said, "the peace is really driving up prices. I've never seen anything like it. Even the beggars are starting to sneer."

"What's the exchange rate?" asked Charlie, thinking of the four hundred American dollars he had in his wallet, and wondering what Krebs had brought with him.

In front of him Manny threw back his head and emitted a rich, full-throated laugh.

"Now?" he said, "Or fifteen minutes ago? I tell you, my friends, it changes by the hour! Dealing with the money is going to be a big part of that orientation I was telling you about. Local currency now is all CNC or Chinese Nationalist currency. There's a lot of paper money, all colors and all sizes, and terribly confusing. What you need to know is that if it says Gold Certificate on it, it's worth fifteen to twenty times what's on the face of the bill. If it says Reserve on it, use it to wipe your rear end."

Charlie and Krebs both laughed, but Charlie was still concerned.

"But American dollars? That's all I got on me," he said.

"Your American money is good," said Manny. "But if you don't spend it down to the last penny they'll cheat you when they give you Chinese back in change. It's best to have American dollars exchanged by someone you trust."

"Don't worry for now," he continued. "I've been instructed to give all the new arrivals seventy-five thousand dollars until they get their per diem money."

"What?" said Krebs. He ratcheted his head, first to Manny, and then to Charlie in the back seat, and then back again, eyes forward. Finally he chuckled.

"I thought you said seventy five thousand dollars," he said.

"I did," Manny said. "But that probably won't last you until the end of the month. Not when a cup of coffee will cost you three hundred bucks."

There was a moment of stunned silence and then all three of them erupted in a trio of hearty laughter. It was a loud, healthy round of laughter, extending itself as it fed on the sound of the others and Charlie felt every last reservation of fear and doubt for the new undertaking dissipate above him in the open air, leaving him breathless and rib-sore, but finally relaxed and eager for whatever would come.

Manny had maneuvered the jeep down the alley and now turned west, back the way they had come, onto the wide thoroughfare that fronted the harbor. The street was a surging swarm of not just cars, old and new, but military vehicles, bicycles, primitive one-wheeled wheelbarrows, two-wheeled rickshaws and three-wheeled pedicabs. People spilled off the sidewalks and streamed suicidally around and in front of moving traffic. It was as if someone had only just tumbled a busy hive and its inhabitants, half human, half mechanical, were emerging shocked and stupefied, angry and lethargic, purposeful and aimless, unified in nothing but the strange buzzing din of voices and horns, grunts and shouts, clanging bells and piercing whistles that was the sum of their activity.

"Geez Louise!" said Krebs after a few minutes. "This has got to be the busiest street in China!"

"Busy enough these days," said Manny. "But just wait a few blocks until you see Nanjing Road."

"This street is known as the Bund," Manny explained. "A lot of what you see here is European or Western investment. Most of old Shanghai's banking interests are here. And the city's best hotels. That one ahead on your left is the Cathay. They say it's the finest in Asia."

Manny shrugged his shoulders. "We could have put you two up there," he said. "But the weather can turn cold suddenly this time of year. And the Japs took out all the radiators."

Charlie and Krebs both craned their necks to look up. This was the art deco building they had seen from the harbor, its magnificent height topped by a four-sided, copper-sheathed pyramid. Charlie's gaze slid down the hotel's gleaming sides to pause at last at ground level, where he suddenly saw a forgotten image from a childhood picture book.

Standing near the curb, before the gold revolving doors of the great hotel, was a tall man—astonishingly tall and fiercely martial—dressed in what looked like the uniform of a Cossack Imperial Guard. He wore a scarlet blouse and tight-waisted tunic, top boots, and tall fur hat. His broad chest was adorned by four descending rows of military decorations. A sheathed sword hung at his hip.

"There!" Charlie shouted. "That man there at the door!"

Manny turned only the briefest glance in the direction of the Cathay. There was some impediment in the traffic ahead of them and they were coming to a full stop.

"Yeah," Manny said. "Colonel Sergei Petrov. Something of an institution on this end of the Bund."

"Colonel?" said Charlie. "You mean he's really a Cossack officer?"

"No. He's not a Cossack. But he *was* an officer. A colonel in the White Russian army. One of those who got out at the very end of the Civil War. Just before the Bolsheviks took Vladivostok. The city is full of these Russians. Some who came early, like that one, back in '22. Another whole exodus later, down from Harbin. Shanghai was a true free-port city then. About the only place that would take them, without papers."

Charlie was intrigued.

"So why is he all decked out like that?"

"That's Victor Sassoon's idea," said Manny. "Sassoon is the Baghdadi Jew who built and owns the Cathay. I guess he figured, old Petrov being a pretty tall fellow anyway, they'd make him even more impressive with the uniform, the tall hat, and all the chest hardware. That uniform isn't authentic. They cobbled it together out of real bits and pieces and got the tailor that does the Pribytkova ballet and some of the Russian playhouses to fix it up."

"But geez," said Krebs, "that must be humiliating for him."

Manny turned to look thoughtfully at Krebs.

"It must be," he said softly. "I think that all the time. Especially when you remember that there are still Cossacks in Shanghai. Real ones, in rags, probably passing him every day. But when you see the state of some of his countrymen, you'll see how he manages it. And why the other Russians wouldn't hold it against him."

Charlie watched the Cathay's costumed doorman with fascination. He was quite an impressive figure really, with a great burly head of course black hair, well-made features, and a large soft moustache that draped gracefully down the sides of a fine and sensitive mouth. There was a regal dignity in his movements and nothing, on the surface, at all pitiable about the tall Russian. But the story had put an achy little knot in Charlie's throat.

"The medals, then," Charlie asked. "And the ribbons. All that glitter he's wearing on his chest. It's all fake, then?"

"Not fake," said Manny. "Some of them are actually his own. Earned in the field in the Russian Civil War. The rest they bought in the shops. No regard for the meaning of the things, you understand. Just for the look. Twenty years ago the city's pawnshops were choked with that stuff. And you still see it around. Not just the medals. But jewelry. Gold imperial coins. Whatever they'd been able to hide on their bodies and carry out with them. They pawned it all, little by little. I don't suppose a hungry baby is much of a match for sentimentality."

"So you've met him, then," said Charlie. "You *know* this Petrov?"

Manny hesitated a moment before answering.

"I know him," he said solemnly. "I drink with him sometimes. He can get a little emotional. The Russians are like that. But this one's stories are worth it."

Charlie watched the tall Russian until the traffic began to move again. Slowly they were creeping upon the sight of the obstruction. A huge wooden wheelbarrow lay on its side in the street, its load—small cages of live chickens—scattered in every direction. Two bearded Sikh policemen, implacable in their white uniforms and scarlet turbans, were using white-gloved hands and furious whistle-blowing to direct the traffic around the mess. Car horns still blew unmercifully at the harried coolie who ran about in futile circles, attempting to collect and stack his cargo, even as dozens of ragged peasants, squealing like hogs at slopping, darted into the street to claim their share of the happy accident.

This was still China, all right. Not so different from Kunming, or Hangkow, or any other place they'd seen. Except that here, in a group of amused onlookers on the sidewalk, Charlie noticed a portly fellow in a full tuxedo, his arm around a beautiful young redhead wearing a full-length ermine coat. Diamonds sparkled at her ears and throat.

There were a surprising number of Navy men on the sidewalks, too, and also the familiar uniforms of the 10th Air

Force. From the looks of things, Shanghai was already lousy with Americans. Clearly they had not arrived ahead of *all* the pack. He and Krebs were going to have some competition for the dames.

Manny wheeled the jeep around the chicken debacle and turned left just past the Cathay. An English sign on the front of a building identified this as Nanjing Road, the street that Manny had promised would be busier than the Bund. The first few blocks here were largely devoted to more hotels, department stores, and elegant European specialty shops. But as they progressed farther down Nanjing Road, the street began to shed its western cloak and to become increasingly Chinese, the shops growing smaller and closer, the sidewalks now crammed with all manner of vendors, the crush becoming so overwhelmingly pedestrian that motorized vehicles, and their drivers, were now the endangered species. Soon they were creeping at a snail's pace, bodies brushing against both sides of the jeep. It was almost sunset now, but if the business day here was winding down, Charlie couldn't imagine what it might look like at its peak. He had never seen so many people in one place in his life.

"Right here," said Manny, "at this intersection with Tibet Road, the name changes. I have no idea why. But from here on the Chinese call the street *Jing'an Si* and the foreigners call it Bubbling Well. The story goes that there was a Buddhist temple somewhere nearby and a bubbling well was one of eight scenic places on the temple grounds. There's no sign of either one now, but the name hangs on."

On their left the road skirted an enormous horse-racing track and Manny explained the Shanghailander's passion for racing, and for gambling on racing.

"They used to run these little Mongolian ponies," Manny said. "Not your Kentucky Derby, of course, but the excitement was just the same. It was mostly about the gambling, anyway. That's really the national pastime. During the war, though, the Japs turned it into an execution field. They allowed the jai lai, but that was about it."

Ahead of them now rose another tall modern hotel and the jeep swung suddenly off the road, lurching to a hard stop directly in front of it. This building seemed nearly as elegant as some of those they'd passed, and Charlie could not imagine that UNRRA would quarter their recruits in anything so fine.

But Manny turned off the jeep's engine and twisted in his seat to face both of them.

"Well, here we are my friends! The Park. I think you'll be comfortable enough. The Red Cross is headquartered next door in the Foreign YMCA. And there's a movie theater just down the street. They'll take care of you at the desk. Just tell them who you are."

Charlie and Krebs exchanged a quick glance. Manny had been great. Not just a good tour guide, but genuine and friendly. Yet both of them, Charlie sensed, after the dizzying excitement of their arrival and their brief titillating tour, now experienced an abrupt puncture, a sudden deflation at the thought that their first day in Shanghai could be so unexpectedly over.

"But listen," Manny continued. "If you two are up for it later, I thought we might rendezvous with a few of the others on staff. Like I said, there aren't many of us yet, but you can meet our Maria, and I know a couple of nurses who could use some R & R."

"*Nurses*?" said Krebs in his best Groucho Marx voice. He flexed his dark caterpillar brows and played an imaginary cigar like a flute at the corner of his mouth. "Did someone say nurses? Why, yes, yes. Now that you mention it, I *am* feeling a little feverish."

Manny laughed delightedly.

"Great." he said. "Do you think the two of you can get yourselves to Jimmy's? We passed it a few blocks back on Nanjing. The food is good. American steaks and all that. You can grab a rickshaw. Or the hotel will call a taxi for you. Ask anybody. They'll know Jimmy's."

"We'll be there," Charlie said, heaving both bags out of the jeep and reaching back in to shake Manny's hand.

"Eight o'clock," said Manny, "See you there."

And then Manny pulled away, leaving the two of them to push through the glass doors into the atrium of a beautiful two-story lobby, to find a friendly and competent desk clerk who would inform them that *yes*, the rooms had spring mattresses, and *yes*, white sheets, and *no*, for the first time in almost a year, they would not be bunking together.

There had actually been eight of them starting out at Jimmy's, but for reasons he would be very unclear about later, Haygood Carson and his mousey, prudish young wife had not followed them on, not even to the second place. By then there had been just Manny and Krebs, the two American nurses, and the Russian girl. Both of the nurses had spent the war in Assam, patching up the 69th, and although Charlie was plenty interested, the place for asking them about their reasons for signing up for UNRRA hadn't really ever presented itself. Nurses were a breed of their own, Charlie knew. That short, rather humiliating, experience in Kunming had taught him to both admire and fear them. Their motivations, he'd decided, were not those of other women.

One of these nurses, the one named *Mary Ann* something, was pretty enough, but a little on the plump side, and probably didn't have a full dance card back home in Idaho anyway. She and Manny seemed to have some kind of a history though. Maybe not a carnal one. Charlie couldn't be sure about that. But they definitely had something in the way of a prior relationship that had put them in confidential head-to-head buzzing all evening. The other one, Julia Kirk, was a real knock-out, but she and Krebs had latched onto each other like magnets right from the beginning. That had left Charlie to entertain the Russian girl—a development that had annoyed him at first, but one, by the end of the evening, had come to feel like the luckiest straw he'd ever drawn.

The Russian girl, Maria, had been hired, according to Manny, by the China program's director, Ben Kizer, to be his personal secretary when he was in town, but to provide general administrative assistance to the rest of them when he was not. Maria, said Manny, had a facility for languages and would be useful to them in innumerable ways.

At first she had looked like just a kid to Charlie. Just a shy kid, hoping to hide her general confusion with the pretense of respectful attentiveness to the others. But whether it was a phenomenon of his increasing drunkenness, or the simple result of watching her—of being *with* her—by the end of the evening he had ditched that first impression. By the end of the evening he had decided that she was something quite unusual. Something altogether different from the women he'd known before.

At the beginning of the evening Mary Ann's maternal voluptuousness and Julia's healthy, beauty-pageant good looks had contrasted sharply with Maria's diminutive size, her small triangular face and delicately chiseled features. This Russian girl spoke a careful, precise English with the smoky trace of a Slavic accent and seemed almost pale and anemic, exhaustedly European, in contrast to the others. At the beginning, the American nurses had struck him as perfect examples of the animal vitality that typified the States, and as clear objective evidence of why the Yanks had won the war. As the evening progressed, however, the American nurses had slowly devolved into something almost crude, something so corn-fed and simple as to be almost primitive. The distinctions between Maria and the American nurses had become the difference between a handmade clay pot and a piece of fine, kiln-fired porcelain.

At the beginning of the evening, before his second cocktail

had even arrived and the conversation had still been on polite and sober topics like the US role in re-building China, this Maria had seemed shy and inarticulate, an adolescent waiting for direction from some adult to know which fork to choose, which joke to dare, whether to laugh or frown. He'd been wrong about that. Dead wrong. True, she had hung back a bit. She had not asked many questions or initiated friendly dialogue with the others. But by the end of the evening he had seen her engage in a dozen conversations, in a half-dozen languages, with an almost bewildering variety of human types. She had handled a delicate situation with a belligerent nightclub proprietor for Krebs, who was showing off for Julia and demanding a better table. She had masterfully smoothed over a disagreement about the currency that had left everyone, even the waiter, happy with the outcome. She had seemed equally at ease with peasants in the street and the several well-dressed foreigners who approached her and called her by name. And she had accomplished all this while seeming to attend to Charlie's every word.

Uncharacteristically, he had talked all night. He had talked about the best and the worst of their missions. About Hazel Grove and his family. Even about Danny Griffin and the accident. She had said enough to convince him of her deep interest and sympathy, but had not offered one word more, or less, than was necessary. Next to this, the noise of the American girls with their giggles and cackles and whimsical juvenile demands, their sudden eruptions of American slang, had somehow become the shrieks and grunts of baboons in a deep, uncivilized jungle.

He had gotten drunk. There was no doubt about that.

But things had happened on his first night in Shanghai. Exciting and exotic things that could never have happened in Hazel Grove, Georgia, and that had fleetingly, because he had not been able to hold any thought for very long, validated his decision to stay in China and made him promise himself to give up his penance to Krebs.

Things had happened. They had seen a fine brawl between a pair of Marines outside a watering hole in the French Concession. He had turned down the offer from a teenage pimp for a "school girl" who looked to be about twelve. They had briefly squatted to play cards in the street and lost money to a sing-songing Chinese card shark. Charlie had bought panties for all three of the women on a street called Underwear Alley or Lingerie Lane or something like that. Other things had happened, too, a blurred tumble of events that came to him now in remembered fragments of color and motion and bits of laughter and talk.

But the most remarkable thing had happened on the fourth stop, at some time certainly past midnight but well before the dawn when Manny and Mary Ann had finally deposited him back at the Park and he had staggered into the elevator alone, not wondering, or caring, where Krebs was, only that he held his own key firmly in his hand and would somehow make it work the lock.

That fourth stop had been the Cathay, the great, elegant hotel which had dominated the skyline from the ship, and which they had passed that morning as naïve tourists in comparison to what they were now. They had gone to the Cathay for the jazz orchestra, which someone had said was wonderful, was excellent, someone had said, although someone else had argued briefly that the one at the Rouge was better, or just as good, and that the drinks were not nearly so expensive. But they had all piled into the jeep and driven back to the Bund, that remarkable main street that presented Shanghai to the world.

Manny had gone to put the jeep somewhere, but the five of them had all spilled out at the curb and there, just outside the golden revolving doors of the Cathay Hotel, Maria had risen on tiptoe to whisper into the ear of Charlie's Cossack. The tall soldier had bent down to her then and Maria had wrapped her small arms around his neck and kissed Charlie's Imperial Guardsman on the cheek.

And then Charlie had taken Maria's hand, because by then he had become terribly smitten and could not, just then, imagine ever walking even a few steps without at least that connection to her. Together they had entered the great lobby of the Cathay, where they would then get the elevator and descend into the bottom— had they really gone *down,* to the nightclub?—where there was the famous and excellent jazz band.

They had already been to another place for dancing, which Charlie had not liked and where he had not danced at all, only ordering another drink each time someone had appeared and asked his permission—as though it were *his* permission to give— for the privilege of dancing with Maria. But there, in the famous hotel with the famous jazz orchestra, he had taken her out on the polished dance floor almost immediately, where they hadn't actually danced, as he was forced to recall it, but only swayed to the underbeat of the music. He had become too drunk by then and even in the swaying he knew he had leaned on her for support.

"Why did you kiss that man?" he had asked her. "Why did you kiss that Cossack?"

And Maria had laughed.

"A Cossack?" she said, "I didn't kiss a Cossack. I kissed only my Papa!"

8 November 1945

I am thinking tonight about this last year and about all of the changes. They began, of course, with Katya's engagement and then her wedding and her moving away from us. It surprises me still, though I can't say why. It seems to have happened so fast. Then it was repére for me and securing the new position right away when I thought I would go begging for months.

None of it though means anything compared to the end of the war. To the changes this is making in the city every day that goes by and not every one for good. Papa has always said that life takes on speed as you go along. I'm thinking tonight that he's right. I wonder about how it will be when I'm [unfinished in the original manuscript]

From the diary of Maria Petrova, translated from the French

Chapter IV.

The bedroom that Maria had shared with her sister—and that now was luxuriously hers alone—was the smallest room, next to the bath, of those in the family apartment. But to both of the girls it had always seemed a little heaven on earth. Until four years ago she had Katya had not even dreamt of a room of their own, having ascended in the last place only to a private sleeping nook closed off by a dull green curtain. Maria had been only thirteen and Katya in her *bac* year when the family had moved to the French section—a move that in Maria's mind seemed to separate *before* from *after*. Their neighbors and the proprietors of the local shops were Russians here, a change that had made Mama much happier, and made them all less worried for Papa. He could now talk his politics and play Durak or chess in one of the nearby cafes and still make his way home safely. If he woke them afterward, with either his weeping or his singing, it mattered so much less. Rue Joffre was a tram route and the school was nearby, which meant they could sleep deliciously late in the mornings, and even after waiting for Mama to finish, could still be home before dark. The building itself had been clean and solid and draftless with good plumbing and heat. They would share an apartment with no one from now on. But the best news of all had come in learning that this little room, from the window of which that first spring could be seen a cloud of pink oleanders blooming in the common courtyard, would be theirs alone, hers and Katya's, to do with whatever they liked.

The room was undeniably feminine, its pale silk curtains and pink counterpane and the small three-mirrored dressing table providing unmistakable testament to its owner's gender. Yet the décor of the room and the objects within it didn't clearly reveal whether its occupant was a child or a woman. Like Maria herself, it was still in transition.

Since Katya had moved out, Maria had made a few improvements. The counterpane, bought with money from her very first salary draft, was new, and though still pretty, and oleander pink, it was much more sophisticated than the one it had replaced. With Katya's things gone she had been able to organize the small clothes cupboard and to arrange her work shoes and the new stilettos for dancing in the space at the bottom that had held toys and childish clutter. But on the foot of the bedpost still hung the embroidered book bag that she had only recently stopped needing for getting her things to school. The little dressing table was cluttered both with the accoutrement of the grown woman's obsession with beauty—the pots and jars and tubes of cosmetics —and the child's love of all things diminutive and fantastical— the miniature teacups, the small plush bear, the collection of tiny ceramic dragons that she could not bring herself to give up. Near a corner of the room, atop a small wooden bookcase, a lined stenographer's tablet and mimeographed copies of minutes from the joint morning staff meetings of the Chinese/United Nations Coordination Committee sat upon a stack of Asian comics, paper-doll folders, and western-styled movie star magazines. Below these, Balzac's *Human Comedy* and Dostoevsky's *The Gambler* sat comfortably together on the same shelf with a half-dozen children's picture books.

But this small boudoir was her own private oasis now and in it Maria had come to enjoy the first domestic privacy she had ever experienced. The room had a solid door under which the long cord of the telephone could be snaked and she sat now on the floor against it, knees drawn up to her chest, the heavy black telephone receiver cradled on her shoulder.

Until the call from her sister Maria had been writing by candlelight in her diary. She had begun the evening habit in the last months of the occupation when the power had been on sometimes no more than an hour a day and almost never in the evenings. The electricity of late had become almost reliable but her pattern had persisted. It helped to relax her and to organize her thoughts. Reluctantly now she closed the little book on an unfinished sentence and turned her full attention to her sister's voice.

"Is he very handsome, then?" Katya was asking. "Papa says he's quite good-looking. And American Army is it? Yes, I remember. Papa said he was an airman. A flyboy. Do you think he will stay in the city? They can send him anywhere I suppose."

Katya spoke in Russian, asking and then answering her own questions before Maria could even respond. The sisters had not seen each other or even spoken in almost three weeks and Katya's urgent curiosity made Maria feel guilty. The new job was taking up all of her days and now Charlie Atwood was taking up most of her evenings.

"Yes," Maria injected. "They can. But we'll be the main

office for China and Formosa. So an assignment here is definitely possible."

"Well, isn't it English then?" Katya rushed on with her questions. "All the time then, I suppose, with these Americans?"

Maria laughed and answered her, deliberately, in English. "Of course it is, Katya, what would you expect?"

"But isn't it tiresome?" Katya continued. "Don't you just get so *weary* in English? Of guarding every word, I mean. Of having to *think* so hard?"

"Sometimes," Maria admitted. "Yes, sometimes." But she felt herself already on the defensive. This line of conversation could well lead down an old avenue. One that she and her sister had explored many times and that was at the heart not just of their differing attitudes about language but at the core of the difference between their personalities. Katya, it seemed, would never understand it. For Maria the acquisition of new words felt like collecting prized jewels. Like gathering blossoms in a rich, exotic garden. She genuinely enjoyed breaking through the fog of language, the thrill of seeing a face light up in comprehension. Especially her own little epiphanies when some subtlety of grammar or idiom suddenly became clear. It was nearly the most fun a person could have. But Katya only saw it as work.

Tonight, though, Katya was too full of other questions to make an issue of American English.

"So tell me about your American! Is he handsome?"

Maria frowned at the question.

"Handsome?" she repeated. "Yes. I suppose he's handsome. Su Mei has met him. *She* thinks he's very handsome. He's been an airman. A gunner. The one who shoots from the back of the plane. His time has been spent in Kunming. His English is very interesting. Slow. And pleasant. It's quite different from the English . . . "

"I don't care about that," Katya interrupted. "Don't be mean! *Tell* me something. How does he look? Is he fair? Or dark?"

"Dark," Maria answered. "At least his hair and his eyes. He has lovely eyes, really. Dark as litchi nuts. And dark hair, too. But he doesn't pomade it or anything. His hair is like Papa's, I think. The kind that will become all gray and stiff."

"Hmmm," Katya sighed, as though Maria had given her something deep to think about. It was the long pensive sigh that told Maria that Katya was alone in the house on Columbia Road. Her sister's voice seemed altogether different when Grieg was at home and when there was a chance that he might overhear. In her husband's presence, Katya's speech took on a crisp, matronly quality, a studied formality that Maria found puzzling. She wanted, Maria supposed, to sound mature and settled, to convey the impression to her husband that she had little time these days for foolishness, especially for girlish gossip. Maria could understand the cause of her sister's affectation. Still, it worried her to think how marriage might alter a person.

"You're in love," Katya said flatly. It was the same tone, exactly, that Mama used to make her own sweeping pronouncements. *You simply didn't study. Green is not your color. You will arrive by ten.*

"I am not in love," Maria replied, trying to be as perfunctory as Katya, but feeling her cheeks and throat grow annoyingly warm.

Perhaps Charlie Atwood *was* handsome. He didn't have a particularly strong face. Not an especially masculine one. He was pleasingly even-featured, but slightly effeminate, with that unassuming thin-bridged nose and his soft, smooth skin, and the delicate, well-defined lips. A "pretty boy," as they said in the American gangster movies.

The other one was good-looking, too. In his own way, Jack Krebs was every bit as appealing as Charlie Atwood. He lacked Charlie's mystery and reserve, but also his wariness and suspicion. Jack Krebs was open and playful, and the way he used his thick caterpillar eyebrows to punctuate his sentences always made her laugh. Actually Maria preferred him, or might have, had it all not been settled that very first evening, without her having been consulted and without any of them even knowing that a momentous decision was taking place. Now it was much too late. She and Charlie had drifted into a kind of arrangement, a tacit understanding that they would be paired for a time. At least until the men were given jobs. Until, as Katya had reminded her, they were sent elsewhere in China. At least until they had learned enough about the city to find other amusements.

She didn't really regret the way things had turned out. She had become interested in Charlie Atwood, curious about the puzzle of him. But she was not in love. And she didn't intend to be.

"You just want me to be an old married hen like you," Maria said.

"I do!" said Katya. "It would be fun to be housewives together!

"I'm having quite enough fun right now," Maria said.

"I suppose you are," Katya replied, almost petulantly. "Meeting all those new men. Dancing at *le cathay grand au milieu de la semaine!*"

"*Un tiens vaut mieux que deux tu l'auras,*" Maria teased back. Katya had slipped into French and those were the rules. Everyone but Papa had always played by them.

Katya became quiet, ignoring the switch to French as well as the suggestion that she might need a little fun in her life. Maria smiled to herself. She knew that her sister understood both quite well.

"So tell me, *devushka,*" Katya pushed on. "Do they pay you in American dollars?"

"Oh, yes," Maria said. "I'm becoming very rich! Two months now I have the pay checks! Soon I'll have enough to buy a grand house like yours and steal away your wash amah. My wages will be better and my panties not so full of stains!"

Katya squealed with delight.

"If that's so then, *porooski*, you little *rich-nik*, you will soon be rich enough to finally pay off your wager!"

Now Maria came near to losing control of her own laughter, hurriedly stifling herself with a fist because she remembered that Mama was asleep, or perhaps not really asleep because Mama never seemed to sleep, but at least she would be resting and could doubtless be disturbed by their silly jabbering.

Katya was referring to a stick-horse race run in a Chapei alley when they'd both been very young. Exasperated by Katya's bragging, Maria had bet her "a hundred million sou" that she would win the next race. Of course Maria had not won, but the audacity of her bet had become a long-running joke between them and for years, at each Yuletide, Maria had made a symbolic installment, of a few coins only, in payment on her debt.

"The sum," Katya giggled, "with interest, of course, must be somewhere near a *billion* sou by now."

"Is that all?" said Maria in mock surprise. "Then you're not taking the inflation into account?"

"Oh, the inflation!" Katya cried, suddenly perfectly serious. "Can you believe what's happening? Last week Madam Chernovsky informed me that the price of shampoo and hairstyle has gone up by half! That's ten thousand CNC in two weeks!"

Maria groaned. This was the married Katya again. She had adjusted so quickly to the little luxuries that her new life afforded. It was almost incredible. The idea of having your hair done every fortnight.

"I'm sorry for you, Madame Sassoon. I can't imagine how you must be suffering."

"Well, it *is* terrible," Katya said, the softening of her voice revealing that she felt chastened by Maria's teasing. "It makes it so hard for . . . the people."

"Yes," said Maria, "it does." For a moment the line went silent.

Maria shifted the receiver to the other shoulder and extended her legs, noting how the wavering candlelight made her legs and bare feet look as though they were floating under water. How lovely it would be to have long legs, like Katya's. What might it be like, to dance with someone who could not rest his chin on your head?

"What do you think is the cause of it?" Katya was saying. "Grieg says it's the Americans."

'I don't know," Maria replied. "Manny says it's many things. Mostly the Nationalists printing too much currency. But every coolie knows the Americans have money and that's certain to drive up prices. The Americans, though, are going to make a lot of jobs in the city. You wouldn't believe the plans that the Agency is making. They're renting warehouses everywhere. They're ordering cables and pipes and tools. Even tractors! They're going to repair Garden Bridge right away. There's even talk about running an oil pipeline under the Yangtze!"

"That will be wonderful. Really." said Katya. "There are so many begging now. More than ever it seems."

Katya paused a moment. When she spoke again her voice was strangely bright.

"In Foochow Street yesterday," she said, "a woman tried to sell me her infant."

"Oh, no," Maria murmured. "What did you do?" It was a sad and terrible story, but not altogether shocking. The misery in the city made anything possible.

Now Katya let out a wild little laugh. "I took it in my arms!" she said. "The mother was thrusting it at me, the little bundle, and I thought . . . oh, I don't know . . . that I would just take a look at its face. I was going to give her the money anyway."

Maria held her breath. Katya's voice sounded almost giddy.

"Of course I wouldn't take someone's child!"

"Of course not," Maria said.

"But the child was quite dead, you see. Long dead, I'd think."

Now Katya began to weep softly. "So *dry*," she said, between her low sobs, "the little . . . thing . . . was . . . so . . . *dry*."

Maria's throat had constricted around an aching lump and she didn't trust herself to speak. Katya was surely crying over something more than the dead baby. Clearly this last year of not conceiving her own child was more troubling to her than any of them had realized.

"Please, Katya. Don't cry," Maria pleaded. "Where is Grieg? Do you want me to come to you?" She could hear Katya's breath coming ragged at first and then slowing, the gulps of air diminishing and at last trailing off to a sigh.

"Don't . . . be . . . a goose," Katya finally sniffed. "You're a working girl now. You have important things to do tomorrow. While I have . . . . well, I have . . . I must have *something* to do!" There was another small shuddering inhalation.

"Where is Grieg?" Maria asked again.

"Oh, another of his endless meetings. I think there's some trouble with the business."

Maria waited quietly, giving her sister time.

"He won't tell me, but I know something's wrong. They were here one night last week. Grieg and Heinz and that short fat one. I could hear them arguing after I went to bed. But the only thing I could make out was *verträge. Die verträge.* So, some trouble with their contracts, I suppose."

"Why don't you come here, then?" Maria asked. "Sidor can bring you." The idea was lovely. To have her sister at home again, even for the night.

But Katya only laughed, easy and natural now. She seemed to have fully recovered herself.

"Now how would *that* be?" she said. "Besides, Mama would send me home again!"

It was true. Mama had done that once. When Katya had been married for only a few weeks.

"Don't worry. I'm fine. It's just my monthly time."

"I suspected as much," Maria said. "And I wasn't worried. I just don't want you to be sad."

"I'm not sad, *devushka*. I'm just silly. But I must say good night now. Grieg will be home soon. I want to wash my face."

For a moment Maria considered objecting, even beginning a new subject to keep her sister on the line. But Katya did seem fine now. And it *was* getting late.

"Good night, then," she said. "Sleep well. We'll talk again soon."

For a long while after hearing the disconnecting click Maria remained on the floor, holding the telephone receiver, still warm from her ear, in her lap. Tonight's conversation with Katya had seemed to mark a change, a peculiar role reversal in their relationship. There had been a time when this shift might have pleased her. When Katya's consuming interest, her little expressions of envy, might have provided the kind of satisfying triumph that a younger sibling dreams about. But tonight they had left her feeling only gloomy and burdened. She was especially uneasy with the role she had played of becoming advisor, of comforter, to Katya.

No one had ever worried about Katya. Either about her behavior or her emotional state. Katya was like Mama. Steady and practical. Katya had never frightened their parents by taking up with strangers or wandering off in the crowded streets. She had never brought home even one bad mark in deportment. And Katya had never been subject to the emotional swings that she and Papa fell victim to—that Mama called their "little Russian fits."

Katya's proposal from Grieg had seemed to prove the value of Mama's way even if she and Papa had been almost despondent about Katya's engagement. Papa had disguised his objections in politics, but Maria knew there was more. Secretly they had made fun of Grieg Waechter, mocking him because he seemed so stiff and humorless. For her own part, she had feared for her sister, who seemed to be consigning herself to a lifetime of dispassionate protocol and lifeless mannerisms. She had never voiced it exactly, not even to Papa, but Maria felt there would be no *fun* in her sister's future with Grieg Waechter.

Tonight it seemed there had been at least some basis for those fears. Katya was lonely. The baby she wanted so fiercely was still not on the way. Her husband left her alone too much. He obviously didn't confide in her, and even if this was to protect her, it was causing Katya pain. Her sister's beautiful new life was proving surprisingly empty.

Maria opened her door narrowly, coaxed the telephone cord from underneath it, and returned the telephone set to its place on the little table in the sitting room. The apartment was dark and still, but a gauzy light from the streets outside still filtered through the front curtains. She could hear laughter and talk on the sidewalks below them, and from farther away the dim whine of a police siren. Shanghai, like Mama, never really slept. And tonight, Maria suspected, she might not either.

25 November 1945

All morning today I unpacked beautiful new typewriters and boxes of office supplies from the United States, though there is still so much that will have to stay in cartons. We have more new things than places to put them! New recruits, too, are trickling in every day now, and Manny is staying very busy collecting them and getting them settled. We are running out of places to put the people, too. This last group has been sent to the old 14th Army barracks. Charlie and Jack are quite vain now about their lovely rooms at the Park.

From the diary of Maria Petrova, translated from the French

Chapter V.

For nearly three weeks, while they waited for an assignment from UNRRA, Charlie and Krebs became quintessential tourists. On most days, without Maria or Manny along to provide any goal or guidance, the two of them drifted aimlessly about the city, allowing impulse to make their plans. Early on they had formed the habit of stopping in almost every morning at the foreign YMCA near the Park Hotel to get the gossip about how demob was going in the China Theater, to play a little snooker, to read the American papers, or at least to catch up to *Dick Tracy* and *Terry and the Pirates* in the comics. They had secured the Shanghai Guidebook put out by the Flying Tigers and systematically ticked off its recommendations for where to eat and drink and shop, taking special pains to visit the places the Guidebook warned enlisted men to avoid. They had discovered the Shanghai Club and spent an entire afternoon and early evening there, rolling Yahtzee dice on what was supposedly the world's longest bar. Krebs thought he had won, but it was hard to say. The game had gone on for a long time and they'd had a lot to drink.

By the end of the second week they were confident enough, at least in the daylight hours, to venture into the Chinese city and to begin exploring the confusing, and redundantly named, Peace Lanes—a fascinating capillary system of narrow alleys and byways where fish scales and rotting vegetables floated in the gutters and laundry flew like banners from bamboo poles. Here old grandmothers still hobbled along on the tiny stumps of bound feet or sat smoking their pipes in open doorways. The centuries of Shanghai's domination by foreign powers, by especially the English, were scarcely visible here. In these narrow streets the only language heard was Chinese—the soft murmuring of Shainghainese or the less breathy, less lovely, sounds of the Mandarin or Cantonese dialects. Even here, though, there were always a few enterprising merchants who knew enough English to make their sales pitch understood and the scantily-clad nymphs leaning out of windows made themselves perfectly clear: "Hey, GI, you want suckie? Suckie you, good. One dollar!"

Most of their excursions were random and purposeless, but not all of them. On one exceptionally windy day in early October, Krebs wanted to make a trip out to the Lunghwa prison camp. In the last days of August, on a fill-in assignment with another crew, Krebs had helped to drop relief rations on this very camp and he seemed obsessed with seeing it, "from the worm's eye view," as he phrased it, "rather than the bird's."

"But what's there now?" Charlie asked him. "Won't it be deserted?

"Not yet," said Krebs. "Not by a long shot. Officially, you know, the camp was liberated in August. But hundreds of allied POWs are still there. Housing's a problem. And a lot of them are still waiting on word from relatives. Help with getting back home.

I mean, you gotta' figure. Their businesses were destroyed. Their homes taken. Hell, some of these people were practically erased by the last four years."

"*Erased.*" Charlie repeated. That was a good way to put it. But the idea hit him with an uncomfortable jolt. Everybody always thought of war in terms of the dead. Or at least of the wounded. Those who had been left crippled. Deaf. Blind. It was natural to think first of the thousands who'd been killed or maimed. But there were millions more whose bodies had been untouched. Who had survived and yet lost everything else. Their homes and villages. Their livelihoods and the positions and titles that defined them. Every single human connection that conveys identity. Their very *place* in the world.

Somehow the yellow hordes of refuges moving through the Shanghai streets, stooped below the dirty bundles that held all their worldly goods, had not really brought this idea home to him. At least not in the way that he absorbed it now, at the thought of white men, of Americans or Europeans, obliged to remain in a liberated POW camp because they simply had nowhere else to go.

The Lunghwa camp, about eight miles southwest of the Bund on Minghong Road, had once been some kind of Chinese academy or university, and was much bigger than Charlie had expected. The place was made up of six or seven concrete buildings and a number of large wood barracks that had originally been built as stables by the Japanese. A high barbed-wire fence skirted the whole compound, but now the big gate stood open and the wooden guardhouse was empty.

They had immediately seen little clots of internees, men mostly, smoking or strolling on the grounds and in the first group they approached they had met a Dutch engineer and a former British journalist who'd been willing to show them around. Most of the camp's dormitory rooms were empty now, but in one, a building called D block, there were still women and quite a few children, too. The women especially looked gaunt and haggard, but at least they were being well fed now and had been given medical attention. The Red Cross was providing movies and books, games for the children, to help stave off the boredom of waiting.

When Krebs had finally gotten around to revealing the real reason for their excursion, Charlie had been relieved to hear that both of their guides remembered the day of the relief drop well. They told Krebs about how grateful the adults had been for the powdered milk, the canned meat and fruit cocktail and the cigarettes, and about how the children had gone crazy over the chocolate bars. Krebs had grinned like a kid on his birthday, even shrugging his shoulders when the Brit mentioned that the chocolate had given the half-starved kids a "docking fine case of diarrhea."

That much had been all right and Charlie had been glad, at least for Krebs' sake, that they'd made the trip. But then, at the last, the Dutchman had ruined it. Tall, blonde and cadaverously lean, he'd walked them back to the edge of the compound.

"Next time," the Dutchman said. "You might give a bit of help to the Johny who worked the design. It killed quite a few of them, you know."

"What do you mean?" Krebs asked. "Who was killed?"

Charlie was puzzled, too.

"Chinese," the Dutchman said, pointing to the open space past the barbed wire fence, just beyond the camp's perimeters. "Bloody heavy, those metal canisters. The shape's why they fell so fast. The little fools ran after them. Trying to catch them coming down. Dropped like stones they did. Bloody heavy, those cans."

Charlie just shook his head. Another sad example of collateral damage. But Krebs had not taken it so philosophically. He had cursed and brooded over it through six or seven dry martinis. The bar bill that afternoon had come to thirty-nine thousand dollars.

There was no routine at all in those early weeks—a radical change from military life that they found alternately liberating and unsettling. By late afternoons, though, they usually found themselves drifting back to the Park for a shower and a shave, a drink in the hotel bar, or sometimes even a short nap before embarking on the evening's adventures. The city's nightlife was not only making demands on their stamina, but it was proving powerfully addictive.

At sunset every night the city became a neon siren, beckoning with every imaginable delight. And there were none of the seven deadly itches that Shanghai didn't encourage you to scratch.

If your cardinal vice was gluttony, the temptations were dizzying. New restaurants and cabarets were opening daily and established ones were doing a booming business. There were tea houses everywhere and Chinese restaurants of every type, offering Cantonese food, Ningpo banquets, or Peking feasts depending on the chef's native province. European and Western fare was readily available. In a club that seated thousands and staged an elaborate floorshow where doll-figured Asian beauties clad in feathers and sequins kicked and dipped to American hits, they had eaten the best steaks of their lives and dropped enough American dollars to feed a native family of five for a year.

The more licentious hungers could be satisfied on a seemingly infinite continuum from the finest Chinese courtesans to the "Jeep" girls that accosted American soldiers on the streets. Your pleasure could be taken as easily in a ten-minute taxi cab ride as in a massage parlor in Blood Alley.

If your dominant lust ran to money or power, there was gambling at high stakes or low. Those with organizational skills, and a little time to invest, could find black market enterprises in almost anything. If you had no desires at all, or at least none that extended beyond the simple wish for temporary self-annihilation, this, too, could be briefly satisfied in the city's many opium dens.

In their second week in the city Manny had told them an old

missionary joke that pretty much summed it up. "Should God spare Shanghai," the missionary supposedly said, "He will certainly owe an apology to Sodom and Gomorrah."

And yet there was beauty, too. The city's architecture was dazzling, the envy not only of every city in Asia, but of the West, in both variety and execution. In the vast ocean of filth and noise and desperation that was Shanghai there were islands of quiet green parks and gardens, native temples and shrines with their round moon gates and zig zig bridges and still serene pools in which brilliant choi swam in mirrors of sky and cloud. In the magnificent guild houses and odd-storied pagodas, in the amazing and colorful bird markets, in the street fares where the jade and copper items and delicate watercolor paintings sold for pennies they had found themselves awed and humbled. This was the oldest civilization known to man and whether or not you understood or appreciated their culture, the Chinese were more than little yellow beggars.

But it was the Russians, Manny had told them—that first wave of Whites fleeing the Bolsheviks, and those Russian Jews who had come down later from Harbin, who had brought western culture to Shanghai. Even on those first ships there had been teachers and artists, musicians, ballerinas, and horsemen. Over time they had learned how to use, and to turn into bread or rice, the skills they carried in the memories of mind and muscle.

These impoverished Russians had taught languages, music, horse-riding and fencing. In all of the fine hotels of the city there were now Russian orchestras and singers. Poets and writers filled the small cafes. There was ballet, opera, and symphony. Shanghai was not merely the Whore of the Orient. She was also the Paris of the East. This city had everything, if you just knew where to find it. And they were learning where to find it.

If Charlie rarely needed his arm twisted to partake of this decadent abundance, Krebs was becoming practically rabid. He was still seeing Julia, the American nurse, but he was spreading himself around, too. He had met a Eurasian girl whose company he also enjoyed, but he wasn't gone on either one of them and still liked to head out stag on some nights so that he'd be free to play the field. On those evenings when Krebs planned to launch the night alone, he could be especially insistent that Charlie come solo too. Sometimes Charlie let himself be persuaded. Krebs, with his boyish grin and calculated innocent rube approach, could often attract a certain kind of woman—exuberant and willing, but still reasonably intelligent and reasonably washed. Charlie had met a couple of such women on those evenings. With one in particular, he'd had himself a pretty good time and still arrived back at the Park by dawn, still possessed of most of his wallet, with a fair recollection of where its missing contents had gone.

Mostly though, when the sun began melting into the river, and the neon fireflies started their twinkling in the city's streets, Charlie found himself thinking of Maria Petrova. He was starting to think of Maria a great deal. Sometimes his thoughts were troubled.

"You know, sometimes I just don't *get* her," Charlie complained one evening. "I don't know what makes her tick."

It was early yet and tonight they had begun in one of the better dance clubs. It was a white tablecloth place with a decidedly Western atmosphere. They specialized in Western-style cocktails with little paper umbrellas or red, white and blue swizzle sticks. There was a glittering mirror ball hanging above the dance floor and the band did a decent job of approximating the tunes of the stateside Hit Parade. The voice of the little Chinese vocalist was a dead ringer for Peggy Lee's, even though, as Charlie had discovered when he had once tried to talk to her between sets, she spoke no English at all. The proprietor was Chinese, wealthy by most standards, but nervous now over what he had invested in the new décor, the new theme, his gamble on American tastes and American money.

The one sure bet he'd put down was on the women. Here the

taxi dancers, or the "hostesses," as this management preferred to call them, were most all of them beautiful Russian girls. They sat ringing the dance floor on high stools, waiting for the next sucker to appear with the string of tickets that would entitle him to dances or drinks and conversation at his table. The dance floor was almost empty this early and you could see the whole bevy at once. Periodically, the girls crossed, or uncrossed, shapely silk-stockinged legs. Feigning boredom, they lit cigarettes with manicured nails, stretching pale throats upward, making calculatedly sensual little red O's with their lips, exhaling thin plumes of smoke toward the ceiling.

Krebs was mesmerized, but he nodded sympathetically as Charlie spoke.

"That's women for you," he said. "You're never going to figure them out."

"No, I don't mean that. I mean like Sunday. She wants to show me this temple, you know. It's old, and really interesting. In the Chinese city. But we're walking along and ahead of us there beside the path there's these two Japs. Sitting on this bench. I know they're Japs because they're still in the uniform. Mostly. One of them has got on black pants and they're filthy, but they're Japs all right. I tell you they're just sitting there on a bench. Like they're taking the sun. And Maria just stops and starts chatting. She speaks Japanese, too, you know. Never studied it all, but picked it up in the streets. It's crazy when you think about it, but Maria was only a kid when the Japs marched into the city."

Krebs was making eyes at a tall girl with a Veronica Lake hairdo and conspicuously fulsome breasts, but he twitched his face in Charlie's direction as a signal that he was still listening.

"Wouldn't you think," Charlie went on, "that after almost four years of occupation, of living under their goddamn heel, that you'd be . . . that you'd be . . . well, hell, I don't know. At least a little *touchy*?"

Krebs considered this for a moment.

"I hate the sons of bitches," he said.

"Yeah," said Charlie. "Me too."

But apparently Maria didn't. At least she didn't seem to. It had been evidence, yet again, of that peculiar quality in her—a characteristic he desperately wished to find attractive, to at least see as innocent or naïve. But he couldn't. In truth, he recoiled from it. She seemed to have no discernment whatsoever where people were concerned. No more discrimination than a child might have. Or a stray dog. A happy cretin! He wanted to see her strange liberality as something innocent and altruistic. But he couldn't. In all other ways, Maria Petrov was one of the most sophisticated women he'd ever encountered. But this particular trait, from the woman he was falling in love with, seemed only simple. And stupid. And dangerous.

It annoyed him that he wanted to discuss such things with Krebs. More, that Krebs had become barely attentive to him. He was bringing Maria up too much. She was taking up too much space in his head. He had come to feel that their time apart was merely a rehearsal for their next meeting. When they were together, it could well be worse. Then it might be anything that bewitched him. The perfect glossy oval of a fingernail. A wispy tendril of hair that had escaped from her upswept hairdo. That dress she had with the little buttons made like seashells. She was spoiling everything. And he was letting it happen.

Now Krebs stood up, thrusting out his chest and distending his belly so that he could tuck and smooth his excess shirt into his belt.

"I think I'm going to cut a little rug, crackerjack," he said. "See anything *you* like?"

"No, not yet." Charlie said. "I think I'll just watch you a while. Take notes, you know."

"Good idea!" Krebs said, snapping his fingers. "You don't get many chances to learn from a master."

Charlie watched as Krebs bee-lined for Veronica Lake, saw

him whisper in her ear and saw her resultant laugh, white teeth flashing and for an instant the drape of hair revealing a second green eye before it fell again, covering her face completely as she took the floor with her partner.

Krebs was a pretty fair hoofer. It was annoying to admit it, but he was. And his talent, well concealed in their months in Kunming, probably accounted to some extent for why Krebs seemed so happy in Shanghai. Why he practically lived for sunset.

Charlie had thought himself a fair dancer in high school. He had learned the Hesitation Waltz, a simplified version of the Foxtrot, and a few other ballroom-type steps in an extramural class that his mother had never known about. It had been good enough for Hazel Grove High. But the Shanghai night life demanded a lot more than his beginner's rudiments, particularly when everybody was watching you. He was getting a little better. But he could not do the more exotic steps of the swing dances that Krebs excelled in or the classic tangos and rumbas that some of the Portuguese and the Italians liked. He was obliged to encourage Maria, who seemed to love it so, to dance with Manny or Krebs or any of the others who liked to show off.

Charlie watched Krebs and the Russian girl. They were dancing to Artie Shaw's "Back Bay Shuffle" and making quite a performance of it. The Russian girl was good, too, managing to kick and twirl and jump even in her tight gown and heels. It was the least expected of these women, he supposed, but Krebs was still sober enough to take some pains with his execution and was in rare form tonight. The other two couples who had been on the floor gave up and backed away, joining the admirers from the other ringside tables who laughed and clapped and lifted their glasses.

Charlie stood up and dug out his wallet. In the chit glass in the center of the table he inserted a few bills for Krebs. He had no idea whether this was too much or little but he didn't much care.

Krebs would either remember to tell him or else he'd forget.

The path to the street door took him across a little corner of the dance floor and Krebs saw him passing and lifted inquisitive eyebrows. Charlie returned a quick little parting salute. Krebs was in his element. For him, anyway, the night would only get better. But Charlie's only goal now was to get to the street and to hail a conveyance that would get him back to the Park Hotel. It was early yet and the city's seductive powers would not peak for hours. But tonight he felt immune to Shanghai's many charms. Tonight his mind was somewhere else.

20 December 1945

The weather has turned quite cold now and bringing winter hardship. Mama is fine at school but Papa must be outdoors in any weather. Even I go from my chilly bath in the mornings, to nearly freezing in the streets, to the stifling dry heat in our offices.

They have begun the work on Garden Bridge and I can watch the progress from the Embankment. Workmen are hanging all over it like insects, chipping at the old paint with little hammers. Some of them have no coats, but I pray that the work keeps them warm.

Katya, I would imagine, will be wearing furs from now on, but Mama is hemming her last good coat for me. I have failed to ask Katya if I might have it. It's too late now.

From the diary of Maria Petrova, translated from the French

Chapter VI.

On the 17th of December they had spent their last night in the Park Hotel. The decision to move had been made largely by Krebs, and not based so much on the fact that the Park had increased its room rates to a hundred thousand dollars a day as because they had jacked up their liquor prices by 50%. Krebs had simply been unable to bear the insult.

They had found other accommodations—Manny had pulled the strings—and were moving to Broadway Mansions, an enormous English apartment house on the Bund. The place was full of diplomats and American journalists and would be even better for getting reliable news than the foreign YMCA. That last morning they had awakened to find the city frigid under a low gray ceiling of cloud and the old man who had regularly begged at the door of the foreign Y frozen dead below a light frosting of snow.

By then they had become inured to it, to the irony of stepping over a trembling half-naked beggar in order to enter a posh cabaret where seven-course meals were served and full orchestras played for men in formal dinner clothes and women in glittering gowns. Little by little, day by day, they had gotten better at it, scarcely noticing anymore the starving and leprous poor. Their sheer numbers were anesthetic, the very breadth of their suffering, numbing. It was impossible to withstand the onslaught of thousands, of tens of thousands. In self-defense one became insensible, unseeing and indifferent.

With the coming of winter, however, there seemed to have come a clearing of the lenses. For Charlie at least the emaciated men, the hollow-eyed women and pot-bellied children, had started to come back into focus. Part of this new acuity corresponded to the change in the weather. For one thing, there were far fewer refuges on the streets now. Many had abandoned the city to return their villages. Numberless more huddled together for warmth in the old Chinese city. Many of those remaining had found permanent outposts for begging and where his own routine and patterns intersected theirs, they sometimes became individuals again. But more of his new focus came from the job.

UNRRAs China Headquarters, intended to serve both the Pacific and the Far East, had moved, too. New offices had been established in an even more mammoth apartment building bordering the International Settlement on the north side of Soochow Creek. The building was known as the Embankment—another of Victor Sassoon's real estate triumphs—and had four sets of lobbies and elevators as well as its own swimming pool. More importantly, for winter in Shanghai, the Embankment also had central heat. The headquarters had now been furnished and staffed, not just with Americans but with a fair representation from all over the globe. There were some Brits, a few Russians and French, a greater number of Portuguese, like Manny, whose countrymen, Charlie had come to learn, had long dominated the better clerical and administrative positions in Shanghai. There was an entire accounting staff of Chinese, clicking their abacuses in a room across the hall from Maria's inner sanctum.

The nurses, Mary Ann and Julia, as well as a virtual avalanche of volunteers in nursing and social work who had come through from the States and elsewhere, had been put to work all over Asia and in all manner of projects from delivering mass vaccinations against smallpox and typhoid and cholera to teaching villagers about hygiene and childcare and food preservation. Haygood Carson and his sanctimonious little wife had been sent to Formosa where they were doing something, he thought, about agriculture.

Through the rather unfortunate accident of claiming on his original application that his specialty was "communications," Krebs had been assigned to the Telephone Section. He had originally been a terrific pain about it, but his grumbling hadn't lasted long. The responsibilities for editing outgoing cable messages and routing incoming ones, for planning and providing telephone service for the thirteen hundred UNRRA employees in China had turned out to be a pretty important job. The added perk of supervising the staff of lovely young Chinese, Eurasian and Russian girls who worked the busy switchboards had eased his disappointment.

Charlie himself had been assigned to the operation that managed the repatriation of displaced persons—a job that on its face seemed as big as China itself. According to UNRRA statistics, about eighteen million Europeans had been uprooted by the war. Eight million of them qualified for the legal definition of DPs.

The first order of business was the matter of the Allied

POWS released from the Japanese camps in Shanghai itself. Some of these were staying on, hoping to rebuild their devastated businesses. Others still held citizenship in Great Britain or other European countries or, almost as good, had funds in foreign banks. These were the easy cases, where UNRRA could provide a form of concierge service, helping with the details of lost papers, finding and communicating with relatives, and arranging transport home. The less well-connected, like those he and Krebs had met still languishing at Lunghwa, needed housing and jobs more than anything else.

Then there was the matter of the displaced Jews. Those who had come in the 30s, and the larger wave of Polish Jews that had come fleeing Hitler after Kristlenacht. The Fuhrer, it was said, had urged his Japanese allies to dispense with the Jewish problem in Shanghai with the efficiency of the "final solution" that the Nazis were employing in places like Auschwitz and Dachau. To his credit, the Shanghai Consul had resisted, instead issuing a Segregation Order confining the 15,000 Central European refugees into a one-square mile section that had become known as the Hongkew Ghetto.

Conditions in the ghetto had improved considerably since Manny had first taken him there some five months ago. Then the district had still been largely a disease-ridden human cesspool, unbelievably overcrowded and all but without clean drinking water. UNRRA had provided Quonset huts to enlarge the Refuge Hospital and helped to supply an outpatient clinic, but the crowding had not been helped by the fact that housing was now being reclaimed by former Chinese owners or conscripted by government agencies.

The Jews had had it pretty rough through the war with limited mobility, rationed food and other goods. But whatever the general attitude had been in Hongkew during the war, it had since altered considerably as they had received news of the grim fates of so many who had not sought sanctuary in China. Many were still looking for lost relatives and friends. For that Charlie couldn't help much, beyond posting the heartbreaking lists.

Through their own efforts UNRRA had managed to repatriate several hundred Austrians and there were plans for Germany to take back some of their own. Australia had stepped up to the plate. It was a big wide open country, that one. But Palestine was balking. And post-war economic devastation was making all of Europe nervous. But at least UNRRA had become a source of employment for the DPs, and for thousands of the Chinese. Everybody in Shanghai it seemed needed something. But he was finding that he could afford to see them again. At least now there was hope.

One plea for help, however, had come from a completely unexpected quarter. One Friday, well before the end of his customary office hours, and almost two hours before their planned rendezvous, Maria had telephoned him, asking that he meet her at a small Russian café in the French concession. He knew the place. He had been there with Colonel Petrov and he associated it with the story that Petrov had told him about the Great Ice March. He had half expected to find the Colonel there this evening, at his favorite corner table with one or more of his Russian cronies, raging about politics. Instead he found Maria sitting at the corner table with her sister Katya and the expressions on both of their faces uncharacteristically solemn.

Both of the women rose, lifting their chins upwards as he greeted each of them with the formal kiss on both cheeks that the French, and for some reason, *this* family, employed for introductions. He noticed again how similar, and yet how different, the sisters were. Katya wore street clothes, a soft and simple dress with those little half-cap sleeves that made one take notice of her broad shoulders and the tanned, well-formed arms. For work in the office, Maria usually wore western-style dresses, belted and short-skirted, or suits with padded shoulders. Today she was already dressed for the evening in a silk cheongsam, the traditional curve-hugging Chinese sheath that could tease or proposition, depending on the figure of its wearer, and on how far up the leg, or hip, those tantalizing slits extended.

"Oh, Charlie!" Maria greeted him. "You are good to meet us. I thought perhaps you could give advice to Katya. At least to put her mind at ease."

They sat down together, all still cordially smiling, and Charlie noticed that they had not ordered even the first drink.

"And how might I help with that?" he asked, signaling the waiter.

"I was telling Katya that you know all the important Americans. I've told her that you know General Stillwell. That you and Jack call him *Vinegar Joe*. The Flying Tigers are heroes to the Chinese. The young boys especially read about him in the comic books."

Charlie laughed. They would have to be more careful about what they said in front of her. Maria interpreted their sarcasm as intimate knowledge of the subject being discussed.

"I don't know anybody," Charlie said. "I have about as much influence on US affairs as you do on the Kuomintang. But surely you can't be worried about anything we Yanks do."

"But I *am* rather worried," said Katya. "Grieg, you see, has already been questioned once by the Americans."

"Questioned?" said Charlie. "About what?"

Katya's face paled. "About collaboration with the Japanese."

Charlie blinked. Now he realized why Maria had been so strange on the telephone. And why the sisters looked so solemn.

Every day for the last few weeks the city newspapers were reporting the developing events in the sensational trial that was taking place in the Ward Road jail. An American military commission had decided to prosecute as a war crime the post V-E Day collaboration with the Japanese of more than twenty-five Shanghai Germans. The Germans had specifically been accused of contributing to the military efforts of the enemies of the United

States *after* their own country's unconditional surrender. He knew of others that had been investigated along the same lines. Some of them were journalists. Even diplomats. But he couldn't imagine how Grieg Waechter could fit into that batch.

"That's ridiculous," said Charlie. And it was. He wasn't particularly fond of Grieg Waechter. He had experienced an almost visceral reaction to Waechter's blonde handsomeness, to the simple fact that he was German. But he had reluctantly acknowledged his prejudice, and the extent to which he, having lived out the war in Burma and China, far away from the European front, had formed his opinions in the same way that the general masses had. From the newsreels and the papers. From the slowly emerging images and stories of the atrocities that had taken place in the German camps. He wasn't crazy about Waechter and, like everybody else, he hated the Krauts. But there was one thing he knew absolutely. However it had gone for the Third Reich, the guidance hadn't come from Shanghai. He didn't especially like Maria's brother-in-law. But Grieg Waechter was nobody.

"Ridiculous!" Charlie repeated. "Grieg wasn't intelligence. He wasn't Nazi or SS. Why should *he* be questioned?"

"It all seems a matter of timing," said Katya. "You see it's because he's a national. And Germany surrendered first. And anything one did after that looks suspicious."

"What do you mean? What's suspicious?"

"Well, apparently *anything.* A sale to the Japanese. Any communication. Meetings and such."

She had dropped her head to fidget with her hands in her lap but she looked up suddenly, directing her remarks to her sister.

"Do you remember, Maria, how we felt? How little it affected all of us? The Japanese of course still held the city. So life went on! For us, the war was not about Europe. For us, the war was still with the Japanese."

Maria looked earnestly at Charlie. "It's true what she says. It was like that. Nothing had changed. We had hope, of course. But nothing had changed."

"Roger that," Charlie laughed. "We celebrated V-E day by firing a gasoline dump!"

Both of the sisters smiled blankly. His attempt at humor had not registered.

"It was like that for Grieg," said Katya. "He simply continued with his business."

Charlie shrugged, and waited.

"But now!" Katya's eyes darted between the two of them. "They are questioning everything! The clubs he belonged to. The newspapers he read. What meetings he attended. His friends. His . . . how do you say it? His *tendances*."

Charlie looked to Maria.

"His habits," she said. "No, not that. The way he is inclined. No! Perhaps the politics? I think it is like . . ."

"I get it," Charlie interrupted.

Maria frowned. She was still grappling for the word she wanted. He knew from experience that she might search for it for hours, days even, but eventually she'd produce it.

"But I *don't* see . . ." began Charlie. He had been prepared to launch into a protestation about how anyone might think a mere industrialist, a businessman, could be involved in anything treasonous, but he stopped himself abruptly, allowing the energy of his protest to trail off as though he had lost the thought. For a split second Katya had caught his eye and he had seen something in her face. It was a face so like Maria's and yet more controlled, less spontaneous, not so easily read. But in that split second he thought had seen something. It had been only a passing shadow, the barest flicker, but he had seen it. There was more here. Perhaps he *did* see. There was some taint of collaboration in Waechter's post-war enterprises. That certainty right now might be resting more in Katya's heart than in her head. But either way, she knew.

"I don't think you should worry," he said calmly, deliberately, for Maria's benefit. "I'll ask around. See if I can find out anything about where they think this thing is going to go."

He was bluffing. He doubted that he would learn one jot more than he already knew. Not half as much as Katya already knew. And that was probably not half as much as her husband knew.

"But maybe," he suggested cautiously, "you should think about . . . about options. This trial is the big one, apparently, and they won't drill down until they see how it goes. But they say it's going to take months."

"Options?" Maria echoed. There was a surprised lilt, a trace of panic in her voice. "What are these *options*?"

"Well, I mean, if you're really worried, you could be well out of here by then. This is definitely no kangaroo court. The Germans on trial have American defense lawyers. And from what I hear, they're doing a pretty good job."

Maria's eyes had grown wide and startled, but when she looked to her sister, Katya only returned a thin, sweet smile. To Katya this was clearly not a new idea.

"We would be grateful to you," Katya said. "For anything you might learn."

They finished their drinks and Charlie called for the check and paid. The waiter, who had served him and Colonel Petrov more than once, gave him an inquisitive look but said nothing.

They had been only moments on the walk outside the little café before the quiet old man, the Waechter's driver, approached them, obsequiously fondling his cap and waiting for instructions.

"Can we drop the two of you?" Katya asked.

"That would be swell," Charlie said. "But won't you join us?"

"Oh, no," Katya replied. "I must be getting home."

"If it's not too much trouble, then. The Seventh Heaven?"

In less than twenty minutes Katya's car had deposited them before the old Standard Oil building. Curiously, her driver, *Sidor* he thought his name was, had kept Charlie fixed in his rearview mirror the whole time.

Charlie opened the huge, many-paged menu and stared at the undeciperhable oriental characters. Manny had recommended the restaurant, intuitively understanding that Charlie had been asking about a really special place for tonight. He had not been surprised then by the lacquered, gilt-wheeled private rickshaws out front. He had expected the quiet elegance inside, even the steep prices. He had not expected a menu without any English translations.

Maria had parted with her sister in French, made brief remarks to Sidor in Russian, and turned within seconds to greet the doorman, the restaurant's hostess, and the white-coated waiters who stood behind each chair, in Chinese. She slipped in and out of languages like a fish, effortlessly tacking into the next current. Charlie would need help even to order his dinner.

Maria opened her own menu.

"Oh, Charlie," she said. "This is very expensive!"

"The prices I can figure out," he said glumly. "It's the rest of it that's Greek."

"Greek?" Maria looked perplexed.

"A figure of speech," he said, and then willed himself to ask the unavoidable question. "Uh, what do you think you'll be having?"

"Hhmm," Maria responded. She tilted her head musingly and touched the edge of her upper lip with the pink tip of her tongue. "The mán yú should be wonderful. And oh, I do love yuao piao tang! If it's not too salty. Or oily!"

Now she turned around to the starch-coated Chinese behind her. For several minutes the two of them engaged in animated conversation, each of them smiling, nodding, and pointing at items on the big menu. Charlie bristled with irritation.

"Help me out here a little, honey! What the hell is *man yu*?"

The little waiter stepped backward, his eyes flying wide. Maria slowly turned back to face him. The expression on her face was of someone who'd just been struck.

Shit! He was going to have to be more careful. Tonight of all nights. He thought now of the pains he had taken earlier to arrange and tidy the new apartment. He remembered the candle he had placed on the nightstand. The stack of clean towels in the bath.

Maria dropped her head. "I'm sorry," she said softly.

Charlie took in a long deep breath and exhaled it very slowly. He reached between the obstacles of glassware to invite her hand.

"No, *I'm* sorry," he said, lifting the tips of her light cool fingers. "I didn't mean to snap. It just gets a little frustrating sometimes. You know? *Please.* Explain it to me."

"Well," she began warily. "Yuao piao tang is a thick soup. Made of mashed fish bladder."

Charlie made the conscious choice to smile. There was Maria in that alluring yellow dress, her small perfect breasts almost resting on the shelf of the table.

"And mán yú is living river eel. It's cooked in rice wine and soy and sugar and ginger juice. Mr. Lu says that they make a cut at the neck of the eel and another cut at its anus and then the chef inserts two chopsticks in the cut at the neck to remove its intestines."

Charlie held his smile. Her eyes were like green mica in this light. The curve of her neck its own seduction.

"They shower the eel with boiling water, wipe off its mucus, clean it with its skin unbroken and then . . ."

"*Great!*" Charlie interrupted, a little too loudly, fighting the wave of revulsion that might easily show up on his face. "Sounds great! I'm thinking, though, that maybe I'll have something simple tonight. Is there anything like . . . oh, I don't know. Chow mein? Chop suey?"

Maria's intent gaze now skipped away from him to focus diffusely on something above his head. She was confused, he could tell. Mildly disappointed. But she nodded acquiescence and turned to engage her waiter in another little conference, the two of them almost whispering this time, their eyes darting back now and then to the ugly American ogre.

"And will you order us cocktails?" Charlie added. "Anything you like."

Surely the worst was over now. He was not about to make a further fool of himself for their benefit.

Maria and her waiter concluded the business of ordering. The waiter bustled away and for the first time this evening they were really alone.

Charlie reached into the pocket of his jacket for a cigarette. The blue flame of an American Zippo appeared instantly before his face. He had forgotten his own waiter, standing sentry behind his chair.

"You look fabulous tonight," he said, suddenly feeling awkward.

"Thank you," Maria replied. "Thank you very much. I wasn't sure you would like the old style on me."

"Oh, but I *do*," he said. "I love it! It suits you perfectly."

Maria colored slightly and he sensed that she was feeling the same awkwardness. It was just so rare for the two of them to be together alone. Without the chatter and nonsense of others.

There was always, he knew, this phase in a conquest. That delicate and tricky little phase in the newness of the thing when you didn't know exactly where you stood. When you suspected that you might possibly be thinking about the girl more than the girl was thinking about you. It was an uncomfortable part, Charlie knew, but a relatively interesting one. And he knew also that the greatest heat, the apex of it all, could follow soon after it.

But this stage was lasting too long. Their relationship had

proceeded slowly. Always, at the end of their evenings, he escorted her by cab or rickshaw to the door of the family apartment in French town where they kissed good night at the door but he was never invited in. Once or twice he had delivered her to her father on the Bund and they had parted by shaking hands. She was managing him quite well. On the dance floor, in those slow dances when his manhood had pressed unmistakably against her, she had always simply smiled, acknowledging his desire as a compliment. This was altogether different from the taxi dancers, the other girls who tended to either make a joke of it or respond with stone-faced, glassy-eyed indifference. That Maria could acknowledge his desire without either mocking him or encouraging him suggested that she had some experience with men. She was scarcely older than a schoolgirl. And a schoolgirl should not know such things. But tonight he would find out. No work tomorrow. Now he had his own place. Tonight he would find out.

Outside the Seventh Heaven Charlie wrapped his arm around Maria's shoulders and paused to breathe in the crisp December night. It was still chilly, but not as bitter cold as it had been earlier in the week. A misty veil hung over the streets, putting all of the signs and electric lights inside a fuzzy circular nimbus and giving a romantic softness to every plane and edge. He felt pretty good. Infused with a sense of animal well-being. The food hadn't actually been that bad. Two drinks had taken the edge off his anxiety but not his anticipation. So far the evening had gone fairly well and he was about to suggest its perfect ending when the worst thing in the world happened.

From across the street he heard his name being called and Maria squeezed his arm, forcing him to acknowledge the hale.

"Atwood! Charlie Atwood! Is that you?"

The voice came from a little group of sailors on the opposite corner. Charlie peered, but the sailors were only a dress blue cluster until one of them stepped forward, dodging across the traffic of the street to spring upon the sidewalk before them.

The sailor was Tom Fritz, a big, soft, baby-faced fellow whose casual acquaintance he and Krebs had made in their last week of morning stops at the YMCA. Shanghai was lousy with seamen right now. The Navy had taken over the old Shanghai Race Track and converted some of it into an Enlisted Men's Club. This one, Charlie remembered, had said he was assigned to the USS Makin Island, the small carrier that he'd seen that very afternoon from the windows of the Embankment.

"Fritz," Charlie said, allowing his hand to be vigorously pumped. "What are you up to?"

"Last night of shore leave!" Fritz said. "We're taking home some boys from the 10th Army next week. We'll be at sea for Christmas, but we'll ring in the New Year in Georgia!"

Now Fritz delivered a brutal self-congratulatory blow to Charlie's back, just between the shoulder blades.

"Good for you," Charlie said, "That's terrific."

"Georgia?" Maria said. "That's Charlie's home!"

"Right!" Fritz said, "Charlie and I are both crackers!"

Maria frowned, but Fritz kept talking.

"Hey! A few of us are heading over to The Phoenix. That place that Sergeant Krebs was talking about?"

"Oh, I know it!" Maria exclaimed "The father of my dear friend, Su Mei, owns The Phoenix. You'll be very happy there. Please give my regards to Mr. Khu. And to Sue Mei, if she's there."

"No kidding!" Fritz said, drawing himself up to surprised attention, pressing both of his soft chins against the stiff uniform collar. "You got connections at The Phoenix? Then the two of you should come along! Maybe you could introduce your friend?" Fritz poked Charlie with an elbow and delivered an exaggerated Vaudevillian wink to Maria. No wonder Krebs and Fritz had hit it off so well.

"Thanks, "Charlie began, "but we're . . . "

"Oh, that would be lovely!" Maria said. "Wouldn't it, Charlie? It's still so early. We hadn't made other plans yet. Had we, Charlie?"

Charlie's brain raced, constructing and then discarding the beginnings of protests that would give him away. He didn't give a damn what Fritz thought. But he needed to be careful with Maria. Fritz was grinning like a baboon and Maria's small chin tilted up at him, her eyes sparkling with excitement.

Hell. It was still early. Maybe they could just have one drink and be on their way.

It was almost three in the morning before Charlie walked, shakily and alone, across the empty echoing lobby of Broadway Mansions and stabbed again and again at the elevator button for the sixth floor. It hadn't at all turned out to be the evening he'd planned.

Everything that he had hoped to avoid this night had still come to pass. Again they'd been surrounded by the chaos of music and laughter and aimless talk. Strangers, uninvited, had dropped down at their table and stayed for the duration. An American general, one of the Chinese sing-song girls, a sailor she'd only just met—they were all the same to Maria and she turned her small smiling face to them just as she did to him, dignifying their shallow remarks with the same earnest little frown that she gave to him, laughing at their stupid inscrutable jokes just as she laughed at his own. Again he'd been victim to that vague sense of panic he felt whenever she went away from him, for one of the evening's innumerable visits to the lady's room, or to chat with some friend she'd seen across the way. Again he'd surrendered her to others who were better dancers or, taking her to the floor himself, had sensed they were all watching him, perhaps pitying her.

For Maria, he knew, it had been a lovely evening. An incredibly *special* evening. She'd told him exactly that. Just before announcing that she would go home with Su Mei. To save him, she said, the bother of taking her home.

In the bedroom of his apartment Charlie removed his jacket and shoes and then fell headlong, still clothed, onto the bed. For a long while he lay face down, absolutely still in the darkness, listening to his own breath, the audible pump of his blood in his ears. Tears, scaldingly hot, welled in the corners of his eyes and began to fall, copious and still warm, across the bridge of his nose to the pillow. At last he turned over heavily, crossed his stockinged feet, aligned his torso, and placed his hands, fingertips just overlapping, flat on the starched surface of his dress shirt, just below the sternum, in the presentation he had seen in half-open-caskets.

His review of the evening had been taking him to a place of decision and now he surrendered to the process, allowing his thoughts, which had crept slowly at first, to accelerate as he approached the truth, moving faster and more surely as he became more certain. Then, in the kind of reckless, almost terrifying leap to awareness that he had rarely if ever experienced, he saw why it was that a man married. His body shuddered slightly as his mind made the great jump and he arrived at the other side, victorious, but defeated, exultant but trembling at what it meant.

He would marry her. It was decided. He would marry Maria Petrov. Because he had to. Because it was simply impossible not to. Impossible to think of her belonging to someone else. To anyone else. Most impossible of all to think that she could go on, as she did now, belonging to everyone else. He would marry this

Russian girl and put an end to her unconscious but reckless behavior. He would save her and also himself. He would marry her. She would have to be his.

7 January 1946

There have been three more workers strikes in the last week, one of them fairly large. The strikes have been difficult for the city and make everyone nervous, but the New Year celebrations have begun early this year and seem to have distracted everyone a bit from all of these other troubles.

The Khus again are planning to hold the reunion festival at The Phoenix and have invited not just Mama and Papa and Katya of course but also Charlie and Jack and some of their friends.

We are all very worried about Katya and her talk of going away. The authorities have made a visit to her home. Only for inspection, Katya says, and pretends not to be concerned.

From the diary of Maria Petrova, translated from the French

Chapter VII.

"The legend," Maria began, "says that long, long ago, there was a monster called Nian. This monster had been born very ugly and so was shunned by everyone. Even by dragons and unicorns! Oh, the people, of course, were very afraid of him and ran away whenever he came down from the mountains and tried to mix among them. And so this monster, Nian, over time became quite bitter and ferocious and angry. Because this is the way, you know, that it will happen. A friendless creature will always become monstrous."

"And vice versa!" said Krebs, who had just returned to the table and could not possibly have any idea what they were discussing.

Maria smiled at Krebs and paused a moment before going on

with her story.

"On the first of each lunar month, it became the habit of the monster to come down from the mountains to hunt people in the village. So the villagers were very much afraid of it and they locked their doors very early, even before sunset on the days of its' coming.

But in the village, you see, there lived a wise old man. This old man believed that it was really the panic in the people that made the monster so bold and furious. Thus the old man asked the people to organize together and to conquer the monster by means of beating drums and gongs, burning bamboo, and lighting fireworks. The purpose was to make a great noise to threaten the hateful monster. And when the old man told people about the idea, everybody agreed on it. And they all agreed to wear the color red, too, because monsters are said to be afraid of the color red."

"I knew that!" erupted Krebs. "Those ole' monsters hate it. They *hate* red!"

"Can it, Krebs!" said Charlie. "Just let her finish."

"So there was one moonless and freezing cold night when the monster, Nian, appeared again. But this time, the moment it opened its mouth, the people burst out themselves with their own frightening noises. They came at him with the fire they had prepared, and wherever the monster went, it was turned back by the terrible noises. The monster ran away. It ran and ran and ran, but the people chased after it until at last the monster Nian fell down in the fields with exhaustion. Then the people jumped up and killed the evil monster! So, you see, that as savage as the monster was, he lost in the end under the efforts from the cooperation of people. And since then the people have kept the tradition of beating drums and gongs and of lighting fireworks at the coldest day in winter to drive the imagined monsters away and to celebrate the victory over it. Today, *Nian* refers to the New Year's Day or the Spring Festival. People often say *Guo Nian*, which means "live the festival." *Nian* also means the year. For an example, the Chinese often greet each other by saying *Xin Nian Hao*, which means *Happy New Year,* or *Good New Year* to you! *Xin* means *new*, you see, and *Hao* means *good.*"

Maria, almost out of breath, finished her tale and looked around.

"Well done!" said Manny, leading by example the table's smattering of applause. "As good an explanation of Chinese New Year as I've ever heard. And I'm almost older than Nian!"

"My sister collects these fairy tales," said Katya, reaching over to pinch Maria's cheek. "She always has! You should get her to tell you one of her renderings of Beautiful Vassilisa and the bad witch, Baba Yaga."

"Oh, do!" laughed Manny. "I'm sure I'd like that one, too."

"Oh, no," said Katya. "That one will have to wait. Come with me, devuskha. I need to powder my face."

The men half-rose for the women's departure and Charlie smiled after Maria. On his last visit to The Phoenix he had been miserable. Tonight he felt only contentment. Everything was different now. Even the looks of the place. For tonight's private celebration the Khus had reconfigured the furniture in the largest dining room. The smaller tables that normally seated four to eight had been brought together, creating a series of long banquet-sized tables. Each of these had its own centerpiece of flowers and its own line of candles burning in red glass snifters. Overhead, the ceiling was festooned with swagging rows of red paper lanterns in which little electric lights glowed like cheerful coals. Beneath the hum of voices and clinks of glassware, the strains of traditional Chinese lute music flowed from some invisible source and outside the restaurant could be heard the occasional shouts or laughter from passersby and the almost unbroken sound of firecrackers going off in loud bangs from streets nearby and in muffled pops from farther away.

There were a few Caucasian faces here, but most of the

guests were Chinese, and family, a mixture of young and old, from the tiny shriveled grandmother who nodded at the far end of the front table to the pair of identical infants who slept more soundly in identical baskets atop the grand piano. Their own group—the Petrovs and Waechters, Manny and Krebs, a few others from the headquarters office—had been thoughtfully seated together and, through the first five courses anyway, they had stayed put, with the exception of Krebs, who had been up and down all evening. Something, or someone, here had put him in a state of high agitation.

Mr. Khu, their proprietor and host, had not been still either. All evening he had bustled about, delivering instructions to his staff, pushing in and out of the swinging door to the kitchen, bringing fingerbowls and towels, filling himself the cups of rice wine that sat beside each plate. Khu was tall for a Chinese and prosperously dressed in a beautiful western style suit in the fabled Shanghai tailoring. But there were small half-circles of perspiration beneath his waving arms and he gave the impression of one who worked hard for his success.

His wife, on the other hand, approached her own duties as hostess in quite another manner. Mrs. Khu, in a shimmering red silk cheongsam, moved gracefully and leisurely among her guests, touching them on shoulders and bending to inquire into their needs, stopping now and again to sit and chat and laugh. A still beautiful woman in early middle age, she had the glassy black hair and smooth, small-pored skin of an Asian. But the round green eyes were clearly occidental. Here certainly was the explanation for Su Mei's Eurasian good looks, and for those of her younger sister who Krebs had hopped up now to visit.

Charlie studied the handsome Khus and their large and animated family and felt a wave of warm nostalgia and a tolerable hint of homesickness. The slower-paced conversation tonight seemed more authentic than what he typically encountered in the city's commercial establishments. Best of all, the dance floor tonight had been covered over by tables.

Manny nudged Charlie and gestured toward the end of their own long table where Maria's parents were now being visited by Mrs. Khu.

"Rather strange to see old Petrov out of uniform, isn't it?"

Charlie nodded. It was strange, indeed. Tonight Maria's father wore a simple dark suit and seemed thinner, somehow shrunken, without his martial regalia.

"You two seem to have hit it off quite well, I've heard."

"I see him from time to time," Charlie replied. "I bought him a few vodkas on Thursday night. He's very disturbed about the Soviets. About their offering repatriation to the Shanghai Russians."

"Offering it?" Manny scoffed. "It was my understanding that they were *demanding* it!"

"Yeah, they are," said Charlie. "But fortunately we don't have to help. Washington dithered over it for a while but they finally announced a policy. Our position is no forced repatriation."

"A lot of them do seem to want to go back, though. You can see them queuing up for passports outside the Soviet Embassy every day."

I know," said Charlie. "And it's making Petrov nearly crazy. He says it's mostly the younger ones that are falling for it. He thinks they'll be picked up as soon as they get back on Russian soil."

Manny clucked and shook his head. "I wouldn't be surprised. The censorship is too tight to get any real news. It may be years before we know what really happens to them."

"But tell me!" Manny went on. "Does the fact that you've spoken with Sergei mean that it's official? Are congratulations in order?"

In spite of himself Charlie felt his face redden.

"I guess so," he said. "I gave her a ring at Christmas and

actually thought we might make the announcement tonight. But when I suggested it, Maria reacted pretty strangely. She said it would be inappropriate. *Impoli,* I think is what she said."

Manny chuckled. "Oh, I don't know about that. This is a family celebration. So it would seem appropriate in that way. And Maria and Sue Mei have been friends since they were small. But the Russians and the Chinese have always been a little aloof from each other. It's funny, really. When you might think they'd have so much in common. But the roots of it, I suppose, go back a long way. When the first ones came it was quite difficult, I'm told. The Chinese had never seen white men beg. They were happy to have something lower to mock."

"Must have been pretty rotten," Charlie said. "Sergei has told me a little, but it's hard to imagine it."

"Oh, well, they got on. The Russians handled it in their own way. They banded together. French town is the evidence of that! And relations are mostly fine now. The young ones have really bridged the gap. But some of the older ones . . . well, I suppose they remember."

Charlie nodded towards Olena.

"She doesn't seem so uncomfortable here."

"She's an interesting woman," Manny said. "Well-educated. Aristocratic. From an old Russian family. I don't really know her well. But if you believe Sergei, she's practically a saint. He certainly credits her with holding them together during the worst years."

Charlie was about to ask a question about those years when the sounds of loud shouting in the street outside turned every head towards the commotion. He and Manny and several of the other men stood up and sprinted to the door.

There had apparently been some kind of traffic accident, but it took pushing into the growing throng before they could see what had happened. It appeared that an American jeep carrying four Marines had struck a pedicab. The pedicab had been mangled, and across the street its young coolie driver lay moaning at the curb. The boy didn't appear to be mortally injured, but a long slash of skin had been peeled from one naked calf and he bled also from a half-dozen lesser scrapes. One of the Marines stood over the injured youth. Another examined the jeep's broken headlight. The other two stared menacingly into the crowd.

For a moment Charlie thought that the biggest Marine was attempting to aid his victim, but instead the soldier drew back a boot and delivered a brutal kick to the coolie's ribs.

"You slope-eyed chink!" the Marine bellowed. "Do you see what you've *done*?"

Gasps of horror escaped from the crowd. A woman shrieked and then a chorus of shouts rose up, unintelligible, but angry. Charlie turned to look for Manny and saw from the corner of his eye that the curtains at The Phoenix's windows had now been pulled back and dozens of the reunion guests peered through the glass.

The youth on the ground writhed in pain, but the Marine apparently wasn't satisfied.

"Stupid yellow jack-off!" he said through gritted teeth, and delivered another kick.

Charlie stood, paralyzed with indecision. Something should be done, but he wasn't about to take on four Marines by himself. Still, someone should *do* something!

A powerful shove from behind whirled Charlie half-way around. When he'd righted himself, he saw Colonel Petrov plowing through the onlookers, advancing into the small center space that held only the boy and his attacker.

"Stop that!" Petrov commanded, planting himself in front of the Marine.

For a moment the burly soldier looked confused, even shocked. But his face relaxed into a widening grin.

"Get out of my way, old man," he laughed. "I've got business with this slope here."

"*Go home!*" Petrov thundered. "And take these other barbarians with you!"

This was the trigger point. The crowd fell completely silent. Charlie's heart hammered, but his body felt frozen in place. He knew he should act, but in the hard knot of his stomach he seemed to already feel the pain of punches landing.

Now Manny Rosario suddenly appeared in the little circle, followed quickly by Grieg Waechter, Krebs, and Mr. Khu. Jolted from his paralysis, Charlie now joined these and the other men who were pouring out of The Phoenix. Together they formed a tight little huddle behind the big Russian in his Sunday suit.

Now the Marine blinked stupidly several times and the grin melted from his face. He glanced around but could not seem to locate his buddies. For an interminable moment he scowled back at Petrov.

"Aw, the hell with it," he said at last, and turned then to shoulder his way back through the crowd. In another minute they all heard the roar of the Jeep's engine and the cries of people scurrying to get out of its way and almost immediately the loud claxton of an ambulance and the wail of a police siren.

Some of the onlookers began to disperse. Others lingered on the sidewalks, discussing the incident in energetic sing-song bursts. But the real excitement was over now, and Mr. Khu beckoned his own guests back inside. His dessert course had yet to be served.

"Aloof?" Charlie said, as he held the door of the Phoenix for Manny.

Manny laughed and shook his head. "Well, of course I didn't mean Petrov."

It was quite warm back inside the restaurant and for a while the guests merely milled about, jabbering excitedly, but gradually they began to return to their places and Sue Mei, her two younger sisters, and Maria and Katya hurried to help pass the gigantic platters of pastries and teacakes, dried and candied fruit, and wrapped chocolates. Charlie settled again into his seat beside Manny and presently began to nibble at a piece of candied hawthorn. But the feeling of easy contentment that he'd savored all evening had all but disappeared. The talk at the other tables had become subdued now, almost confidential. He could understand little of what was being said, but he sensed that everywhere the conversation remained stuck on the incident in the street. Clearly the Chinese coolie hadn't been the only victim of the accident. The States in general, the American military in particular, had also taken a beating in many of these minds. Each time he looked out he saw accusing almond eyes directed at him. Even the beautiful Mrs. Khu turned abruptly away when he smiled at her.

###

April had begun with four days of chilly, unrelenting rain, but two days before the Quin Ming Festival the sun had broken through, ensuring that the day, as the festival's name promised, would indeed be clear and bright. The rickshaw workers strike, which had all but immobilized the city for days, had ended, or been called because of the Festival, and the girls had easily found a coolie to bring them most of the way to the cemetery.

This would the fourth year in a row that Maria had accompanied Su Mei for the sweeping of the tombs, but the first in which Katya would not be coming along. Su Mei's own sister had abandoned them this year, too, apparently for a date with Krebs, and Su Mei had been out of sorts about it all morning.

The walk to the old public cemetery was steeply uphill but it was good to be outdoors after the gray days of rain and everyone they had met had seemed friendly and pleasant this morning. Su Mei carried a woven basket of hand gardening tools. To Maria she had given the small cotton bag that held the food and other paper-wrapped gifts for the dead and the enormous bouquet of fresh flowers they would distribute among the favorites of Su Mei's ancestors. The two women joined the line of others moving up the hill, stepping carefully to avoid the puddled ruts in the poor road. When they had reached their own destination, near the center of a long row of tombs at almost the highest point on the terraced hill, both girls dropped their bundles and stood to look about.

There were many families here already, some in their festive best, others in the plain cotton tunics and black pants that were the uniform of China's peasants. Children scrambled up and down over the terraced steps of the cemetery, laughing and chasing one another or flying one of the many colored kites in varying shapes and sizes that dipped and swooped in the cloudless blue sky. Maria saw designs made to resemble frogs and dragonflies, birds and bats, even a crab and a stork. The green hillside itself was also punctuated everywhere with bright spots of color—with the reds and whites and yellows and purples of the floral offerings, the spirit money and other gifts that had been laid about the headstones.

"It's a beautiful place," Maria said. "Your ancestors must be happy here."

Sue Mei put her hands on her hips and heaved a dramatic sigh.

"Oh, sure," she said. "It's all in harmony. The cemetery faces south, of course, which is very, *very* important. Then there are the surrounding aspects. The hills, you see. And there's the little stream down there." She pointed just past the highest ledge where the ground fell away to dense growth and one could hear the light gurgle of running water.

"And then there are the groves of pine trees. All of this creates the best flow of *chi* to keep the ancestors happy." Su Mei rolled her eyes and shrugged, as if to mock the words she'd only just spoken. To suggest that she herself didn't necessarily believe in the old feng shui folklore. And yet Maria knew she didn't necessarily *disbelieve* it either. That was the way of the young women in China. Especially the educated ones.

But it *was* a beautiful place and Maria felt a melancholy envy. Her own family had no places like this. Or if they did exist, somewhere in Russia, there was no means by which they might visit them. And the final resting places of so many would be lost and unmarked.

The Chinese believed that the spirits of deceased ancestors looked after the family. If that were true, Maria could only imagine the restless wanderings of their own ancestral dead.

"Do you think it matters?" she asked aloud. "Do you think it matters to the ancestors if the family moves away?"

"What?" Sue Mei said. She had begun pulling cotton gloves over her beautifully manicured fingers.

"Oh. I see. Of course it does. It's not at all unusual for families who must go away to take the bones of their ancestors with them."

"Take this one here," she said. Sue Mei pointed to a small moon-shaped headstone that bore no discernable inscription but had already been honored with little packets of pork, a few flowers, and several fluttering bills of spirit money held down against the wind by pebbles.

"He may have been left behind," she said. "This one we just call *Old Ancestor*. Nobody even remembers who he was! Father says perhaps he is dead to us. Because we've failed to remember. But that doesn't mean we're dead to him."

This time there was no hint of sarcasm at all in Su Mei's voice. She had stooped beside the stone to extract the clumps of dry autumn leaves that had accumulated at its base.

Maria bent to retrieve the bouquet of flowers she had carried up the hill. She selected a few of the very best stems and placed them atop the decaying headstone.

Yes. She could understand Mr. Khu's logic. A person couldn't really die, not really, as long as there was someone who remembered him. In their own family it was Papa who did the remembering. For them it was Papa who called up the names, the memories, of uncles and aunts and cousins—that horde of invisible *others* who had once populated the family tree and to whom she and Katya owed their very being.

Papa, she thought, hadn't let anyone go. He still remembered, of course, the names of fellow soldiers who had died or disappeared. But he had also told them the story of their grandmother, Valentina, who had made them leave her behind on the frozen lake. The enemy was gaining. Valentina was too ill.

It was because of Papa, too, that they knew about Mama's sister. About how the filthy Bolshevik, merely for Ana's impertinence to him, had hurled her from the moving train and they had watched her small body tumble, bouncing like an acorn, down the steep ravine.

Many of Papa's tired old tales had bored his daughters. All of them had annoyed his wife. But for the first time in her life Maria felt a warm rush of gratitude for her father's stories and the ones he'd kept alive.

Su Mei moved on, skipping a pair of older stones here on the highest tier, but stopping at another ancient marker, this one's identification not quite so obscured by time.

"This is my Auntie Meng" said Su Mei. "And *she* isn't dead to me. I remember her. I do. Her feet had been bound as a child and I have no memory of ever seeing her walk. But she always sat at the window in Deshi's house and she rested those tiny little feet on a silk pillow and let children on her lap. Father says I was too young to remember. But he's wrong. Auntie Meng smelled of sandalwood. And I remember."

Maria placed a few more blooms atop the crumbling headstone in remembrance of Auntie Meng and followed again behind Su Mei who seemed to pick up speed as she descended the terraced rows.

They had not come early to the cemetery. Most of the graves here had already been swept, and few, if any, lacked tributes. Su Mei's work for the most part now was only symbolic gesture, but she paused from time to time to comment on the occupant of a grave and Maria listened thirstily to the little stories that Su Mei told of the relatives she did remember, the inherited anecdotal tales of those she didn't.

Su Mei's mother was only half Chinese. She had no maternal ancestors in this cemetery. But somewhere in the city another branch of the family was undoubtedly sweeping other ancestral tombs. The Khus had filled the Phoenix at the reunion celebration. They were a large prosperous family with a venerable history. With excellent memories.

In Maria's own family there were only four now. Only four, possibly, who still remained of two long lines of blood and tradition. Of Papa's three brothers and his many cousins, almost all of them soldiers, all felled by differing enemies on various battlefields. Of Mama's ancient family, the line easily traced to the days of Peter the Great who had given them the lands of the Rose Palace and the responsibility of an entire village.

Only four! And now Katya was leaving. It seemed she *must* go for Grieg's safety and perhaps even her own. Then they would be only three.

The sun had scarcely passed its brilliant height and only the lightest of breezes ruffled the grass and leaves, but Maria now began to feel that she was moving in shadow and each light task of their grave tending added to a chill that could not be explained by the bright spring weather. Around them children laughed and birds twittered, but with each step Maria felt the thought, the presence, of their own unknown, unremembered *others*, wrapping her like a cool, cottony cloud.

It was not entirely new, this felt presence. She had sensed it before and so, she knew, had Katya. They had even tried to conjure it up as children, telling each other their own ghost stories, made from the fragments of their father's tales. They had even played at Ana's death, using their dolls to act out her murder and her body's cascading fall into the gorge. It appalled her now to remember their macabre play and Maria shivered in the sunlight.

And yet, perhaps, it was not really so awful. They had, after all, been born and had grown up in China. Among people who venerated, even worshipped, their ancestors. Perhaps she and Katya had done no harm. At least they could remember those whose deaths they had play-acted. And, in remembering, perhaps they had kept them alive.

"Do you think of them as ghosts?" Maria asked Su Mei. "Do you think they walk among us?"

Su Mei stood up slowly, the weed she had just pulled from the side of a headstone still dangling from her hand.

"Maria!" she said. "How morbid you are today! I've never known you to be so preoccupied with the dead." She knocked the root end of her weed clump against the headstone, dislodging a shower of dirt.

"I'm sorry," Maria said. "I don't feel morbid. But I can't seem to help it. Being here, I suppose. Thinking of all the ancestors my parents had to leave behind."

She paused for a moment and swallowed hard.

"Thinking of Katya leaving. Wondering if we'll ever see her again."

Su Mei tossed her weed away and hurried to Maria. The friends embraced and Maria let her head rest on Su Mei's shoulder.

"Oh, dear," Su Mei said. "Of course that makes you sad. But you mustn't think that way! Of course you'll see her again. Of course you will!"

After a moment Su Mei pushed Maria gently away.

"But you should be happy!" she said. "You're about to

become a bride! What shouldn't you be happy?"

Maria smiled. "I'm happy," she said. "I'm happy."

Now Su Mei began hurriedly returning her tools to the basket. From Maria's hand she plucked the last flowering stem and plopped it unceremoniously on a nearby stone. In single file they began moving along the terraced step in the direction of the little road.

"You do like him, don't you?" Maria asked of Su Mei's back. "I know you think it's too soon for us. But you like him, don't you, my Charlie?"

Su Mei didn't respond. Perhaps, walking ahead as she was, she hadn't heard Maria's words.

Maria tried again, a little louder this time.

"You like him, don't you, Su Mei?"

Su Mei walked on a few more paces and then stopped, turning round on the narrow row to face Maria.

"I don't know," she said at last. "I'm of two minds."

"Two minds?" said Maria. She was not certain about the expression.

"I want you to be happy, my friend. I want only the best in this life for you! But your Charlie is an American. I'm finding I don't like the Americans so much."

Maria thought immediately of the ugly incident at the reunion feast. It was the only such scene that she herself had actually witnessed, but the rumors of bad behavior by the Americans were increasing every week. There were stories of café brawls, fights with police, even assaults on Chinese women. The attitude among many, though it was quite absurd, was that one occupying enemy had merely been replaced by another. She had even started to see signs, posted prominently in public places, telling the Americans to get out of China. To go home.

But they weren't all like that. Charlie wasn't like that.

"You can't think that Charlie and Jack are happy about these things. Charlie is a good man."

"I know," said Sue Mei earnestly. "But I worry for you. Maria, I love you. I have other sisters. But you have always been the sister of my heart."

"Of course you were born here," she went on, "just as I was. I understand that this is the only life you've ever known."

Now Su Mei lifted her gaze to follow the stuttering descent of a red and gold butterfly kite being reeled in, or falling, to earth. When she spoke again her voice was distant and strange.

"But even you, Maria, are not Chinese. And Shanghai is changing. *China* is changing. I try, but I don't see how you and your American will belong in the China that's coming. I try. But I can't see your future."

For another moment they both stared at the sky and the plunging kite and then wordlessly they moved on to join the foot traffic in the cemetery's road. Some were still coming up the little road but even more now were going home. They made their descent down the hill in silence, each fearing to add to what had already been said.

At length they came to the bottom of the hill.

"You will come, though?" Maria said. "You will come to my wedding?"

Su Mei laughed.

"Of course, little sister," she said. "Of course, I'll come! I've already chosen my dress!"

12 June 1946

Having Katya at home again for this short time before they sail has been a great comfort to Mama. They talk all the time like two old ladies and have done everything for the wedding. I can't remember quite where Grieg is spending his own last days here, but we see little of him and he only calls when there is some question about their papers or baggage.

Papa, though, has been almost a wild thing lately. He weeps for Katya in one moment, he laughs for me in the next. I'm not sure this wedding should be happening so soon but I feel I must give them some small happiness in the face of their great loss.

And I do <u>so</u> want Katya to be here to see me marry. I can't believe that she's truly going. And Argentina. So far!

From the diary of Maria Petrova, translated from the French

Chapter VIII.

"Heavens!" Olena exclaimed. "We'll be two more days righting this kitchen!"

Katya pushed the last sheet of pastries into the oven and turned to survey the damage. All morning they had been making lepeshki, the sweet little sour cream biscuits that Maria loved and had requested for her wedding feast. Almost every surface in the little kitchen was powdered with flour and sugar and the floor below them crunched from the fallen flakes of almonds.

Katya looked around and laughed.

"Oh, Mama!" she said. "I'm such a messy baker. I throw everything around! And I've been so spoiled, you know. I make the mess and the amah cleans it. But I'll clean this one up. Go and rest a bit."

Olena still smiled but the reference to Katya's old life, so recently lost, brought a quick little clutch to her heart. For three weeks now, since Katya and Grieg had quietly vacated the house on Columbia Road, their Katya had been here, as of old, sharing the room with her sister and working industriously alongside her on the preparations for Maria's wedding. Katya had been gay and stoic about her changed circumstances and by unspoken agreement they had all avoided the subject of Grieg's troubles as well as the uncertainty of the couple's future. But the coming separation lay between them, a yawning wound too tender to touch.

"I hate to abandon you, kiska," Olena replied, "but I do think I will. You're still young. I don't suppose your back feels like mine."

"Oh, *do* go," said Katya, her face puckered and frowning like a guilty child's. "It won't take me long. I promise!"

Olena slipped off her bibbed apron and moved out of the little kitchen and across the narrow hall to the sitting room where she dropped herself, not at the end of the dilapidated settee where she usually read or graded her papers, but in Sergei's own chair where she could still catch angled glimpses of Katya, crossing between table and sink. Olena sighed and settled deeply into the big chair, feeding while she still could on the sight of Katya's quick, graceful movements.

How fast it had gone! All of it! Their infancies and childhoods. Their passionate, confusing adolescences. And how slight, after all, had been the pains and sacrifices of bearing and rearing the both of them—sacrifices, it seemed to her now, that she had worn like a martyr's stripes. How silly, now in the face of losing her, seemed the trivial arguments she'd had with little Katya. Over games or dolls. Over grades or deportment. How harsh she had been to her! Over nothing. Over the failure to decline a noun properly. Over the great unforgiveable sin of improperly washing her hands.

Olena squeezed her eyes shut over the threatening tears and let her thoughts drift backwards to that time of Katya's birth.

They had been two years in China then. Two years of bewildering confusion, of moving from place to place and rarely knowing what the next day might bring. At first, when the menses had not come, she hadn't worried. It happened to many of them in those early years—to those women who worked too hard, became too thin, who lived in unrelenting fear. But this time it had not come for another reason and she had begun praying almost immediately that, *if* His will be done, the child's soul might be taken to God.

But that, apparently, had not been His will. She had not understood it, or been grateful for the fact that her pregnancy had persisted. That she had grown round and full and heavy in spite of being hungry all of the time.

She had accepted the pains of her long labor with almost animal resignation and stoically prepared herself to meet the news of the child's stillbirth, or the awful monster her sin of wishing it dead had spawned. Instead there had been the surprise—the glorious, almost cruel surprise— of seeing the wet and wriggling infant lifted up, a thin-limbed and pot-bellied girl child, mottled and squalling, but undeniably, *furiously* alive.

And perfect, they said. Perfect! Down to the miniscule digits of fingers and toes.

Like a ship whose limp sails are billowed by a sudden squall, she had felt herself that day, just so recently emptied, now being filled again, the whole of her being stretched to a new expansion. Like a ship, too, she sensed that she had now been given direction, set on course with not merely a reason, but a drive to live. *Here was this child!* Against all odds and in spite of her horrible, secret wish that it would die, here *was* this child.

She had become a mother. Four years later, a mother again, in the easy delivery of little Maria, but by then her true course had been set. Her own growing strength had surpassed Sergei's, who in time became childlike himself to her, and certainly to them. He had been the one to indulge their childish imaginations in play. The one with whom they could build castles and make fairy tales and the one they ran to for comfort. She had become the disciplinarian, the one to make the rules and the one to enforce them—the punisher, though she'd never laid a hand on them, or even a student, in her life. But she had seen, early on, what the dangers were in this place, this city where a white woman could be bought for the night for the price of a loaf of bread. She had willingly become the bad witch, the Baba Yaga, for their sakes, and thought it had been necessary. But now she saw that her long posturing had made her seem hard, even loveless, to them. Suddenly she saw her mothering as a long series of needless cruelties and that with Katya at least it was too late to be forgiven.

Across the hall Katya was now washing the cleared surface of the kitchen table, humming a little tune as she worked. Olena watched her, her own thoughts echoing Sergei's anguished questions, moaned softly to her last night in the privacy of their bed. *How will we bear this? How can we lose our child?*

Still posturing, she had pretended to shame him. They were not losing this child! Not really. How could he say such a thing? Hadn't they stood, many times, alongside others who had actually suffered that most horrible, unnatural grief? Had he forgotten the Khavins? The Tomilins who had buried two in a month? This was nothing like that! Their Katya lived, and *would* live. Safely, in Buenos Aires. In a place and among a people that, while they could not really imagine it, would nonetheless be real and alive. Thus this was not the worst. This pain of this departure, however hard, was not as great as a parent's might be.

This was the cold logic she had offered the father. And yet the mother knew, as surely as if she were closing a casket upon her daughter's face, that they were nearing the last glimpses they would ever have of their firstborn. The distance between Buenos

Aires and Shanghai—more than ten thousand miles they said—was impossible. Even if by some miracle she and Sergei could procure papers, the money would never be found. And in spite of everything the Americans and their allies had done, they had not finished the war here. The peace agreement between Chiang's forces and the communists had already collapsed and the next war, an internal one bringing its own turmoil, had already taken the stage.

They were growing old here. Already she had stopped bothering the doctors with the frequent lightheadedness, the birdlike fluttering of her heart in its cage. Sergei was stronger perhaps, more virile and energetic, but he was not immortal either. Here is where they would die. In Shanghai. This place that Sergei, after all these years, still thought of as a way station, a temporary fallback before the next victorious charge.

Katya would be lost to them. Their cross now was to not pin their hopes too desperately on Maria. To not so burden the child with their own fears that her life too might become small and circumscribed. For Maria's sake, and the new life she was beginning with her young American, they could change nothing. It was too late to alter any of their patterns, the formula that, however misguided, had served to rear their girls safely, virtuously as far as she knew, and competent in several languages to present themselves among cultured and civilized people.

They should do nothing to alert Maria to their terror, to make her feel the weight of their need. Sergei must be allowed, even encouraged, to go on with his weeping and laughing and dancing, his wasting of money in the cafes, his friendships with like-minded fools which made him believe that he was effecting, could effect, the course of war and politics. And she would go on as she always had. Letting them think her cold and severe, indifferent to the life of their imaginations, the flights of their insubstantial dreams and their girlish, human, hearts.

From her vantage in Sergei's chair she could see a batter-laden ladle dropped at the foot of the kitchen table and a dusty patch of flour that Katya had missed near the door. Cleanliness, she had always told them, might not be quite so dear to God's heart as everyone supposed, but He certainly didn't love filth. And simple sanitation was a good practice for health. Katya was going soon to a new place and strange people. She would need reminding.

Their wedding would take place in the Church of St. Nicholas, the church which the early Russian émigrés like Maria's parents had built with their hoarded pennies back in the thirties, and the only church that Maria had Katya had ever attended.

"It's dedicated to the czar martyr," Maria had told him.

"To who?" Charlie had asked. Maria was always assuming that he knew things he really didn't.

"To Saint Nicholas," she had said. "The passion bearer. The last czar. Oh, it's beautiful! You'll see. There are wonderful frescos."

Actually he *had* seen the church. On a late-night pedicab ride. He thought he recalled a small stuccoed structure with a tall peacock-blue onion dome rising above its modest height, but he'd been a little tight that night and couldn't trust his impression, let alone remember the exact location. Maria had suggested that on the day of the wedding he and Krebs should approach the church on foot, perhaps gathering their wits and having their last bachelor conversation in the little park that was only a short alley's distance from St. Nicholas.

"They call it French Park now," Maria had said. "But Mama and Papa call it *Kukaza*. It's Number 18 Rue Corneille."

They had found it all right. Manny had dropped them off, ridiculously early, and then he and Krebs, stiff and careful in their full dress uniforms, had found themselves using its little walks and benches to perform an anxious comic ballet of pacing and smoking, sitting and standing, pacing and smoking again.

Strangely Krebs seemed almost as nervous as Charlie was. And not just jumpy, but irritable. Charlie thought perhaps it was the fresh haircut which had left Krebs with little white half-moons around the top of his ears.

"Son of a bitch!" Krebs suddenly burst out when they had just completed their third lap around the park's perimeter. "Don't you love the irony?"

"Irony?" Charlie repeated. "What irony?"

"The irony of jumping out of the frying pan into the fire! It was all your idea, you know. To come to this fascinating cesspool! What was it? Just eight or nine months ago? You were desperate to do anything to keep from going back stateside where that little cheerleader could ball and chain you. And now look at this!"

Charlie had to smile. So maybe it *was* ironic. But there was nothing comparable between Bonnie Jo Richards and Maria Petrov.

"Guess you gotta' figure it was destiny, right? All the way from finding that notice on the mess hall board to standing here, half an hour away from tying the big knot."

"Destiny." said Krebs. "Sure."

Again Charlie heard the irritation in Krebs' voice.

"What's the matter, old man? You're not worried about me, are you?"

"Worried? About you?" Krebs now ground the dead cigarette butt he'd been carrying viciously into the lawn.

"What are you saying, then? Do you think that I would . . . that I'd . . . that I'd do anything to *hurt* Maria?"

"Aw, I don't know," said Krebs dismally. His face had taken on a look of dull confusion. Heavily he sat down again on the little iron bench.

"I don't know," Krebs said again. "Maybe you wouldn't mean to. But you can be a selfish son-of-a-bitch, Atwood. Remember the girl from Akron? And the nurse at Kunming? "

"Well, sure," Charlie said. "But that was . . . "

"The hunt!" Krebs said brightly. "I remember you saying that. That the catch was always a disappointment. It was the hunt and the chase, you said. Men were made for the hunt!"

Charlie was growing annoyed. He didn't remember any such conversation. It was Krebs, really, who'd been the big ladies man in Shanghai. And he didn't appreciate being castigated by Krebs on his wedding day.

Suddenly, as though the little iron bench had somehow ejected him, Krebs jumped straight up onto his feet.

"Geez Louise!" he said, looking wild-eyed at Charlie. "Did you even *tell* your family? Does your mother even *know* about this?"

"I told her," Charlie said. "I sent her a wire last Thursday."

He had meant, for weeks, to write letters to all of them. He had even made fumbling starts once or twice. But the time had somehow gotten away from him and he hadn't written. Now he realized that his succinct, economical cablegram had probably broken his mother's heart. *Marrying Maria on Saturday,* he had cabled. *Small church wedding. Will get pictures.* There was going to be a ton of repair work to be done if he ever went back home.

"Thursday," said Krebs. "That's great. You tipped 'em off on Thursday." He sat down with defeated resignation, but then tilted his head up quizzically.

"And you wrote it yourself?"

"Yeah," Charlie replied. "I thought you'd like the part about the church wedding."

The church wedding part *had* actually been the kind of thing that Krebs would have included. Particularly since his mother's letters lately had been consumed with questions about Maria's "faith" and her "family background." He was pretty sure that

Estelle Atwood—who didn't even approve of Methodists or Episcopalians or Presbyterians—wouldn't be warm to a Russian Orthodox ceremony. He had heard her more than once refer to Catholics generally as "idol-worshipping papists." And frankly, he, too, was a little put off by their mumbo jumbo, their ikons and rosaries. But at least they weren't Jews. For that his mother would never have forgiven him.

"So what's this thing going to be like, anyway?" Krebs asked.

Charlie hesitated. There had been no rehearsal. Everything he knew about today's events had come through Maria.

"I don't know much, really. There's a priest and all. Maria says that in the ceremony the groom and the bride are crowned. Like the king and queen of their own little kingdom. The priest takes the crowns and holds them above the couple and says, *the servants of God*—and he puts in our names—are *crowned in the name of the Father, and of the Son, and of the Holy Spirit. Amen.*"

"That sounds OK," said Krebs. "Maybe the crown part is a little creepy."

"Yeah," said Charlie. "Maybe. The crowns are supposed to represent martyrdom or something. Maria says it's because every true marriage involves self-sacrifice on both sides."

"Both sides," said Krebs. "Right."

"Listen," said Charlie. "Do you have some kind of a problem?"

"I don't know," said Krebs, "Maybe."

Charlie felt himself tense but the anger that he had seen flare in Krebs' eyes died almost instantly away.

Krebs sat down again. He shook his head.

"She's such a little butterfly, your Maria. That's what she is! A butterfly. And you're . . ."

"I'm what?" Charlie said. "She's a butterfly. And I'm what?"

Krebs didn't answer.

"*What?*" Charlie demanded, "A *pig*? A bull in a china closet maybe? A *dog*? What am I, Krebs?"

Krebs looked up. He still hadn't answered, but the familiar twinkle had appeared in his eyes.

"What?" Charlie asked again, not quite so insistently. He was trying to ignore the devilish twinkle, the fact that Krebs was now doing that ridiculous elevator thing with his eyebrows.

"A jack ass!" Krebs said gleefully. "You're a jack ass and you know it!"

Charlie tried to react, but his protest dissolved into wordless sputter. Krebs was rocking with laughter now on the little bench, his polished dress shoes rising from the ground and thudding down again as he pounded both knees with his fists.

"A butterfly . . . and a . . . jack . . . ass! What a match!"

For several seconds Charlie merely gaped at Krebs, reveling in his absurdly juvenile joke. He felt every right to be angry. But there was Krebs, just being Krebs, and enjoying it immensely. Unwillingly Charlie felt the contagion of the humor taking hold of him. In another second he was laughing himself, nudging Krebs over on the bench.

For several minutes they laughed uncontrollably, attracting the attention of a few others in the park and frightening two small children in school uniforms who ran wailing to their mother.

At last Krebs produced a pocket handkerchief and they each used it to wipe their eyes.

"Are you scared? " Krebs said, breathless but finally calm.

"Yeah," said Charlie. "I'm scared."

"But I can do this," he went on. "I'll get through it."

And he knew that he would. As skittish as he felt, as surprisingly animal-frightened as he'd ever been, there was another aspect of him, another corner of his nature, that was certain and committed. This had to be done. There were a hundred places in the world, a thousand, *a million* places perhaps, where he would rather have been on this bright and beautiful Shanghai afternoon in the twenty-fifth year of his life. But none of those other places were going to get him Maria.

At precisely three forty-five the two of them walked silently side by side through the short alley and approached the church, timing their arrival perfectly to be met and then led inside by a young acolyte in white robes who had been stationed there for the purpose.

Maria had tried to prepare him for the elegant beauty of the small church. Still he was mildly shocked, slightly taken aback by the artistry in even the preliminary frescos in the little vestibule, by the decorative richness of the place, the carvings and gold ornament that represented the obvious sacrifice of these lost Russians. He had expected to see beauty and to feel some emotion on this his wedding day. He had not expected to be made so vulnerable, so sweetly raw by the strains of dimly heard music and the high delicate voices of the choir. He had not expected to take the sight of Maria almost as a blow, to feel his head go light and his knees made watery at seeing her in the simple white dress, her pure angelic face glimpsed only hazily through the lacey veil. He had not anticipated how grateful he would be for the brief ring-blessing ceremony in the vestibule that would allow him to hold her hand for the whole rest of the service.

Apparently the Russian orthodox ceremony didn't require the long march of the bride and her attendants that he was familiar with and he found himself, rather suddenly and without fanfare, standing alongside Maria before the high gilded altar at which the richly robed priest presided, intoning cryptically—was it Latin or Russian?—to the gathered congregants who Charlie sensed, more than saw, behind them.

He understood but vaguely the meanings involved in the several blessings, the lighting of the candles, the wrapping of the embroidered scarf over their intertwined hands, but he was deeply affected by each of these rituals and not unconscious of the fact that he was playing a part in a very old play.

Now the robed priest, his face a wrinkled pink under the

strange stiff hat, his hands pale and lovely as they flitted in and out of the elaborately brocaded vestments, made the sign of the cross before them. Standing behind Maria, glimpsed only in the corner of his eye, Charlie saw Katya lift and suspend a bejeweled crown over Maria's head and felt, though he could not see it, Krebs raising its counterpart over his own. The crown had not touched him but he felt his scalp tingle and the hairs on his neck rise upward.

Soon the priest tugged at the scarf that lapped their hands and began to lead them with it around the altar. Round they went, the priest leading them like gentle sheep, three times around the altar with the tether of the scarf. All the while the choir sang and the priest droned his mystic incantations.

Charlie would never know exactly where in the exotic but beautiful service that he and Maria had officially become man and wife, but at some point he felt that he had become enchanted, fallen completely under the spell of the candlelight and music, the strange religion and its rituals. He might easily have stayed there forever, doing whatever was asked of him by the siren voices of the choir and the genial, beguiling priest.

It was only afterwards, in the flurry of congratulations, the hearty back-slapping from Krebs and Manny and Murdoch and the others, in being kissed by relative strangers and smothered in the ample bosoms of old women he'd never seen before, that Charlie came to himself again. He seemed to wake, fully relaxed and smiling, genuinely pleased and humbled by what had been accomplished. He was married now! All of the agonies of indecision were over. A great dark weight had fallen away and he felt light, buoyant, and happy.

There were a few formal portraits inside the church and then almost the entire assemblage gathered for a group photograph on the steps outside. For the first time that day Charlie embraced his new in-laws. Olena and Sergei had not attended the ceremony. One of their strange superstitions degreed that it was bad luck for the bride's parents to attend the wedding. But they were here now, having waited outside the little church through all of it and Sergei Petrov especially seemed as weepy and sentimentally affected as if he'd been inside.

The photographer lined everyone up on the shallow steps, pushing and pulling at his subjects until he was satisfied, snapping a picture or two and then rearranging them again. In every configuration Charlie and Maria were at the center of the group and Sergei Petrov, taller by a head than any of the rest, stood behind at the apex. In the last portraits the photographer called for only the small wedding party and "family," and Maria smiled and pressed his arm at the word. Charlie felt a strange self-consciousness, as though he himself looked through the camera's eye or already held the yet unrealized portrait in his hand. Could life really be so marvelously strange? Was this really him? A shy, fatherless boy from Hazel Grove, Georgia, standing here, alongside a Russian bride in Shanghai, China?

When the photographer at last released them and everyone laughingly exhaled and began to move away, Charlie grabbed Krebs by the elbow of his dress uniform and pulled him bodily against him.

"I love you, man," Charlie said. "Thanks for being here."

Krebs, obviously touched, but surprised, too, by the gesture, only patted Charlie's back awkwardly.

Charlie tightened his embrace.

"And I love her, too, Jack," he whispered into his friend's ear. "Don't worry."

The wedding feast was to be held at the Cathay Hotel—that scene, the exact place, where Charlie had first seen his future father-in-law and formed his first impression of the sad and romantic complexities of the family he would inherit. The expensive rooms—a good-sized banquet hall and a small anteroom for cloaks and packages—had been discounted, but not made a gift of, to Sergei by his employers. Charlie had been allowed to make a small contribution to the expenses of the wedding. Krebs had asked to chip in his pot from an especially good night of gambling, and Grieg Waechter's contribution, everyone knew, had been generous and considerable. There was a long white banquet table along the wall, loaded with food, much of it supplied not by the Cathay but by the Petrov women and others from the church.

Sergei had hired a traditional balalaika orchestra—he hadn't needed anyone's help with that—and the musicians were already playing when the guests began to arrive. Three of the musicians, one of whom was said to be a virtuosa, played the triangle-shaped instruments, but there was also a guitar, Russian accordions, and a long-necked three-stringed thing that Maria told him was called a "domra." The sum of the instruments produced music that was either Gypsy-wild and frenetic or else so sweetly wistful and sadly romantic that it was almost painful to hear. As with everything else this day, Charlie found it exotic and wonderful.

He ate heartily although he was almost unconscious of the process as friends and many strangers interrupted constantly to wish them blessings or to make jokes that were almost shockingly lewd. The music, though, seemed more central to the celebration than the food, and their guests—the young and strong as well as the old and easily winded—waltzed and tangoed, did raucous polkas and a surprising number of renditions of modern American dances.

In Su Mei's sister, Lily, Krebs had found perhaps his perfect partner and they spent almost the whole of the evening in the center of the polished dance floor. But Charlie found he didn't mind. Even the laughter that erupted when he tried to follow Maria's lead in the Russian folk dances didn't bother him tonight.

He found himself clowning for everyone's benefit.

###

It was almost midnight as Sergei watched his wife, the mother of the bride, cleaning and clearing, as though she were a common domestic servant. He sat now, both hands around a glass of vodka, at one of the small tables along the wall, leaning his great head against the hotel's moiré wallpaper. He would have liked, with the guests mostly gone now, but the musicians still booked for at least another quarter of an hour, to celebrate privately a little with his wife. It had been a triumph, he thought. As fine as Katya's wedding, though the circumstances then had been much different.

Olena, of course, would not want to celebrate with him and he could not imagine himself asking her. He could not recall when, or where, he had lost the ability to speak plainly to his wife, but he had long ago despaired of telling her his feelings. In the last years especially, whenever he had been brave enough to try, he had been fumbling, inarticulate, impotent. It was his life's debt to her, he assumed, compounded again by the way she had managed this wedding and was shoring them all against Katya's leaving. His gratitude, inexpressible, had served to make him mute. And yet she suffered him, fool that he was.

Sergei swallowed the last of his vodka and leaned again on the wall, closing his eyes to savor the orchestra's playing of *To Nie Vetier*, the beautiful old tune that had always torn at his heart. The haunting melody seemed to be carrying him away. It was transporting him back to another ballroom, much like this one, but not quite the same. Here, too, was the polished parquet dance floor, the massive glittering chandelier overhead, but along the walls of this great room portraits of the czars hung in massive gilded frames. This hall was filled with beautiful women in elegant gowns and handsome young soldiers in uniform.

He was not asleep, but he saw it as in a dream and smiled to himself. *Ah, yes*, he thought. *The Rose Palace.* The night of our engagement ball. The orchestra had just begun to play *To Nie Vetier* and he saw himself searching the faces of the guests for his betrothed. From a rustling group of ladies Olena stepped forward, radiantly beautiful in a gown of emerald satin, her own eyes also seeking. Ten steps in his thin-soled cavalry boots and he had been rewarded with her luminous smile, taken her gloved hand in his own, and drawn her onto the floor.

In the dream that was not a dream he felt the warmth at her small waist, the light weight of her hand on his shoulder as they began to move, easily and gracefully, their bodies in perfect harmony, gliding as if on ice to the sad, sweet waltz. In the dream that was not a dream he had achieved heaven, the pinnacle moment of sublime happiness in a life that, once this night was over, would rarely know happiness again.

From outside his reverie a voice spoke to him.

He had no wish to be anywhere other than behind his closed eyes. He thought he might be assumed asleep, but the voice came again, a woman's, speaking in Russian, and reluctantly he opened his eyes to see that she, the very one of whom he'd been dreaming, stood over him.

"Stand up, old man," said Olena. "Your wife wishes to dance."

3 October 1946

I will miss our Jack terribly. But Charlie will miss him more. I'm not sure that they are parting as exactly the friends they began but then nothing really is the same as it was and all of us are much changed.

There is almost no cooperation from the Chinese now for the American mission. The joint meetings, when they don't postpone them over something slight, are a poor farce and there is nothing now that the Americans send that is not filtered through the black market. Even blood plasma sent by the Red Cross has shown up in the pharmacies, selling for twenty-five American a pint.

No one will speak the truth, but the war turns in Mao's favor. Su Mei and her university friends seem glad of it. She has been to visit me only once and talked only of politics.

The rumors are that we will be closing down before the end of the year. I can't think where either of us will find work if this is true. They say also that the American consulate has begun urging all Americans to prepare to go. Charlie talks of our going, too.

But how can I leave Mama and Papa? And how can I stay where my husband is despised?

I find myself in the place of Katya some few months ago. Like Katya, I will have to decide.

From the diary of Maria Petrova, translated from the French

Chapter IX.

Kreb's official farewell send-off had been the night before, with twelve of them gathering at Jimmy's to a hilarious review of every transgression that Krebs had committed in Shanghai, from losing himself for a whole weekend in Nantao, to needing the shots for clap. Several girls from his telephone staff had been there to balance anecdotes of Krebs' wolfish behavior with evidence that he'd not been such a bad boss after all, that he'd actually done wonders in setting up and managing their section. Near the end Manny had stood up to deliver a sincere and moving toast to Krebs' accomplishments here and to his future successes and each of them then had briefly followed suit, doing their best to mix humor with honest tribute. Finally Krebs, too moved and affected by that time to play the thing straight, had wound it all up, telling everyone, including Jimmy, who stood smiling in his white apron against the bar, that he never intended to give any of them another moment's thought and that he fully expected, by God, that Manny would pick up the night's tab.

That had been the official farewell. But tonight was Krebs' last night in Shanghai and they had reserved it for themselves alone, the two of them heading out solo, just like in their early days. Charlie had been quite forceful about urging Maria not to wait up for him, but his insistence had probably been unnecessary. In the last few weeks she often went to bed only an hour or two after clearing their dinner and yet she still claimed that at work she often fought to keep her eyes open. Sleepiness, apparently, was a symptom of pregnancy.

Today Charlie had left the Embankment early, arranging to meet Krebs in Bubbling Well at UNRRA's street office where only months ago he'd often helped out with certifying DPs. He'd heard that the staff here had been cut back and thought they might use him today. But the long queues of DPs waiting to be certified were gone now. Only a manageable few still milled around the little office and his services weren't really needed.

Krebs had assessed the situation immediately and greeted Charlie cheerily.

"You folks have just about worked yourself out of a job!" he said.

"Yep," said Charlie, shaking his friend's outthrust hand.

"Mission almost accomplished. At least for the Jewish refuges anyway. I was just telling Manny yesterday that I really can imagine it now. The day that every last one has left Shanghai."

"Well, good for them," said Krebs. "And good for you, too. I didn't expect it would fall into place so quickly."

"No," said Charlie. "I guess I didn't either. But they certainly had the world's sympathy. You know, as the news got out. And the Jews were already pretty well organized in Shanghai to begin with. Maybe you didn't know it, but the AJDC sent regular status reports on the refugees, collected money from the states, all through the war. It finally got down to a matter of logistics. And paperwork."

They had begun walking east down Bubbling Well in the direction of the Bund.

"I don't suppose," said Krebs, "once everything's well and done, that any of them will be sorry. I mean the way it went in Europe after all."

"No," said Charlie. "I don't suppose. They've been very modest about it. Wanting to get out, of course. Upset sometimes with the bureaucracy. But they know. I guess, in looking back, they'll all be glad for Shanghai. That it worked out the way it did. We laugh sometimes, our little crew, what's left of us, thinking about it. About what they'll take away. Do you think they'll like Chinese Food? Do you think they'll ever play Mah Jong again?"

Krebs tilted back his head and smiled broadly into the skies above the street.

"I'd bet on it!" he said. "The influences will show up. So maybe the grandkids won't know why Grandma is crazy for willow pattern china. I'm betting, though, that it won't all be lost. The important thing, though, is that they weren't. I mean, *they* weren't."

Charlie nodded. Clearly Krebs understood what he'd been trying to say. What his own little bunch, busier now in second-guessing themselves than anything else that UNRRA had lately assigned to them, now spent most of their time on.

They walked on, some invisible magnet drawing them toward the Bund and the harbor. Bubbling Well, always crowded, seem unusually so this evening. There had been a massive street demonstration protesting China-American policy earlier in the day and although it had broken up hours ago there were still stragglers moving in the crowd, some still carrying signs or banners. This evening Krebs was back in uniform, his street clothes and other belongings having been already sent ahead to the ship. It was probably the uniform that provoked the three across the street. They were boys really, too young to be university students. They pointed, raised fists at Krebs, and began to shout.

"Foreigners!" one of them cried out. "Yankees! Get out, Yankees!"

"Get out!" the other two chimed in. "Tsor-lor! Tsor-lor!"

The busy human traffic on the sidewalks seemed to stop. A space opened up in the buzz of noise.

"*Screw* you!" Krebs yelled back. "You ungrateful yellow bastards! We're going! We're *all* going! See how you like it then!"

The youths had stopped in their tracks, flinching a little at Krebs' retaliation and Krebs had begun moving in their direction, about to cross the street. The smallest boy turned and ran immediately but the other two unsteadily stood their ground, their eyes searching the crowd for reinforcements. At the curb beside them a coolie without a passenger lowered the traces of his rickshaw and stood up to look. Others on the sidewalk had also stopped to watch.

"Let it go, Jack," Charlie said, grabbing firmly at Krebs' arm. Krebs tried to shake him off but Charlie held on, practically dragging him into the door of a nearby watering hole.

The place was small, very dark inside for so early in the evening, but it didn't appear to be a complete dump. Dust motes floated lazily in the colored light in front of a new-looking jukebox. Two attractive young sing-song girls looked up and giggled at the end of a polished bar.

Charlie pushed Krebs down into a chair at one of the tables. Krebs was visibly upset, fairly vibrating with anger and frustration, and for a moment Charlie thought that he might actually cry. He recalled the visit to Luangwa so many months before and the hours it had taken to calm him down.

Charlie kept one eye on Krebs and yet managed, to the barkeep, to communicate a request for a full bottle of Scotch and two reasonably clean glasses. These were produced quickly and Charlie slid them onto the table and dropped into the chair opposite Krebs.

"The little worm's turned, my man," Krebs was saying. "The worm's turned and the dove is pecking back."

"What?" Charlie said. "What the hell are you talking about?"

"Shakespeare," said Krebs. "Henry the Sixth."

"Right," said Charlie, "Shakespeare."

He opened the bottle of Scotch and filled the two glasses. *God, where had Krebs found the time to read all that crap?* Maybe it explained why, at Kunming, Krebs had been so lousy in the base softball games. It didn't explain, though, where he'd found the time to learn to dance.

"Can you believe it?" said Krebs. "Not so long ago, we were the conquering heroes. Don't you remember? We were the goddamn conquering heroes! And now we're nothing. They think we're nothing! Nothing but . . . " He let his thought trail off in favor of tossing back half the contents of the little glass.

"Yeah," Charlie answered. "I do remember. Seems like only yesterday this whole town was painted red, white and blue."

Krebs laughed wickedly.

"Well, it'll be red all over soon enough!" he said. His eyes swept the dim bar to see if anyone else appreciated his wit. But the joke, even for him, collapsed almost instantly. He dropped his gaze again to the table and his glass.

"We botched it," he said glumly. "We botched the whole damn thing, didn't we?"

"Maybe," said Charlie. "It's beginning to look like it."

"I hear Sassoon's pulling out," Krebs said. "Selling everything. Even the Cathay. Going to the Bahamas they say."

"Yeah. I heard that too. A bad sign I guess. Must make the Old China Hands nervous."

"The old hands!" said Krebs. "Hell, there aren't many old hands them left! They closed the banks again, you know. Nationalized the assets. Shit. It was over for the Old Hands before it was over for us."

Charlie considered this for a moment.

"I guess so," he said. "I suppose it really was."

He hated that it was going like this. That Krebs' last night in Shanghai might be spent wallowing in self-pity and recrimination. For a moment he wondered if the two Chinese kids might still be outside. If it might not be worth it, for Krebs sake, to give them the beating of their lives.

"It wasn't all bad," said Charlie. "We had some times."

Krebs said nothing, still staring grimly down into his glass, but then a grin began to spread at the corners of his mouth.

"Hey! Do you remember that night we paid those two rickshaw boys to race us in Chinatown?"

Charlie smiled. He'd almost forgotten that night. And he couldn't recall now how it all had come about. He only knew that someone's drunken challenge had resulted in a series of hilarious Roman chariot-style rickshaw races in an alley that five or six of them had commandeered in the Chinese city. It hadn't just been the matter of paying the coolies for each increasingly more expensive sprint, but the wagering on the whole stunt. Even the locals had been laying down bets in the street.

"We nearly killed those guys!" said Krebs.

"Maybe," said Charlie. "But they were well paid for it."

"How much did we drop on that, do you figure?"

"I don't know. Maybe a hundred grand."

"Who won?"

"I don't remember."

Krebs filled his own glass again and Charlie's. For a time they sat silent.

"I liked that part, you know. I liked being rich."

"We weren't rich," Charlie said. "Nobody was rich."

"Maybe not, said Krebs. But we *felt* rich! And it was a helluva lot of fun! It amounts to the same thing, doesn't it?"

"I guess," said Charlie. But he didn't believe it. He'd agonized a lot lately remembering the dough they'd thrown around. Now that he had a wife, a baby on the way, and no real plan for the future. It wouldn't have been that hard to save some of that money.

"But you're not broke or anything, are you?"

"Almost," said Krebs. "How about you?"

"Almost," said Charlie.

Krebs was holding up his small empty glass, rolling it slowly back and forth between his fingers. Then, quite suddenly, he popped it over one eye, scrunched his face and held it there, a telescoped monocle.

"I can see it all!" he said suddenly, nearly toppling his chair to stand up, to lift both hands theatrically into the air. "I see it all! The future of Shanghai! I see it as through a glass. Clearly."

Charlie chuckled and settled back in his seat. This was going to be good.

"I see Victor Sassoon and all the other foreign taipans. I see them packing up. The English bankers and the Swiss financiers and the Belgian brokers and all the rest of them. The smug Old Hands. And they're all packing up! I can see them stuffing their wads of money in their crocodile attaché cases and kissing their skinny yellow mistresses goodbye and telling their fat pink wives and their fat pink children to pack up. And I see them driving their big Packards and their Buicks and their armored Lincolns down to the docks and putting everything on a big ocean liner. And I see them sailing away!"

Charlie laughed again and noticed that the little sing song girls were now playing close attention. He doubted seriously that they understood any of this but they were certainly interested in the performance.

"I can see Hongkew!" Krebs said, getting louder. "That miserable hell hole where the Japs kept the Jews caged up. And I see that it's empty! All the Jews are gone! They've gone to Australia and Palestine and America. And they're glad they were here, of course. *Considering.* But they're glad to be out of here and they don't look back."

"And now I see the French," Krebs continued, affecting a passable French accent. "Zees French. They are very *sensitiff.* Zees Shineese have taken back zee land! Zee pretty French Town. There eez no future anymore in being French without a France in Shina! And so, zees French? They pack and they go!"

Charlie was almost convulsed with laughter, but Krebs showed no sign of stopping.

"And now I can see Uncle Sam!" he said, the accent now become a Texas drawl. "He's swooping down on his big ole' eagle wings." Here Krebs flapped his arms and weaved his head, but the glass monocle stayed in place.

"And that ole eagle, why he reaches right down. He's got his gigantic talons and he plucks 'em all up. He plucks up the sailors and the soldiers and the admirals and the generals. The doctors and the nurses. The silly missionaries and all the rest. *All* of his little Yankee Doodle Dandies, and he flies west with them. Over the ocean. Back to the nest."

Now Krebs paused, sat down again at the table, briefly removed his monocle, and saw that he had a drinking problem. Charlie pushed his own glass over to share it, but instead Krebs took a long pull directly from the Scotch bottle, coughed, and popped the magic monocle back into place in his eye.

"And then one day," he continued, not standing up again but leaning intently over the table to Charlie. "*One* day! One gray morning. I see all the little yellow beggars in Shanghai waking up. I see them waking up. They wake up and look around. And you know what? You know what they see? Nobody! Nobody else. Just them! The Chinese. All nine million of them. All *alone*."

Charlie dissolved into laughter. But as he recovered himself, as he filled both their glasses again and lifted a toast to Krebs' hilarious theatrics he could feel the truth he'd been denying for weeks spread like an icy pool within him. Krebs was right. The Chinese were taking their city back. It was time to get out of here. Before it was too late.

For a long time they sat quiet, drinking companionably, one or the other of them periodically chortling aloud at some private remembrance which caused the other to smile but didn't provoke conversation.

At last Charlie asked the question that had been plaguing him for days.

"Are you sorry, man? Do you wish I hadn't talked you into this?"

Krebs made a face of comic, exaggerated disgust.

"Sorry?" he said. "*Hell* no! Not a bit sorry! What was *I* going to do anyway? Besides, I've had the time of my life. "

He paused and his voice became low and sober.

"If I've got any regrets, you know, that's it. That I'm not even thirty and I've already *had* the time of my life."

They had not quite come to the end of the Scotch bottle but in a few minutes more, by some unspoken agreement, they both stood up. Charlie threw a few bills onto the table and nodded over to the smiling, kowtowing bar keep.

Outside it was full dark now. The street, alive with noisy activity, looked no different from the way they had first encountered it more than a year ago and yet as Charlie stepped into the street to hail a cab and give pidgin English directions to the driver he saw that it was in no way the same. Little in Shanghai seemed strange anymore. Now that their visit was coming to an end, the exotic had become familiar. What had felt foreign now felt like home.

In the taxi Krebs was quiet, looking straight ahead through the cab's windshield with an unfocused glassy stare.

"Let me take you to the Palace!" Charlie said. "We'll have shark fin soup and feel rich."

Krebs smiled but shook his head.

"I don't think so, man. I'm really not that hungry. And I've got this feeling, you know. Like I've worn out my welcome. I think the old whore's had enough of me. And I've had all I'm going to get out of her."

Charlie didn't try to argue. Again Krebs was probably right.

In little more than half an hour Charlie had deposited Krebs at the top of the wharf, shared a final handshake, and watched his friend's back descend and disappear. Their last exchange echoed in his head.

"If you ever get to Georgia," Charlie had said, "Look me up."

Krebs had hiked both bushy eyebrows in surprise.

"You've decided then! You're sure?"

"Yeah," Charlie had answered. "I'm sure. We'll be right behind you."

"Good," Krebs had said. "I'm glad."

For a long while after Krebs had disappeared in the shadows below him Charlie stood at the top of the levy, feeling loose-ended and directionless. He had not expected the evening to end so quickly. He had not expected it to end on such a somber note, one that now seemed to have colored his whole experience here and made him eager to be following Krebs.

Behind him was the broad glittery Bund and the row of great

hotels where he could easily find a rickshaw or taxi. But the trip home would be made too fast then and he needed more time to think. He turned south and began walking.

Ahead of him he could see the twinkling arcs of Garden Bridge and beyond it the rows of lights in the nineteen stories of Broadway Mansions. He didn't try to calculate which one of those floors was the sixth, or which window might be their own, but he suspected that even this early that one would be dark. Even if Maria were still awake she'd have lit her candle by now, using the time and the quiet to scribble in that little journal of hers. He wondered what she wrote there. If she confided things to her diary that she couldn't to him. If she told her diary that she was content now, the wife of an American serviceman. Or that she missed the attention of other men, the glamour of the city's nightlife. He didn't suppose he'd ever know for sure. He couldn't read a word of French.

Tomorrow he'd have to tell her. And she would have to tell her parents. He felt suddenly sick at the thought of it and the black irony of Sergei and Olena's situation. UNRRA had accomplished the largest human transport in history. He'd personally certified and secured visas for hundreds, perhaps thousands of Russian refuges. Even old Sidor had gone to the States. But all of these had been Jewish first, Russians only second. There was nothing he could do for his wife's own parents. They were still paperless, citizens of nowhere. The one place in the world that would welcome them was Soviet Russia. And before that Sergei would sooner die.

Consciously now he noted that he had begun walking faster but he stuffed both hands down into his jacket pockets and lengthened his stride even more. Now that the decision had been made he felt a pressing urgency, almost a panic, to be acting on it. Tomorrow he'd tell his supervisors and inquire about passage. He might have tickets within the month. He'd send cables back home so that his family would know their plans.

There was the possibility, of course, that Maria would argue with him. That she might even try to refuse. He would have to be ready for that. To be strong if she, or even Sergei, came at him with tears and pleading. He slowed the pace of his walking. What if she wanted to wait? Until after the baby came? He didn't know how long these things took. How long it might be for a woman to recover and an infant to be old enough to travel. He tried to perform a swift calculation but shook his head at the effort. *No!* They couldn't wait. Tonight had shown him again how hostile the city was becoming to Americans. And Krebs was right. The Reds were winning the civil war. Who knew when Mao's army might march into Shanghai?

No. They needed to go. As soon as possible. Before it was too late.

18 November 1946

I am as tired tonight as I can ever remember but will write because I've neglected to do it and cannot know when I will find the chance again. There has been so much to do in a small time with all of the packing and moving out of our little place. Our apartment has gone to newlyweds also, a young pharmacist from Chungking and his sweet, shy wife. I am glad for them but full of envy because we were so happy there and I'd thought to stay forever.

I have said good bye as often, and to as many, as I can bear. Manny has taken us three times for a last farewell dinner with others and the friends from the school and from St. Nicholas have been kind and generous in trying to make me fat. Even Su Mei and I have had our own dear parting and our troubles seem all forgotten.

In three days we go. We will be almost two months on the ship that docks in seven ports before we arrive in the city of New York. From there we go by train to the capital of America in Washington where Charlie will get the papers to say he is no longer a soldier. We will take another train then to his family in the southern parts and if Dr. Gormachevsky is correct in his calculations that will be just in time. My baby will be born American by their laws and a citizen from his first breath.

It is this finally that has persuaded me, although Mama has argued with Charlie from the beginning and at the last, even Papa. Of all that has happened this has been the most surprising. That they would send me away for the sake of a faceless, unborn babe.

But I begin to see. My child moves within me and already I seem to know his moods and whims. He dances between my ribs to Tchaikovsky and does somersaults in the noisy streets. He goes quiet for Brahms, but still I think he will be an athlete. He will be strong and fast like Katya and Papa.

We have had one cable from Katya and nothing since. She must be busy in her new life, and happy, I think, but the silence is hard to bear.

From the diary of Maria Petrova, translated from the French

Chapter X.

Maria had been spent her entire life seeing, and yet not seeing, the teeming activity in Shanghai's busy Woosung harbor. It had always held war vessels—the destroyers, warships, troop carriers, gunboats, freighters and cruisers—even if now their population was dominated by American and allied vessels rather than by Japanese. She had always been aware of the busy commerce, of the merchant and cargo ships waiting to be loaded, of the tea and silk and cotton waiting on the wharf, bound for ports unknown. Wistfully, almost since childhood, she had watched the tenders bringing in passengers from the great ocean liners anchored to river buoys in midstream, or taking travelers out to board away to places she could only imagine. This harbor had always moored a hundred types of craft, all of them coming and going, sporting flags of a hundred nations. It was the living center, the very beating heart of Shanghai, and it would have been impossible not to be aware of its importance to the city, to the Orient, and to the world.

Yet curiously she had felt all morning like she was seeing it for the first time. She had been surprised by the realization that, with the exception of a single summer afternoon spent in a rowing skull with a British lieutenant in the public park in Pudong, she had never really *been* on the water. She had dreamed of it, but never fully imagined that she would one day find herself aboard one of the huge passenger steamers, pulling *away* from the crowded quay, out of the Woosung harbor and on downstream through the narrow straits of the Whangpoo, headed for the yellow Yangtze and then on to the open ocean.

They had been brought to the ship in mid morning after all

the fuss at the steamship office of producing tickets and papers and arranging for the baggage. She had parted with Mama and Papa there, at the jetty at dockside, predictably letting herself be doused by Papa's tears, allowing the poor old thing to ruin her hairdo in the crush of her head to his heart. Mama had been predictable, too. Quiet and stoic and dry-eyed, but in her own way, Maria had finally come to see, just as broken-hearted.

This morning's *au revoire* had been only the dreaded formality. She and Mama had said their real goodbyes on the evening before last, the two of them sending Papa and Charlie away to the cafés where Papa might have his last mournful vodka with Charlie and she and Mama might be alone. The men had been gone only minutes when Mama had called Maria to her, to come and sit beside her on the spring-broken little settee.

"*Dochinka maya,*" Mama had said. *My little girl.* "I have something here to give you."

She had extended to Maria a small shapeless parcel, wrapped in red tissue.

Maria had peeled away the layers of tissue, so old and wrinkled they felt almost organic, like soft thin layers of membrane, or leaf. Inside she had found a heavily lacquered wooden egg that had been brightly painted to represent a woman, or a girl.

"How lovely!" Maria said, cupping it in her palm, relishing its smooth surface and its fundamental shape, the cunning little face and clothes painted on the colorful egg.

"What is it?" Maria had asked.

"Matryoshkhas," her mother had replied. "Nesting dolls. These were made in Sergiev Posad by the artist Maliutin who was a friend of our family. When Ana and I were young your grandmother Valentina would let us look at them from time to time. But we were never allowed to play with them. They were among the few things I escaped with. These and some stupid, worthless papers. A little jewelry and rubles that went in the first year."

"This is she," Mama had said, twisting and removing the top of the little doll to reveal another, slightly smaller but nearly identical doll inside. "And here I am."

Maria had gasped in delight at the cleverness of the snug design, the surprise of the little wooden doll begetting another so like it.

"And this is you," Mama had continued, opening the next doll, and the next, lining them up on the battered tea table. "And the one inside, *your* child. And the one inside this, the child of your child perhaps."

"Oh!" Maria had said. "I see!" And she had seen. The reason that her mother had thought these little toys worth saving. The reason why she had kept them hidden and was bringing them out and making a present of them to her, only now, on the eve of her departure for America. Why the beautiful little dolls, more properly belonging to Katya, as eldest, were being given to her instead. Why Mama, who had seemed so stricken by Katya's leaving, had seemed almost to encourage her own.

There had been little talk between them after that. Maria had laid her head in her mother's lap and her mother had stroked her hair in the way that she'd done when she and Katya had been quite small. On one of those nights when the Japanese soldiers shooting at rats in the dark streets had disturbed their sleep and Mama had soothed them with stories of the Rose Palace. The two of them had still been there, silent in the dark flat, when Charlie and Papa had come in the door.

The leave-taking was over. The last sleepless nights of indecision passed. And yet this morning's rush and confusion had seemed all for nothing. She and Charlie and the other passengers had waited an hour before the river pilot who would guide them up the Whangpoo had finally come aboard, and then almost another hour before the ship had finally cast off its moorings and gotten underway. The two of them had spent a little time checking their cabin, exploring a bit of the ship and exchanging casual greetings with other passengers before Charlie had gone off to see about the extra trunks, leaving her, for the first moment since sunrise, alone with her thoughts.

There were certainly things to do in the cozy little cabin that had been assigned to them below. Nothing in their bags had been unpacked, none of their toiletries, the new clothes Katya had given her, or the wedding lingerie she had been saving, just in case. Becoming the bride of an American soldier had always meant possibility, the chance that sooner or later she would be going somewhere and she had put back a few things, saving them in their newness against the possibility of adventure. She had never expected, though, that it would be an adventure so large, or so soon. That it would fill her with such a strange mingling of excitement and despair.

The passage across the Atlantic, Charlie had said, would take them fifty-six days. That was plenty of time for settling themselves into their little nest below and for talking about what lay ahead. For now she felt that she had to be here, leaning on the guardrail of the ship's observation deck, looking and thinking backward. Saying goodbye, for now, to Shanghai.

Maria watched fascinated as the tall buildings on the Bund began to draw farther and farther away. The ship passed the mouth of Soochow Creek where the river flowed under Garden Bridge and an entire floating village of colorful junks and sampans bobbed and bucked on the waves. Most of its inhabitants had been born, would live, and die, on the water, but this was her first time to be here, *with* them as it were, and the sight, familiar since childhood, of an old man skipping briskly from one sampan to another, seemed suddenly fresh and marvelous. Too soon it seemed the river began taking its sudden hairpin turn. She glanced down as the ship lurched in the wake of a passing tanker and on looking up gasped and felt a fluttery panic on seeing that her new perspective of her city and its magnificent skyline had been suddenly, completely, lost.

Now she began to observe the thinning of the oil slicks, their surfaces making iridescent whorls of rainbow colors. She noted the clots of floating garbage in the water beginning to diminish, and followed, almost the last thing, the bloated body of an old woman riding a bier of paper flowers disappearing in the distance. For perhaps the first time ever she became fully aware of the city's distinctive perfume, an aroma of rotting fish and petroleum, of rancid cooking oil rising from the sampans, as a new and different air began filtering the old familiar one out of her lungs and nostrils. The birds that circled the harbor—that had been there, always, since the very beginning of the beginning of memory—now circled their own ship slowly, and for the first time in her life she took notice of their sharp, urgent cries.

At last they had left it all behind, the warehouses and factories, the belching smokestacks that she knew well but had never been so keenly aware of until this morning of going away. Time passed and Charlie didn't return. There was no reason to move from her observation point and in a little while the scenery began to change again, gradually becoming something else she knew but didn't know. Slowly her view became the familiar scenes of the painted plates, the watercolor renderings of country life that she knew from fabrics and carvings, the traditional rural still-lifes etched in the consciousness of all who have lived in the Orient. Lush farmlands and glistening rice paddies passed now on either side of the river and from time to time a bending pen-and-ink peasant stood up in his field, faceless below his wide straw hat, to lift a hand to wave. Maria waved back.

Suddenly there was a hubbub on the deck. A rush of boys and men came running to her rail, shouting and pointing at something ahead in the river. Apparently someone had sighted a mine, or what might be a mine, and the vibration of the engine slowed beneath her feet and the ship moved closer to shore. But from the voices of the sailors, in the several languages she could understand, she concluded that the object in the river had been only carrion, the top of a mast perhaps. A number of Japanese ships had been sunk along here, they said. Pieces had broken off in towing them away.

It will be good to leave the war behind, she thought, the idea an echo of something Mama had said, in one of their troubling discussions of her future and the dilemma that her American husband had presented. *It will be good to leave the war behind.*

But what did that mean, really? *Leaving the war behind.* For one thing, it depended upon some memory of *before.* Of a time when there had been no war. Maria could scarcely resurrect such a time. She had been very young when the city had been taken, and before that the war that her parents had fled had invested and imbued every moment of her early life.

She had a few notions of what that might mean. Some of these had been absorbed from the talk of Charlie and Jack and the other Americans. More had come from the American cinema and the newsreels. From pictures of lovely warm homes inhabited by beautiful, smiling families. From their images of wide, clean streets filled with new automobiles and well-dressed pedestrians, but absent of hungry beggars. Scenes in which people traveled freely and no one wore armbands or carried papers. Where there were no camps or armed soldiers on every corner.

If only it were that— just that—she was leaving behind. Only the ugliness and violence of war that she sensed slipping away, gliding backwards beneath the ship's iron hull in the roiling yellow wake. But of course it was more. It was also Mama and Papa. Her friends and her city. Her childhood.

The memory of Katya's departure, only months ago, was sharp in Maria's mind. She had been focused that day on her own grief, her own almost suffocating sadness at the loss of sister, and friend. Now she replayed it, that scene of farewell, and saw it altogether differently, putting herself in Katya's place, seeing all that had happened through Katya's eyes, and feeling this time for her sister instead of for herself. Katya, too, had been sailing into a great mystery. But Katya's notions of South America were certainly cloudier than her own of the United States. And Katya, the sturdy practical one, who had never been thrilled by strange languages and strange people and never valued adventure over safety, had probably not felt this strange admixture of aching regret and heady anticipation that Maria was laboring to reconcile. Katya, below her placid exterior, had probably been purely and simply afraid.

The last eight weeks, beginning with the night that Charlie had come home frothing to leave Shanghai, had been a confusing blur, made worse by Mama and Papa's unexpected reaction to Charlie's plan. Maria had not always behaved so well these last weeks and now felt a deep shame over her selfishness and regret for things she had said. She had resisted seeing what was self-evident to them. That she was in fact far luckier than Katya. That what she would be leaving behind was far less important than what she would be taking away.

There was a new life inside her now. Someone else to consider. The hope that all of them would continue, that the breaking and scattering of their family could end, rested now with her. With her and with Charlie. One day they would all be together again. Someday, perhaps soon, there would be a change in the ways of the world. Mama and Papa would be able to get papers and Grieg's situation would be understood and forgiven. Everyone then could come to America. She would want to be ready for them.

"All right then, *papooshka*," she said softly, placing her hand on the firm mound of her abdomen. "Here we go. To America."

"You, *my bebe,* will be an American!" she continued, laughing aloud now. "Do you believe your good luck? You will speak English like your father and French like your babushka, and I will see to it that your Russian is better than Papa's."

"You can be anything there!" she said, not even looking

around to see if there was anyone to wonder at her madness. "Anything you wish! And no one will ask you about your papers. Or your politics. Or any questions at all. And if they do, you will have the answer."

Maria relaxed her grip on the iron deck rail and felt the struggle that she had endured these many weeks resolving itself, evaporating like river mist almost before her eyes.

"You will tell them, *I am an American*," she said defiantly, "and there will be nothing more to say."

Part II.

Maria's Doll

12 January 1947

I have packed again for us by the bathroom light and in my rummaging have found my book. It was lost even on the ship and gone forever, I thought, but now as it turns out only in the wrong bag.

My darlings still sleep soundly in the bed—better I think now that I have given it over to them completely. The hotel here was unable to find us a crib and whenever I lie down with them, I drift into terrible dreams. In the last one I imagined that I had rolled on the baby and got up then, seeing it was no use. I will have my turn to sleep perhaps tomorrow on the train.

Charlie has cabled to Mama and Papa and Manny that we have a sweet and perfect little girl and I expect they were all surprised to learn that she insisted to be born in Washington. I would give anything to see their faces and to know also if they've heard anything from Katya. Already it seems I've been gone so long. What it would mean to hear Mama's voice! Or to see Papa holding our little one in his arms.

From the diary of Maria Petrova, translated from the French

Chapter XI.

"There!" Charlie shouted. "There they are! Abby's come, too. Look at the crazy hat! Aw, you're going to love her, Maria. She's a lunatic!"

Maria looked where Charlie was pointing and momentarily saw them too, three female figures standing under the streetlight just beyond the tall fence, all of them disappearing as the bus swung away and turned into the station. Two of that trio had seemed much alike, leaving her unable to guess which of the staid black-coated women might be her new mother-in-law. The third figure, taller and younger, wearing a white coat and a brilliant red cloche hat and bouncing up and down on tiptoe, had obviously been Abby, Charlie's sister, the lunatic he was promising.

In the damp, aching crook of Maria's arm, the infant stirred and she looked down at its face, wondering if her body had somehow telegraphed her own anxiety to the child. For days now, certainly for these last interminable hours, she had wanted nothing more than for their long trip to be over. But now that they were finally here she felt a gathering apprehension.

She was nervous about meeting them. She had expected to be. But she had not expected that events would have arranged themselves so that the person she would be presenting to them would not be herself at all. There was still the watery bleeding, the pain when she walked or urinated, the heavy ache in her lower parts. It had only been two days since their release from the hospital in Washington and she had slept fitfully there and really not at all last night in their small hotel room. They had risen early this morning to catch the train to Atlanta and every moment since had been consumed with attending the baby—in feeding or soothing or diapering or cleaning, in either actual custodial activities or the exhausting hyper-vigilance that seemed to have been delivered to her with her child.

She had not anticipated that in their last leg of the trip—that hurried dash in Atlanta from train station to bus terminal—she would be unable to wash her hair or properly tend to her face. She knew that her clothes—the dark crumpled skirt and the only buttoning blouse she had brought that worked now for discrete nursing—were not bright or cheerful enough for first impressions. They were not even especially fresh, and she wondered if they would think her unclean.

In the last dreary miles, while Charlie and the baby had slept peacefully in the darkening evening, Maria had mentally fondled a whole rosary of worries. She was worried about what they would think of her. About whether the gifts that she and Charlie had brought for his family were appropriate. She wondered if they would have privacy in his mother's home. Selfishly, she worried about when she might sleep—if motherhood meant never really sleeping again—and where she would find the reserve, the strength, to be herself.

A journey well-planned is a journey well-ended, Mama had always told them. Good advice, Maria thought, although Katya had been the one to take it most to heart. But she could not see now where she had failed in her preparations or why she already felt so defeated. Dr. Gromachevsky's calculations had been close. Just not close enough. Their child had arrived whole and healthy. This most difficult part had gone well for them. *Except.*

She had not presented Charlie with a son, but with a daughter, and he'd poorly disguised his disappointment. Almost two months on the ship and they'd never even considered the possibility that their child might be a girl.

"I'm thinking of Ana," she'd said. "That was the name of Mama's only sister. It will please her, I think. To learn that we've remembered her this way."

"That's fine," Charlie had said absently. "Anne is fine."

"*Ana,*" she had corrected. "Her name was *Ana.* But Charlie! If there's another name? If there's something you like. A family name perhaps? I'd thought a boy, too. But we have a girl. And she must have a name."

"No. That's fine. Whatever you like."

This was one of the beads she'd been fondling. The sense that she'd failed. It didn't help that her memory held clear images of the little bundles along the Shanghai streets. The cast-off females to be picked up with the morning's trash.

She would not have arranged it so, but the arrangements had been made. Certainly it would all work out. This was not China, after all. A girl could do many things here. In time Charlie would come to see the comforts that a daughter could bring to a man's life. In time her new family would forgive her this sad first impression and commiserate, perhaps even laugh, with her over her ordeal.

"So here we are, papushka," she said, gathering the child close, standing up stiffly and edging toward Charlie as he moved into the bus's narrow aisle. For an instant her head swam dizzily, but as it settled itself, she smiled. The journey was really over now. In a few minutes more she could fall into welcoming arms. There would be the support and understanding of other women, the relieving comfort of family, even if they were Charlie's family. She would not make the best first impression perhaps, but there would be plenty of time to repair it. This family was hers now. *Theirs.* For the time being anyway, the three of them were home.

Abby stood for another moment, glancing just once more between the thin mound of the girl's body in the four-poster, the infant's curled hand through the spindles of the crib, before backing quietly out of the bedroom and pulling the door shut softly behind her. Both mother and child were now resting and, though Maria still sniffled now and then against her pillow, her eyes had been closed for several minutes and Abby thought she would soon be fast asleep.

Back downstairs in the parlor she saw that their company had made a hurried departure, but the rest of them still stood around. Even Rowena, her eyes huge and blue-white in her shiny black face, stood knotting her apron nervously in the frame of the kitchen door.

"She'll be all right," Abby said. "She's just exhausted. We need to let her rest."

Estelle Atwood glanced back up the stairway and frowned.

"What a *strange* little thing," she said. "I can't imagine what set her off like that."

Abby turned to look at her mother.

"Well, I can!" she said. "And you can, too, if you think about it. She's just given birth, if you remember. And then my darling little brother puts her right off on a train and then a bus and throws her into a bunch of strangers who swarm her like hornets with their stupid questions. Passing her baby around like a hot potato! She told me that she hasn't even bathed in two days. Didn't want to get into our clean sheets to sleep!"

Abby paused and swept their eyes with her own.

"I don't think, under the circumstances, that a little crying jag is the least bit surprising."

"Why, the poor little thing!" said Aunt Cassie. Her face, which only a second ago had still been rigid with shock, now relaxed into sympathetic comprehension and she lowered herself into an armchair.

Abby took a step toward them into the center of the room.

"But good grief, Mother!" she said. "What was the idea of the tea party? Inviting the preacher in for their first night home. And the *Richards*, for God's sake!"

Abby was trying to keep her voice down but she had managed to keep her fury coming through and was not surprised to see the flash of Rowena's white apron fleeing into the kitchen.

Their mother let out an annoyed little huff.

"Why, I can't *imagine* what you mean," she said. "Brother Stiles has prayed for Charlie all through the war. And Amanda Richards is a friend. She's been eager to meet Maria."

"Oh, I'm sure she has," said Abby, making no effort to conceal her sarcasm.

"And you!" Abby hissed, whirling to face Charlie. "Hauling out the goddamn high school yearbook! Giggling with Bonnie Jo over your sweetheart pictures while your wife is . . . is practically *expiring* in the corner."

"Jesus," said Charlie, taking a cringing step backwards. "I didn't think . . . "

"No," Abby began, "I don't suppose you did." She was about to say more, but their mother advanced on them, her jaw clenched and a finger pointed at Abby.

"Stop it, Abigail!" she said. "*You're* the one being hysterical now. There was no harm at all in having a few people in to welcome Charlie home. No harm at all. And if either one of you take the Lord's name in vain, *even one more time*, I'll have to ask the both of you to leave my house!"

Charlie dropped his head. From the front hall the grandfather clock begin chiming the hour and the three of stood in tableau, listening. S*even, eight, nine, ten.* When the last vibration had died away, Abby dropped her shoulders and sighed. This wasn't helping. *The more things changed, the more they stayed the same.*

"Don't worry, Mother," she said, "I was going anyway."

"I'll walk you to the car," Charlie offered, grabbing up Abby's red hat from the lamp table and hurrying to follow her through the dining room and into the kitchen.

In the kitchen Abby found Rowena sitting before a large bowl of shelled pecans, pretending now to be picking debris from the shelled nuts.

"Rowena," said Abby, putting a hand firmly on the girl's shoulder, "I'm counting on you to see that Maria and the baby are not disturbed. Can you do that for me?"

"Oh, yez'm," said Rowena. "I kin do it."

"And she'll need a big breakfast tomorrow. Even if it's noon."

"Yez'm. I'll feed 'em. Don you worry none."

"And a bath!" said Abby. "Help her out if you need to, with the baby. So the girl can get a bath."

"Yez'm," Rowena said again, nodding her head vigorously.

"Good," said Abby. "I'll see you sometime tomorrow then."

Charlie opened and held the kitchen door and Abby crossed

the room, stepping quickly down the little stoop and out into the chill December night. Behind her Charlie closed the door and then paused, thrusting his hands deep into his pockets and tilting his head skyward.

"Gosh," he said. "I'd forgotten how dark it gets out here in the country."

Dark enough, Abby thought, but this time she said nothing. Her car was halfway down the long gravel drive and she headed for it, crossing the wide back lawn obliquely. The frozen grass crunched loudly beneath her feet.

"Abby!" said Charlie, hurrying to catch up. "Hold on. We didn't even get to talk. I want to know . . . "

Abby kept her stride but tossed her head to address Charlie over her shoulder.

"Talk?" she said. "*Now* you want to talk?"

Charlie had caught up with her and Abby stopped suddenly.

"You know, little brother, you only wrote me once. One lousy letter in almost two years! And I got tired of wasting my time writing you. But if you had bothered to communicate, I would have warned you. I would have told you that she wasn't taking it well. She didn't take it well at all."

"What do mean?" Charlie asked. "Take what well?"

"You know exactly what I mean. The Richards. The embarrassment you caused her in front of her holier-than-thou friends. The fact that you married this foreign girl. Do you have any *idea* how many times she's said that? A *foreigner. That foreign girl!*"

Abby saw her own breath coming in frosty, annoying, little puffs. She moved on again, her trajectory straight now, the sound of her steps changing in the loose pebbles on the drive.

In a few yards more she had reached the car and opened the door to retrieve the white wool coat she'd left in the driver's seat. Charlie helped her into it and straightened the collar, holding to the coat's lapels until Abby looked up at him.

"Don't be mad at me, Ab," Charlie said. "It's not my fault she's like that. What do you want me to do?"

Abby groaned, but Charlie's face was open and earnest. She had almost forgotten how handsome, and how charming, her brother could be.

"If you want my advice," she said, "you'll get your wife and that baby out of this house as fast as you can. Tomorrow wouldn't be soon enough!"

Charlie dropped his hands and took a step backwards.

"But Abby, that's crazy! We just got here. I don't even have a job. And Maria could use a little help right now. Maybe it'll take Mother a little while to come around. Maybe it will. But Rowena and Aunt Cassie . . ."

"*Aunt Cassie*," Abby scoffed. "Aunt Cassie hasn't had an independent thought in thirty years. You know damn well that Mother thinks for both of them. And Rowena! When does anyone ever know what Rowena is thinking? But she won't cross Mother. That's for sure."

Charlie dropped his head again. It was the same gesture he'd used as a little boy whenever he was being scolded.

Abby moved close and placed a hand gently in the center of his chest.

"Listen, little brother. I'm glad you made it through the lousy war. I am. You'll never know how we worried. But you can't let her do to you what she did to me. What she did to Daddy."

Immediately Charlie lifted his face and for a split second Abby saw the warning flash in his eyes. *Watch it, Abby. You're going too far now.*

For a long moment Abby held his gaze, stubbornly refusing to flinch.

Suddenly Charlie laughed.

"You worry too much, kiddo," he said, reaching up to squash the red cloche hat over her hair. "Leave everything to me."

At the end of the long drive Abby gave the horn a sharp little tap by way of farewell, or apology, to her brother, but she turned the wheel quickly and didn't look back to see if Charlie had already moved toward the house or was still standing, pondering her acid words and her unambiguous advice. There was nothing the least bit unusual for her to be leaving the old home place mad as hell. It was rare enough these days that she and mother could get through a routine visit without cross words. But she was not angry, not really, at Charlie, and she felt now more than a little ashamed of herself for how hard she'd been on him.

Tomorrow she'd drive the sixty miles back to Hazel Grove to check on Maria and the baby, but now she only wanted to get home. Alan would be asleep by now. The lights would be off and the doors locked, but in all probability he'd forgotten to feed the dog. That's what happened when you left everything to men.

13 March 1947

Ana laughed out loud today. It was Rowena who made her laugh first, but then Ana looked to me as if to say, "Isn't she funny? Do you think she's amusing, too?" And when I smiled back at her, Ana laughed again.

It's strange, but there are times that I feel that all of my life, before Ana, was somehow spent asleep. I was asleep, really, and while I believed that I was learning, and had fine plans and was becoming quite clever, I was only walking in a dream, waiting to be awakened by this small, helpless child.

There is a terror to it that overtakes me at times. I wish desperately to speak of it with Mama and want to tell her that I'm coming to understand and how sorry I am for everything I caused. I think of the day that I followed the boy with the goat and Mama, when she found me, raised her hand, but didn't give me the blow that I deserved. Mama only dropped down in the dirty alley and began to cry.

Oh, Mamushka! I miss you so and want to tell you how sorry I am. But I couldn't have known, really. Because I wasn't yet awake.

From the diary of Maria Petrova, translated from the French

Chapter XII.

She had made a bad start that first night, with her little Russian fit. Even Charlie, he'd told her the next day, had been frightened to see her almost collapsing over the baby in her lap, her shoulders shaking and her sobs coming in ragged gulps. They had attributed her breakdown to fatigue. And she certainly *had* been tired. In that last hour especially she had come to feel herself a hollow, intangible thing, a ghost who could not eat the loaded plate they had brought her and who heard their voices as if coming from another plane.

But the cause of her breakdown had really been something else. Something she had not even tried to explain to them. Its source had come from the big mahogany secretary beside the chair where she sat. On its shelf there had been a crowded display of family pictures, assorted portraits and photographs in small guilt or carved or velvet frames. There were several pictures of babies in long gowns, and children pictured alone and in groups. In one of them she could identify Charlie in cowboy costume sitting atop a small pony. She had smiled at a photo of a toddler with a kitten and at a young couple at the beach in antique bathing garb. But in one faded oval a mustached man in military uniform had looked strikingly like Papa. In Abby's wedding portrait, she had been posed exactly as Katya had been in her own, and in a photo of three young graduates in black robes, Su Mei had floated up, a puzzled frown on her face.

Maria had certainly been tired. And later she would see that the resemblances of the smiling American faces to people at home had not really been so uncanny. But that night the gallery of family pictures had somehow ambushed her, triggering from nowhere a wave of homesickness so huge and smothering it had simply engulfed her, and she had been as surprised as the others were to hear her own moan, and to feel herself going under, drowning, it felt, under the weight of sadness.

Abby had rescued her from their shocked faces and solicitous murmuring, whisking the two of them upstairs to the big bedroom where a lovely old crib had already been installed for the baby. That night she had finally slept. For the first time since leaving the Washington hospital she had slept deep and dreamlessly and in the morning had awakened stronger and with a ravenous appetite. No one, besides Charlie, had ever mentioned the incident again.

But she knew she'd made a bad start. They seemed to be a little afraid of her now. All of them, but especially Rowena, the Negro girl who cooked and did the cleaning, treated her with a strange deference and unwarranted formality. In a few weeks only Rowena had become confident and playful, even sometimes a little boisterous, with the baby. But to Maria she still spoke softly, with a look of pained sympathy in her eyes, as though she were addressing an invalid.

These people were strangers and she had expected there to be some distance between them at first. But she sensed now that they thought her fragile, even a little mad perhaps.

Charlie had told her little about them. Even on the ship, when she had questioned him about his family or pressed him to talk of his childhood, he had been reticent, usually yielding only specific answers, volunteering little more. He had not given her much by which to guess their natures and omitted several important facts.

He had told her that his mother and aunt were his grandparents' only children. That Cassandra Whitaker's fiancé had been killed in a hunting accident long before he was born and that the sisters had since been inseparable, still living together in the house that his grandfather had built. He had mentioned, Maria did remember, that his mother and his aunt looked very much alike. But he had not prepared her for a resemblance so astonishing that to Maria they seemed like identical twins.

Both of the women dressed in black, or a gray so deep it was almost black, only venturing into navy blue on Sundays or festive occasions. They both wore dark, semi-opaque stockings and sensible black oxfords of the type that Eleanor Roosevelt had worn in the poster in Maria's school. Neither wore jewelry or make-up and they wore their hair identically, rolled around the crown and secured by hairpins, marcelled into neat finger waves in the center. They were patrons of the same salon in town, Maria would learn, and weren't the only women of a certain age to wear the style.

Charlie's mother, Estelle, was the elder by some six years. She was slightly more solid, a bit wider in the hips than her sister, and shorter by perhaps an inch or two. In time, Maria would come to see that the maiden aunt's limbs, especially her wrists and ankles, were thinner and more delicate than Estelle Atwood's, that her step was quicker and lighter, and that free of her sister's influence she had a musical laugh and a taste for simple, childish jokes. But it would take some time to make these fine distinctions. In the confusing early days Maria rarely knew which of the sisters was addressing her or how to tailor her response. For almost a month, perhaps more, Charlie's mother and Aunt Cassie were virtually indistinguishable. When she encountered one of them singly, in the kitchen or parlor or passing on the wide stairway, she rarely knew which of them spoke to her and a few early mistakes had reinforced their notion that she was perhaps weak-minded, at the very least a little strange. In the evenings, at meals, or at any time when both were present, Maria had come to rely on their voices alone to tell the two women apart.

In Margaret Atwood's voice there was always a tone of authority—that same quality that Mama had possessed and which, annoying as it had been when applied to trivial things, had sustained them in great and trying things, melting their fears in the face of her certainty. Already Maria understood that this was a good mother's ploy, possibly even her burden.

But unlike Mama, Charlie's mother seemed more fixed on communicating command than on conveying assurance, more critical than comforting. Her directives, whether they were to Rowena about plans for the week's meals or to Charlie about his future, never admitted of self-doubt or questioning. They were not open to dispute or debate. In the intimacy of their household she ruled supreme, and to a great extent spoke to all of them, even to Charlie, as though they were consummate fools.

In the family business, too, the elder sister seemed dominant.

The sisters ran a hardware store, another bequest from their father, just off the town's main street. Charlie had taken Maria there in the first week, on the same day that he had shown her his old high school and stadium, and they had toured the town square. In the tidy store, stocked with tools and garden implements, paints and oils and small machines, and rows upon rows of little wooden bins filled with nails and screws and bolts, they had found Aunt Cassie wearing a canvas apron and waiting on customers on the selling floor. Madam Atwood at first had been nowhere to be seen until Charlie had pointed up and waved, and Maria had seen her then, peering down at them from a small glassed-in office perched at the top of a wooden staircase. Aunt Cassie, as Charlie explained, was in charge of sales and "customer service." His mother managed the books, the purchase of inventory, the reporting of sales and taxes, and was generally, in Charlie's words, "executive management." The arrangement seemed natural to Maria, given what little she had already discerned of the sisters' temperaments, but she wondered how it must be for Aunt Cassie—and how it had felt for Charlie as a youth—to always be working below Madam Atwood's vigilant eye.

For the first weeks in her new environment, in the evenings and on weekends, the parade of visitors that had begun on that very first night continued almost unabated. The Atwoods, like the Khus, seemed to have a great many friends and a prominent standing in the social community. Many congregants from their church dropped by to welcome them, to peek at the baby if she were sleeping, or to take a turn at holding her if she were content and happy. There were also many of Charlie's old classmates and friends from his and Abby's childhood. Some of these visitors, Maria sensed, harbored rather strange notions of Asia in general, and of China in particular, and often asked her questions about hygiene or social customs or religious practices that were truly bizarre. Some found it difficult to understand how a white woman could have been born in China, and one of Charlie's friends had even remarked to her that she "didn't look Chinese." For the most part, though, they were kind and friendly, and frequently brought little gifts for the baby and left virtual banquets of food.

On Sundays they all attended church together and Maria looked forward to the social aspects of the day even though she found the service itself rather lacking in beauty and ritual. This Baptist priest delivered his sermon in a business suit rather than in clerical vestments and, except for the choir's white robes, there were no liturgical trappings of any type. Saving two stained glass windows done in meaningless colored mosaic and a bare wooden cross hanging above what appeared to be an empty aquarium, there was not even any art in the big church—no paintings or frescos or ikons of any kind. She could scarcely absorb this contradiction in that the church seemed obviously wealthy. There was lush new carpeting everywhere, electric water fountains, and huge, separate bathrooms for men and women with sparkling fittings and tiled floors. There was a nursery for the children and a fully equipped kitchen. But all of it was sparse and modern and unadorned.

Maria felt that Mama might not approve of the American church, but she took comfort from those elements of the sacraments that she could recognize and loved seeing the beautiful clothes. She had been introduced to several young women at the church, a few who were even young mothers like herself, and two or three had proposed outings or made promises to take her shopping or to the cinema, but as yet none of the invitations had materialized. It was Charlie who entertained her and Charlie who took her everywhere.

It was his turn now to be the teacher, the one to explain the customs and folkways of this new place and he seemed to relish his new role and to delight almost equally in educating and in mystifying her. In their brief stop in New York, and the half day they'd had in Washington before her labor had begun, she had already been amazed by the cleanliness of the cities, the new automobiles in the wide streets, the size of the shops, and the array of goods they sold. There had even been a shop in which food sat behind little windows and could be purchased, automatically, with coins. But now Charlie introduced her to the life of small towns and to the farms and the farmers that filled the bellies of these amazing United States.

It might be true, as Charlie reminded her, that she had come from one of the largest, most cosmopolitan cities on earth, but she was still a city girl and knew little of rural life. For many days he took her on long drives through the Georgia countryside where she saw not only American plentitude but the seemingly boundless space from which it sprang. Here there were poultry and hog farms as big as a village and fruit and nut orchards that ran for miles along the road. Cattle ambled lazily in acres and acres of empty green, and corn and cotton fields stretched almost as vast as the ocean. There was no rice grown at all here, but an abundance of other crops, and all of them seemed to thrive in the dry, rust-colored soil.

It was an exhilarating, nearly blissful, time for Maria. She loved touring with Charlie, walking arm in arm in the little towns where they stopped, and greeting the friendly locals who were kind and curious and almost never too busy to talk. But by their second month Charlie had become serious about looking for work and all his time was soon being spent speaking on the telephone or writing letters or the interview excursions that took him away from home at first only in the daytime, and then overnight, and gradually for several days at a time. It was a small village, this Hazel Grove, and there were not many opportunities for young men as clever as Charlie. There was still a lot of competition, too, from the swarms of servicemen who had returned from the war. There had been a discussion at the dinner table about the resentment at a local cotton mill where the women were being laid off in order to give their jobs to the men. Abby and her mother had disagreed about the way the matter was being handled. Maria, familiar with silk factories, but not with cotton mills, had embarrassed herself by wondering aloud why men would want such work. But Charlie wasn't interested in that kind of job anyway, and everyone, particularly his mother, encouraged him to take his time, to find a position suitable to his talents.

Maria's days were now spent at home with only Ana and Rowena. The care of their child consumed a fair amount of Maria's energies but the infant still slept much of the day and, while only Maria could feed her, Rowena often insisted on being allowed to bathe or dress or change little Ana herself. Indeed, while Rowena often begged for these duties, Maria was clearly not expected to help Rowena with her own work. Rowena had been rebuked once for allowing Maria to bring in laundry from the line, and again for merely letting her sweep the wide front porch. The situation was quite confusing, but Maria reminded herself that this was Madam Atwood's home, and she had no wish to make trouble for Rowena, who still held her at a distance.

To stay busy Maria used the newspaper and Sunday School pamphlets to study the written English and she listened to radio jingles and news broadcasts to learn the American slang and idioms. But she also told long fairy tales and fables to Ana in Russian and French and, when she was certain that no one would hear her, even babbled to her in Shainghainese. Still, the days began to feel astonishingly long and a restlessness overtook her that often made her irritable as well as a little ashamed. There was nothing here to complain of. Charlie's family was much wealthier than she had imagined. The big old house was solid and warm and filled with graceful furnishings. The bedroom they'd been given for themselves was comfortable and spacious. But she missed the tiny little flat that had been their first home. She missed the work that she had done for UNRRA and the feeling of value it had given her. She had heard nothing yet from Mama or from Katya, and tried hard not to think of any of it, but there were times when homesickness plagued her like an aching tooth and she could not keep her thoughts from probing the source of her pain.

Often, in the evenings, after their dinner had been cleared and Ana had been put to bed and the older women had settled themselves in front of the television set to watch Mr. Ed Sullivan's show or to cluck at the news reports, Maria found herself wandering outside, into the twilight space of the evening, to marvel at the blackness of the sky and to grieve, alone, in the quiet.

It was the remarkable quiet here, more than any other of her American experiences, which seemed most novel, and which seemed to speak to her, far more than the watery miles of ocean they had crossed, of just how far she she'd come.

She missed especially the street noises. The blare of automobile horns and the screeching of brakes. The rattling of the rickety old trolleys running down the Bund, the mechanical clang-clang of their bells, and the shrill piercing whistles of the traffic policeman. She longed, too, for the river sounds, and on closing her eyes could hear the tinkling of sailboat rigging in the harbor, the mournful bellow of the steamer's horns, the rush of the wind and the slap of the waves along the wharf. She imagined that she could hear the pigeons cooing in the park, and the cicadas shrieking from the parasol trees.

She ached for the human sounds, too. The noises of Shanghai's fourteen million souls. She missed the chatter of voices, the half-dozen languages heard on virtually every corner. She missed the grunts and pants and cries of the coolies, the slap of their bare feet or the clap of their crude wooden shoes on the pavement.

And then there was the music. In the daylight in Shanghai there had always been the loudspeakers roaring Chinese opera from storefronts. There had been the high, sing-song entreaties of the ubiquitous beggars striving to be heard above the din. The clappers of the street peddlers, clacking beneath it all.

The night had held its own music, especially those nights from the time that she and Charlie had courted, and every evening had been filled with jazz or swing in the big dance clubs, piano or violin in the smoky cafes. And below this, always, the music of laughter and talk and ice tinkling in glasses.

Shanghai had been a bedlam of noises, a discordant riot of sound. And yet, to one accustomed to it—to one so far from home—it was a symphony of all she'd ever known. Against the noise of her birthplace, that cacophony of remembered life, there was almost nothing here, almost nothing at all. Georgia evenings engendered only an eerie antiphonal chorus of invisible insects in the deep brush, the rare ghostly call of an owl or other night bird from the wall of the black pine woods. Against the noise of Shanghai, this new place offered a sepulchral silence—a lonely, deafening quiet, not of peace, not of death exactly, but of the very absence of life.

There was nothing here to complain of. And she knew what her mother would say.

As long as the sun shines, don't ask for the moon.

But it was Papa, not Mama, who she knew would understand the dark melancholy that had taken seed within her, and Papa's voice she often heard in her head.

Chas ot chasu ne legche.

Some things don't get easier by the hour. Some things go from bad to worse.

11 April 1948

We have Charlie's small phonograph in our room now and a few recordings. Ana loves listening to the music, but especially Dvorak, which will calm her when nothing else will. She will hold her own little hands and stare into space, as serious as a monk. But she likes my singing, too, and doesn't care at all how terribly I perform. She likes Twinkle Star best when I sing in Chinese. She frowns when I turn it to English.

She is fond of stories, too, both Rowena's and mine, but I know that her favorite is Beautiful Vassilisa.

From the diary of Maria Petrova, translated from the French

Chapter XIII.

Many years ago, in a small village there lived an old couple who had only one child, a daughter who was called Vassilisa. The family lived very humbly, but they were happy and comfortable, until the day that sorrow came to them. The mother fell ill and knew that she was nearing death. She called her daughter to her and gave her a small doll.

"Dochinka maya," she said. "Take great care of this little doll and keep it secret from anyone else. If you ever get into trouble, give her something to eat and ask her advice. She will eat the food and will help you in any trouble that comes."

The mother gave Vassilisa a last kiss, and soon after she died. Although the old man mourned the loss of his wife, after some time he married again, thinking he would find his daughter a second mother. The new wife had two daughters of her own who were stupid and cruel, but their mother spoiled them and allowed them to make Vassilisa's life a misery. They were always scolding her, treating her unkindly, and working her hard. They did their best to spoil her good looks by exposing her to the sun and the wind.

All day the girl heard nothing but, "Get on with cooking the dinner, Vassilisa! It is time you swept the hearth. The fire is going out. Fetch some firewood! Have you milked the cows yet? Don't just stand there doing nothing!"

Vassilisa was very willing to do everything they asked, was always trying to please them, and she found the little doll of great help in managing the work. Early every morning Vassilisa went to the pantry to give her doll some milk.

"Drink little, Dolly," she said to it each day, "and help me in my troubles." The doll drank the milk and comforted the girl, and did all the work for her. Vassilisa would sit quietly in the shade while the doll weeded the flower beds, fetched water, lit the stove, and watered the cabbages. The doll even showed Vassilisa certain herbs that would protect her from sunburn, and so the girl grew more beautiful than ever.

A day came when her father had to be away from home for some time. It was almost winter, and dark outside the cottage. Rain fell and the wind howled. The stepmother and her daughters would not set foot outside the house because all around the village was a deep forest and in the forest lived the witch, Baba Yaga, who ate people as if they were chicks. The stepmother gave all the girls work to do. One daughter was to make lace, the second to knit stockings, while Vassilisa was to spin. Then the stepmother put out all the lights except one small glimmer where the girls were working, and lay down to have a sleep. But the birch splinter which the girls were using for light soon sputtered and went out.

"Now what are we to do?" the daughters wondered. "There is not a light anywhere in the house, and we have our work to do. Someone must go to the witch Baba Yaga and get light."

"I shall not go," the elder stepdaughter said. "I am knitting lace, and the crochet hook gives me all the light I need."

"And I won't go either," the second stepdaughter said. "I'm knitting stockings, and the needles give me all the light I need." And they both cried at once, "Then Vassilisa must go for the light. Go to the witch Baba Yaga, Vassilisa!" And they pushed the girl out of the house.

All around her Vassilisa saw only the dark night and the deep forest. She heard only the angry wind. She burst into tears, and took the doll out of her pocket.

"My darling Dolly," she said, "they are sending me to the witch Baba Yaga for light. And the witch eats people and crunches the bones."

"Don't worry," the doll told her. "As long as you have me, no harm can come to you."

"Thank you, Dolly," Vassilisa said, and she set off for the witch's hut.

All around her the forest stood like a wall. She could see no stars shining, and the bright moon did not rise. She walked along trembling, pressing the doll to her breast. Suddenly a horseman galloped past her. He was dressed in white, riding a white horse, and the horse's harness was glittering bright. Dawn began to break. As Vassilisa went on she stumbled and fell among the roots and vines that snagged her. The dew clung to her hair and her hands were icy with cold.

Suddenly a second horseman galloped past. He was dressed all in red. He was riding a red horse with a brilliant red harness. The sun rose. It warmed Vassilisa and dried the dew on her pigtail.

All day she walked on. At evening she came to a glade. She looked into the glade and saw a hut surrounded by a fence made from human bones. On the fence were human skulls. Human leg bones served instead of a gate. The bolts were bony hands and sharp teeth acted as the lock. At this sight the Vassilisa was terrified and stood rooted to the ground. Suddenly another horseman rode past. He was dressed entirely in black, riding a black horse wearing a black harness. He galloped up to the gate and vanished as if he had been swallowed into the earth. Night came on.

As darkness fell the dead sockets in the eyes of the skulls on the fence began to glow and soon made the glade as light as day. Vassilisa trembled with fear. She wanted to run, but her feet would not carry her away from the fearful spot.

Suddenly she heard a terrible noise and the earth began quivering and shaking as though rocked by an earthquake. It was the witch on her way home. She was riding in a mortar, using a pestle to urge it on, and sweeping away her tracks with a broom. As she rode up to the gate she screamed.

"Phew! Phew! The place stinks of a Russian soul. Who is here?"

Inside Vassilisa was trembling, but she approached the witch, bowed very low, and spoke to her humbly.

"It is I, Granny," she said. "My stepmother's daughters have sent me to you to get a light."

"Ah, yes," the witch said. "Your stepmother's a relation of mine. Well, you can stay and work for me, and then we will see about the light." Then she shouted to the horrible fence made of bones.

"Powerful bolts, unfasten yourselves! Open for me, broad gates!"

The gates opened, and the witch rode in. Vassilisa followed her, but near the gate a birch lashed out at her with its branches.

"Birch tree, "the witch said. "Do not whip this girl. I have brought her in."

A dog lay at the door. It jumped up and tried to bite the girl.

"Do not touch her," said the witch. "I have brought her in."

In the porch a snarling cat tried to scratch the girl.

"Do not touch her, snarling cat, I have brought her in," the witch said again and she turned to Vassilisa.

"As you see," she said, "it is not easy to get away from me."
She went into the hut, stretched herself out on a bench, and in a
moment called out.

"Swarthy child, get me some food."

At once a swarthy young girl ran in and began to feed the
witch. She had brought a cauldron of beetroot soup, a bucket of
milk, twenty young chicks, forty ducklings, and two pies, as well
as endless quantities of kvass, mead, and beer. The witch ate and
drank it all. She gave Vassilisa only a crust of bread.

"Now, Vassilisa," she said, "take this sack of millet and sort it
out seed by seed. Take out all the black seed. And if you do not
get it all done I will eat you." Then she lay down, and soon
started to snore. Vassilisa took the crust of bread and set it before
the doll.

"Dolly, Dolly," she said. "Eat the bread and listen to my
troubles. The witch has given me a difficult task, and she says she
will eat me if I do not get it all done."

But the doll replied, "Don't cry, Vassilisa. Go and lie down to
sleep." As Vassilisa dozed off she heard the doll cry: "Little
birdies, fly in a swarm. Fly here and save Vassilisa from harm."

At once all sorts of birds came flying up in great numbers.
Trilling and cooing, they set to work to sort the millet, putting the
good grain into a sack, and the black grains into their crops. They
sorted out all the grain seed by seed, and cleansed it of all the
weed seeds. Just as the task was finished a white horseman
galloped past the gates. Dawn came. In time the witch woke up,
and at once questioned Vassilisa.

"Well, have you done the work?"

"It is all done, Granny," Vassilisa answered.

The witch flew into a rage, but there was nothing she could
do.

"Well," she grumbled, "I have to fly off now to fetch
something. Take that sack over there. In it peas are mixed with

poppy seed. Sort them all out, seed by seed, and put them into two heaps. And if you do not get it done I will eat you."

She went out and whistled, and the mortar and pestle rolled up to her door. A red horseman galloped past. The sun rose. The witch seated herself in the mortar and rode out of the yard.

Vassilisa took a crust of bread, fed the doll, and said:

"Have pity on me, Dolly dear. Help me."

The doll cried in a loud voice, "Hurry to me, little mice!"

The mice came running up in multitudes. There were field mice, house mice, and granary mice. In under an hour they had sorted all the peas from the poppy seed.

Late in the afternoon the swarthy child laid the table, and waited for the witch to return. A black horseman galloped past the gate. Night fell. In the skulls the eye sockets began to burn, the trees creaked, the leaves rustled. Baba Yaga, the bony-legged witch, was on her way home.

"Tell me, Vassilisa," she asked as soon as she came in. "Have you done all the work?"

"It is all done, Granny," the girl answered.

The witch was furious, but she could do nothing.

"In that case," she said, "go to bed, and I will lie down in a moment."

Vassilisa lay down behind the stove but before she could get to sleep she heard the witch say, "Swarthy girl, make the stove hot. Get a blazing fire going. When I wake up I will cook Vassilisa." Then Baba Yaga stretched herself out on a bench, covered her feet, and started to snore so loudly that she could have been heard all through the forest.

Vassilisa lay in her corner, for a while only weeping. At last she remembered and took out her doll and set a crust of bread before it.

"My darling dolly," she said. "Eat the bread and listen to my troubles." The doll ate the bread, and then told Vassilisa all she had to do in order to escape from the witch. So the girl went to the swarthy child, and bowed to her.

"Help me, swarthy child," she pleaded. "Don't burn the wood, but only wet it to make it smolder. Here, take my silk handkerchief as a present."

"Very well," the girl said, "I will help you. I will take a long time lighting the stove, and rub Baba Yaga's feet to make her sleep more soundly. You run away home, darling Vassilisa."

"But will one of the horsemen will catch me?" Vassilisa asked anxiously. "Will they come back?"

"Oh no," the girl answered. "The white horseman is the broad daylight, the red horseman is the golden sun, and the black horseman is the dark night. They will not hurt you."

Vassilisa ran onto the porch. The snarling cat rushed at her and tried to scratch her. But she threw it a patty, and it did not touch her. The dog jumped up and tried to bite her. But she threw him some bread and the dog let her pass. In the yard the birch tree tried to lash her eyes out, but she tied it with a ribbon, and the birch let her pass. The gates wanted to swing shut against her, but she greased their hinges with grease, and they opened for her. But now the black horseman galloped past; in the forest it grew darker than dark. How could she ever find her way home without a light? Her stepmother would beat the life out of her if she returned without it. Once more the doll instructed her what to do. She took a skull off the fence, and set it on a pole. The eye sockets in the skull shone so brightly that the dark night was lit up like day and Vassilisa ran through the forest.

After her nap the old witch woke up and stretched herself. She went to catch Vassilisa to cook her, and ran into the porch.

"Snarling cat," she said. "The girl ran past you. Why did you not scratch her?"

But the snarling cat answered: "I have served you for ten years, Baba Yaga, and you have never even given me a crust. But she gave me a patty, so I let her pass." Then the witch rushed into the yard and cried: "My faithful hound, why did you not bite the disobedient girl?" But the dog answered:"I have served you all these years, and you have never even thrown me a bone. But she gave me bread, so I let her pass."

The witch screamed hoarsely, "Birch tree, my birch tree, why did you not lash out her eyes?"

But the birch tree answered: "I have been growing in your yard for years, but you never touched my branches. She bound me with ribbon, so I let her pass."

The witch ran to the gates. "My evil gates, why did you not shut on the disobedient girl?"

But the gates answered her: "We have served you so long, and you never even poured water on our hinges. But she greased them with grease, so we let her pass."

The witch was furious but there was nothing she could do.

Meanwhile Vassilisa ran all the way home. When she arrived she saw there was still no light in the house. Her stepsisters ran out and swore at her. "Why have you been so long bringing the light?" they demanded. "We simply cannot keep any light going in the house. We have struck and struck the flint against the iron, but it never gave a spark to set the tinder alight. We hope the light you have brought will stay alight."

They carried the skull into the best room, and there the skull's eye sockets glared at the stepmother and her daughters so fiercely that they were caught on fire. By the morning they were burnt into cinders.

In the morning Vassilisa took the skull and buried it in the ground, and a crimson rose bush sprang up in the spot. Then she gathered her few belongings and went to the town where she took lodging with an old woman in exchange for work.

The old woman was kind and the work was light but Vassilisa soon grew restless. One day she said to the old woman: "Granny, I am bored with sitting here doing nothing. Buy me some flax, the very finest you can get."

The old woman bought the flax, and Vassilisa sat down to

spin it. The work flew so fast in her hands that the spindle hummed. The thread came away even and fine, like golden hair. She wove into linen as soft as silk and bleached the linen whiter than snow.

"Now, Granny," she said, "go and sell the linen and keep whatever you get for it." The old woman gasped at the linen.

"No, I shall not sell it," she said. "It is too good. Only a prince should wear such linen. I will take it to the prince."

When the prince saw the linen he was astonished at its quality. "What do you want for it?" he asked. "Such linen is without price," the old woman answered. "So I have brought it to you as a gift."

The prince thanked her and sent her home with presents. The servants wanted to make a shirt for him from the linen, but when they saw it no one would undertake the task: It was too fine for them to handle. So the prince sent for the old woman again.

"As you have been clever enough to weave such fine linen, now make me a shirt from it." But the old woman answered. "It was not I who spun and wove it, my prince. It was the girl Vassilisa."

"Then she must make the shirt," the prince said.

The old woman went home and told Vassilisa what the prince had said. The girl made the shirt, trimmed it with silks, and decorated it with seed pearls. Then the old woman carried it back to the palace. Vassilisa sat down at the cottage window to do more sewing but in a short time she saw one of the prince's servants come running down the street. He hurried up to her window, and told her:

"The prince requires you to go to the palace." So she went to the palace. And when the prince saw how beautiful she was he stood rooted to the spot.

"I do not intend to let you go away," he said. I want you to be my wife." He took her white hands, seated her at his side, and there and then they celebrated the wedding. In time Vassilisa's father returned from his travels, and came to live in the palace with his daughter. The old woman who had helped Vassilisa was taken into her service and held a place of trust and great friendship. Vassilisa and the prince were very happy. And for the rest of her life she always carried the little doll in her pocket.

15 June 1947

Charlie seems happy with the new job and with the automobile, a fine one, almost new, that comes with it, but Ana and I are not always so happy ourselves. He is traveling on the road all the time now. Sometimes even until Saturday morning. Ana is frightened of him at first when he comes home and for this somehow he becomes angry with me. She is not six months old and will soon grow out of it, of course, but at times he seems a stranger to me, too, and like Ana I want to howl.

I wither here. I shrink. I dream that I have become small and made of glass.

Last Sunday Charlie helped me and together we placed a transatlantic call, but they said there was no number for a Petrov on Rue Joffree. I can't think what it means and only hope that Mama and Papa have not given up their flat. Mama had everything just to her liking and Papa his great chair and I need to see them there in the pictures in my head. Charlie says that we will try to call again soon. He thinks the operators are simply lazy and there is no reason to worry, but worrying is the only thing I can do in this place. I don't know why no one answers my letters. I fear something is wrong.

Perhaps I am only lonely tonight and my mood is just foul. It has rained for days and Ana and I could not even walk the yard and the road. I had just found a place where I could hide the pram in the brush only a hundred meters before the bus that goes to town. It will be better when the rain stops. We'll learn to go places then. And tomorrow, Abby comes! She brings me sunshine, whatever the weather.

From the diary of Maria Petrova, translated from the French

Chapter XIV.

"Will you carry, me?" Maria asked, knowing that the question she posed of Abby contained an element of risk. The gamble, though, had more to do with language than with the possibility that her request would be denied. Abby was like Su Mei, rebellious and outspoken, but always kind, and Abby would be forthright if the favor was inconvenient. But Maria was also testing her use of the verb. She had observed that the verb use encompassed not just the meaning of gestation—as *porter* did in French—but also that here people "carried" not only objects, but adult individuals. Rowena, for example, had voiced a need to "carry" her mother to the doctor. Maria was doubly pleased by Abby's response.

"Of course I'll take you," Abby said. "Goodness knows, you're cooped up here all the time. But what's so important about tomorrow?"

"Here," said Maria. "See it for yourself."

She handed to Abby the typed letter she had received from Mr. Gordon Stiles, Editor of *The Hazel Grove Standard.* After a moment Abby began to read it aloud.

Dear Mrs. Atwood

Several months ago our paper ran a feature on war brides who are making their home in our county. We are interested in following up on that story. As we've learned that you have since come to us from Shanghai, China, we would like to add some details about your experience and to photograph you, along with the others.

Abby lowered the letter and smiled.

"Of course!" she said, "I remember that article! It ran at just about the time that we learned that you and Charlie were marrying. Believe it or not, I was already thinking about you."

Maria felt a thrilling little flush rise to her throat and cheeks.

"Am I anything like what you were thinking?"

Abby frowned and tilted her head as though seriously considering the question.

"Not really," she said at last. "Charlie always liked redheads. With *huge* bosoms!"

Now they both laughed gaily and from the kitchen a low, barely audible chuckle told them that Rowena was eavesdropping again.

Abby pressed a finger to her lips, motioning with her head towards the kitchen.

"I'd be happy to carry, you." Abby said, a bit loudly. "We'll let Rowena watch the baby. And after you've been to the newspaper office, we'll do a little juking."

Maria was suppressing her laughter for the sake of the joke, but the odd word caught her.

"Juking?" she asked. "What is this *juking*?"

"Juking!" Abby said, "You know! Go to a juke joint. A honkey-tonk. A bar! A place where we can have a few drinks and find us some men. You like to dance, don't you?"

Again, Maria was caught off guard.

"Oh, yes!" she said, "I love to dance! At home I danced all the time. There were wonderful places, you know, where we went dancing almost every night. The Portuguese and Italian men are very good at the tango. The rumba. The Americans throw you around, of course. But the English like the dances to hold a woman close."

Abby, who only a few moments ago had been half supine and relaxed on the sofa, now sat up and began writhing like a snake. Twice she clapped her hand over her giggles before finally taking a deep breath and speaking again in a businesslike voice.

"Well great, then. It's a date! I'll pick you up tomorrow afternoon. You can do your lovey-dovey, war-bride bit, and then we'll go find us a place where we can be real loosie goosies."

Now Abby stood up, pointed toward the kitchen, and beckoned Maria to follow her to the front door. It was rare that Abby used this door to come and go, but Maria thought she understood. At the door Abby gave her a warm hug, and then a broad wink, before skipping happily across the wide porch and down the steps to the walk. Even before she'd reached the drive, Maria could hear her begin to laugh aloud again.

Maria watched until Abby's car had almost reached the end of the long drive and then she closed the heavy door and for a moment leaned against it, exhaling a deep, satisfied sigh.

Juking? Honkey-tonk? Loosie goosie? What delicious fun! Not simply the delight of the new words, but the joy that Abby always brought her. The joy of speaking freely.

In her old world she had never thought to be afraid of speaking. Her natural garrulousness, the fearlessness with which she had plunged into learning other tongues, had been her strength—a weakness for Katya who was always afraid of making a fool of herself. But in this world, their world, Maria had become rather silent. They contributed to her silence and she felt this somehow an intention on their part, but with all the words at her disposal she could not have explained this to Charlie.

In Shanghai she had believed that her English was good. Her marks in school had been almost as high in English as in French and she had felt completely at ease conversing even with the native British. She and Charlie had courted in English and used it for their private love-making. It was the only language now that she had to speak with anyone, the only agent that could possibly assist in her own American assimilation.

She knew that she had not mastered all of the idioms. Certainly not the syrupy, drawn-out patterns of delivery. There were many times that she and Rowena had nearly reached impasse in their exchanges. But she was accustomed to making mistakes with language and had never been afraid to make them. It was different here. Here her mistakes were not met with the laughing delight of schoolchildren or natives. Not even, what she would have been inclined to expect, by the dry didacticism with which Mama had always corrected them. Here her mistakes were usually met with chilling recoil, a reaction almost of disgust, or horror. She was *foreign* as she'd heard them say, and she was coming to understand that, in their world, the word was fraught with meanings as yet too subtle to grasp.

In the beginning, her curiosity about this place, these ways, had been almost inexhaustible and she had been prone to sudden eruptions of questions or exclamations of confusion or delight. She had seen that these little explosions of hers had startled and embarrassed them. That her intensity had seemed to them assaulting, her excitement completely out of proportion to the ordinariness of its subject. It was a factor of culture she understood, a function of their reserve, and she vowed each time to control herself. But this strain contributed also to her silence and she could feel herself, in their world, becoming increasingly silent.

It was only with Abby that her tongue, and her heart, were not bound by confusion. In truth, Abby had become her one and only friend here, and Maria was terribly grateful for her friendship. If only Abby came around more often. If only she and her mother didn't quarrel so. But tomorrow, at any rate, she would be with Abby again, and out of the house, where they could truly speak freely.

It was scarcely three-thirty when Abby pushed open the store's street door and heard the little brass bell signal her entry. She had stopped at the drug store, lingered to chat with Hugh and

Alma Patterson, and then taken two turns around the square to kill more time. But Gordon's letter had said he'd need Maria for at least an hour. Mother already knew they were downtown today, and failing to drop in would cause more trouble than it was worth. The ticket was to make this short and sweet, and to not let Mother get her goat.

The store was almost empty this late in the day. Two little boys were feeding pennies into the gumball machine and just at the door Sam Yardley and Earl Wilson were apparently arguing.

"That Robinson fella's sure got the goods," Sam was saying, but he paused to acknowledge Abby, politely touching the brim of his hat.

"Don't make a damn," Earl shot back. "Afternoon, Miz Abigail."

"Gentlemen," Abby said, nodding as she passed between them, taking in the stench of Earl's sweat and the face, abnormally red, even for Earl.

"Don't make a damn," Earl repeated. "They's gonna' come at him spikes first. They's gonna' throw at his head until he's a slobbering fool. Ain't nobody gonna' set still for a nigger playing in the majors."

Down the second aisle she saw Aunt Cassie putting nails on the scale for a tall gaunt man in overalls. Abby waved and blew a little kiss to Aunt Cassie before crossing the wooden floor and heading for the stairs.

Inside her little cubicle Mother sat behind the big oak desk, the telephone receiver anchored on one shoulder, both hands sorting papers.

"Very well, then," she was saying into the receiver, "I'll expect them by the twenty-fifth. But this time I mean it! If I've got to wait three weeks anyway, I might as well order from Atlanta."

Abby sat down in the only chair provided for visitors and dropped her handbag, feeling a genuine twinge of sympathy for the supplier her mother was haranguing. The family business had suffered, as many had, during the war. Except for gardening supplies, there had not been a lot of interest in the last few years in the kind of small repairs and maintenance projects that were the lifeblood of a small town hardware store. For some time now the vendors' wartime production, particularly of metal goods, had given them the upper hand with the Dragon Lady—the nickname they'd given Mother almost from Grampy's death. But that advantage was being lost now. People were fixing up again. Many of the boys, only idling until they found real work to do, were using their time to mend roofs and fences, to paint and patch on the family homes and farms. Mother would be enjoying the little building boom and the opportunity to take a little revenge.

She ended her call and turned to look at Abby.

"Well, I presume you've delivered our little war bride?"

"Yes," said Abby, ignoring the icy edge in her mother's voice. "Maria seemed quite excited about it. A little nervous maybe."

"I'm surprised she agreed to it, really. She's such a timid little mouse."

Abby smiled, remembering their ride into town and Maria's magpie chattering.

"You know, Mother, that's a funny thing. I don't find her timid at all. She's just new to all this. And you can be . . . well, I suppose *all* of us can be, a little bit intimidating."

Behind her desk her mother stood up and flashed a quick frown, but she said nothing, moving instead to the far corner of the little office where two battered gray filing cabinets held the receipts and paid invoices for Hazel Grove General Hardware. Abby watched her mother wedging the green receipts into the bulging folders and recalled, unpleasantly, her own experiences with the heavy drawers and her mother's incomprehensible, but uncontestable, filing system. For one summer, as a teenager, Abby herself had briefly held the position of assistant bookkeeper and file clerk, but her mistakes had resulted in a spectacular, and tearful, termination. Charlie had held on all through high school, but Abby, like her father, had given up the hardware business abruptly and forever.

"And she's just so young," Abby went on. "I mean, eighteen for crying out loud."

"Yes," her mother said languidly. "But I was only nineteen when you were born."

"She's pretty sophisticated, though," Abby offered.

A file drawer slammed loudly and Abby flinched at the sound. Mother had turned to her now, her thin brows arched high in surprise.

"Oh, yes, she's *very* sophisticated. Why, just last night she chose to offer us a little gardening lesson. She explained the preferred method of crop fertilization in China. Apparently something called a "honey cart" comes around each morning to collect the . . . well, the human *excrement*. To transport that filth into the countryside. Imagine that! And she shared this little revelation at the dinner table. It was quite sophisticated. Quite!"

Abby bent to the floor to retrieve her purse. There was a nail file in there somewhere and pretending to look for it would cover her grin. *God! That must have been priceless! It would have been wonderful to have been there. To have seen Mother's face.*

Having located the nail file and escaped her mother's glare, Abby kept her voice deliberately light and casual.

"I was thinking, you know, more in terms of her own accomplishments."

"Accomplishments?" her mother echoed, "I don't what you mean. Unless it's snagging your brother. Getting out of that filthy, heathen country. Getting citizenship, I suppose, for her child. What has she *accomplished?* Other than that?"

Abby looked up, shocked by the patent unfairness, more by the undisguised vitriol in her mother's words. This was the place, if their pattern held, if they followed the template of their endless jousting—a template now ten years old but long ago disassociated from the event that had made it—where Abby could well stalk off in a huff. She might be expected—Abby usually did—to deliver one more thrust or parry. She might rage, or swear. Scream or bellow. Step very far over Estelle Atwood's low threshold for the profane or obscene. It would likely be useless, even comical.

Abby's nail file, her poised fingertips, trembled a little above her lap and she made soft fists of her hands to hide them.

"Mother, she speaks half a dozen languages. She had a job. A career. She was . . . she was a *professional.*"

The word, the mistake, hung in the air between them. Abby saw her mother's sly smile slide into place and waited, expecting to feel the child's impotent rage, the feeble fury aroused by adult trickery. Instead, as she looked now, at this slight woman in her grass-widow black, at the furrow of her frown, the deep marionette lines etched beside the thin mouth, she was suddenly filled with unexplainable sadness. *How had it come to this?* Her mother was getting on in years. Her battles, most of them anyway, seemed won. She had survived, even triumphed, over the humiliation of a runaway husband. She'd proven them wrong when they said she couldn't make a go of Grampy's store. She certainly had enough money to live comfortably, and the respect now—or at least the healthy fear—of most of the town. *What did she want? What was enough?*

"Can't you just give her a chance?" Abby pleaded. "She's a sweet girl, Mother. She loves Charlie! And I think he loves her."

"And now what do you mean by that? Give her a chance, indeed! She's here under my roof, isn't she? I feed them, don't I? And the girl doesn't have to lift a finger."

"Yes, but . . . Mother, you know what I mean. Just give her a little time."

For another instant their eyes remained locked and Abby saw the uselessness of even this simple appeal. The black telephone on the desk rang and they both started at the noise.

"I'm late," Abby lied. "I really must run. Maria will be waiting for me by now."

She closed and shouldered her handbag, stood up, and then impetuously stepped forward, putting her arms around her mother's shoulders and bussing her cheek with her lips. For a second her mother seemed to respond to, or at least to tolerate, the light embrace, but she broke away quickly, hurrying to the ringing phone.

On the sidewalk outside the store Abby felt the familiar weakness, the enfeebling exhaustion that always seemed to follow her visits with her mother. She had kept her vow today, but still it had been a battle. One she had lost, it seemed, where Maria was concerned. The situation for Charlie and Maria was worse, much worse, than she had even imagined. And Charlie's new job was keeping him completely oblivious to their mother's hostility to Maria. She would have to find a way to talk to him again. To remind him, again, of what was at stake.

Across from the Standard building Abby found an empty meter and eased the car into the angled spot. She turned off the engine and was about to rummage for a nickel when the door to the newspaper office suddenly opened wide and a group of laughing young women poured out onto the sidewalk. Gordon Stiles, too, had followed them out. Abby watched him become the hub of the little group, shaking hands with each of the young women in turn, smiling his broad, beautiful smile and bending his tall lean body down to speak intently to each of the women.

In the little huddle Abby found Maria, easily the prettiest in the lovely little bevy, and watched her return a fat, bonneted baby to a raven-haired girl who kissed the baby's cheek first and then Maria's own. Abby removed her keys from the ignition and was reaching for the door handle when a figure approaching on the sidewalk across the street caught her eye. Walking down the sidewalk, unhurriedly, but with the same cocky saunter she remembered from high school, was someone who looked a lot like Eddy McQuiston. The black hair was a little shorter, the body a bit trimmer and harder. But the expression was the same, in a face that could be called handsome, were it not for the snide, crooked smile, the look of defiant arrogance in the dark, narrowed eyes. It was definitely Eddy. And except for the addition of a large tattoo on his forearm, a snake-wrapped anchor, he looked exactly as she remembered him. Exactly.

A flutter of motion down the walk returned her attention to the newspaper's door and she saw that Gordon Stiles had caught sight of her. He tapped Maria on the shoulder and pointed to the car. Maria waved happily and the two of them began making their way across the street.

At the passenger side Gordon helped Maria into the car and then leaned in to greet Abby.

"Well, from the looks of you two, I'd say your interview was a success," Abby said.

"Oh, it was lovely!" Maria burst out. "There were two girls from England. And while they didn't know each other, at least not before, these came on the very same ship. For brides!"

A ship for brides? Abby smiled and gave Gordon a furtive little wink. Maria communicated very well, but she could still mix things up sometimes.

"She's right," Gordon said. "The U.S. Military and the Red Cross had several of those operations. War bride ships. Really! And two of these ladies, one from Dorchester and one from London, actually came over together on one of the later ones. Their husbands served with the RAF."

"How interesting!" said Abby, "I'd heard nothing about it."

"Oh, there's a lot to learn around a newspaper, Abby. You should try it," he said, giving her a devilish little wink.

"Oh, they speak beautiful English, of course!" said Maria. In the passenger seat her head darted between Abby and Gordon. "And there was another, an Italian girl from Naples. She has married a soldier from here, a soldier of Italian descent. Her name was Luisa, I think?" Now she looked to Gordon.

"That's it," Gordon said. "Luisa DiSalvo. Some trouble with the language there, but Maria helped. Your sister-in-law is quite the linguist."

"She is, indeed," said Abby, thinking again of how little Mother valued this accomplishment.

"We were getting nowhere with one of them, a Chinese girl, until Maria stepped in. You should have seen her face light up then!"

Maria smiled shyly and reached to touch Abby's arm.

"Li Chin!" she said. "She comes from Canton. The dialects are very different, but we could talk a little. She hasn't much English."

"Li Chin is her name," Maria said again, a touch of irritation in her voice this time. "But she says she will be called Mary now."

"Yes," Gordon said, his tone strangely sarcastic, "Mary."

"But are they getting on?"Abby asked. "All the girls I mean?"

"Most of them, I think. The English girls, certainly. And the DiSalvos are great folks. I'm sure Luisa will be fine. If she can get used to the smell."

Abby laughed. Gordon wasn't really making a joke. The DiSalvos had a pretty large, but very aromatic, hog farm about twelve miles west of town.

"I expect it will be a bit more difficult," he said, "for . . . for Mary."

Gordon now leaned deeper into the car and directed his gaze strictly at Abby.

"She's married Eddy McQuiston," he added.

Abby took in an involuntary gasp of air.

"She lives in the town of Morgan Hill," said Maria. "I've promised to visit. Is it very far, this Morgan Hill?"

Abby saw Gordon wince.

"No," he said gently, "only about twenty miles or so. But Morgan Hill isn't exactly a town, Maria. Not really. It's a mill village. The place where the cotton mill workers live."

"The workers have a village?" Maria asked.

"Oh, yes," said Abby. "The company rents them small houses. They have a store and a church. A school. Everything."

"Everything one needs to live in servile squalor," said Gordon brightly, standing up suddenly to lift his face above their view through the window.

Maria turned a puzzled frown to Abby.

Exposing conditions in the mill village was a long-running crusade for the paper. And Gordon Stiles had become the resident thorn-in-the side for Morgan Textiles. She could explain all this to Maria someday. But not just yet. Not now.

Abby shrugged her shoulders and let the awkward seconds pass.

Gordon bent down to them again at the window.

"Well, it was wonderful to meet you, Maria," he said, "and to have your help today. May I call on you again should we need a translator? The Standard would be happy to pay you."

Maria blushed visibly, clearly flattered by Gordon's offer. For a moment Abby thought she might be too embarrassed to speak, but a dancing little twinkle lit the green eyes.

"Oui," Maria said. "Oui. C'est gentil. Merci!"

Abby and Gordon laughed together while Maria, between them, sat quietly, an impish smile on her face.

"And Abby!" Gordon said. "It was certainly nice to see *you* again. You shouldn't be such a stranger. No reason that old friends couldn't have a cup of coffee now and then, is there?"

Abby hesitated. Of course there was a reason. And Gordon Stiles damn well knew it.

"No," said Abby, "No reason at all."

24 October 1947

Rowena is still in Macon caring for her mother. This is my third day now alone in the house. I had thought to make good use of my time as mistress, but most of it has gone badly. I seem to put everything in the wrong place. I have put too much bluing in the laundry and can see from their faces that they don't at all like my cooking. I expect that there are other errors ahead of me, too, but still I'm glad that Rowena is gone for a while.

I'm not quite sure that I've completely forgiven her. There was such a terrible row after she told Madame Atwood that Abby and I had gone dancing with men. It was not true, of course. We went only a little way over the line of the county where we had only one cocktail. I don't remember that we spoke to anyone else at all. But even Charlie pretended to be shocked. Madame Atwood spoke of spirits, of evil spirits, and I was slow to discover her meaning. They think it sinful to drink even wine and will not allow it in the home or in the church.

I do love Rowena. She would not have told but for her own trouble. The new television is quite nervous and she had been told not to touch it. If only I had spoken up and taken her part we both might have been spared much worse.

From the diary of Maria Petrova, translated from the French

Chapter XV.

In the very beginning, after the difficult delivery and before her strength and energy had fully returned, Maria had been glad to be here in a house with three other women who knew something about the mysteries of babies. She had been happy then, at times almost tearfully grateful, to surrender the child into their competent arms for the chance of getting even an hour of uninterrupted sleep. It had taken only a little while for her to begin to feel quite differently about their help and she had come to realize that in accepting their aid she had unwittingly surrendered something of inestimable value.

In those first months, when the child had been colicky, crying too long and stiffening when she tried to calm it, the older women had been careful about making suggestions, asking if they might be permitted to try some experiment or other, some trick of infant soothing that had worked for them before, in other lives and with other babies. But in a short time it had become common, at the first sound of Ana's crying, for one or the other of them to simply pluck the child from her arms, flashing Maria a swift, disapproving frown as though they had just rescued the baby from some threatening danger.

After only four months Maria had abandoned the breastfeeding, letting their fears about whether or not it could be getting enough nourishment from the "skin and bones" of her body, to infect her, too. They had felt thoroughly vindicated when, after only a few weeks, the baby had begun to put on weight. More than once after that Maria had awakened, startled by the time on the clock and the thought that little Ana had slept through her feeding, only to find the crib empty and downstairs one of the women already in the rocking chair, feeding a bottle to her bundled infant, singing it a strange hymn or an unknown nursery tune. Now the ease of the bottles and powdered formula made everyone as capable as she was of feeding her own child. Aunt Cassie had made the last bottle of the day her own duty and now put Ana to bed herself.

There were other things, too, some so slight as to seem almost imaginary. For three Sundays in a row they had changed items of the baby's clothes—the shoes or bib or bonnet that Maria had just dressed her in—for no apparent reason, or at least none that anyone bothered to explain. They had become wordlessly critical, exchanging between them knowing little glances they had stopped trying to conceal from her, but offering her nothing constructive in return.

She felt that they were usurping her motherhood, taking her child from her by a strange gentle theft that she herself scarcely understood and could not articulate even in her own thoughts, certainly not to anyone else. The one time only that she had tried to complain of it to Charlie she had become terribly muddled, stuttering out a list of offenses that had sounded merely petty and ridiculous. He had laughed at her and she had dissolved into tears of shame and frustration, falling asleep on her damp pillow wondering if perhaps he could be right. Maybe she *was* a little crazy.

But there was nothing anymore that could prevent the feeling of dread that descended upon her each weekday evening at about six o'clock—the hour, except on Wednesdays, when the black Oldsmobile bearing the sisters home from their workday, pulled into the long drive. These evenings, without Charlie or Abby, had become almost unendurable and she had exhausted all ideas for breaking their bleak monotony. There were two cinemas in Hazel Grove and one of them even now was running a new film starring Rita Hayworth—the most glamorous, Maria thought, of all the American stars. The sisters, however, could not be persuaded to attend. Going to movies, like dancing or playing cards, was somehow morally out of bounds and Madame Atwood thought the American Hollywood was filled with anarchists and Reds. Aunt Cassie would sometimes agree to dominoes, but she was not clever at the game and Maria felt cruel in beating her.

At the end of the summer she had finally secured the bus schedule, and about once a week she managed to walk the three quarters of a mile down the blacktop road to the place where the bus stopped twice a day. On her own she had found the town's little library and was working her way through its small collection of books. Occasionally she visited the newspaper office where Gordon was always happy to see her and often had big city papers to share. She had once been fetched by Antonio DiSalvo and spent a delightful day with Luisa.

The days at least were bearable, but it still had been wonderful in Rowena's absence to have the house, and her child, all to herself. For the first time in her life she was discovering that being alone was not at all the same as loneliness. She was enjoying doing things to her own liking and had made almost a game of it, going out of her way to re-order tasks, to drink her tea hot rather than iced, to leave the baby barefoot and dressed only in diapers in the overheated house.

Today she had spread an old quilt in the center of the parlor floor and brought down the cushions from the sofa to make a soft playground where the two of them had spent the afternoon. The pallet was strewn with toys and books and the scraps of the lunch they had rebelliously eaten, also, on the floor. It was terrible mess, but there was plenty of time for clearing it and for hiding all evidence of their unconventional day.

For the last half hour Maria had been telling Ana, in Russian, about the wonders of the Rose Palace, a place neither of them had ever seen, but whose description had become so ritualized for the two of them that Ana had learned where to clap her hands or to widen her eyes—Charlie's eyes, dark and fringed with black lash—or to make her baby *ahhhh* sound in the places in the story that had been designed to elicit her sympathy. She especially liked the end, the description of their favorite room, the great ballroom, because it typically involved mother and child circling together beneath the great chandelier, dancing their own twirling waltz to the sound of the orchestra. Ana knew the Rose Palace, as Maria did, and when no one else was listening, they went there often.

But the story had ended some time ago and for the last few minutes Ana had been left to her own devices. Tired of toddling back and forth between toys and books, she was rather listlessly now lining up the wobbly nesting dolls on the edge of the carpet, picking one or the other of them up occasionally to give it a sweet spontaneous kiss, or else to simply test the ovoid lacquered surface with a wet, inquisitive mouth. In a few minutes more she had grown tired of even this and took two toddling steps toward a sofa pillow where she dropped on her bottom, leaned back, and allowed her eyes to blink, droop and briefly resurrect again, before finally closing in easy, natural sleep.

Maria, who had been watching her daughter's antics with a mother's fascination, now smiled, stretched on her own pillow, and waited a bit before moving to scoop up her sleeping child, pick her way carefully across their cluttered play space, and carry her up the wide staircase and down the hall to her own little crib in their bedroom. She was about to tiptoe out when the tissue-papered airmail letter on the dresser caught her eye. For the third time this week she picked it up and began to read again.

Dearest Maria,

Your father and I greet you in fair health. There are shortages of everything now as more and more goes to the soldiers and only bribery will get you anything. I have paid cumshaw to the postman, but still can only hope that this letter eventually reaches your hand.

We have been relieved to learn that the new owners of the hotel will keep your Papa in his place but the wages are much less than before and the hours longer. There is a photographer in the hotel now and they pay him to pose in pictures. He brings home the copies of these when the fools neglect to pay. On the table here is one with a large florid woman with a small dog in a jeweled collar. There is no end, I fear, to the humiliations that your father must suffer in this world, but still we are far better off than most in the city and will find our ways to economize. I have already had the telephone service removed as my girls are no longer here to gossip. My pupils and their parents were finding it far too much of a convenience at any rate and I'm sure I'll not miss it.

Frugality, my darling, as I'm sure you know, is a virtue in a good wife. You must do all that you can to be saving so as not to be a burden to . . .

Here Maria tossed the letter down again and involuntarily stamped her foot. There was some comfort in Mama's familiar tone. And it was a relief to know that the telephone, and not the flat, had been sacrificed. But elements of the letter were also confusing, and annoying. She was rather insulted that Mama had seemed to suggest that she was extravagant. There had been no mention at all of Katya, and no answer to Maria's third or fourth request for Katya's permanent address. She was perturbed by the post script, presumably dictated, where Papa was apprising her only about politics. She would never get her own letter from Papa, of course, because he wrote only in Russian and was ashamed of his small, scratchy penmanship. Still, she had hoped that he might speak to her of something more than his distrust of Joseph Stalin.

The date of the letter was now more than eight weeks old. She had asked at the little post office about other letters, but had been assured that all of the mail, every bit of it, was collected each weekday by someone from the hardware store. They had no explanation for why this one letter, delivered to her by Madame Atwood's hand, should have come to her so tardily. Most disturbing of all was the clear sense that Mama had missed certain stages in their dialogue. Maria had written at least half a dozen times in the last few months, to tell about new teeth or to brag that Ana had begun walking and was learning new words every day. But Mama had no response to any of this news.

Maria turned to take one more look at the sleeping baby. For the first time she observed that the gold chain, bearing the tiny Coptic cross that had been hers as an infant and that Ana had worn since her own birth, was almost buried in Ana's fat little neck. It was beautiful against Ana's tawny skin, but she was outgrowing the necklace, and perhaps it posed a danger. Maria cupped the baby's head, lifting it in order to tease the chain's clasp forward, finally managing to unlock the clasp and to release and retrieve the chain. Once in her hand she gave the little cross a quick, reverent kiss, promising herself that she would buy a longer, safer chain. She pulled up the light blanket to cover Ana's bare shoulders.

It was Wednesday, a prayer meeting night for the older women, and as often as not they took their Wednesday dinners in town before going directly to the church. Ana could be fed her small morsels of solid food later. There was nothing to do about dinner, but still, tea might be nice. She might even start another letter or write more in her journal.

Once downstairs Maria returned the sofa cushions to their rightful place, collected Ana's toys and story books and packed them in the wicker hamper, and finished clearing and inspecting the parlor. She was just going to make tea when she heard a light knocking at the back door. She crossed to the kitchen and opened the door.

At the bottom of the three-step brick stoop stood a slightly built Negro man, ragged but not dirty, in a flannel shirt, a well-worn corduroy coat, and dark trousers supported, not by a belt, but by a piece of frayed rope. The man had knocked, Maria was sure of it, and yet he seemed surprised to see her in the doorway and immediately swept a tattered wool stocking cap from his head, meeting her eyes with his own and then casting them down again, several times in quick succession.

"Hello," Maria said.

Between them now was only the light frame of the thin screen door, no barrier at all for a man of any strength, but it did not occur to her to be frightened. She had lived in a desperate city in a desperate time and understood clearly what desperation might drive a human to do. She had also absorbed something of the contempt, and fear, directed at dark-skinned people in America. But she had relied since earliest childhood on a host of subliminal signals for evaluating danger and there was nothing about this man's bearing or countenance to raise even the slightest alarm.

"I beg yo pardon, ma'am," the man said. "I'm sorry to disturb. I was just passing along and I was wondering if y'all might have any work."

"Work?" Maria echoed. *Work?* It was a simple English word. One that she thought she knew well in all its connotations, and yet now, in this particular situation and context, she found herself grappling for meaning.

"Yez'm. I can do most 'bout anything."

"Well, you see," said Maria, "this isn't really my home. Well, perhaps it's my *home* for the time being, but it's not really my *house,* you see. My mother-in-law, Mrs. Estelle Atwood, owns this house, and she is in town this afternoon. I don't know what work there is to do about the place, but I'm sure that if you came back tomorrow, or perhaps later his evening, she'd be glad to discuss the possibility of employment with you."

"Yez'm," he said. "Yez'm." He persisted in skipping his eyes between her face and the ground as though her glance were hot and he could not tolerate it for very long.

Her intent had been merely to shake his hand in parting, but in the opening, and scraping, of the screen door, the man jumped, almost violently, and then Maria understood. In the sharp backward step, the reflex of a beggar about to be struck, a fallen coolie who already felt the stick to come, she saw for the first time what was before her.

"You're hungry," she said. "You want to work for food."

For the longest moment yet he met her eyes and then again he cast them downward.

"Yez'm," he said softly, talking to the ground. "I'm powerful hungry. "

"You should have told me!" Maria said. "There's food enough in this house. Come in." She pushed the screen door wide.

"I thank you, ma'am," he said. "I'm powerful grateful." He took several more backward steps now, placing himself truly in the back yard.

"I'll be right here!" he said, suddenly excited, pointing to the big flat tree stump that stood almost central in the manicured back yard.

"Why that's silly!" Maria laughed. "It's practically freezing out there! Come inside. It will only take me a few minutes."

"Oh, no'm," he said again. "I 'preciate it. I do. But I'll be right out here."

"Come *in*," Maria said firmly, pushing the screen door wider. The man's eyes would not meet hers, but Maria continued to hold the door and after much hesitation he came forward again, accepting her invitation to step into the kitchen.

While her nameless guest sat in the white kitchen chair at Mrs. Atwood's white kitchen table, Maria bustled about preparing his meal. From the refrigerator she retrieved the ample remnants of last night's beef pot roast and the large leftover caches of lima beans and carrots that had come from their own garden. While she was still not perfectly familiar with the arrangements in the Atwood kitchen, she managed to light the gas stove and to find pots and stewers and the other implements she needed. In a very few minutes she had placed a heavily laden plate of meat and vegetables and a side saucer of leftover blackberry cobbler before her guest.

The small dark man blinked once and began to eat. He had brought his chin down almost to the level of his plate and still his hand trembled as he scooped food into his mouth. He was trying hard, she could tell, not to appear ravenous, and yet he was, and could not help himself. She watched as tears welled in the corners of his eyes and heard his breath coming animal-like as he ate.

This was familiar, too. She had seen, more than once, a half-starved human being eating like this. In Shanghai it had most often been the result of an accident. A turned-over cart, a spilt sack in the street, had often created a desperate opportunity and the need for uncivilized haste. She worried that he would choke himself

Maria waited until the man's urgency had slaked a little and he had begun to take full breaths between his loaded forkfuls. At the corner of the table she pulled a chair for herself and sat down.

"So you're passing through?" she asked him. "Then your home is not here?"

"Oh, no'm," he said. "I'm from down Augusta way. I come up to see 'bout could I get on at the mill."

"You're a spinner, then. Or perhaps a carder?"

Maria didn't actually know what either of these words meant. Only that they described duties performed inside the gloomy two-story brick building at the back of the mill village. She had collected the words, and perhaps a half-dozen others, in two visits with Li Chin, now Mary McQuiston, who had no Cantonese equivalents to explain the work of her husband and father-in-law.

"Oh, no'm. I weren't looking for no work like dat. They's let colored folks clean up some. Unload and open the cotton bales. Outside, you know, on the dock. But that's 'bout all."

"I see," Maria said, although she didn't quite. She knew that the mill jobs were quite hierarchical, that there was considerable competition for the better paying ones, and a good bit of nervousness and insecurity among the mill hands now that wartime production had dropped. It didn't surprise her greatly that the Negros would be the last to be hired. She assumed that her guest had not been lucky.

Maria sat quietly while he finished his meal, rising only once to fill his glass from the tea pitcher. It was difficult not to stare but she returned a friendly smile whenever he looked up, and she noted that his shoulders had lifted and that he could now afford to pause from time to time to blot his mouth with the napkin. In a few minutes more he had emptied his plate and turned to address, with full composure now, the overflowing dish of blackberry cobbler. He took one bite, chewed slowly, then closed his eyes, moaned softly, and shook his head.

"This here is jes 'bout the best cobbler I ever et," he said. "I do believe it is! You shore do make a fine cobbler."

"Oh, I didn't make it," Maria said hurriedly, "although I did help Rowena to pick the berries. July, I think it was. Or early August. But I didn't enjoy it very much and I really don't think I'll do it again. I was scratched all over by the thorns, you know, and suffered for days from the chickers."

The man tilted his head quizzically and frowned.

"Chickers?" he said.

"Oh, yes!" Maria said. "If you'd ever had them, you'd know. You don't see the little beasts at all, but they bite you everywhere. And in the most embarrassing places. I thought I'd *die* from the itching!"

The perplexed frown and narrowed eyes remained frozen for several seconds, but slowly the furrows in his brow relaxed, a wide smile spread to alter his face, and he began to laugh, with only a chuckle at first, but then an increasingly robust crescendo that soon had him rocking sideways in his chair.

Maria stared at him, still smiling, but confused. It had been an awful experience really. How could he find it so amusing?

"*Chiggers*," he said at last, stressing the guttural consonants. "I believes you mean *chiggers*."

"Oh!" said Maria. "Yes. Of course! Not chickers. But chiggers."

"Chickers!" the man said again, laughing even more energetically, and Maria began to laugh too, seeing that her mistake *was* rather funny, but happier still that the frightened little man had now been so transformed.

"Chickers," Maria repeated, for his benefit and for hers, because again she had unraveled one of the delightful puzzles of language.

"Chickers!" he echoed, and they laughed together now, each slapping the table in glee, bouncing the empty plates and crockery and filling the kitchen with their sound.

And that is how they would be found, when Mrs. Atwood and her sister walked into the family kitchen that gray October afternoon. There was Maria and a nigger, Maria's fine blonde head and the stranger's nappy black one only inches apart where they sat, conversing congenially at the white kitchen table, the two of them laughing together like grand old friends. Laughing so loudly that they had not heard the baby, little Ana, who had been retrieved from her crib, practically naked in October, and wailing forlornly, a sodden diaper drooping between her legs.

13 March 1948

I read in the papers that the winter offensive has gone well for the communists. Their armies are already at the Yangtze. I can almost hear Papa raging over it, but there has been only one letter more from Mama and she makes no mention of it at all. She sent me no birthday greetings either, but the letters come so slowly that I haven't yet despaired. My birthday passed unmarked here, but Mama would never forget.

At least she has sent me a little news of Katya. I am happy that again she has horses to ride and that she is playing tennis again. But by this I know that there is not yet a baby on the way and I can't rejoice over that.

From the diary of Maria Petrova, translated from the French

Chapter XVI.

The reaction of the women, the looks of horror on their faces, and the verbal assaults on her visitor, had made it quite clear to Maria, even before the small dark man had turned over his chair in running for the door, that what she had done this time was no mere *faux pas*, no simple social breach or error in judgment. Aunt Cassie had only stood mutely by, nodding her head and sniffling a little, but Madame Atwood had pelted Maria with questions. *What was the meaning of this? Didn't she know that Negroes raped and murdered white women? Was she not aware of their filth and diseases? Had she no regard for the safety of her child? Had she meant to have all of the valuables of the household stolen? If not now, then later, when he might return with accomplices?*

In fact Maria did not know any of this, nor did she believe it, still trusting the instincts which had allowed her visitor in. But she saw that in their minds she had been reckless and foolish. That this mistake would be harder to live down than others she had made. It had taken until Sunday, though, four days after the incident, to understand the full repercussions of her mistake and the real damage she had done.

The sisters had left for services early and alone, a rare development, and one that Maria assumed had been prearranged by Charlie and his mother. In their bedroom Charlie had also surprised her by beginning to pack early for the week ahead. He had been striding purposefully between the closet and dresser and bed where toiletries lay scattered beside his leather traveling valise. Maria sat meekly at the foot of the velveteen chaise and Ana stood in her crib, tracking him with her eyes. Her lower lip protruded and quivered slightly. She had registered the tension between her parents.

"I can't *have* this!" Charlie was saying. "I won't! I've got to work. How am I supposed to concentrate, to keep my appointments, if I've got to be worrying about you all the time?"

"Don't *go* then," Maria pleaded. "You promised me that we would have a place by now. A little house, I don't care. A room only. I can live anywhere."

Charlie frowned as he jammed balled socks and a hairbrush into the valise.

"Maria, you're being ridiculous," he said. "I've got to think of the future. One more big order and they'll give me the Atlanta territory. We can move to the city then and . . . "

"Then take us with you!" Maria interrupted, springing up and running to the big bureau where she kept the baby's things. "We won't be trouble. Ana is good. We'll only take enough for the week. I can be ready quickly. I can . . ."

At the top of the bureau she wrenched open a drawer and began removing little garments, piling them in stacks on the top of the chest.

"Are you crazy?" Charlie shouted. He stepped forward and grabbed at one of the little stacks, tossing the whole bundle angrily at the open drawer. "I live in hotel rooms. How are you going to take care of the baby in a hotel room?"

"Then Abby, then! We'll go to live with Abby. Oh, I know that she'll agree to it. Abby loves Ana. And her house is big! Large enough for the three of us. We will go to live with Abby."

"We'll do nothing of the kind!" Charlie fired back. "You've already got Mother and Abby going at each other all the time. You've got to stop it, I'm telling you! You're tearing my family apart, Maria."

Maria froze. There was some truth in Charlie's words. She knew that the rifts between Charlie and Abby, between Abby and her mother, were growing wider, and that she somehow was a contributor. There was too much to say to this. Nothing she really could say. Her reply came in a childlike whimper.

"Your mother hates me," she said. "I can do nothing to please her."

"She doesn't hate you," Charlie thundered. "It's just your crazy stunts. What was the idea of letting in that drifter? He could have robbed us blind, you know. You might have been killed. Or worse!"

In her crib now Ana began to cry in earnest.

"Baba yaga!" Ana wailed, pointing a small index finger at Charlie, "Baba, baba . . . yaga."

"What is that?" Charlie asked. "What is she saying?"

"She thinks you're bad," Maria said, hurrying to lift Ana out of the crib. "That you're acting the bad witch."

"What nonsense! Why do you fill her head with all that worthless junk? And I want you to speak English to her, do you hear me? You promised! I've told you for the last time. English!"

Maria stiffened, tightening her hold on Ana. It was ridiculous, this provincial theory of theirs, that Ana's English would be impeded by hearing a Russian fairy tale or a few simple words in French. As though Ana's mind, as though anyone's, was too small for a second tongue. Perhaps she had promised Charlie. *Had* she promised him? It had not really seemed serious then. And her polyglot play with Ana, for the most part, had been private. But Ana was talking now, and had begun to repeat not just words but whole phrases she had learned from her mother.

Maria intended to advance a rational argument. She was thinking of reminding Charlie of the cosmopolitan nature of UNRRA, of Shanghai in general, where language skills had been a distinct advantage. Of the fact that her own skills had secured her position in the headquarters office and been the cause of their meeting, the initial catalyst of their romance and the union that had given them Ana. But as she struggled to compose her appeal, a long-smoldering anger and frustration overcame her. For the first time ever she raised her voice, against her husband, and in Ana's presence.

"She's my child, too!" Maria screamed. "You'll not tell me how to speak to her! You're never even here!"

For an instant Charlie seemed stunned. For a long moment he stared at her. She watched as his eyes, wide and startled at first, narrowed into slits and began to burn with anger, or contempt. He bent to the bed, snapped his valise shut, and slowly stood to face her. When he spoke again his voice was unnaturally calm, alien, and icy cold.

"And from what I understand," he said, "you're not around much either."

"What?" Maria asked incredulously.

Charlie smiled now, but the look in his eyes hadn't changed.

"I'm told that you gallivant all over these days," he said. "Running to the mill village. Visiting Gordon Stiles? Stopping at roadhouses, I'd guess. Now that Abby has introduced you to the local culture."

Gallivant? Maria didn't know the word. She had never heard of *roadhouses*, either. But she understood clearly what she was being accused of and the source of Charlie's information.

"What would you have me do?" she asked." In Shanghai at least I could go about. I had friends and things to do."

Charlie answered her through gritted teeth.

"This *isn't* Shanghai, Maria," he said. "You need to get that through your head!"

Now he swept the valise off the bed and took the few steps necessary to reach her, to take her jaw between two fingers and forcefully lift her face to his. The pressure of his thumb at her chin was painful. She wanted to wrench herself away, but she remained still, afraid of frightening Ana.

"This isn't Shanghai!" he said again. And with that he had turned and left them.

This quarrel had not been their first one. They had argued before, lively little spats, from which they had recovered quickly, often treating each other afterward with solicitous tenderness for days. This had been different. She was haunted by the look she had seen in Charlie's eyes that Sunday, and felt that the entire tone of their relationship had changed. Over the next weeks he seemed more absorbed by his work than ever. He was tired and listless when he arrived at home late on Fridays, and increasingly there were more and more Mondays when he pulled away again, the entire weekend having been spent without any intimate discussion, without their having made love. They had been in his mother's house now for almost two years, a betrayal in Maria's mind, since she believed, although she couldn't be sure, that Charlie was earning a decent salary and there seemed to be no expenses which Madame Atwood would let them bear. But she didn't question him anymore and he offered no hints as to plans he might have for their future. As far as Maria could see, the situation was permanent and her duty was to resign herself to it.

With the exception of Christmas week, when she had seen Abby briefly and a few family friends had dropped by to visit, the winter passed in gray isolation, but she made no more trouble for herself. From October to February she made one trip only to town—a sanctioned luncheon with Charlie's old friends, Bonnie Jo Richards, and her mother—but she had come directly home afterwards so that there would be no doubt in anyone's mind. She had not returned to the library, and soon devoured what reading material there was in the house—a small collection of leather-bound children's classics, a book on fishing, and a sociology tome—she could not imagine how it had come to their library— on English feudal society.

In the newspaper she still read reviews of the newest movies and books, but she kept her interest in them to herself, never asking even Rowena what she'd heard about the new Huxley novel, or if she'd seen *Key Largo*. For the most part she kept her promise to Charlie about speaking only English to Ana. Instead of their fairy tales and songs, the imaginative play that they had indulged in before, she and Ana and Rowena now watched *Howdy Doody* and *Kukla, Fran and Ollie* on the television, and Ana's chatter reflected the American influences.

Through all of that winter Maria worked hard on affecting a manner of chastened humility, speaking only when spoken to, volunteering no opinions on anything, even on the smallest domestic matters, and making a point to defer to the older women on everything from Ana's dress to the family's preference for cold tea over hot. It seemed to be working. They were softening to her. Madame Atwood seemed less critical and rigid, even at times almost friendly. Their weekday evenings now were still formulaic, but cordial, and Aunt Cassie was teaching Maria to crochet. They were "getting along," as they said here.

After many of those evenings, though, after Maria had kissed Ana goodnight and crawled, alone, into the big four poster, she lay awake, tortured by doubts that her ploy was making genuine progress. It had not convinced Charlie who seemed more distant than ever. It had not really convinced Madame Atwood who might pretend also, but still despised her. Charlie might deny it. He almost had to. In a recurring nightmare she dreamt that Nian was coming down from his mountain and that there was no one at all to stand beside her.

Perhaps worst of all, her efforts had done nothing to quell her own restlessness, the hunger for sights and sounds, but especially people, which her situation here seemed to deny her. She could see the awful joke of it, the irony of having come so far, to a land of overflowing plenty—a place where they were safe and comfortable and had no material wants—only to wither and die like an uprooted vine. She tossed and turned, hating her own nature, and vowing to change. But she could not think her way out of her dilemma or will herself to joy.

The winter had felt like a dark passage, an airless tunnel through which she had moved in dreamlike slowness without much confidence that she was even progressing at all. But in the second week of March, the spring came. It came suddenly, overnight it seemed, in a shock of white and pink dogwood in the woods, of clumps of yellow daffodil in the yard, and the general explosion everywhere of pastel buds and tender green shoots that had simply not been there yesterday. It was almost enough just to be outdoors again, but in the next week Abby called. She had an errand near the mill village and would take Maria along if she wanted to go. That evening Maria slept with the window open. The softened breeze carried the scent of warming earth and in the morning she woke to a riotous trill of birds.

"Up here!" Gordon shouted over the noise of the presses, beckoning Abby and Maria to follow him upstairs to his own office. Abby followed along behind him through the maze of desks and machinery and on up the staircase, but Maria turned off, heading for her pal, Joe Lawler, who had immediately stood up to beam and wave to her from the back of the main floor pressroom.

Upstairs Gordon lifted a small stack of newspapers out of a chair and tossed it onto his desk, already buried under a good half foot of newsprint and other papers.

"Take a seat if you can find one," Gordon said.

Abby sat down and looked around her. It was a big airy room, its high ceiling a labyrinth of pipes and ductwork, the walls, except the long windowed one that overlooked Main Street, crowded with photos and plaques. It was quieter here on the second floor, though the hum of the presses could still be heard and the bare wooden floor still vibrated underfoot.

Abby had not been up here for perhaps a decade. This office had belonged to Gordon's father then. Gordon himself had still been in college, a junior at UGA, but he had been at home that weekend for the town's Independence Day celebrations. He had invited her up here, he said, to watch the fireworks, but they both knew it was really to neck and they'd been pretty well along with it before the town's deputy had seen a shadow and begun shining his flashlight in the upper windows. That night had been the first time that a man had ever touched her bare breast. She still associated the smell of printer's ink with the 4th of July. With summer heat and the tender ache of first love.

Gordon himself may have been recalling something of that night. When she looked up at him, he was staring intently, a strange wistfulness in his eyes.

"So, how's our girl been getting along?" he said. "We haven't seen her in ages."

"It's not been a good run for her these last months," Abby said. "Some dumb mistakes, she'd tell you."

"Dumb?" said Gordon, frowning and drawing himself up a

little. "Hard to think of Maria as dumb. I find her quite intelligent. She used to come in here and just pore over the metropolitan papers and the wire service issues. She's got a grasp for international politics that nobody on my staff can rival. She was really following those last Nuremburg trials. And Senator McCarthy's hearings."

Abby shook her head in annoyance.

"Oh, she's smart enough! I didn't mean that. But there's something about her. I can't quite put my finger on it. She's naïve in the oddest of ways. People, mostly. You'd think that where she's come from, what she's seen, she'd have developed a little healthy cynicism in regard to people. I mean, she actually thinks Bonnie Jo Richards is her friend! And Mother has been a witch to her. An absolute witch! You wouldn't believe the way she contorts even the most innocent things into something vile and sinful."

Gordon looked at her blankly for a moment and then returned a sad, thin smile.

"Me?" he said softly, "Now what would I possibly know about that? I'm the one with the Jewish mother, remember? A Christ-killer."

Abby dropped her head and felt her stomach take a small, sickly elevator plunge. It had been a long time since she and Gordon had been able to relate again in any meaningful way. It had only happened in these last two years and only thanks to Maria. She had missed Gordon. And she didn't want to go back to the old awkwardness. To crossing the street at his approach. To averting her eyes whenever they found themselves in the same place. Perhaps there could only be friendship between them now. But she wanted that friendship.

She looked up again, but Gordon had charitably turned his back to peer out through the street-side window.

"But yeah," he was saying. "I think maybe I do know what you mean. It worries me a bit that she hasn't picked up on the

McQuistons. That little Asian wife of his has landed herself in a real viper pit. Old Daddy Mack is the king of serpents himself, and Eddy didn't fall very far from the tree. He's playing that union appointment for all it's worth. Loving the publicity and the power play. But nothing on earth could make me believe that Eddie McQuiston gives a damn about the mill hands or anything else. Maria would do well to stay away from it. From all of it! But she's asked me to take her out there twice and I think she's been by herself, too."

"She has!" Abby said. "A couple of times. It's quite a trek for her, what with two bus transfers and all. And it makes Mother crazy. If she takes the baby with her, Mother complains of the heat and the dirt, and all the diseases she imagines that Ana could catch from the filthy poor. But if she leaves Ana with Rowena, they all act like she's an unfit mother. You know how it is," she began, realizing almost immediately that she was doing it again. Of course Gordon knew how it was.

Gordon turned from his window to look at her again and this time there was neither sorrow nor accusation in his expression.

"So where is Charlie in all this?" he asked. "What does your brother think?"

Abby twisted in her seat.

"I'm not sure," she said. "He seems magnificently detached. The job seems to be going well and it gets him out of here, you know. Out of Hazel Grove, which was always a priority. I try to talk to him, Gordon, but the old stuff gets in the way. I think he may even be seeing someone."

Gordon walked to his desk chair and sat down with a slow, deliberate heaviness. He looked across to her and seemed about to speak. But something stopped him.

"What?" Abby said. "What is it?"

"You might be right about that, Ab. I wasn't going to say anything, but . . ."

"What?" she pressed him. "Say anything about what?"

"Well," Gordon said, "Do you remember Johnny Blakely?"

"Yes," she said. "I think so. Class below mine, wasn't he? Big fellow. An athlete. Basketball guard or something."

"A forward," Gordon said. "A good one. All county in '43. He got a full ride out of it to Georgia Tech. They won the conference title his senior year. Blakely probably could have gone pro if he'd wanted it."

"Gordon!" said Abby in exasperation, "What does this have to do with Charlie?"

"I ran into him last week in Atlanta. Blakely, I mean. He's the sports editor now for the Journal. We got to talking about the old gang, you know. He mentioned that he'd seen Charlie."

Abby waited, her pulse quickening.

"At the Kimball House Hotel. Having dinner with his wife."

Gordon paused and took in a long, slow breath

"I don't suppose," he said, "that Maria was in Atlanta with Charlie last week."

Abby laughed.

"No, of course she wasn't. She was here. But you already knew that, didn't you?"

"Listen," said Gordon. "It may not mean anything, Abby. The woman could have been a customer."

"Sure," said Abby."She could have been anything. She could even be his . . . detachment."

"I shouldn't have told you," Gordon began, but he stopped in mid sentence, his face brightening suddenly. Abby half-turned to see that Maria, flushed and smiling, had appeared in the office door.

"Have I kept you waiting too long?" she said. "Mr. Joe was showing me the new Linotype machine."

Gordon laughed. "Old Joe's going to make a newspaper woman out of you yet, Maria."

"I would like that," Maria said. "But there seems so much to learn."

"Well, you'll have to learn it another time," said Abby, standing up, "We've got to be going."

Gordon rose, too, and followed them to the door, one hand resting lightly on Abby's shoulder.

"Can I buy you ladies some lunch?" he said. "It's Thursday. Meatloaf on the menu at Ruby's."

"Oh, thanks," Abby said. "But Rowena fed us like royalty this morning. And I've still got to drop Maria off at the mill. We'll let you buy next time, OK?"

"You bet," he said, smiling down on them as they descended the stairs. "Next time."

On this morning's short drive to town they had babbled like schoolgirls, even talking over each other at times in their effort to catch up, to cram everything possible into their time together. On the drive to the mill, though, Abby seemed strangely preoccupied, deep in her own thoughts.

Maria took her cue from Abby, staying quiet herself but enjoying the drive, the views from her window, and the renaissance that spring had brought to the countryside. The fields that she had last seen stubbly and dry were emerging now in yellow-green brilliance and in the pastures she saw new calves and foals, standing close to their mothers. There were splashes of color from climbing vines and wildflowers in the ubiquitous pine woods and passing one neat farmhouse she gasped at an astonishing patch of red Dutch tulips, planted generously beside the road. She read the signs, advertising patent medicines, painted on the sides of barns, and an entire little poem, spaced out on small boards along the road, for something called *Burma Shave*.

In no time it seemed Abby was turning between the tall brick columns at the front of the village, stopping just at the place where the bus had deposited Maria those times when she'd come on her own.

"Three o'clock, then?" Abby asked, as Maria opened the door."I'll pick you up here."

"Three, then," Maria returned. "But won't you come with me? You would like Li Chin, if only you knew her."

"I'm sure I would," Abby said. "And I will. I promise! But I've got to pick up this thing for Alan, another thirty miles east. And I expect I should get you home before dark."

Maria agreed, nodded and waved as Abby pulled away, but she stood for a moment, pondering Abby's promise. She was not sure she could really imagine Abby, always so beautifully dressed, always trailing a cloud of expensive perfume, actually sitting down in one of these houses to visit with a mill hand.

The development here at the front of the village was commercial, and civic, the small solid buildings here all seemingly built at the same time and all of the same angry red brick. There was a tiny post office, a proper barber shop, and just down the road, an elementary school with a grassless fenced play yard and a flagpole, its quilt-sized American flag whipping in the March wind. Old men played checkers in front of a small grocery, which Gordon had told her that the company stocked and managed. Gordon had also told her that Hazel Grove's citizens preferred that the mill hands stay out of town, except, of course, on payday.

The mill building itself was possibly the biggest building in the whole town. It loomed large but uninteresting at the far back of the village, though all of the roads and several well-worn foot paths led to it. She had never been inside the mill, but it seemed somewhat malevolent to her. It evinced a low mechanical hum like a hive of deadly insects. At one end was a dock where Negro hands unloaded and opened the bails of delivered cotton. The activity there, she assumed, was the source of the white tufts which collected like the last drifts of melting snow at the edges of every solid obstacle and even hung from the few scrubby trees like wispy white blossoms.

The houses within the village were identical, all one-story and wood frame, set close together in perfect geometric rows on straight narrow streets that were paved, but without curbs or walks. Some of the houses distinguished themselves with outbuildings for storage, meat houses, or small lean-tos, but these, too, were painted the same battleship gray and the general effect was of dull and colorless conformity.

Behind the houses was a community grove or pasture in which a few indolent milk cows swished their tails, ambling among the remnants of vegetable gardens, now barren and scraggly after the winter. Part of this grove had been converted to a softball field and on a previous trip she had seen a rousing game being played, attended by quite a few enthusiastic spectators. Today it was empty and the red earth on the field looked raw and muddy.

On her first visit it had taken her much wandering and backtracking, as well as intent questioning of the children she encountered, to finally discover the exact house where her new friend lived. Today she knew where she was going and walked briskly and directly to one particular house near the center of the third nondescript block. The door was opened by the old man, Mack McQuiston, Li Chin's father-in-law, who stood in the doorframe in a dingy grey undershirt, frowning into the sunlight.

"Good afternoon," Maria said. She had reminded herself, and was about to inquire as to whether *Mary* might be at home, when McQuiston lifted a stained handkerchief to his face and began a paroxysm of coughing. He was ill, Li Chin had told her, dying of the lungs, and while Maria had heard the phlegmatic evidence of this on her last visit, she had never witnessed it face to face, or had to stand, watching his eyes bulge, then close, at each painful exertion.

At last the old man wiped the spittle from his mouth and stepped aside, pointing in the direction of the kitchen.

"In there," he said.

Maria stepped into the house. The small living room was surprisingly dark for the bright spring day and the air inside was close and foul, a dank mixture of cooked cabbage and tobacco smoke. There was no city water or inside plumbing in the houses yet, but even the electricity that had been brought in during the war years was used sparingly. The only evidence of it here was the glowing green dial of the big radio which sat in the corner beside Mr. Mack's battered chair.

In the kitchen Maria found Li Chin sitting at the white enamel table, the light from the window behind her illuminating the cuff of a man's white dress shirt on which she was making small quick stitches. Other garments lay piled on the table and on one of the chairs.

"Maria!" she said, dropping her work and starting to rise in greeting.

Maria stepped forward, stopping her with a hand to the shoulder, but leaning down to kiss her friend's cheek.

"Hello, my friend," Maria said, in Cantonese, "You're looking very well."

Li Chin smiled, tucked a tendril of black hair behind her ear and waved a hand over the table.

"I might have looked better, had I known you would visit. Please forgive my appearance and the state of my humble house."

Maria laughed at the familiar, ritual greeting, and felt an instant wave of warm nostalgia. There were no people in the world, really, so polite or modest as the Chinese.

"You look lovely," said Maria, pulling a chair for herself at the table. "And you're keeping yourself busy, I see. What *is* all this?"

I sew a little," said Li Chin, shrugging her shoulders. "For the Woos. They have the Chinese laundry. On the end of Sessions Street?"

"Oh, yes," said Maria, recalling the little shop with   its

Chinese red signs. "I've seen it. But I thought you had just found a job with the mill!"

Li Chin sighed.

"At first, yes," she said, picking up her cuff again and dropping her head over it. "I did. Yes. I worked for ten days, I think. To make the cloth. The same as the other women."

Now she lifted her head again and looked quite deliberately at Maria. The expression in her dark bright eyes was strange, the look almost accusing.

"But my English is not so good as yours, "she said. "People complained."

"Oh, well," Maria laughed. "You would learn! It wouldn't take you long."

"Perhaps," Li Chin said, still pinning Maria with her gaze. "But they said also that I was not white. That this could bring trouble."

Maria frowned. She was not completely clear on the meaning of Li Chin's words.

"My husband, my Eddy, is a leader of the workers," she said. "It would be bad, you see, to bring this kind of trouble on him."

Li Chin picked her cuff up again, took the needle between her thumb and the silver thimble on her finger, and made a quick stab into the cloth.

"So now," she said, "I sew."

Maria sat silent, not knowing what words to offer.

Li Chin was a few years older than Maria and not well-educated. She had come from a large farming family, but gone to the city quite young. In China, she and Li Chin would probably have had little in common. But here—in the fact that they both *were* here—Maria had thought they now had everything in common and she had felt an intense sisterly bond from the moment of their meeting at Gordon's paper. Now, for the first time, she wondered if she had misinterpreted that bond. That she had exaggerated it. Or else, even sadder, that the bond itself was being dissolved by their individual experiences here.

"I can't sew at all," Maria said. She could think of nothing else to say.

Li Chin had made tea, deliciously hot and sweetened with a taste of honey, and for the remainder of their visit Maria had tried to talk of China, of politics even, and of Ana's humorous antics. But to every subject Li Chin had returned some remark that, while not quite hostile, was somehow sour or disinterested. There was resentment here, and anger, and Maria could not find the way to dilute it.

It had been almost a relief when Li Chin's husband, Eddy, had appeared at the kitchen door and greeted them, surprising Maria a little with the enthusiasm of his welcome. He had stayed to sit at the table and to take hot tea, and asked interested questions about her family, but especially about Abby, who it seemed he had known in the high school. He was a handsome man, this American, and in every word he said, his every motion, Li Chin's eyes had followed him, but Maria could not decide if Li Chin was in love with him or if her nervous attentiveness meant something else. It was reassuring when Eddy had insisted that they walk her together to the street and pleasant to look back at them, standing together, their arms around each other's waists, waving and smiling until she turned the corner.

But the feeling with which she had begun her day—that sense of spring-like renewal and energy with which she had risen, that had still been with her in her time with Abby and Gordon, and that she had carried into the drive here and into her visit with Li Chin, was gone now. She was uncertain about how she had lost it. About what exactly in Li Chin's remarks had drained her of hope and optimism. But in her short walk back to the front of the village she felt the return of her winter mood.

It was not her nature to be philosophical. She did not ordinarily plumb the deep mysteries of the human condition. But now she felt deeply reflective, her thoughts turning inward and images that she had taught herself to forget rose up from the mists of her memory. For some reason she saw a small Jewish boy crying outside a bakery, his clothes only filth and tatters, but the armband affixed to his ragged sleeve absurdly bright and new. She squeezed her eyes shut at the remembrance of the dock coolie, being beaten into unconsciousness after falling beneath his load. She shook her head to see that ahead of her, the tall gates of the Morgan Hill village reminded her of those surrounding the Luangwa prison camp.

20 March 1948

Nothing has been said about last Thursday. I assume that they don't know that I went to the mill or that no one is angry about it. I'm glad, no matter, that I made the visit to Li Chin, although I expect it will be my last for a while. There was more unsaid than spoken aloud between us, but I think now that I am not the best one to comfort her. Her husband, Eddy, seems nice enough. He was very kind to me and sat with us quite a while over tea in the kitchen. Abby has promised to send her all of her own sewing, but that is all, I suppose, that can be done just now. Li Chin will manage, as I will, if we put our minds to it.

I have new books now, four of them, and Abby has given me an excellent English dictionary. There is plenty to read now, but I'm not so in need of it, because it's so beautiful here just now and Ana and I are in the garden every day. Rowena is quite smug, teaching us about the vegetables, and she delights in mocking my ignorance of everything. It is good in the days now. Not so hard in the evenings. I will manage. If only I put my mind to it.

From the diary of Maria Petrova, translated from the French

Chapter XVII.

Maria felt under-dressed in the thin summer frock she had chosen only for its coolness. The Atwood sisters had both added small black hats to their black Sunday dresses and each had white gloves on their laps. Everyone, in fact, who had come to the revival, seemed well scrubbed and wearing their Sunday best, and the general air beneath the big tent was almost holiday festive. In the milling crowd Maria recognized quite a few townspeople and members of the Baptist church as well as a startling number of mill hands whose faces she recognized, though she didn't know their names. Clean-shaven men in dress suits or starched overhauls moved along the aisles or stood at the tent wings, shaking hands and talking. Neatly coiffed women embraced one another as they led duckling lines of children into the rows of folding chairs. Just across the aisle a long row of teenage girls with crisp bows in their hair giggled and twisted in their seats, responding to the pokes and teasing from an almost equally long row of well-groomed teenage boys seated just behind them.

The layer of sawdust which had been spread all around the big tent was deep and drifting in the aisles and here below their seats. Its fresh pungent smell filled the tent, mixing with the sweet scent of honey-suckle wafting from somewhere across the dark field. There was the same air of anticipation that she recalled from Shanghai, thrumming through the audience before a ballet or concert, and she realized how very long it had been since she had attended any type of live performance, any entertainment really, that had not come to her over the television or radio.

Initially she had not wanted to attend the revival. Abby had only returned a scoffing laugh when Maria had asked if she would be going and by being here, on a Friday night, she was likely to miss Charlie's homecoming. But the sisters had seemed to assume her attendance and despite Abby's reaction Maria had developed a vague curiosity about it. That curiosity was turning to excitement now, and she found herself genuinely annoyed by the handsome slick-haired man who had been interminably testing the microphone, holding back the scarlet-robed choir members who were all in the places on the little stage and seemed eager themselves to begin.

The aura of excitement had apparently infected little Ana, too. She had been quiet and awed at first when the three of them had taken their places, to the left of the wide center aisle and only five or six rows from the wooden stage. But that had not lasted long. For some time now Ana had been restlessly fidgeting, once asking to be put down into the aisle where she had squatted to scoop loose sawdust and then been very unhappy to have it dusted from her hands. Since then she had been mischievously conducting a deliberate and occasionally painful march across their laps, not staying long enough with any of the three of them to allow herself to be stilled or distracted.

Suddenly the microphone erupted in a loud static puff and the slick-haired man began an official greeting, welcoming them all and promising that great things would happen tonight for the Lord. Another man then took the podium to read a Bible verse and lead a prayer, and then at last the choir rose. The song was called "What a Friend I Have a Jesus." She had heard it before, and even sung its simple lyrics with the others in the Atwood's Baptist church. But tonight the song was performed in lovely harmonic parts, and though there could not have been more than a dozen voices in the little choir, their sound was rich and full. The music, Maria always thought, was the best part of the American church.

Through all of these preliminaries, Ana had stood erect in Aunt Cassie's lap, steadied by the clump of hair she held at the back of her great aunt's head, staring in fascination at each new player on the stage, even swaying a little to the choir's song. But as the preacher began his sermon, her attention waned and she began to whine and fidget again.

"Where is it?" Madame Atwood hissed, realizing at the same moment that Maria did, that the quilted bag containing Ana's things—a light blanket, her small traveling toys, and the bottle they'd prepared for putting her to sleep—had not made it to their seats.

Maria had carried Ana on her own hip from the place where the cars were parked, across the wide field to the tent. The other women had carried only their own handbags and their bibles, but it was natural that Maria would be blamed for forgetting the diaper bag.

"I'll go, "she whispered, casting her mother-in-law a quick, apologetic glance.

"Here!" Madame Atwood said, pulling a set of jangling keys from her purse and passing them to Maria, just out of reach of Ana's grasping hand. "There's a fooler, too! On the front seat, I think."

"I'll get it," Maria said.

"Hurry!" one of them whispered.

Maria edged to the aisle and made her way to the back of the tent, but once outside she was disoriented, unsure of even the direction they had taken in coming from the cars. She had almost completely circled the great tent before she recognized an enormous tree on which an electric light had been mounted and remembered that they had passed it. She headed for the tree, stumbling now and then in her progress. Beneath the sawdust the ground was uneven, hard and still rutted from its long ago plowing. Behind her the amplified voice of the preacher sounded across the field. She could not make out all of his words, but his tone was angry and scolding. These American preachers seemed always mad about something.

She had arrived at the parking lot now, but saw that this was a problem, too. She had never owned or even driven an automobile and paid little attention to makes and models. How would she identify the right one? A great many of the vehicles were trucks, or old cars, too battered and dirty to belong to Madame Atwood. These she eliminated easily, but still she had cupped her hands and peered into the interiors of nearly a dozen others before she found the familiar upholstery, and Ana's bag, in the back seat of the Atwood sedan.

In the dim interior on the car she rummaged through the bag, not finding the rubber fooler that had supposedly been in the front seat. It was not in the back seat either. Not lodged in the cracks of the car's upholstery, and not, as far as she could tell, anywhere on the floorboards. She felt that she had been gone a good while already and she could almost see Ana's restlessness and sense Madame Atwood's building agitation, but she was afraid to return without her mission completed. They would behave as though she had been sent for this object alone. It seemed an unlikely place, but there was still the glove box to search and she rifled Madame Atwood's keys, testing several before one magically sprang the lock and the box flipped open.

There was no rubber fooler in the glove box. There was nothing, in fact, in the glove box but an ordinary screwdriver, a lady's white handkerchief, and a small packet of loose letters. There were perhaps five or six of these and they bore what appeared to be Chinese stamps.

Maria snatched up the packet and held it near the windshield where the light from the tree made the address, the postmarks, barely readable. Almost immediately she felt her heart start to race and her pulse begin to pound audibly in her ears. Yes! These were *her* letters! Her own letters! From Mama, and from home.

These letters had been kept from her. Someone had opened and read them and then hidden them away. There was no other explanation—nothing in the world that could account for their presence here.

In a dreamlike stupor Maria slid out of the car, leaving the door ajar and the bag she had been sent for forgotten on the ground. Slowly she began walking, reading only a line or two from one of the letters before she tore at the next, her staccato progress toward the big tree and the electric light halted, again and again, by the words she read.

We are losing pupils at the school as their parents flee the city . . .

Su Mei has asked about you and I have given her your address . . .

The new owners of the hotel no longer feed the workers, but . . .

His old friend Yuri has broken his ankle and your Papa thinks to mend it by buying him Vodkas.

The letters were filled with these small bits of news, some of which seemed to assume some previous knowledge on Maria's part. With a sickening shudder, she realized that, if some of Mama's letters had been withheld from her, if they had been selectively censored and only fed to her based on their contents, then some of her own letters—the dozens she had patiently written and then trustingly handed to Madame Atwood or Aunt Cassie for posting in town, might not have reached Shanghai either. Her brain raced, trying to remember any unpleasant remarks she might have made about her mother-in-law, about America or Hazel Grove, about her growing disappointment with Charlie and their marriage. There could not have been many. Mama didn't suffer complaining, and Maria had tried to put the best face on her life here. *But there must have been something.* Perhaps a few uncomplimentary remarks? And those, she now realized, could explain the odd gaps in their communication.

She had now reached the place where the electric light from the big tree seemed to cast its most illumination and she brought the last letter to the top of the packet. This last one was different, the handwriting and stationery unlike the others. This one had not been opened at all. Its date was recent, only a few days old.

Maria used her thumb to rip at the letter's flap and opened it, recognizing almost immediately that it was Manny Rosario's hand, and Manny's voice, speaking to her across the miles.

Dearest Maria,

I write at your father's request to bring you the saddest of news. Your dear mother, Olena Petrova, has been called by the angels, passing peacefully in her sleep on Wednesday last. Sergei wants you to know that your mama did not suffer, nor was she alone, as he woke to find her in their bed, a beautiful smile on her face. The funeral mass was said at St. Nicholas . . .

The handwriting on the letter extended for the rest of this page and half of another, but Maria stopped reading, letting her arms fall slack at her sides. There could be no small details here that could add a jot to the weight that now descended on her, crushing all of the air from her lungs and welding her body to the ground where she stood. *Mama dead? Could this be true?*

From just ahead a man's voice spoke to her and she sensed a shadowy presence.

"Well, what do we have here?"

The voice seemed familiar, but she couldn't make out the speaker's face. He spoke from beyond the big tree and her own tears had already clouded her vision.

From out of the shadows now, Eddy McQuiston, the husband of her friend, Li Chin, stepped into the pool of light and approached, moving to stand directly before her.

"Eddy," she stammered, looking into his face. "There were . . . letters. In the car . . . My mama . . . my mama . . ."

"Yes, yes," he murmured, wrapping his arms around her, "Hush now. I'm here. It's all right."

For a long while he held her, forming a brace against her shaking body and letting her weep against his chest. Maria's sobs now came on in huge, strangling gulps. She was almost unaware that his hands had begun moving, gently at first, in slow circles on her back and then lower. Suddenly he cupped her buttocks fiercely in one hand and at the same time crushed her against him with an encircling arm. Maria pushed back, gently at first, and then hard against his chest.

"Eddy?" she said, "Eddy! Stop!"

She squirmed out of his embrace and broke away, running in the direction of the tent and of Ana, but the snakelike root of the ancient tree writhed up to clutch at her foot and she fell, hard, the ground rushing upward to slam at her cheek, her head bouncing fast the first time, but slower the next, and the next, so that soon it was nothing, only soft reverberations against the pillow of the world. At last it stopped and a colorful confetti snow, the red and blue chevrons of airline letters, began to fall from the edges of a white sky.

Dochinka maya,

. . . my little girl.

Come sit with me.

I have something here to give you.

On some level she was aware that he was on her again. She could feel the great weight of his body and the sour-sweet smell of him, but it seemed too difficult, too impossible, to move. She felt sleepy, and closed her eyes, but a chorus of loud shouting went up, and laughter, too, and he rolled his weight away and scrambled to his feet, his heels flicking bark and dirt into her face.

She opened her eyes. Three young boys stood over her. They giggled and pointed down.

On the hard ground she turned her head languidly to one side and saw a man and a woman, other strangers she didn't know, standing below the great tree. Her eyes found Aunt Cassie, the wide-eyed Ana on her hip. In the corner of her vision she saw Estelle Atwood, running here and there like a thin black chicken, stooping to peck at spots on the ground.

She would not remember—she would never remember clearly—the events after that. There had been a great commotion of talk and shouting, but she had at last found herself in the back seat of the big sedan and felt the sleepy monotonous lull of the road and the murmuring hum of the tires. The long ride home had been quiet. Ana, exhausted at this late hour, slept peacefully in Aunt Cassie's arms in the front seat and no one had spoken.

In the bright light of the kitchen she had been shocked to see that her hands and arms were smeared with dirt and blood. Her summer frock was torn at the neck and there was a deep gash at her ankle. But the blood there looked old and dirty, like the results of an injury that had happened long ago.

In the parlor Charlie was reading the newspaper by the hurricane lamp. He lowered his paper as they entered and smiled out at them, his expression turning to puzzlement as he watched Aunt Cassie, Ana still on her shoulder, sweep on upstairs without even stopping to greet him.

He looked now to Maria, taking in her disheveled state.

"What's this?" he said, tossing the paper aside and rising to his feet. "What happened here?"

"We found her like this," his mother answered. "Rutting on the ground. With one of those mill hands."

"What?" Charlie laughed. His grin returned now, large and gleeful, in anticipation of the rest of the joke.

In the center of the parlor hall, Maria had also just watched after her daughter, disappearing upstairs on Aunt Cassie's shoulder. She had intended next to head for Charlie, the balm of her husband's arms, but she stopped now, turning, not her head, which seemed too painful, but her entire body in Madame Atwood's direction. *Rutting?* What did it mean? *Rutting?*

"We came on them," said Estelle Atwood, placing her handbag on its side at the edge of the dining room table, aligning her white gloves carefully on top. She lifted her chin then and deliberately drew herself up, crossing her hands daintily below her stomach and turning to look directly at Charlie.

"Your wife and that Eddy McQuiston," she said. "They thought they were safe, I suppose. The revival had barely begun."

Maria struggled to understand. It was all so hazy. But the mention of Eddy McQuiston had triggered something and she remembered the worst of it.

"Mama!" she said, running to Charlie. "My Mama is dead. My mamushka has left me!"

Charlie opened his arms and enfolded her, stroking her hair with his hand.

"Oh, Maria," he said. "I'm sorry. I'm so very sorry."

He held her, for the first time in many months, and in the old way. The solid warmth of him, the genuine tenderness in his touch, flooded her and she began to cry again, softly against his chest.

"But how do you know?" he said. "Who told you?"

Maria turned her face up to look at him. How *did* she know? Had Eddy told her? How *did* she know that Mama was gone?"

"My letters!" she said, some of the pieces of the dark puzzle falling into place.

Charlie drew back slightly. "Your letters? What letters?"

Suddenly Maria remembered. She remembered the black chicken, plucking her letters up from the ground.

"Ask *her!*" she wailed, turning to point to her mother-in-law.

The big house seemed to reverberate from the sound of her voice. A long moment passed and the clock ticked audibly in the room.

"Mother?" Charlie said.

"I have no idea what she's talking about," said Madame Atwood, shaking her head, turning a bemused, pitying smile on Maria. "But what would *letters* have to do with anything?"

Now she removed her small black hat. This, too, she added to the organized cache on the table before speaking again.

"The fact of the matter, son, is that your . . . your *wife* is a woman of easy virtue. Everyone knows it, really. Everyone else. Only *you* hadn't the sense to see it."

Maria felt her jaw go slack and a burning heat run from her chest to her face. She fought with an urge to laugh out loud, and with another to scream. Instead, she turned to her husband.

"Mi amor?" she said, moving toward him again, lifting an open palm. "You know this isn't true. You can't *believe* this. You know this is a lie."

Charlie stepped back from her. He did nothing more than step away from her, in either revulsion, or doubt. But in his small movement, that crystallized instant, she saw that she had lost. She saw that he had chosen, and that she had not been his choice.

She would hear them, for hours it seemed, arguing muffled and inarticulate below her. Long after she'd bathed and tended her wounds, she would still hear Charlie's feet, crossing the parquet foyer in his pacing. She would hear their voices rise and fall, Charlie's angry and belligerent at times, his mother's for the most part calm, but now and then surprisingly shrill. She didn't even try to make out their words. What they said to each other now didn't matter. She had already formed her plan.

She would not be able to get everything they needed. With Ana, and the pram, it would be impossible to manage more than one small bag and what she hadn't packed already would have to be improvised. Tomorrow was Saturday. Rowena would not be here. It was the only day of the week they allowed themselves the luxury of sleeping past seven o'clock. Charlie, left alone, might sleep for hours more. No matter. Whether they rose early or rested long, it would be too late for them. She had already formed her plan and by then she would be gone.

5 April 1948

We live, Ana and I, completely on Abby's generosity. She found us, after three days, in the same way that Charlie could have found us, had he really wanted to. The crumbs of my trail were clear. I went first to the hotel on Moore Street, which was full, and then by way of Rutherford's taxi to the boarding house on Lincoln where they called Charlie's old friend, the deputy sheriff, who was the one to bring us here at last. I had pocket money only. I don't know what I was thinking. I've always been impetuous. But I had to leave and don't regret it. I could not have stayed.

I have been dull here and slow to begin thinking again. But I begin to sort it out and see what is before me. Twice now in the last week I have been to the Church of the Ascension to light candles for Mama and to say novenas. I am more comfortable there and think it would make Mama happy, though I don't go for my own soul and haven't asked for confession. I could not go on without believing that Mama is there, looking down on us from heaven. But I don't need God in my heaven. Only Mama.

From the diary of Maria Petrova, translated from the French

Chapter XVIII.

Like a shell-shocked soldier, she had kept her feet, marching doggedly forward under the demands of Ana's care, and yet strangely disconnected from the rest of the physical world. In the place where they had settled, The Candlelight Inn, she and Ana had learned to function. They ate and slept, she dressed and bathed Ana, and even played games with her, acting by empty rote the roles they both remembered. There was some semblance of routine, but nothing felt normal. For a while she felt nothing at all.

It was nearly two weeks before the first prickling sensations of pain began to return, bringing with them the first unwelcome reminders that she was still alive. First to surface was the sharp grief for Mama, mislaid on the day of her exodus. For long days she thought only of Mama, replaying whole dialogues with her from memory and creating new ones in imagination. In her head all day she talked to Mama, but in her dreams at night she recovered her mother's living presence, hearing her voice, still young, chiding them for abusing a schoolbook. She felt Mama's soft warmth as they huddled below her coat in the rain, waiting for the trolley. She came upon her in the little kitchen in the dim early morning and heard her whispering her fervent prayers into her teacup. In her dreams at night, Maria could regain her mother. In the mornings, she woke, again and again, to her loss. For a time she moved completely in a black fog of sorrow and was simply unconscious, until Ana reached up to wipe her face, of the endless stream of silent tears.

Gradually, another grief, this one more confusing and harder to address, began to subsume the other. She had expected that Charlie would come for her. She had been certain that once he had fully realized that her flight had not been a demonstration— that she would never go back to that house—he would come to fetch them. She was sure that Charlie was already making plans to settle them in a small, clean place where they might begin again, as their own family. She was confident that he would see through his mother's poisonous lies and come to her, contrite and ashamed. But the days had gone by. She had become less certain.

The only bridge to her husband now was Abby, who had come to them at once, and been thoroughly supportive, if not quite encouraging. Abby had found it difficult to talk to Charlie alone, and, since this last eruption, impossible to speak civilly with their mother. At the end of their third week here, Abby had arrived one evening, seething with anger and mortification. Her car was packed with only a few of the things that Maria had requested, and desperately needed, for Ana. But tellingly the Atwoods had released virtually every item of Maria's own belongings. Both of them knew that Charlie had cooperated in some way in the gesture.

Her feelings for Charlie were much confused, but for Estelle Atwood they were not. For the first time in her life, Maria felt in her own person the passionate focus, the boiling malevolence, of hate. It was an altogether new experience, at the same time terribly frightening and enervating. She had, a thousand times in her imagination, contrived elaborate retributions for the Bolsheviks who had murdered her daughter's namesake. She had re-written, in the book of her mind, other endings, different bloody victories, for many of her father's battles. As a child she had seen the senseless cruelty of ordinary people to neighbors and to animals and even prayed the child's prayers that these villains would get their just reward. As an adolescent, she had been shocked by the barbarism of the occupying Japanese, the cavalier manner in which they had lorded their power over the peasant Chinese and the Jews and she had wanted to lash out, to make some demonstration, even at the risk of hurting someone, to make the important point. But all of that had somehow been abstract and diffuse, an ill will directed somehow at ideas or institutions, but not really at persons. She had never felt anything like the hatred she now felt for Estelle Atwood. She was awed and horrified by this newfound passion and recognized it as purely evil. But it fortified and fueled her and she had no wish to release it, to have it corrected, or forgiven.

For much of the time in those first few weeks, she fed and nurtured her hatred for Estelle Atwood, remembering the details of little injuries that at the time had seemed merely hurtful or confusing, but which she now recognized as part of an obvious pattern. For the first time in her life, she had a personal enemy and realized that Estelle Atwood had perceived her as one from the very beginning.

Whenever she could tear herself away from this new obsession, she reverted to the practical, trying to imagine the next steps in her plan. By now she saw that that she'd really had no plan at all on that morning that she had run away, the wound of Charlie's betrayal propelling her down the road to the bus stop, the taxi stands, the doors that she'd found closed to her before finding this place. That flurry now passed, she found herself in the plight of every abandoned mother of small children. She needed to find work. She needed to find some means to feed and clothe and support her child. But the child itself was an obstacle, the very barrier to its own survival. Who would tend Ana if she did find work? What kind of job could she do here, and who would hire her?

Charlie had been right about one thing. It was difficult to take care of a child in a hotel, although the Candlelight Inn was not really a hotel. It was a motor court, a "motel" as Abby called it, a series of a little bungalows organized around a public lawn. But she and Ana had a bath, at least, and a tiny kitchenette, and the grassy public area had a swing set and sandbox where Ana could play and they both could take the sun. It was Sunday. For the second time today they were here and Ana had already begun her strange practice of trying to swing herself with her tummy hung over the seat. Maria sat in one of two metal chairs, a copy of *The Standard* on her lap. The large headline, TRUMAN SIGNS MARSHALL PLAN, marched below the paper's banner, but Maria ignored the story, thumbing instead for the single page of classified advertisements that might hold some hope. She had only just found it when Ana jumped away from her swing.

"Beebee!" Ana shrieked, pointing to the highway where Abby's big Oldsmobile was turning into the drive beside the tall neon sign.

Maria smiled, but felt the usual twinge of guilt. *Darling Abby.* She still came, almost every day, even though she had amply supplied them with groceries and already paid for the cottage a month in advance. Abby came to them now with no particular mission. Only because she was a friend. The only one, it seemed, that Maria had left in the world.

Ana had already begun running to Abby, her strides sure and astonishingly graceful for a toddler, and for an instant Maria saw the young Katya, long-legged runner, winner of races, being scooped up onto Abby's hip and felt an aching clamp in her throat. She watched as Ana kissed Abby noisily on the face, squirming in her arms as they approached and Abby dropped beside her in the other metal chair.

"What did you bring me, Beebee? " Ana demanded, reaching across for Abby's handbag.

"Ana!" Maria gasped, "Shame on you!"

Abby laughed and shook her head. "Don't fuss at her," she said. "I've done the training here. I would never come without bringing her a little something."

Now Abby produced a small wind-up toy, a tin rooster, which Ana seized upon, jumping down with it from Abby's lap.

Maria watched Ana run to the swing and sighed.

"You've already done so much for us. I hate thinking about how much trouble I've caused you. The problems I've made in your family. Your mother so angry and . . ."

"Oh, hush," said Abby. "You take too much credit, Maria. Old Stella and I were at loggerheads long before you hit the scene."

"It was Gordon, wasn't it?" asked Maria, surprising herself with the presumptuousness of her question. She had wanted to ask it for a long time, though she was reasonably sure she knew the answer.

Abby laughed.

"Of course it was Gordon!" she said. "She just simply

couldn't abide him. And to this day I'm not really sure why."

Still smiling, she titled her head, lifting her gaze toward the sky and the evergreen spires across the road. In a moment the smile dissolved and she turned back to Maria.

"Well, maybe," she said. "Maybe I get some of it. I mean Gordon's *prospects* as Mother said, weren't all that wonderful. He didn't really know what he wanted to do then. There was the paper, of course. But Gordon's father hadn't become ill yet. He was still running it, you know, but that little newspaper wasn't any great shakes anyway. So there was that. But she just didn't *like* them. Any of them, but especially Gordon's mother. She was Jewish, you know. A beautiful woman. Cultured. And funny! I adored her. But Mother didn't. She was still trying, back then, to rise above her small town humiliation. She'd turned to the church and gotten all these . . . ideas. But Gordon and I just couldn't leave each other alone."

Now Abby leaned forward slightly in her chair, seemingly intent on telling the rest of her story.

"She didn't know what to do with me, you know. She didn't want to send me to UGA. Gordon was there. She decided I needed a change of scenery. Some culture, she said. A *real* education! So she packed me off to Europe. To London, and I went kicking and screaming. But not for long. I met some people. Lovely people. In the same shape, you might say, that I was. Oh, Maria, it *was* lovely! We took chances. We took lovers. I was deliriously happy when she pulled the plug."

"Pulled the plug?"

"Cut off the money," Abby said. "She'd changed her mind about Europe. About her confused educational philosophy. About what she thought I needed. About everything! She'd gotten her own footing by then, and wasn't so afraid of my scandals."

Maria sighed. This was the stuff of fiction. Of the layered emotional complexities in French and Russian novels. She sympathized with Abby, but only a little. In the families of the poor, it was always simpler. In the bad times, you cooperated to stay alive. You clung together. In better times you dared to hope a little. In the best times, like those after the war when she had met Charlie, you began to indulge the long view. To actually plan for the future and to think that your planning could matter. Suddenly she recalled something she'd written in her diary, long, long ago. *Mama has lost too much to believe in happiness. But I do. I intend to be happy.* She could not write that now. She had lost that certainty.

"So what did you do then?" Maria asked, curiously obliged to see the discussion through, but knowing its end would somehow lead here, to this place, and to Abby's essential unhappiness, too.

"Well, of course, to spite her, because I was angry, and because the opportunity presented itself, I married money. More money than she'd ever see! And I thought that would be the end of it. I'd have nothing more to do with her. Last laugh, you know. *Screw you, Mommy!*"

Maria flinched a little at Abby's slang, at the sting in her voice. But she saw, too, the moisture at the corner of Abby's eyes and heard her next words come low and soft.

"It *was* the end of it, too," Abby said, "Until you, Maria. Until you and that baby got off that bus. And I saw how young you were. How fragile."

"So, you see," Abby said, standing up now, smoothing the front of her linen skirt. "We're only a few squares back now, mother and me. You really shouldn't take so much credit."

Maria thought a moment.

"Abby, you believe me, don't you? You don't think I was unfaithful to Charlie?"

"I believe you," she said. "I do. But I'd still be here if I didn't."

"Which reminds me," she said, unlatching the clasp of her patent handbag and reaching to dig inside it. "I've brought something for you, too. You're going to need a lawyer. Here's a name. I've already spoken to them and they know I'm good for the legal fees. You should call right away."

Abby handed Maria an engraved business card bearing the inscription, *Ramsey & Lowdermilk, Attorneys at Law.* Maria stared at it, her eyes widening.

"A lawyer?" she said. "But surely you don't think . . ."

Abby wrapped her fingers firmly around Maria's wrist.

"I *do* think," she said. "I do! You mustn't let them, Maria. I mean, you can't just give in. You need to protect yourself."

Maria frowned, but said nothing more. Abby engulfed her in a long, tender hug and then took the few steps necessary to stoop and hug Ana, too. Ana turned up her cheek for the good-bye kiss but kept her attention on the tin rooster. It lay on its side on the swing seat in a little nest of plucked grass.

Maria stood and watched as Abby strode to her car, waving as Abby pulled down the drive and turned out onto the highway. Dusk was coming on now and the tall neon sign at the highway sparked and crackled once before humming into red and green electric life. Maria collected her newspaper and the few stray toys before hiking Ana onto her hip and heading across the lawn to the cottages. Abby's perfume still clung to the top of Ana's silken head.

They had been only minutes inside, enough time for Ana to strip off her shoes and carry the tin rooster to her own little corner where she had made a play place already stocked with a few toys and some odd kitchen utensils. There was a knock on the cabin door. Maria froze. She had not secured the chain latch. It was growing dark outside and she certainly expected no visitors. *Abby*, she thought. It was probably Abby returning for something. It might even be— her heart bounced at the thought—that *Charlie* had finally come for them.

She opened the door, smiling, to find a tall man in military uniform standing on her stoop. *Jack?* The soldier resembled Jack Krebs.

"Hey, there, butterfly!" he said. "What's cooking?"

There it was! The familiar voice. The familiar face. Those eyebrows! In another instant they had embraced, rocking in delight at the sheer joy of reunion.

"Quelle surprise! Combien merveilleux!"

"Good to see you, butterfly. Been a while, hasn't it?"

When they finally drew apart to study each other's faces, Maria reached out, placing a hand on the breast of his uniform.

"You're still a soldier!" she said.

"Yep," said Krebs. "Ridiculous, isn't it? Certainly not what I'd planned. But I ran into an old buddy in D.C. who said they were looking for folks who could do a little word smithing. Public relations for Uncle Sam. Anyway, he'd talked me into it. No real soldiering. I just shoot ink now."

"Oh, Jack! That's wonderful. And it's wonderful to see you!" She looked down now at her cotton dress and ran a hand through her hair.

"But I look a horror! If only I'd known. If even Charlie had told me."

Krebs shifted his weight from one foot to the other.

"Well, he couldn't have, really. Because he didn't know I was coming either. I wanted to surprise him."

Now he cast Maria a sheepish glance. "I guess I was the one who was most surprised."

"Yes," Maria answered. "I, too, am surprised. I think that I'm living a very bad nightmare. That soon I'll wake up and . . . but Charlie! Charlie told you I was here?"

"No, not exactly. He just said that you were out at this little motor court on Highway 92. It wasn't that hard."

"He didn't send you, then. He doesn't know?"

Krebs shook his head. "He doesn't know. I don't suppose he'd like it. I didn't stay long with them. It was pretty damn awkward if you know what I mean. But I wasn't going back until I saw you."

For a long moment he held her eyes and she felt his concern, and his pity.

"Listen!" he said. "Let me take you somewhere. We'll get a bite to eat. I passed a couple of places that looked OK. We can talk better over some grub."

Maria shook her head.

"Oh, I couldn't," she said, turning to look at Ana who stood a few feet away, staring up at them, her expression wary, but curious.

"Well, sure you can!" said Krebs. "We'll take the kid along. I mean, what would be the harm?"

Maria looked past him, over his shoulder to the dull vacant courtyard of the Candlelight Inn, into the gravel crescent of the empty parking lot, to the two-lane highway beyond, unlit at the moment, by a single traveling headlight.

"Very well," she said. "Give me a minute to fix my face."

The cabin door still ajar, she retreated into the tiny bathroom, rushing to run a brush through her hair, to apply fresh lipstick and a little pressed powder. Beyond the door she heard Krebs introduce himself to Ana, his voice formal and respectful, and she heard Ana replying in kind. She smiled to herself and tarried unnecessarily when she heard Ana ask Krebs for help in finding her shoes. When she emerged, they were hand in hand, both of their faces smiling and expectant.

The place where they stopped, Grover's Family Dining, was not a place that Maria knew, but it was warm and comfortable inside and no one seemed to find their entrance unusual or suspect. A plump middle-aged woman with thin white hair over a bright pink scalp led them to a booth and produced a high chair for Ana. Jack lifted her up and seated her, and Ana, once ensconced, turned a beatific, almost comically theatric, smile on their male escort.

"Geez," said Krebs, chuckling, actually blushing from Ana's attention, "She's beautiful, Maria. I don't see a bit of Atwood's ugly mug in her."

Maria laughed. "But she has Charlie's eyes, don't you see? *Son teint?* His color? But I think she favors my sister. Papa, a little. But mostly, Katya. She'll be tall, I think. I'm happy for that."

"Well, tall is nice," said Krebs. "But good things come in small packages, too," and again he flushed.

"What do you know of the city?" Maria asked. "Tell me everything."

Krebs shrugged. "I don't know all that much. I know it got pretty rotten there at the end. The censorship was just iron clad and Shanghai had been pretty much blockaded for months. I think most everyone was relieved when the communists finally came in, but nobody I knew was still there by that time. I don't even know how long Manny hung in. After they closed UNRA down, officially, you know, I got only one more letter from him. That was almost a year ago and he was already talking about going back to Hong Kong then. I guess he did."

Maria smiled weakly.

"No," she said. "He was still there in April. When Mama died. He wrote to me. For Papa."

Krebs' jaw dropped and his eyebrows lifted high. "Geez, Maria, I'm sorry. God, I didn't know."

"No," she said. "Of course you couldn't know."

"But Sergei?" said Krebs, dropping his gaze to his lap and then lifting it immediately. "I mean Colonel Petrov. That's awful, I mean. I mean, how is *he* doing? That's a terrible thing. I mean a . . . a terrible loss for your father."

In his eyes, darting and skipping, seeking a place to land that was anywhere but her face, Maria saw his anguished sympathy. She wanted to reassure him and thus to comfort herself. She wished they were not here, in this public place, so that she might fall on him, and they both might grieve for Papa. She saw now that she had neglected to do it. It was almost unbearable to think of Papa alone. To think what might become of him.

"I don't know," she said at last. "I don't know about Papa. The telephone has been taken out. The new address for Katya is gone. I expect that Manny wrote to her also, but I can't know. Madame Atwood was getting my letters, you see. She has some of them even now. Maybe more than I know, but she denies it and makes me the one gone mad. No one believes me but Abby, but it's true! I write to Papa now, but he doesn't answer. Perhaps he can't. He might never answer anyway."

The food that they had ordered—she could not remember choosing anything—was now placed before them and Maria composed herself, smiling for the waitress and for Jack. For a while they ate almost in silence, using the device of ministering to Ana, the cutting of her food, the retrieval of the dropped napkin, to make talk and to fill the quiet.

It was a long time before Jack spoke again.

"Listen, Maria, I don't know how easy it would be to get back in. I'd have to investigate. But if you want to go back, I'll try to help you."

"Go back? To Shanghai?" For a moment she felt an involuntarily lift, a vital surge of the blood as sights of the city, a flash of beloved faces, the texture and smell and sounds of Shanghai flooded her memory. But the phantasm disappeared almost as quickly as it had come.

"Oh, no," she said. "I couldn't! I can't leave Ana. Oh, Jack, it *would* mean leaving her. They would never let me take her. And she is the only thing left. The only thing that still makes any sense to me."

Jack reached for her fluttering hands, capturing them both and covering them gently with his own, like one rescuing a frightened bird. His brows were furrowed with concern.

"I'm sorry," he said. "I didn't mean to upset you. Of course, you're right. I understand."

Ana, who had already begun nodding in her highchair, was fast asleep on Jack's shoulder before they had even reached the car. The drive back to the Candlelight Inn was oppressively somber but Maria had somehow lost the will and energy for conversation. At their cabin she unlocked and opened the door and Jack swept past her, carrying the sleeping Ana to the farthest twin bed, already prepared with Ana's pink quilt and the favorite ragdoll, Vassilisa. Maria tucked her in and they both stood for a while looking down.

"She had a grand time," Maria whispered. "And so did I, Sergeant Krebs. We thank you very much."

"My pleasure," said Krebs, reaching into his uniform pocket.

"Listen, butterfly. If there's anything you need. If there's ever anything I can do for either of you, just give me a call." For the second time today Maria was presented with a small engraved business card.

"Thank you, Jack," she said. "I will."

At the stoop again in the open door, Jack wrapped his arms around her.

"I'm sorry, butterfly," he murmured into her hair. "I'm so sorry for the way it's going for you. I'm sorry for your loss. For *all* your losses. Maybe it will still work out for you and Atwood. Maybe it would be better if it doesn't, I don't know. But you haven't lost everything. You've still got friends."

He laughed suddenly, a wicked little chuckle, the mischievous laugh of the old Jack she remembered.

"Why, you've still got me!" he said, dropping his arms to point a finger dramatically at the center of his chest. "That's a helluva lot!"

Maria laughed, too, grateful for the gift of his humor and happy that their reunion might end with this lightness.

He hugged her once more, tight this time, and kissed the top of her head before stepping out and melting into the night.

"Bye bye, butterfly," he sang over his shoulder, "Tsai chien!"

"Bon près, cher ami!" she called back. *Goodbye, my friend.*

When she could see him no longer and the sound of the engine, the tires on gravel, had been replaced by silence, Maria closed and locked the door, remembering this time to secure the night latch. On the bed behind her Ana stirred and moaned and she turned to look. But the child slept peacefully, the very picture of innocence, and Maria remembered Jack's comforting words. *No,* she thought. *I haven't lost everything.*

26 August 1948

The deputy came today bringing the papers. Charlie has filed to dissolve our marriage, but Abby had warned me of it and I was not surprised. I have not even cried over it. I don't cry anymore.

From the diary of Maria Petrova, translated from the French

Chapter XIX.

Her first visit to Ramsey & Lowdermilk had been short and preliminary, spent mostly in filling out forms and a brief discussion with Wilton Ramsey's legal secretary. Until today, she had not met the man himself, or formed any notion of him, but she was shocked just the same by the mammoth figure who rose out of his chair to greet her.

"Mrs. Atwood," he said, stepping around the corner of his desk and extending a hand to her. He was some past middle age, perhaps fifty or sixty, only a few strands of dark hair pasted across his glistening scalp. But there was something youthful, babyish even, about his round face, the plump, apple cheeks and small red mouth. The eyes, too, were small—dark, bright little buttons pushed into the upholstery of his face—but his nose was big, too big, a doll maker's joke that made it difficult to look at him and difficult to look away. His tan summer suit was cut large and fit him loosely. The cloth of his trousers puddled above his shoes, but his vest rode high over the girth of his stomach and the buttons seemed dangerously strained. He was easily one of the largest men she'd ever seen.

Maria held out her own hand to him and he took it solemnly, briefly clasping it between both of his own. It was a strange, ecclesiastical gesture that made her think of the gentle priests she had known back home as a child. His fingers were short and puffy, but his hands, like theirs, were as soft as silk.

For a second he studied her face. The tiny mouth pursed, then smiled.

"Wilton Ramsey," he said "At your service."

"How do you do," Maria said, "It's good to meet you."

"Take a seat, darlin'," he said, motioning her to one of a pair of green armchairs aligned in front of his desk. "Would you like a Coca-cola?"

"Oh, no," Maria replied. "Thank you, but I'm fine."

"Well, that's good," Ramsey said. "But we got cold ones. Cold Coca-colas right here in the box!"

"Thank you," Maria said again. "I do enjoy them sometimes. But I'm fine now. Thank you, Mr. Ramsey."

"Well, all right, then," he said, turning back to his desk, lowering himself into a high- backed leather chair. The chair squeaked indignantly, but he leaned dangerously backward in it, blotting his brow with a white pocket-handkerchief. He was sweating rather heavily and Maria thought it curious, in light of the fact that the day was overcast and the big fan overhead was stirring up a whirling current of cool air.

The office was spacious and sumptuously furnished, the big desk and other furniture all of the same gleaming mahogany, but it gave the impression, if not of clutter, of incongruity, as though two very different individuals shared the space, or the prior occupant's possessions had not been completely removed. It seemed impossible to her that Mr. Ramsey could be a hunter. But on the wall behind him the stuffed head of a deer stared down with piteous eyes. On one of its antlers hung what appeared to be a lacey woman's garter. The tall bookshelf on one wall held neat rows of matching law books. So neat, in fact, that they appeared unused. But on a few middle shelves she saw other books. A three-volume Shakespeare, a match-bound set by someone named

Louis L'Amour. A copy of Mr. Whitman's *Leaves of Grass*, and much to her surprise, the *Kama Sutra*. A shelf low to the floor held a sloppy pile of yellowed newspapers and hunting magazines.

Ramsey cleared his throat.

"Well," he said. "I've had a long talk with Lester Clovis about your case. Lester's the attorney for the plaintiff. The plaintiff being, you understand, Mr. Charles Atwood, Junior, your husband?"

"Yes," said Maria, "I understand."

"Well, Lester pretty much laid it out for me," Ramsey said. He mopped his brow again and squinted up at the ceiling fan. "Seems like what we're facing here, pretty much, is a kangaroo court."

"A kangaroo court?" Maria repeated. She had heard this expression before. In Shanghai, she thought, though she couldn't be sure. She could not quite remember its context or the situation, but for some reason an image of Katya flashed in her mind.

"Kangaroo?" she said again. "I'm very sorry. This I don't understand."

Ramsey looked at her curiously for a moment and then laughed a loose, crackling laugh. The laugh set him to coughing and Maria waited while he hocked into his handkerchief, his big body bouncing in the chair.

"Lawd! I'm sorry." he said, when he had finally recovered himself. "It's a strange sayin', I guess. I got no idea where it come from. What it means, though, is that this thing ain't gonna' be fair. Leastwise to you."

"Fair?" Maria repeated. He was teasing her, of course. One's own lawyer didn't begin by making such an admission. Certainly not in America. He was joking with her for some reason. *But why?*

"Well," said Ramsey, "I mean there's a hill to climb."

Maria waited, knowing the metaphor was only a delay.

"The first strike against you," Ramsey continued, "is the judge we've been assigned to. We don't have but two of them, you see, and it looks like we pulled the short straw. Now, Jasper Lamar's a good man. I'd say most of the time that he's fair. But Jasper, you see, is an old friend of your husband's family. Jasper's mama and Miss Estelle? Why, they went to school together. And Jasper's a deacon in your mother-in-law's church. So you can see, can't you, that he ain't going to be predisposed to our point of view."

"Predisposed?" Maria said. "To our *point of view*?"

Now Ramsey gave her an annoyed frown. He thought her stupid. And she was behaving stupidly. There was no reason to parrot everything he said.

"Well, yes," he said. "I think you're gettin' it. But I hate to tell you darlin', it's worse than that."

"Worse? In what way, worse?"

"They're going to hit us with a whole lot of stuff. With your evidenced association with unsavory characters. With desertion of your spouse. With the suggestion . . . oh, *more* than the suggestion, of infidelity. And with neglect of your child."

"But that's not true!"Maria protested. "None of that is true. How can anyone . . ."

Ramsey flicked a hand in front of his face as though batting a swarm of gnats.

"Oh, they's got some witnesses, he continued, "A certain domestic, in your mother-in-law's employ."

"Rowena?" Maria offered. But Ramsey hesitated only a moment.

". . . who alleges that you are disposed to visiting roadhouses where you drink and dance with men."

"Oh, no," Maria laughed, relaxing a little. "That was only a joke we played. You see, Abby and I knew that Rowena was listening and we . . ." But again, Ramsey plowed on.

"And this witness will attest to the fact that you confided in her. That this was a practice of yours in your previous life in the foreign capital of Shanghai, Chiney."

Maria felt a welling panic, but she knew he would press on. This was not a dialogue, but a speech, and Ramsey would not be deterred by anything she might say.

"Your mother-in-law herself is prepared to testify that you entertained men in her own house."

Now he abruptly leaned forward, his desk chair creaking in loud complaint.

"Negro men!" he said, with genuine anger. "They're going to make it up like you're a nigger-lover, darling. And a communist, to boot."

"A communist!" Maria exclaimed, half rising now from her chair. "A communist! I'm not a communist! I've never been a communist. How can you say a thing like this?"

Ramsey actually chuckled.

"Oh, pshaw," he said. "It ain't *me*. I never said you were. And you know what? Why, Lester don't think so neither. "

Now he offered her a sympathetic smile and stood up. From the top of his desk he retrieved a sheaf of papers, bringing it along as he slowly maneuvered his bulk from behind and around the desk, settling it again in the matched chair beside her. He mopped his brow and neck again, and then leaned in, very close, to her face. His nose was pocked with blackheads and his breath was both foul and sweet, a mixture like mint and manure.

"But darlin'," he said, "It just ain't gonna' matter. They's a whole lot of ignorance down here. And you being a Ruskie and all, it's going to be all the same to them. Ruskies are commies. And 'bout the only thing that riles up folks down here more than uppity niggers, is commies."

"I ain't gonna' lie to you," he went on. "They's gonna' get the baby. The only thing up in the air right now is whether or not you ever gonna' *see* that baby again. Whether you get some kind of Christian visitation."

"What?" Maria gasped. "See my baby? *See* her?"

She gripped hard at the wooden arms of the chair. Her head spun and every object in the room seemed to take on animate life. The walls pulsated like a beating heart. Books on the shelves seemed to move and swim. The wet eyes of the dead deer looked down in panicked horror.

"But . . . but . . . you can *help* me? Surely you can help me!"

"Well, yes ma'am," Ramsey said. "I think I can. I can definitely get you some weekends. And holidays. I'm gonna' work on it. I'll do the best I can."

"But I can't believe this," said Maria. "Are you telling me, in truth, that I will only *visit* my Ana?" The word, even her own voice, sounded completely alien. She was certain there was some trouble with the language. With the way that the lawyer was using the word.

"A few days at Christmas, for sure," he continued. "Thanksgiving. Something can be arranged. And the summer! At least a week. It's contingent on the school term, of course. Your daughter is young. That gives us an advantage."

"But . . . but Charlie," Maria stammered. "My husband! Charlie would not take Ana away from me! Surely *Charlie* wouldn't want this."

"Oh, yes ma'am," Ramsey said emphatically. "He does. Indeed. You see, Lester's already sent me this here agreement. And your husband has already signed it."

Now he dropped the set of stapled papers on the edge of the desk in front of her. The typed, capitalized title read, *Agreement of Divorce.*

"This here's got it all worked out. It stipulates that you agree to the terms of the divorce and to the amount in alimony that Mr. Atwood is offering you for a period of two years in exchange for relinquishing custody. Now, you don't have to sign it. That's strictly up to you. But I think it's very fair under the circumstances and my best advice to you is that you do. We can stay out of court that way and you can avoid all that . . . well, all that *embarrassment*, if you know what I mean. "

Maria had taken the document in her hands and now lifted each of its pages in turn until she arrived at the last one, where Charlie's unmistakable signature was inked above the typewritten words, *Charles Atwood, Jr., Plaintiff.*

"I see," she said weakly. And she did. None of the accusations, the absurd lies that Ramsey had mouthed, spoke half so plainly as Charlie's name, written by his own hand on the last of these pages.

Now Ramsey stood up again and stepped toward the door. There he turned, pushing both hands into the pockets of his voluminous trousers. He rocked slightly backward on his heels, jingling the loose change in his pockets. He was dismissing her.

"You take that on home with you now," he said. "You read it over and you take some time to think about it. We can play this out any way you want to. Anyway you say. But I'd be remiss in my duty if I didn't tell it to you straight. They's gonna' win it. They surely are. For your own sake, and your baby's, you oughta' take the deal."

Maria stood up. There was her pocketbook to retrieve from the carpet at her feet, and the papers to tuck under her arm. She managed both, though another wave of vertigo took her and now nausea was threatening. There was still the lawyer's soft, moist hand to shake once more and a tight, reflexive smile to be turned on the secretary. But she managed. She managed the ten steps necessary to cross the reception area and she found the strength to open the glass and mahogany door that led to the street. Outside, she managed even a few more steps before staggering against the red brick building that saved her from collapse.

She had anticipated Abby's reaction and assessed it correctly, even if Abby's explosive fury, the characteristic barrage of American curse words, her threats to do all manner of horrible things to her mother, to Charlie, to "that fat assed faggot of a lawyer" had been louder, more intense and colorful, than even what Maria might have expected.

Don't worry, Abby told her. *Don't worry*, she'd said, again and again. "We'll figure this out. We'll beat them."

But for the first time Maria felt that Abby was the naïve one, the innocent who failed to grasp the true ways of the world. Abby had not been there, to hear the fat lawyer deliver the facts, and to see, in his face and demeanor, that these were the real facts and that her cause was doomed.

In the next weeks she allowed Abby to assume command of her defense, becoming her voice and the liaison between the ostensibly warring attorneys, who ate lunch together, at least on Thursdays, at Ruby's diner near the library. Abby had gone twice in person to argue with Wilton Ramsey and had made quite a scene apparently in the middle of Hazel Grove Hardware. Maria listened only half-heartedly to Abby's reports and her ideas. But for the rest of the summer and early fall, whenever she was instructed to do so, she dutifully appeared at the law offices to sign some worthless papers—a request for temporary support, a modification in the visitation arrangements, anything that might buy her a little time, but only a little time.

Charlie had not come, or even called. He had not seen his daughter in eleven weeks and little Ana had stopped asking her heartbreaking questions. With the divorce still unsettled, Charlie had sent her no money and Abby still supported them. The Atwoods, of course, knew this. For Ana's welfare at least, they would have no concerns. As for Maria, they intended to wear her down. And they were succeeding. Before long, she knew, she would have to "take the deal."

Maria lay in only her slip on one of the cabin's unmade beds. The bed's surface was littered with the scraps of their cloistered life here, the bits and pieces that had made up the day, or the day before, or the day before that. There were scattered sections of the week's newspaper, a half-eaten apple, the crushed box of animal crackers, and odd pieces of clothing. She lay at an angle among this debris, staring in the general direction of the small television set on the dresser. Its picture, only a black and white snowstorm of static, rolled between frames. It was the news hour and she recognized Murrow's voice. He was droning on about the Soviet blockade between West German and Berlin, but his words scarcely registered in her consciousness

She was thinking again about running. About taking Ana and fleeing to Atlanta or to another big city where the two of them could simply disappear. For weeks now, she had been wrestling with the idea, though its logistics seemed overwhelming. There would still be the same problems. She would have to find a place to live. *How would she know where to begin looking? How much would this cost? And how much extra would she have to pay, without references, or any records?* She would have to find work immediately. *Would she need papers for this? What kind of papers would these be, and how could they be acquired?* Ana must be kept safe while she managed it all. But who could she trust? How did one know, in a city, a country, of strangers, who might be a danger?

But none of that was the worst of it. The worst was losing Abby, her only friend, her last source of love and support. For her own sake, Abby could not be a part of it. Whatever Maria did, she would have to do alone.

In her own little corner, Ana was playing by herself. Maria turned to look at her, glad to hear her animated jabber. Ana, too, had been quiet and listless in the last weeks, as though the strange suspension they hung in was draining her own energy, too.

Maria studied her now and saw that in one hand Ana held up Vassilisa, the favorite ragdoll, and with the other she was pressing a broken animal cracker against the doll's red, chain-stitched mouth.

"Eat, little dolly. Eat it up. *Please*, little dolly. Please."

Maria frowned. There was the oddest tone in Ana's voice. A note of almost desperate pleading. Maria sat up and edged to the end of the bed.

"What is it, Ana? What do you want the dolly to do?

Ana froze. Her small back went rigid, but her hands, and the doll, didn't move.

I've embarrassed her, Maria thought, sensing all at once how rude this intrusion must seem to the child. After days of benign neglect. After the countless hours, in this last week alone, when Maria had not laughed with her or played the old games, not even spoken aloud to her. But in a moment Ana turned, lifting her gaze to her mother. The little face was solemn and sad. The long, dark lashes were heavy with tears.

"Home," she said. "I want to go home."

2 May 1950

This will be my last time to write here. I intend to leave this book and the last of my foolish thoughts with Abby, who can do with them what she will.

For more than a year now I have tried to satisfy this American justice, but the situation grows worse. Ana grows more distant and treats me more and more the stranger. They have poisoned everything. She has forgotten our happy times and our visits distress her so. However much I resolve not to do it, I cry and cling to her. I make her afraid of me.

Gordon has found a job for me to work as a translator in an export firm. It is California. On the other side of this vast country. But the pay is good. There is no work for me here, and no one who will risk Madame Atwood's displeasure to hire me. If I can save enough money, I will come back and find a city lawyer to see if anything can be done. If I cannot, I know that Abby will watch over Ana.

From the diary of Maria Petrova, translated from the French

Chapter XX.

Here is your bus ticket," Abby said, pressing the ticket, and another rubber band-bound packet of papers, into Maria's hand. "And your plane ticket's inside here, and all the information for your flight from Atlanta to San Francisco. Gordon's friends will meet you, but their number is there just in case. There's some extra money, too. It should last you a while. If you run out, then you must call me."

Maria's pale cheeks colored slightly but she took the packet and they watched her stow it safely in her handbag.

"You've been very good to me," she said. "I won't forget. And I'll repay it. I promise!"

"Oh, shush," Abby said. "I don't care about the damn money. You just take care of yourself."

"I have something for you, too," Maria said. "It's the last of my little journals. I've kept them since I was girl, though I wasn't always faithful to write."

Abby took the thick little book, its cover bound in brilliant red Chinese silk, a golden phoenix stamped on the cover.

Maria drew her own hand away but still leaned toward Abby's open hand and the strange, thick little book she'd delivered. She shook her head slowly,

"There are months, I'm afraid, when I wrote nothing at all. And then there were many days in the same week when I scribbled like a fool. But in my own way, I've kept the habit. And this is the last of them."

Gordon looked on while Abby casually put a thumb into the book, allowing it to flip open to a tissue-like page filled with neat, inked handwriting.

"French? You write in French?"

"Yes. My Mama proposed it. A good exercise, she thought, when Katya and I were young. I don't know about Katya. Whether she stopped after school. But I've kept it up. In my own way."

Abby looked down at the page again and laughed wryly.

"But Maria, you know I don't read French."

"Oh, no," Maria said hurriedly. "I don't expect you to read it! Perhaps no one will ever read it. But I know it will be safe with you. And perhaps someday you'll give it to Ana? You'll know when it's time."

Abby looked up to meet Maria's eyes and saw the mist there, but only a mist. Maria's jaw was set, her expression stoic and controlled. The small triangular face was still lovely, the skin clear and taut, but its sallowness made the green eyes stark in their sockets and the nimbus of gold hair that had always made Maria seem an impish angel, now looked brittle and limp. Her clothes were neat and clean, and yet they hung almost clownishly on her depleted body. Even her shoes looked too big.

All of this Abby took in, realizing with a shock that this girl, this woman, was quite different from the Maria she had first met, only a few years ago. That Maria had been tired and drained, too. From the months of travel and the birth of her child. She had not been the best, the real Maria, either. But even the eyes of that Maria had widened and sparkled as she surveyed her new surroundings. This one's eyes were glassy and distant. Everything about the demeanor and appearance of the woman who stood before her now seemed hollow and empty. Drained, not just of youth, but of hope.

"I'll take care of it," Abby assured her. "When the time comes . . . *if* the time comes, I'll give your diary to Ana."

The three friends shared a last embrace and Maria walked away, joining the little queue that had formed to board the bus.

"Oh, God," Abby sniffed. "Have we done the right thing? Were we wrong to let her go?"

Gordon stepped close, producing a pocket handkerchief and putting an arm around her shoulders.

"Hell, I don't know, Ab," he said. "How can we know? But the situation here was intolerable. I don't see that she had much choice."

"But California! I wish it hadn't come to that."

Gordon dropped his head.

"I know. I know," he said. "I wish I could have done better. But the opportunity to use those language skills of hers is just better on one of the coasts. And you know there's a large Russian community in Frisco. She may even find someone she knows. At least she'll make friends. And Mark and Valerie will take care of her until she can get her own place."

Abby made the effort, and smiled. Gordon was right. The situation had been intolerable, the solution the best they could devise. *Still*.

The seat that Maria found was halfway down the aisle, next to a window, in much the same spot where she had sat on her last bus trip, the one that had brought her to Hazel Grove. For all she knew this was the very same one, the exact same noxious, lumbering vehicle that had brought her here, at the beginning of her American odyssey.

For this trip, however, the bus was more than half-empty. Most of the other passengers sat alone, too, and she saw that her handbag and little train case could stay on the seat beside her. The driver closed the door. The bus began to move. In only seconds it had heaved itself out of the depot and turned the corner and she felt a fluttery panic as Gordon and Abby, standing stiff and forlorn, disappeared from view.

She watched as the now-familiar buildings and storefronts of Main Street began to move slowly past her window. She looked down on the tops of cars and into the beds of pickup trucks parked at angles at their meters. They bumped across the railroad track and in the center of the green town square, she saw a flock of pigeons briefly rise and settle again on the lacey white gazebo. On the sidewalk outside the drug store, she recognized Alma Patterson and Mrs. Wiley, the librarian. Reflexively she lifted a hand to wave but she stopped herself, letting her hand float back to her lap. There was no one else to say goodbye to. At least no one else who cared. She had spoken to Charlie, twice in the last week, by telephone, but all of their exchanges now were brusque and businesslike, this last one the more painful for his "wishing her luck." Even Ana, on Thursday evening, had been restless and cross with her, too happy to finally escape her arms and run down the walk to Rowena.

The bus had reached the highway now and between the sparse houses and barns the open cropland began to roll past, a brown-green undulating sea. For a long time she watched it, allowing the sweep of the land, the vibration of the engine, the monotonous rush of the highway beneath them, to almost mesmerize her and to feel it begin to tug at a memory she could not quite reach. There was something there. A newsreel perhaps. A passage from a novel. Something bittersweet, but important. Lovely, but dangerous.

And then she saw the girl. Standing on the deck of a great ship. The girl was swollen with the child inside her, but heavy, too, with hope and anticipation. She saw that girl. And felt a mocking pity for her. *What a little fool!* Standing there, fraught with dreams. The dream of reuniting her family in America. Of someday holding Katya's child. Even the hope that the world had outgrown its lust for war. All of the doomed fantasies of a naïf. China was in the hands of the communists now, behind an iron curtain of censorship. Mama was gone and Katya lost. The soviets had tested their own atom bomb.

In her handbag she fished for the new vial of the nerve pills that helped her to sleep. She smiled to herself, remembering how easily Dr. Horner had been persuaded to make the prescription unlimited this time. She was going a long way. It would take time to get settled and to find a good physician. It would take time to begin a new life without anything to live for.

From the train case she removed the little flask of vodka, quickly uncapped it, and washed down the two pills with a burning, icy-hot swallow. In a little while these medicines would begin to work their magic. Soon the cottony drowsiness would come on her, dulling her senses and softening the sharp edges of the world. It would push the pain farther away and make bearable that last image of little Ana, running away from her on quick, strong legs.

Part III.

Ana's Doll

Chapter XXI.

There might be another stoplight now before the Hazel Grove exit. The speed limit along here had been raised again, and for the last five miles the highway had been cluttered with billboards, with unfamiliar stores, and new fast food outlets. This used to be the place, anyway, where she had always checked her appearance before Grandmother's inspection. Where she'd spritzed herself with a little cologne and popped a piece of chewing gum into her mouth to mask the smell of cigarettes.

Reflexively Ana grabbed up a lipstick from the console, tilted the rear view mirror slightly, and looked in at her reflection. The face in the mirror was not a college co-ed's. She'd quit smoking ten years ago. And Grandmother had been gone even longer than that. *Objects in the mirror may appear closer than they are.*

How did that work, anyway? How could it be that every trip back home made her feel like an adolescent again, resurrecting the old anxieties, even the shame? Where did that power come from? And why, at nearly forty years old, was she still so vulnerable to it?

She guessed that she had been pretty lucky in avoiding it. She had not had many reasons in the past years to return to Hazel Grove. She had come back, of course, for her grandmother's funeral, and again for the reading of the will. She had come for Aunt Cassie's services, following predictably close, but not too close, to those of the sister she had shadowed all her life. But the signing of the final papers for the sale of Hazel Grove Hardware had been managed in Atlanta. And the old house? She'd been lucky about that, too. Only two quiet tenants in almost a decade. You really couldn't ask for more than that. There'd been a few problems, maybe. A new roof in '82. That thing with the furnace last winter. Minor issues that the family attorneys had found too complicated, too human, to handle on their own. But Aunt Abby or Uncle Gordon had managed most of those. She'd been lucky. With few exceptions, she had avoided these pilgrimages back to Hazel Grove.

This might be the last one. Really the end of it this time, now that the last tenant had moved out and she had decided to sell the property. Her relationship with her great grandfather's house, with the little town where he had built it, might really be ending this time. But she'd thought that before. Endings, it seemed, were rarely neat or clean, not even finite. Rather they tended to be taffy-like, a stretchy and sticky and messy process that was hard to make a ceremony of.

The light turned green and Ana adjusted her mirror again, tossing the uncapped lipstick back into the console. Lipstick wouldn't help much. She knew hardly anyone in Hazel Grove now anyway. The few friends she'd made in high school had moved on long ago, or, being female, had changed their names, making it hard to identify their achievements in the *New Hazel Grove Standard*, or even *The Hazel Grove Shopper* which had a much wider circulation than Gordon's paper had ever laid claim to. She was not likely to be recognized. Lipstick wasn't important.

In another mile she had pulled off the highway and turned onto the access road that led directly to Hazel Grove's main street. There were more small changes along this route, too, but none that lifted her gloomy nostalgia. The Esso service station, she noted, was now an Exxon. Mackey's fruit stand had been replaced by a Dairy Queen. Filbert's was completely gone, only a pile of cinder blocks and graying lumber marking its former spot. On Main Street she saw that Quality Furniture was now a Savings & Loan with a bright new façade that ruined the look of the block. The drugstore, like Hazel Grove Hardware, had become a small link in a big national chain. The town square and the courthouse looked the same, but Sally's was empty, a big *For Lease* sign and dozens of smaller advertisements pasted across its dusty glass storefront.

In a few blocks more, she turned away from downtown proper, moving first through the old residential district where most of the town's prominent citizens had once lived and beyond it into the less affluent neighborhood known incomprehensibly as Arcadian Heights. The land was still flat here, the streets still narrow and shady, the annoying proliferation of stop signs the only signs of change.

She was glad now that she had started early from Atlanta this morning. She still had two more hours left before meeting Aunt Abby at the house. That meant time for a quick lunch later, but enough time now for this—a surprise visit with Arden Sessions, the only resident of Hazel Grove, Georgia she cared at all about seeing.

This street, anyway, had not changed much. There were the same crumbling sidewalks beneath the mammoth oaks and magnolias and the same tidy little clapboard bungalows, looking well kept, most of them, behind the trimmed hedges or low fences that separated their small front yards from the street. It felt like ritual, pulling into the short drive, tracing the mossy stepping-stones from the drive, to the walk, to the porch, feeling the old tingle of anticipation when she rang the bell, knowing its chimes would return the first notes of *Claire de Lune* and summon her old teacher to the door.

But the face that greeted her was not Mademoiselle Sessions'. It was a stranger's face, that of a white-haired woman with twinkling blue eyes. This face bore a striking familial resemblance to her dear French teacher's, but it was not a face she knew.

"Good morning," Ana said. "I'm Ana Atwood. I'm a friend, a former student actually, of Mademoiselle Sessions. I was hoping to catch her in."

"Oh, goodness!" returned the woman, "Ana! Of course! I know all about you. I'm Millicent Adams, Arden's sister. Please come in. Come in!"

She held the door wide and Ana stepped into the familiar room. It was a lady's parlor, still fussy with claw-footed furniture, with needlepoint pillows and Victorian prints, and the hand-painted ceramics that had been acquired abroad. The parlor, with the exception of a large stack of cardboard boxes on the dining table, looked, and felt, exactly the same.

"You know me?" Ana asked. She felt childishly flattered by the warm enthusiasm of Mrs. Adam's welcome, but this woman had to be in her seventies or eighties. Most likely she was merely confused.

"Of course I do! You're *Ana of the diary*. My sister's favorite pupil! Did you finish it, by the way? I'm not sure that I *do* remember that."

"Well, yes," Ana replied. "I came here after school, off and on, for over a year. Arden was helpful, but brutal. She made me do all the work myself."

"Well, certainly," Mrs. Adams said. "That would be Arden's way. And she wanted nothing in return of course. Except making of you another French teacher. For life!"

Now she laughed gaily and Ana joined in. It *was* rather funny, put that way. The notion that Arden Sessions had extracted a lifelong commitment in payment for a little after school tutoring. It was not true, of course. Neither of them had known then that the process of translating her mother's journal would spark an interest in languages, a particular fascination for the French. But Ana's decision to carry on with her studies was something that Arden Sessions had taken pride in. She had told Ana so often over the years. Apparently, she had told her sister, too. This woman *did* know about her. Perhaps she knew a great deal. But at that moment, in the midst of their shared laughter,

Ana looked around, realizing that something was wrong. The answer to her unspoken question came gently.

"She passed away in February. I'm sorry you didn't know."

Ana took a step backward, lowering herself onto a dainty Victorian chair.

"No," she said. "I didn't know."

But I should have. I should have! I hadn't called her in months. How long has it been? Did I even send a Christmas card this year?

"What was it?" Ana asked. "Was it sudden?"

"Sudden?" Mrs. Adams echoed, as though it were an odd, somehow an amusing, question. "I don't know whether you'd say so. She caught a cold. It went to pneumonia. She died in the General Hospital here. Not sudden, I don't suppose. Arden was seventy-six. At our age, darling, nothing is sudden. But it was fast enough. She had a few bad days. But not many. It was fast."

Ana swallowed hard over the ache in her throat.

"I'm sorry," she said. "You know, we kept up for years. But I guess I lost track lately. I haven't been very good at . . ."

"Oh, sweetheart!" Mrs. Adams interrupted. "You mustn't feel bad. Arden was very proud of you. You were special to her. And she knew you'd come round again. She left you the kitten."

"The kitten?"

Ana followed Mrs. Adam's gesture to the velvet settee, where an enormously large yellow cat sat licking a white-tipped paw.

Mrs. Adams laughed delightedly. "Well, of course she's not a kitten anymore. As cats go, I suppose, she's nearly as I old as I am. That's Giselle."

"Giselle?" said Ana, moving cautiously toward the big cat, who acknowledged her approach with a blink. A basketful of baby kittens had often been an extra attraction of the Sessions house, but she didn't remember anything that even resembled this huge yellow feline.

"Well, actually, that's *Giselle Dieux*. The last of the last litter.

Arden had the idea that her cats spoke only French. I don't think very much of the theory myself. In the time I've been here, Giselle and I have gotten along pretty well with *here, kitty, kitty*. But that was Arden's notion anyway. And she told me, whenever you came round, to see that I gave her to you. "

Ana sat down, carefully, beside the cat on the small settee. The cat rose, and for a moment it seemed that she had startled the animal, but Giselle, after stretching luxuriously, only took two dainty steps onto Ana's lap, where it sat down again, facing her, nearly eye to eye.

Ana looked in astonishment at the big cat's face, back again at Mrs. Adam's. Both of them seemed to be grinning.

They had shared coffee and sandwiches, some sparse, polite details of each other's lives, and anecdotes about Arden Sessions, their true mutual interest. Several times in their conversation Ana thought about explaining why she couldn't take the cat. She lived alone and spent most of her time at the university. She'd never had pets and wouldn't be good with them. She traveled occasionally and knew no one she could ask to care of it in her absence. These were practical objections, needing only to be phrased diplomatically. But more than an hour went by without her raising any of them. When she finally left the Sessions house, scarcely thirty minutes before time to meet Abby, the trunk of her car had been loaded with toys, an ample supply of cat food, and an enormous bag of kitty litter. In the passenger seat, Giselle settled down immediately, curling herself into a big, furry comma.

Ana started the engine. From the doorway, Mrs. Adams, looking more than ever the image of her dear French teacher, sent her a last little wave before turning back into the house. But Ana had seen the wink, the sly, sweet smile, and knew she read her thoughts. *Well done, Arden. Now you've made her a cat lady, too!*

It *was* funny, really. Ironic. Maybe even a little sad. But she felt no resentment at all at the notion that Mademoiselle Sessions had bequeathed to her another improbable legacy. An inheritance was not necessarily a curse. An influence was not a cause. Whatever the effects of her long friendship with Arden Sessions had been, they had not made her the woman she had become.

She put the car in gear and began backing out of the narrow drive, but at the street's edge she stopped, looking back again at the little house. This was an ending, surely. But she recalled another one. That balmy spring evening when she had actually thought she was coming here to say good-bye. That spring when all the pieces in the puzzle she called her life would show their color and outline. Where they would begin to find connections, meeting each other to form discernible fragments of the picture they would one day make. The picture of Ana Atwood. *Middle-aged female. Divorced. Childless. French teacher.* And now, *cat lady.*

All the pieces had come out of the box that spring. There was the diary, and Mademoiselle Sessions. There was Billy Shumer, the son of mill hands, the boy who wore his hair too long, his pants too tight, and was crazy for rock and roll music. The boy who Grandmother thought "vulgar," but whose lips and gentle, inquisitive hands Ana had found irresistible. There was Aunt Abby, and the diary. There was the bad timing, or good, of the sale of Gordon's paper. That piece had meant that he and Abby would be able to take their five-month tour of Europe. But that piece had also meant that Abby, the only one who might have made a difference, wouldn't be here when Ana needed her.

There was Daddy, too, in the puzzle, and the new stepmother, the second one, that spring. But the experiment of living with the first stepmother had gone badly. And once the wedding was over no one had expected anything more of Ana. That piece, anyway, was insignificant, a small tessera, lost in the picture's edge.

It was the diary, really. If her life indeed was a puzzle picture, a mosaic that had come together that spring, and that while forming a cohesive whole, still showed the fracture lines of its elements, then the diary would be the centerpiece. The diary, perhaps, was responsible for everything that had happened.

She had not discovered it that spring. Abby had given her the diary almost a year before, on the occasion of Ana's fifteenth birthday. Abby had accompanied its presentation with a strange, teary little speech that had left Ana feeling uncomfortable, and more than a little annoyed. It was not like Aunt Abby to get all weird on her like that. Ana was not much interested, anyway, in the thoughts of the woman who had abandoned them. And the book was written in French, inscrutable after only one year of high school Latin. She had put it away, in the China Box, that quaint wooden repository holding the few pictures and trinkets that had belonged to the mother who had forsaken her.

But the diary must have called to her. Somehow, even in handling it, in turning only a few of its cryptic, tissuey pages, in the exposure of putting it away, it must have infected her with some virus of repressed curiosity. Why else, at the beginning of junior year, had she enrolled in Mrs. Sessions French class? Why else would she be so drawn to the teacher and the subject? In a short time she had brought the diary out again, curious to know if her developing skills could make any meaning of its hieroglyphics. They could. At least a little. On its very first page she had translated a line or two. *Mama has lost too much to believe in happiness. But I do! I will be happy.* And that tantalizing little bit had been just enough.

By the time she had come to say farewell to Arden Sessions that spring evening—to tell her honestly why she would be going away for a while and would not likely be back in time for the beginning of senior year—there were no real secrets between them. By then they both had already come to see that everything Ana had been told—everything her family had allowed her to believe—was a lie.

From the diary she had learned how her parents had met, something of their brief courtship and wedding, and the more important fact, for a girl of sixteen, that, once upon a time, her mother and father had been deeply, passionately, in love. She had discovered that she was the namesake of another Ana, her Russian grandmother's sister, who had died tragically, but mysteriously, not even in China, but in Russia. She had learned a great deal about her mother's own sister, Katya, whose physical likeness to Ana herself was a recurring theme in the diary. And she had seen, on page after page, expressions of her mother's anguished longing for the ones she'd left behind.

It was startling and cruel that these small facts, at least some of which they surely must have known, had been kept from her. But the terrible lie was elsewhere.

The woman who she had been told was uncaring and indifferent had recorded minute details of her child's development. She had remarked on teething and crawling, celebrated milestones in walking and talking, and presented dozens of other small events as monumental achievements.

The voice of the diary had gradually revealed itself. It spoke with a mother's pride and a fierce maternal love. Interwoven in the details of Maria Atwood's attempts to assimilate, her struggles to understand and to please them, were patterns that Ana recognized from her own life. A loneliness and confusion that Ana would come to share. Some people, it seemed, however strong their resolutions, were simply not meant to be happy.

Ana shook her head, scattering the broken bits of memory, willing herself back to the present.

"I want this over!" she said, startling herself with the sound of her own voice, startling the cat, too, who lifted its head and stared.

"Sorry," she said. From the steering wheel, she unclenched a white-knuckled hand, stretching it to stroke the cat. "Didn't mean to scare you."

Under her fingertips, the cat's body began a gentle, humming vibration.

"But this is it!" she said. "Really. This time, I mean it! I'll give that damn house away if I have to. I need an ending to all of this. I want it over. I don't want to come back to this crummy little town again. I don't want to remember it anymore. I want it to end."

Chapter XXII.

It was not that easy, with a cat in your arms. There were the keys to find and juggle, the lock to turn, and the heavy door to push open into the empty house, but she managed it, and Giselle, once released onto the wide wooden planks of the foyer, gave one look over her shoulder and set off on her own leisurely exploration. Ana hesitated a moment before following the cat inside, stepping gingerly into the center of the foyer, but stopping there, in the safety of the sunlit shaft of brightness made by the open door.

The house was vacant, as stripped of furniture and decoration as one would expect it to be, but the eerie emptiness of the rooms was still shocking, somehow not quite believable. Almost instantly she imagined muffled footsteps and heard female voices, the low ghostly murmur of conversation coming from no particular direction, and in another trick of the senses, impossible after all these years, she breathed the scent of the lilac toilet water that Grandmother and Aunt Cassie had both worn.

Don't do this, she thought, shaking her head. *It's just a house. An old house.*

Deliberately she drew another long, deep breath and this time there was the scent of floor wax, the stale, ashy odor of the fireplace, and a damp hint of invisible mildew. She looked around her now, resolving to study the rooms objectively.

The place seemed clean enough. Remarkably so, considering. But the old house was also showing its age. There were cracks in the plaster here and there and two large yellow stains marred the dining room ceiling. The rectangles and ovals of long-gone pictures decorated the walls with their pale geometry. The finish on the hardwood floors was scratched and splotchy, except for those places where the grandfather clock, the china cabinet and other larger pieces, moored to their spots for decades, had left it unworn and shiny.

Slowly she began walking through each of the downstairs rooms, trying hard to assess them through a buyer's eye. She opened closets, finding them clean and empty. She inspected the kitchen, finding modern appliances and bright new linoleum—something else that Abby or Gordon had managed on her behalf. She examined the pantry and canning porch and took in the view of the deep back lawn and the fence, weathered, but still functional, that surrounded the vegetable garden. She had returned to the foyer and was considering climbing the stairs when the tap of a horn sent her back to the front door. Abby's Lincoln was coming to a stop in the driveway.

The car door opened and Ana watched as Aunt Abby's beautiful legs—slim, still toned, and tapering to a high-heeled finish in dark boots—swung out and touched down on the macadam drive. In another second the legs had straightened to support the whole of her aunt's trim form, definitely thinner, somehow smaller, but impeccably clad in a short hounds-tooth skirt, black turtle neck sweater, and designer leather jacket—all of it accessorized by gold lavaliere, earrings, and bangle bracelets.

Geez! You had to count on Abby to dress for any occasion.

Ana looked down at her own faded jeans and grass-stained sneakers. Where, exactly, had the communication gone wrong? How had Abby imagined that she was wearing the perfect attire for spending a long afternoon rummaging through the dusty detritus of a 150-year-old house?

"Hulloo!" Abby called, catching sight of her now on the long porch, slamming the car door behind her in a way that would make any man, even Uncle Gordon, cringe.

"Hey there!" Ana called back, and then, too eager to wait, she jumped the short steps and raced down the walk.

In a moment they had connected, embracing each other in the old jubilant way, finally turning to walk arm in arm up the walk and onto the porch.

Ana pushed open the old front door, but Abby stopped short.

"Sheesh," Abby said. "Haunted house!"

Ana saw her actually shiver, and had to laugh.

"Don't you *dare* think of backing out on me!" she said. "I can't do this by myself!"

"No. I won't." Abby said definitively. "Put me to work. What's the plan?"

Well," Ana said, "It's mostly the attic. It's been locked from the tenants all these years and I don't even know what's up there. But the real estate agency wants it empty, so we've got to clear it out."

"Great!" said Abby, rolling her eyes, "Then I guess we'll do the attic."

Together they ascended the stairs to the second floor and walked halfway down the long hall to the door that led to the attic's own staircase. A blackened skeleton key already protruded from the door's original keyhole, but Ana fished her key ring again for the one to the more modern, but still greening, Yale lock. At the top of this next flight, which now put them high in the house's gabled eve, there was the smell of dust and mothballs, but there was plenty of headroom, at least in the center, and sunlight from the gable window washed all but the deepest reaches.

Ana surveyed the space. Maybe this wouldn't be too bad. But most of the attic's contents was stored in nondescript crates and boxes. They should probably go through all of them.

"How about this," she said. "We'll stack what we're going to keep over here. On either side of the door. That can be your side. If there's anything that I want, I'll put it here. Everything else, we'll just get hauled away."

"Sounds like a plan," said Abby, who had already begun rummaging in a box of school yearbooks.

Over the next hour they uncovered an old wooden ice cream freezer, a crockery butter churn, a portable sewing machine, a box of rusting tools, and other antique or curious odds and ends, all of which, they admitted, might have some value to someone, but not to either of them. Neither of them had really found much at all worth saving and their little personal caches on each side of the staircase door seemed hardly worth the effort. Abby had found some old costume jewelry, two boxes of Christmas ornaments, a crocheted shawl, and a few other oddments. Ana's own pile contained only an ancient book on gardening and a battered three-legged stool.

"Oomph," grunted Abby, dragging forward a wooden apple crate from under the low eve. "These are obviously Charlie's things."

Ana turned to watch as Abby held up in turn a ball glove, a stained baseball, a red tin fire truck, and then a yellow Duncan yo-yo.

"Anything there he'd want?" Ana asked, instantly seeing Abby's puzzled frown and sensing the foolishness of her question.

For a moment they were trapped in each other's gaze, each of them, Ana suspected, privately imagining Charlie Atwood in his room at the Autumn Breeze Rehabilitation Center, seeing him, on the side of his hospital bed or seated in the chair by the window, puzzling the tactile mystery of a Duncan yo-yo.

"No," said Ana. "Leave it for the trash."

Abby exhaled a slow sigh and pushed the box with her foot, almost violently, toward the growing heap of clutter they had designated as trash.

For another hour more they worked quietly, both of them, Ana sensed, growing a little melancholy now, and perhaps getting a little tired, too. She had become cursory in her own inspections, scarcely peeking into the boxes and bins before rejecting them outright, when she saw the wicker hamper.

She recalled that the large woven basket—the *toy basket* they had called it—had occupied a long-standing place in the parlor on the edge of the musky-smelling hearth. There had been good things in the toy basket. Familiar and pleasant objects to entertain a child. But she associated it also with discipline, with "cleaning up" and "being good" and making the grown-ups happy. Its attraction was strangely ambivalent, but she drew it toward her, lifted its hinged lid and looked in. Her adult heart fluttered at the sight of a grimy little ragdoll, half-buried by blocks and puzzle pieces.

"What have you got there, kiddo?" said Abby, picking up on her frozen posture.

"My doll," said Ana. "Beautiful Vassilisa."

"Ah," said Abby. "Yes. I remember it! You were crazy about that doll."

Ana lifted the doll from the hamper. It was smaller than she remembered, limp and almost weightless in her hands, and the little doll's features, its embroidered blue eyes and cartoonish smile, looked simplistic and garish. How could the name, and the memory, of this simple, faded toy ever have been *beautiful?*

She felt Abby's eyes, the weight of her own silence, but for a long moment the only life in the old attic was the lazy swirl of dust motes in the slanting beam of light.

"It's strange," Ana said softly. "All this junk. All this family history. But nothing of *her*. Nothing really. I mean, they're no pictures. No clothes. Nothing! This little doll. It's the first thing I've come across that even makes me . . . remember."

Abby stood up, moving to bring a small hatbox to add to her salvage pile. She tossed it down, bending to retrieve the three-legged stool from Ana's own cache. She pulled the stool closer to Ana and sat down on it, making it clear that she was willing to talk, or to listen.

"What do you remember, darling?" she said. "Tell me what you remember."

In spite of herself, Ana emitted a pained little groan.

"I don't really know," she said. "I mean, I really couldn't remember much, could I? I was, what, five, when she left us? But the strange thing is, I *do* seem to remember it. Or some of it. When they say I really couldn't. Because I remember these dark nights. We would go outside, you know, and she would talk to me. I remember dancing with her, too. In a castle made of roses. We'd go round and round and fall down laughing. There are other things, too, but I don't trust them."

"Trust them," Abby said. "Tell me what you remember."

Ana hesitated. She wasn't sure now that she wanted to go on. But there was Abby, her face open and expectant, her own eyes misting over, too.

"Well, I guess I remember the last best. I remember the phone calls. I remember them waking me up and calling me to the phone."

"To the phone?"

"Yes. The dogs were barking outside. Or maybe they weren't. But that's what I associate with it. She was dying, you know, Abby. I didn't realize it then. I didn't put it together for a long, long time. But she was dying then and *they* knew it, of course, which is why they woke me up. Why they let me talk to her." She paused again.

"There was that last time. The last time she called. I remember that she was crying. Not much. It was not so much that I could hear her crying as that I could sense it. She was very sad. I knew that she was sad, and that she felt like crying and then . . ."

She had never put words to the memory before. And certainly never put voice to the words. The memory, if that's what it was, had been only a cluster of feelings, a tangle of regret and guilt and longing. Ana felt warm tears begin to slide down her cheeks.

"Keep going," Abby said. "Tell me."

"Then *you* came on the phone! I was crying, too, you see, but you talked to me and I felt better then. I suppose I made that part up. I guess I put you, *your* voice, *that* piece in there later. When I got old enough to realize what those phone calls had really been about. When I'd finished all of the diary, Abby, and when I knew . . . when I *knew!* "

The words had rushed out, but she paused now, gathering her breath to speak slowly so that Abby would understand.

"I couldn't bare it, Abby. When it started to come together. I couldn't stand thinking about it. Thinking that she died alone. So . . . young. So far from home."

"Oh, Ana!" Abby cried, sliding off the little stool, dropping to her knees before Ana like an anguished supplicant. "There isn't anything wrong with your memory! It happened just like that. Of course, I was there! I thought you knew that. All these years and you didn't know? Of course, I was there. And her friend, Jack Krebs. We were both there. At the very end. "

They both cried then. On the attic floor, in the old house where they had both grown up, two adult women cradled and rocked each other like a pair of abandoned orphans. They each wept for their own reasons, but those reasons were as intertwined as their clinging bodies. Within the circle of Ana's arms, her aunt's bones felt frail and fragile beneath her stylish, youthful clothes, and for the first time Ana felt that she was also consoling Abby, the source of her own comfort all of her life. She had known, for years, the guilt that Abby bore for her mother's sake. And for her own. Abby had never forgiven herself for letting Maria go, or for being in Italy, rather than Hazel Grove, in Ana's own time of need.

Abby was not responsible for what had come to either mother or daughter. They had spoken of it, carefully, circuitously, over the years. But they had never cried together before. This catharsis was overdue—decades overdue—and Ana felt it lightening, lifting and healing both of them. But their exchange had done something more. For Ana it had excised the dark thought of a young mother—the Maria of the diary—drawing her last breath alone.

Their sobs, at first unashamedly loud and plaintive, had quieted to sniffles when Abby suddenly yelped and jerked away.

"What the hell is *that*?" she shrieked. A trembling finger pointed to a big yellow cat.

Ana had forgotten Giselle, who had shown up now to investigate the lamentations in the attic.

Laughing, Ana wiped her nose on the sleeve of her shirt.

"That's a cat," she said. "Mrs. Sessions left her to me."

"*Left* her? You mean . . .

"Yes. In February. I stopped by to see her this morning and got the bad news from her sister. I also got the cat."

Abby eyed the cat suspiciously.

"Well, that should be . . .uh . . . lovely for you."

Ana laughed again and reached out to stroke Giselle, who had now insinuated herself between them. Abby stiffened, but Giselle took no notice of the slight, slowly weaving between the two of them, brushing her silky flanks against one then the other, emitting a deep mechanical purr.

When at last they stood up again, swacking dust from their clothes and grinning sheepishly at each other's tear-streaked faces, they both knew that all interest and energy for completing the project was gone. By mutual agreement, they declared the entire attic's remaining contents "trash," and in a few more minutes had closed the door behind them, leaving the key in the lock. Maybe her relationship with the house wasn't really ending yet. But Ana knew she had stretched it much closer to disconnection. And this part, anyway, was over.

It took only two trips to load Abby's dusty treasures into the Lincoln and for Ana to toss her book and the three-legged stool into her own trunk. Giselle and Vassilisa went into the passenger seat. Her parting with Abby, as always, was a mixture of teasing and tenderness, but this time Ana felt a solemnity in her promise to call next week, and took the suggestion to "think about September" as a serious obligation.

She waited while Abby started her car and began backing down the long drive. In the rearview mirror, she caught sight of her own face and gasped. The face that stared back at her now was red-eyed and swollen. Her normally tawny skin looked drained and colorless.

"Well, what do you think now?" she asked the cat. "Do I need lipstick now?

The cat's eyes narrowed into drowsy slits.

She tried again.

"*Rouge à lèvres? Est-ce que j'ai besoin de rouge à lèvres?*"

This time Giselle lifted her chin and the tip of a pink tongue whipped across a white muzzle.

Ana smiled.

"Very well," she said, reaching for the lipstick tube. "I suppose a little color wouldn't hurt."

Chapter XXIII.

Dusk was already coming on as Ana reversed her morning's route back into town, drove slowly through the thin traffic down Main Street, and turned onto the access road that would leave Hazel Grove behind. She had lost interest now in looking for signs of the town's progress or decay, and once the old highway had merged with the interstate, there was nothing to see anyway. After thirty miles or so on I-75 North, she settled in, moving the seat back a few inches and rummaging in the well of the console for a cassette tape to replace the radio's static. Her fingers selected a tape and she pushed it into the car's player, listening while it made its ratcheting little adjustments. She smiled when the strains of Dvorak's Ninth finally came, the second movement at the beginning of the largo, with its haunting French horn solo.

Goin' home,
Goin' home,
I'm a goin' home.

How beautiful it was! How exquisitely sad, but still hopeful. There was something about this melody that had never failed to calm her, to soothe her nerves, and quiet her thoughts. She sensed it working even now, the tension flowing out of her back and shoulders, her arms and hands on the steering wheel softening almost at once.

She had eaten nothing since lunchtime and in the deeps of her stomach there was a yearning little ache, not painful or urgent, just insistent enough to keep her from fully relaxing. It probably made sense to stop, to get a quick bite to eat and perhaps top off the gas tank somewhere on the road back to Atlanta. But she drove on, reading, but ignoring, the signs that promised food, or gas, or clean restrooms in only a few miles. There was the cat to deal with now, and she knew anyway that the gnawing sensation in her stomach wasn't really hunger at all. The music, with its yearning melody, had merely drawn her attention to it again. But she had felt it off and on all day, gnawing away inside of her.

She was familiar with this immaterial hunger. There had been times when her entire life had seemed characterized by this craving. By this compelling, incessant desire for *something*. Maybe it was like that for everyone. Surely it was for some people. It was the reason they ate too much, drank too much, became deliberately self-destructive. But what was it they wanted? Was it different for everyone? And what was *she* really craving?

It was the big question, really. The one that she had taken to Greta, off and on, over the course of fifteen years of ragged, intermittent therapy.

"What do *you* think it is?" she could hear Greta asking, in that infuriating way that Greta had of ping ponging every question right back at her.

She had groped toward the answer in their sessions, varying the approach depending upon where she'd been in her life at the time, and on what crisis had driven her to run to Greta yet again.

In grad school it had been mostly grandmother. The struggle to gain acceptance, to do anything at all that Estelle Atwood could fully embrace, or approve of. Later on, it had been Jeff. The bitter disappointment of the miscarriages. The confusions of their short, failed marriage. In between, for diversion, and to fill in the gaps, they'd talked sometimes of her Daddy. Of his seeming indifference to her, and the constant womanizing.

Well, *love*, of course. Love was the universal hunger. The craving that Grandmother had fed through religion. That Daddy had tried to satisfy with casual liaisons. But there was no breakthrough there. She hadn't gone to Greta to be reminded of the obvious. *Had she?*

Across the median, the lights from a southbound car winked at her and she looked down at her own dashboard. It was getting dark now. Well past time for headlights. She reached now to turn her own lights on, casting a quick apologetic glance at her passenger.

Only once or twice in the whole trip had the yellow cat even moved. Once Ana had noticed it stretching its front legs out stiffly, spreading its white-tipped paws. Once it had dropped briefly to the floorboard, nosed around a little, and then returned to the seat, circling one time before settling down again. This was a traveling cat, for sure. If Giselle's road trip behavior was any sign of things to come, they would get along all right.

Ana shook her head in amazement. There had been quite a few surprises today. The uncomfortable one, this morning, when she'd seen how Hazel Grove could still affect her. The sad one, on learning of her dear teacher's death. The redemptive one, in the attic with Abby, when she learned that her mother's passing had at least been comforted by friends. None of them, though, seemed quite so amazing, so completely unpredictable, as the prospect of returning home with this huge yellow cat.

The Dvorak tape, at half an hour each side, had gone round twice now, but the music suited her reverie and she made no move to change it. She drove on, sticking to one lane, keeping a safe distance behind the car ahead, not bothering to pass other vehicles.

The imaginary dialog with Greta felt unfinished. There was something unsettling there and she tried to remember their last session. Six years ago? Seven? She had left angry that time. And she'd never gone back.

"What about you? Greta had asked. "What's *your* substitute?"

She had not liked where Greta was leading her. The implication that she was like them. Perhaps her studies *had* been consuming her. The foreign language program had been difficult. It had taken work to distinguish herself among others, probably brighter, but not so dedicated. But she had a few friends on the faculty. She'd dated, a little. And once she got tenure there'd be less pressure. She could relax a little then. Concentrate on other things

Ana sighed. She'd been tenured for five years now. What had filled the void of all that time?

She turned again to glance at the cat.

"You may have made a huge mistake," she said aloud.

Giselle opened one eye, twitched an ear, returned to her catnap. Ana smiled, finishing the thought.

"But I'll try. If *you* will."

It was full dark now. A wafer moon, invisible earlier in the glare of highway and streetlights, had suddenly appeared at the top of her windshield and with a self-conscious shock, she saw that she was turning onto her own street. She had been driving unaware for hours. There was no memory at all of how she'd managed to travel at least the last fifty miles. And now there was another shock.

There were lights in her house! Lights in the living room and in the kitchen. She had not expected to be coming home this late and knew positively that she hadn't left any lights on in the house. The neighbor's houses all looked normal. Quiet and dark. *A prowler*, she thought. But what kind of prowler, after picking an empty house, would switch on the living room lights?

For a moment she considered driving on by, finding a phone where she could call the police. But then she saw it, Richie's battered old Mercury, parked just across the street. *Richie!* Of course. She'd forgotten that Richie still had a key. And Richie's arrivals, like his departures, were always unexpected.

It was terrible, really, how easily she could block Richie from her mind. And not just the reason she'd hired him. There had been a time, years ago, when the unexpected fortune from her grandmother's will had given her hope of solving some of her life's great mysteries. Richie had been her champion then. The handsomely rumpled *film noir* detective whose unconventional methods would open doors she couldn't.

That hadn't worked out. He'd tried hard enough, she knew. Maybe he was *still* trying. Occasionally he still sent her a cryptic, poorly documented statement for his time and expenses. Eight years ago she had even paid for a trip he'd made to Buenos Aires. But the doors hadn't opened. Nothing had come of any of Richie's detection.

Somewhere in the world Ana had a maternal aunt—her mother's sister, the beloved Katya of the diary. Perhaps now there were also grown cousins. And Richie's other quest? The baby that Ana had given up. She would be grown now, too.

But Richie hadn't managed to find any of them, and they'd stopped talking about it long ago. The professional aspect of their relationship had reached closure. It was the personal part that they hadn't managed to tie off. Each time that Richie went away, she was sure that it was over. Each time he showed up again, she saw that it wasn't.

In her own driveway now, Ana cut the engine and looked over at Giselle, yawning now that the pleasant vibrations of her road trip had ended.

"Looks like we've got company," Ana said. "*Invités?*"

Now the porch lights came on, too, and her front door swung open, revealing Richie, sleepy-eyed and boyish in tee shirt, jeans, and white socks. A section of newspaper dangled from one hand. She felt him watching as she circled the car and opened the passenger side door, retrieving the rag doll, which she secured below one arm, needing both of her hands to lift and extract the big cat.

"What in the world is that?" Richie asked, scowling at her approach.

"Obviously, a cat," Ana said, tilting her cheek for his quick little kiss before pushing past him into the house.

"Well, damn, that's weird!" said Richie. "I never figured you for a cat person. If you wanted a pet, why didn't you get a dog?"

Ana deposited Giselle gently on the carpet, propped the rag doll in a chair, and handed her car keys to Richie.

"And why don't *you* unload my trunk?" she said. "I'll make us a drink. Have you eaten anything?"

"I found the ham," said Richie. "I made a sandwich."

He started for the car, but at the front door he turned, frowning back at her over his shoulder. "But you're out of Dijon," he said accusingly. "That regular stuff is boring."

"Dijon," Ana mumbled. *Dijon, indeed!* But once in the kitchen she lifted the stub of pencil tied to her grocery tablet, and added "Dijon" to the list. And then, as an afterthought, "flea powder."

Richie had left all the elements of his sandwich making—the platter of ham and head of lettuce, an open loaf of bread and an uncapped jar of pickles, as well as an ice bucket and tongs and the bottle of Jim Beam, strewn across the kitchen counter. A big yellow dollop of the mustard he didn't like clung to the lip of the sink.

It was annoying, his sloppiness. As irritating to her as her own obsessive need for order was to him. It was this, or something like this, that had provoked their last argument and sent him away the last time. Something trivial and stupid—an excuse, seized upon because one or the other of them was finding the spell of intimacy too scary. Because *she* wouldn't make love with the lights on. Because *he* had dog-eared a book. Always they came to that place where they'd blow it up. To that afternoon or evening when she'd come home from school to find Richie simply gone, the house empty and quiet.

In the sink, she wet a dishcloth and used it to wipe the mustard. He would let her know presently if he planned to stay the night. But she wouldn't drive him away just yet. Not over a dollop of mustard.

The rest of this mess, though, she could clean up later. Right now she had to find something to use for a litter box. And maybe Giselle was hungry. How often did cats eat anyway? And how much? Next week she'd check the university library. Maybe they had a book on how to become a cat lady.

From the cabinet she took down two cereal bowls, a white and a yellow. The white one could be for water. Yellow for food. They would do for now. Maybe next week there'd be a trip to a pet store, too.

Richie had returned from the car, his arms filled with the box of cat toys, the sack of food, the gardening book, and the three-legged stool.

"Listen, Ana," he said, dropping the whole lot on the kitchen table. "There's something I want to talk to you about."

"The big bag?" she said. "It's cat litter. Will you get that, too?"

"Yeah, "said Richie, "I was going back. It's just that I wanted to talk . . ."

"I really need it," she said. "The cat probably wants to go."

Richie rolled his eyes, but he turned and headed back toward the living room. In another few minutes, he had returned with the cat litter.

"In there," she said, pointing to the pantry. "Do you think I should find a veterinarian?"

Richie took a step backward.

"Why?" he said. "Is the cat sick?"

"No! Of course not," she laughed. "But if she *gets* sick. Why, then I'd have one. I wouldn't have to . . . "

She stopped, letting her voice trail off, busying herself in the cabinet drawer where she kept the kitchen shears. This was another danger zone. Another place where the differences between them could loom too large. Her wish, always, was to plan for the unexpected. He was more spontaneous, haphazard it seemed to her, in his approach to everything from balancing his checkbook to oil changes. He had even gone to South America without vaccinations. She looked up nervously, expecting at least to see his crooked grin, an expression of exasperation. But this time Richie didn't react.

"I guess," he said flatly. "I guess that's a good idea. But Ana, we really need to talk. I've got something important to tell you."

"Of course," she said, placing the kitchen shears, the heavy ones that could be used to open the bag of kitty litter, onto the countertop.

She was pretty sure that she knew what Richie wanted. He wanted to say he was sorry. He had prepared his formal apology for whatever little snit had exploded into their last separation and he wanted to deliver it. She'd let him. She'd missed Richie, too. And she'd certainly admit her own part. They'd make it up again. And if the pattern still held, they'd end up in bed. But there were still things to do first. Before she could concentrate.

"Of *course* I want to talk," she continued, using the sympathetic, faintly patronizing voice she used on her students. Just before they asked for a make-up test, or tried to explain why an assignment was late.

"But would you mind doing one more thing? Would you mind looking around in the garage to see if you can find something to make a cat box out of? Something not too deep, I'd think."

Richie gave her another pained frown, but he shuffled off again, still shoeless, through the laundry room and into the garage.

From the garage she heard the sounds of his rummaging, the loud clatter of something metal hitting the concrete floor, and a short burst of profanity. She grimaced, wondering if she should go herself, but in another minute there was Richie, holding the shallow plastic pan she had once used for potting plants.

"That's perfect!" she said, taking the pan. "I'm going to put it on the sun porch. When it's very cold out, I'll have to keep the door closed. I don't know how we'll manage that. But for now, it'll be more hygienic out there. Don't you think?"

"Ana, please! Can't you just be *still* for a damn minute? I've got something to tell you."

The pan seemed clean enough, but it wouldn't hurt to give it a quick rinse.

"All right, Richie," she said. "I'm sorry. I'm listening."

She was startled by the irritation in his voice, guilty for postponing him. She hurried now to rinse the pan, to give it a quick swipe with a drying cloth before turning to look at Richie. She stood still now, and smiling, and yet still not fully attuned to him. She had not cleared a space for what he was about to say.

She would remember, later, that even then she'd been thinking about what a long day it had been. She had just glanced at the kitchen clock and would remember that it read 9:17, exactly. Her day of endings, and near-endings, had consumed something like fourteen hours. She had actually made that quick calculation, and would recall with crystal clarity that her next thought had been about a shower. The most important things in the world to her just then—the thing that she thought she craved—had been hot water and shampoo.

"All right, Richie," she said. "I'm sorry. I'm listening."

But Richie hadn't answered right away. He had stood, waiting, until their eyes had locked and he was sure that he had her undivided attention. He moved toward her then, taking her elbows in his hands. Even then, he'd waited another second, two, before he spoke.

Just before dawn, at 5:21, exactly, she would slip out of bed, careful not to disturb Richie or the big yellow cat sleeping at the foot of the four-poster. They had not been resting long. Even Giselle, during the long hours that she and Richie had talked, had stayed awake, too, pacing in front of them, a vigilant, restless tigress. They both slept now. And they deserved to. She wanted to be alone anyway. To replay again, for the hundredth time, that moment, just after 9:17, when Richie had demanded her attention.

"I've found her, Ana," Richie had said. "Your daughter. I know where she is."

Chapter XXIV.

It had rained all that day, but not heavily. There'd been no lightning or thunder until at least ten, when lights were supposed to be out anyway, and most of them were already asleep. But then the storm had come. A furious electrical storm that would fracture her memories into staccato flashes of impenetrable blackness and blinding light. She had been alone in her room then, writhing silently in her bed, when the storm and her pain had converged, reaching a violent crescendo that had made the hall lights blink on and off and the sounds that she'd been stifling erupt into a piercing scream.

It wasn't supposed to be this way. Babies weren't supposed to be born in the Florence Crittenden Home. This was a place for waiting. For hiding away. For repenting one's sins. But it was not meant for delivering babies. When a girl went into labor, and when the labor was deemed authentic enough, an ambulance was summoned and the girl went away. The girls went to Crawford Long or to another local hospital to deliver their babies. Only in the rarest of cases did they ever come back. Whatever they had learned about how it actually felt to give birth, to labor and deliver, and then to surrender their baby, was not shared with those still waiting back at the Home.

Ana had understood the protocol. Her last roommate, Robin, had "gone out" as they said here, only two weeks ago. Robin had delivered a healthy baby boy, they said. She'd had an easy time. But the information came second hand. Someone else had come to pack up Robin's things. They had not spoken again.

She had expected that her own case would be like Robin's. The contractions would begin. Dr. Henson or one of the nurses would examine her. They would tell her that it would be a while yet. To stay calm. To try to relax between contractions. If she were lucky, one or two of the other girls might be allowed to sit with her. They'd laugh and make jokes, all of them pretending they were old hands at this and that nobody was really afraid. Finally, when it was time, and the ambulance had been called, they would follow her into the hall, calling out their good wishes as the wheelchair or stretcher wheeled her away, or maybe even, as she walked out all on her own, leaning on the arm of one of the black-robed nuns for the sake of drama only.

She had envisioned that scene. Or something very close to it. As for the next one, and the one after that, she had no clear notion. Girls who went out didn't come back.

But no one had told her about back labor. None of the books, or the gritty black and white film they'd been shown, had mentioned anything about those cases—not rare at all as it turned out—of women who took their labor in their backs. Without the obvious contractions. Without the long, paced labor they'd all been led to expect.

Yesterday her assignment for household duty had been the common bathroom on the second floor. They were expected, of course, to clean the toilets and shower stalls. But this time Sister Veronica wanted special attention paid to the floors. These floors, she said, were being neglected with their lazy wipes and swipes. This time she wanted these floors *really* scrubbed.

They'd scrubbed. For three hours or more, mostly on hands and knees, she and Judy had worked on the filthy lines of grout, brushing and gouging, soaping and rinsing, until the little octagonal black and white tiles in the floor had begun to lift and float in Ana's vision and she could barely straighten herself up. She had blamed those tiles for the back pain that had wakened her from sleep that night. For the nagging ache that had persisted the next morning and all afternoon, growing and grinding into her spine, belly, and legs, until her scream had brought the flash of lightening, the crack of thunder, and then the shadowy darkness.

The baby had been crowning before they had finally come with their candles and sent for a gurney. Before she knew the first thing about back labor or that all births weren't alike.

Babies weren't supposed to be born in the Florence Crittenden Home. The little examining room in the infirmary, where every week the girls had their weight and blood pressure checked, where old Dr. Henson treated their head colds or bandaged small injuries, had not been intended for the delivery of babies. Certainly not during an electrical storm. Not when the telephones were out, too, and no ambulance had been summoned at all.

But most of it, by then, had been over anyway. Sister Martha had been there to bark orders to Sister Alice Claire and to the young colored girl they called Sissy who had been summoned from her bed and mostly stood and blinked. The women had stripped her panties, mopped her brow, trapped her flailing arms to check pressure and pulse. Dr. Henson, his pajama top showing beneath his white coat, had caught the baby and cut the cord. But for the most part, it was already over. And for the most part, she'd done it alone.

In the quavering shadows of candlelight, she had seen Dr. Henson lift up the tiny wriggling form, seen its frog legs bounce and spring, and heard the baby's lusty squall. She had held out her arms spontaneously, a reflex as old as time itself. But the doctor passed the baby to Sister Martha, who took it in a towel, engulfing it all but the top of a dark, waxy head, and handing it off then to Sissy, who had taken her baby away.

A few minutes, Sister Martha had said. A few minutes. We have to clean her up. And you, too! You can see her in a few minutes. We'll send for you. In a few minutes.

Several lifetimes, it seemed, had already passed in waiting. She could wait a few more minutes.

But the few minutes had become half an hour, three quarters

of an hour, then more. She was tired. Weak as a kitten. But back in her own room, she found herself unable to lie still, and too sore and too restless to simply sit and wait. She washed her face and brushed the sweaty tangles from her hair. She put on a clean cotton nightgown and the bathrobe she'd brought from home. On the bed, in readiness, she laid out the two objects—the gifts she would give her baby. One of these was the yellow blanket she had crocheted in her time here. It wasn't quite perfect. Aunt Cassie would have found the few places where she'd failed to make the last extra stitch before turning the row. But it was soft, and buttery yellow, and she had made it with her own hands.

The other object was the little necklace. A tiny Coptic cross on a delicate gold chain. It had come to her in the bottom of the China Box, and for most of her life had been only a pretty, puzzling trinket. Last spring the diary of Maria Petrova had unraveled its mystery. Ana had memorized the passage.

Mama's cross was not lost after all, but removed by Madame Atwood. It is the wrong kind of cross, she says, though I don't understand what she means. It may have become a danger anyway. Ana is growing so fast that it had almost disappeared in the folds of her fat little neck. I will put it away for her. She may want it someday for her own child.

The *wrongness* of the cross was mysterious to Ana, too. There were crosses like this one—ornate, with fancy little trefoils, all over the Florence Crittenden Home. But the fact that her mother had preserved the little necklace for her, the fact that she herself had worn it as an infant, had made it precious to her, and this, too, would be a gift.

In the corridor outside her room, the lights blinked and she hurried to the door, leaning out into the hall. The lights blinked off once more, then on again, this time holding steady. The storm was passing. Or someone had found the way to make the generator work. But every door on the corridor remained closed. She heard no voices. No female heads poked out, no faces to register curiosity or shock that she should be standing there, her belly flat, alien and dead-feeling to the touch, but obviously emptied. It was eerie, and unreasonable, that this could be true. That she could have given birth less than two hours ago and there was no one to know, or care.

In the distance now she heard the dim whine of a police car or an ambulance and the sound filled her with panic. What if Sister Martha had forgotten her promise? What if they were already coming for her baby? Quickly she turned back into the room, snatching up the little necklace and the yellow blanket, stopping only a moment to blow out the candle that had burned to its last inch.

It was not easy to hurry. It hurt, a little, to walk at all, even more to walk fast, but in a few seconds she had made the stairwell and managed the one flight back up to the third floor where the infirmary area occupied the corner space at the juncture of halls. Ahead of her, she could see the gray metal desk where one of the sisters always sat, even at night, to keep the infirmary log, to guard the infirmary's little cache of drugs and antiseptics, or to dispense, on some nights, advice or the occasional aspirin. Tonight's duty shift must have fallen to Sister Martha. It explained why she had been there for the delivery and her take-charge attitude. But the station was unattended now and the desk's brass reading lamp was unlit. In both directions, the long dim corridors were empty.

Curiously, she approached the examining room, that small theater where the biggest drama of her life had so recently been enacted. The knob turned beneath her hand and she opened the door. She groped for the light switch and flipped it, illuminating the small room with a bright white flare. The room was empty. And clean. Immaculately clean. The counters were bare and white. The small rolling stool on which Dr. Henson had perched between her legs was now in a far corner, only an accessory to the room's sparse décor. Even the linens on the examining table had been changed, the narrow berth made ready again for checking a sprained ankle or scratched knee. There was no trace of her blood or her sweat. There were no gloves in the empty wastebasket. There was no sign at all that anything of importance had ever happened here. She surveyed the examining room, a dizzying wave of lightheadedness taking her. Had she made it all up? Could someone *dream* that they'd delivered a baby?

She had taken two steps back into the empty hall. She had looked once more down the empty, silent sweep. And then she had done the only thing she knew to do. She had closed her eyes, taken in a great breath, thrown back her head, and begun to wail. The loud, bellowing bawl of a wounded animal.

Oh, they had come running then! Not just Sister Martha, but others who she wouldn't remember. In only seconds they appeared, a small crowd of black-robed nuns and barefoot pregnant girls in nightgowns, all standing around her, their eyes wide in horrified confusion. Someone had stepped forward, taking her by the shoulders and shaking her like a rag doll.

"Shush, child! Have you lost your wits? You'll wake the dead with that howling."

But she hadn't stopped. She had kept up her wailing even when Sister Martha began dragging her by the sleeve of her robe, pushing her at last into a tiny broom closet of a room, furnished with only a narrow cot, a plain crucifix, and a rocking chair.

"Sit there!" she was told. "I'll be back in a few minutes."

Alone in the rocking chair, with only the crucifix, the pinioned Jesus, for focus on the blank white wall, her wails had diminished to rhythmic moans, interspersed by quick little breathy gasps. She was readying herself for the next assault.

But this time Sister Martha was true her word. In a few minutes, really this time, she had come back through the door, carrying a swaddled bundle.

"Your baby," she said, lowering it into Ana's arms.

"Oh," Ana said, and "Oh."

"I'll leave you alone, dear" said Sister Martha, and for the first time there was almost no anger in her voice. "But I'll be back in a few minutes."

She had turned away then, but at the door she stopped, looking back at Ana, who held the baby stiffly in the rocking chair, staring into its small round face.

"Ana," she said. You're a smart girl. And you can forget this. You can go home now and start over. You must put this all behind you."

Ana didn't answer. The baby was wide awake. It stared placidly up at her with bright dark eyes, the expression knowing and solemn.

"I wouldn't put her to the breast," Sister Martha added. "The doctor will give you pills to stop the milk."

Again Ana said nothing, but in a moment she heard the door bump softly and knew they were alone. When the nun had gone away, she moved the baby gently to her lap.

There had only been a few minutes, really, to unwrap it. To discover the umbilical clamp and peek into the diaper. To catch up the longish-looking little feet and count the pink beads of toes. To examine the curling hands, and to be astonished by the miniature perfection of the fingers, the tiny fingernails and hairline creases of joints and knuckles. To look into the intricate whorls of ears, and trace the pale downy arch of real eyebrows.

When she had inspected everything, assuring herself that every part of this small new creature seemed normal and well made, she drew the little gold necklace over the baby's head and tucked the tiny gold cross furtively inside the knit undershirt. She bundled the baby again, wrapping the yellow blanket around the thin flannel one, and lifting the whole light bundle to her shoulder, where she could breathe in its scent and her lips could just rest on the top of its small, warm head.

In the time remaining to her she would begin the motion of the rocking chair. She would find an ethereal little lullaby, ready-stored in her head to hum. It was a familiar little melody and yet one she had not been conscious of knowing.

Bayuski, bayu,
Bayuski, bayu.
Close your eyes and go to sleep,
Bayuski, bayu.

In the last of the last few minutes, she would close her own eyes. The memory of her daughter would be almost totally sensate. It would recall the whispery sound and motion of the child's light breathing, its rise and fall almost immediately entraining with her own. It would record the inconsequential weight on her shoulder, the warmth of the cheek and the sweet silken smoothness of skin. It would note the sound of the rocking chair's runners on the linoleum floor.

When Sister Martha had come back, bursting into the little room on a wind of authority, her face already set for the trouble she expected, Ana had given her none. In the last second before the warm life that she had created had been lifted away, leaving her shoulder, her neck, her heart, with a cool, ghostly emptiness that she would feel for the rest of her life, there'd been only time enough time to whisper a few words into a scrunched pink ear.

"I'm sorry," she said. "But I won't forget you. I promise. I won't forget."

Chapter XXV.

Abby had never liked Sundays. As a small child they had always seemed only dull and idling to her, but later, certainly by the time she'd become an adolescent, there was reason to dislike them intensely. By then Mother had found God, and the entire day could be wasted with Sunday School and church, the stream of tortuous visitations and righteous company. They were whole days then to be lost to your own plans and your own friends. To any hope, usually, of hanging out at the drugstore, or of riding with the rest of the gang in Butch Lipton's new convertible.

Sundays had been a problem, too, through all the years of her marriage to Alan Greenberg. There was something about Sundays, so curiously fraught with the expectation of intimacy, which had somehow made her loneliness even more acute. On Sundays, their separate islands had always seemed more distant than ever.

Gordon, at last, had changed all that. For two Sundays a month now there was sleeping late, leisurely breakfasts, the companionable sharing of the newspaper. On some Sundays they went to the lake. In the springs, they gardened together. Best of all were those Sundays when they never advanced beyond pajamas and the entire day was spent in a slow adagio of reading and listening to music, of talking and walking and holding hands. Gordon, at least, had redeemed half of her Sundays. But there were still the other two. On the other two Sundays she was obliged to visit Charlie.

It was a duty that Abby didn't hate outright. She was glad to split the month of Sundays with Ana and felt considerable guilt because Ana wouldn't allow her a greater share of the burden.

But Abby still approached her Sunday duty with a feeling of dread. And usually, once she had fulfilled it, she wasn't even sure that her visit had really mattered.

On this particular Sunday at least, her spirits were marginally higher. The ninety-minute drive to Atlanta had gone quickly, her thoughts preoccupied with last night's phone call from her niece and with Ana's startling news. It seemed too good to be true. That Richie had actually found Ana's child. She had listened carefully while Ana explained the solid basis of Richie's evidence and she had heard the trembling hope in Ana's voice. Abby wanted to believe it. Certainly for Ana's sake, but also for her own. Maria had asked her for one thing only. That she should watch over Ana. But in that one thing only, Abby had failed. There was no way to know, now, what might have been different. How much that broken promise had altered Ana's life.

Abby shook her head, trying to chase away her pessimism. Ana had been disappointed before. But she was a strong, practical girl. She would manage, again, if Riche were wrong. And this time, if Richie should be right, it could change everything. It might bring the healing that Ana—that both of them—needed. For now, anyway, it was all only conjecture. In the meantime, it was still a beautiful day.

She had determined to make this Sunday's visit with her brother a pleasant one. On the seat beside her she carried a cookie tin of the imported shortbreads that Charlie liked, and she'd resolved today to try to get him outside for a bit. They'd walk the grounds a little. Talk in the sunshine. And no matter what happened, she'd be patient with him. No arguments or explosions today. Just a nice, pleasant little visit.

The Center's parking lot was almost full today—a surprise, in a way, since poor weather, not good, usually inspired the relatives and friends of patients in the Autumn Breeze Rehabilitation Center to sacrifice their Sundays. Today it took two passes around the sprawling two-story structure before she found a place to park, collected her things, and traced the sidewalk up to the Center's main lobby.

She pushed through the glass doors of the Center, her feet sinking into the deep pile of the lobby carpeting and her smile already in place for Lindy Myers, the pretty young receptionist who sat, on Sundays, at a Queen Anne desk, anchored on one end by a vase of fresh flowers. The young woman's only job, as far as Abby could tell, was to operate the buzzer that allowed visitors, but not residents, to exit the Center. Today, though, Lindy actually seemed busy. Recruiting, most likely. A middle-aged couple stood at the corner of her desk, studying the Center's colored brochures. Abby gave Lindy an encouraging little wink, breezed past, and turned into the east corridor.

The first rooms on this hall, numbers 104 and 106, were empty this afternoon, but through the open door of 108, she waved at Helen Decker, who was spoon-feeding her husband something from a white bowl. The Deckers were in their 70s and had recently celebrated their fiftieth anniversary here in the Center. But Marcus Decker's last stroke had made it a sad milestone. Marcus could not even speak coherently anymore. Helen said he'd mostly stopped trying.

In a few more strides she had passed Room 110, where Benny Pintor, a quadriplegic, sat alone in his wheelchair, his head lolling unnaturally to one side. The Autumn Breeze Convalescent Center was euphemistically named. The majority of the residents here were elderly, not really convalescing from anything. They would not recuperate from old age, or from minds and bodies that had reached, not the autumn, but the winter of their lives.

There were certainly a few exceptions. An eighteen-year-old had gone home last month after recovering from a horrible bicycle accident. There was Benny Pintor here, and in the east wing that sweet Millie Harrell, a Down's syndrome victim who was probably not twenty years old. Charlie, too, in his own way, was something of an exception. At 64, he was far younger than most of the Center's other residents. But Charlie had lived, at least. He'd had a chance at least, at his own success and error. Maybe Charlie was part of the pathos in these halls. But these young people seemed the real tragedy.

She wondered how she would find him today. In a way, *who* she would find today. Like most of the patients here, Charlie had good days and bad. On some visits she would find him alert, coherent, seemingly in the present. He could question her then about some current event, recall the names and personalities of the third, even the second, wife. At other times he seemed locked in another decade, obsessed with the Korean conflict or the Watergate scandal, a World Series, or an old girlfriend—games that had played out ages ago.

Most of the time he lived in a place where past and present were mysteriously fused. Where the redheaded charge nurse was someone he was dating on the base at Kunming. Or the glass paperweight atop his stack of newspaper clippings was a sales award he'd only just received. His own ancient history could be very close to him then and sometimes he recalled details from it in startling clarity. But there were definitely some memories that he couldn't access. Or that he wouldn't. Not once had he ever mentioned Ana's mother—a fact that probably shouldn't be surprising, since all of them, except Abby and Gordon, had stopping speaking of her long ago. But it did seem, though, as often as Charlie's mind had lately begun returning to his youth, to the war, and to Shanghai, that the name or memory of Maria Petrova would sometimes surface.

Abby had worried at first, for her own sake and for Ana's, about what the creeping dementia might herald for the two of them. There was a genetic component to Alzheimer's, they said. It ran in families. But she was the older sibling, and had shown no signs. Gordon was convinced that President Reagan suffered from Charlie's disease, but he insisted that Abby herself was merely "a beautiful scatterbrain." And Grampy Atwood, their mother, even

Aunt Cassie, had kept their wits to the end. The doctors had concluded that Charlie's injury, the midbrain trauma from the accident, had led to the mental, and now the physical, deterioration. Charlie had begun to wet himself lately. The motor skills were going.

She had now reached the middle of the corridor and could hear the clicking of Mah Jong tiles and Mrs. Weinstein's deep, throaty voice coming from the Day Room. Charlie never played the game himself, but he had a curious fascination for it, and Abby stopped at the door, expecting to find him in a chair at the edge of their table, watching the women's speckled hands flit across the ivory tiles. But Charlie was not in the Day Room.

She continued on to the end of the hall and to the last patient room, the corner one, more spacious, and more expensive, than all but one of the others on the main floor. She never entered it without thinking about Estelle Atwood's will. About the irony of being eliminated from the will herself, only to become her brother's guardian in another two years. This, anyway, was how she spent her brother's money. With any luck, it would hold out.

She found her brother reading the Sunday paper. He was dressed and clean-shaven, wearing matching socks and polished loafers instead of the usual bedroom slippers. His salt and pepper hair was parted on the wrong side, giving it an unusual pompadour look, but still it was tidy and trimmed, and the faint aroma of talcum scented the room. He looked pretty good, actually. The caught breath she'd been unconsciously trapping escaped her with a sigh.

"Hi, there!" she said brightly, dropping her cookie tin on the bedside table. "Whatcha' up to? Catching up on the headlines?"

Charlie stretched his chin above the paper, looked lucidly into her eyes, and smiled back.

"No," he said. "I'm looking for a new car. That old Impala of mine is a wreck. The '86 models are coming out, and boy, are they beauties!" He turned the newspaper in her direction, revealing a half page of bold numbers in headlines and poor, inky graphics of automobiles.

Abby felt her jaw go lax, the breath catch again, and her brief optimism evaporate. She searched her brother's face for clues to where he was and to how their Sunday might proceed. Charlie had referenced the right year. That was tremendous, the doctor's said. On those tests of orientation to person, place, and time, Charlie rarely scored two out of three. And he was certainly correct about the Impala being a wreck! She winced at the remembered image of it that night, hours after the accident, but still there on the side of the highway, a twisted mess of steel and glass, glistening under the streetlights in its reflecting pool of gasoline and blood.

Charlie's smile seemed sincere. He wasn't making a bad joke. In whatever world he inhabited today, he was actually shopping for a new car.

"Good idea," she said, dropping to sit on the edge of the bed. "Your last road trip was a smashing success."

Charlie lowered his newspaper a little more and tilted his head quizzically.

"Where's Alan?" he asked.

"Alan?" Abby repeated. Now *that* was interesting. He had never asked her about Alan before. His mind these days was like an apothecary cabinet, little drawers of information opening randomly, snapping shut again for no apparent reason. Today, evidently, the Alan drawer was open. Gordon was likely locked away.

"You know," she said. "I'm not really sure where Alan is today. He probably has something exciting to do. A tax return to file, maybe. Shoes to polish. Something."

"That's OK," Charlie shrugged, lifting his paper again. "I just wanted some advice. I think he used to be a General Motors man, but I don't know anymore. Tell him, would you, to give me a ring when you get home?"

For a fraction of a second she considered reminding him that she and Alan were divorced. A very long time ago. You remember, don't you? The craziness! How everyone pretended to be shocked, when no one actually was. How easily Alan capitulated. How relieved he really was.

She decided to let it go. The doctor had told them to challenge him. That it was good, sometimes, to try to force him back into the present. And sometimes it worked. His face would cloud with consternation, but he would listen patiently while you explained, again, that Mother, or Aunt Cassie, was gone. That he was here, "recovering" from an accident. That it was not, after all, the sixties or the seventies. Not 1959. Or 1974. That the war with Korea was over. That Nixon had resigned. That Diane, his third wife, had really left him, and not the other way around. He could handle it, sometimes, even if afterwards he sat brooding, a wounded, confused child.

As often as not, though, those challenges could backfire. The small, seemingly palatable dose of reality you offered to him would provoke a violent, irrational rage. His anger could roar down the quiet halls of the Center, frightening the patients and bringing the attendants running. You had to pick your battles. This one wasn't worth the risk.

"Sure," she said. "I'll tell him."

"But listen," Abby added cautiously, "you want to take a walk or something? It's really beautiful outside."

Charlie lowered the paper slowly to his lap. He closed and folded it carefully, once, twice, three times, making it a fat package there on his knees.

"Why not?" he said at last. "I suppose I've got time. I need to stop at the commissary anyway."

Abby frowned. There was, of course, no commissary here. But the fact that Charlie had agreed to go meant that half the battle was already won. In only a few minutes, she had him out of the chair, his rubber-tipped cane in his hand, and they were walking, fairly steadily and at a decent pace, down the hall toward the double glass doors that led to the Center's large open atrium. As they passed the nurse's station Mattie Grayson looked up, giving Abby a pleased little smile and a wink. Charlie immediately elbowed Abby in the side.

"Did you see that?" Charlie said, his voice a lecherous rasp.

"Yes," said Abby, "I saw it."

"That woman's crazy for me!" Charlie said. "But it's a good thing you're here. I'm not of a mind to fool with her today."

Abby sighed. She would never understand her brother's peculiar attitudes toward women. He had always been focused on conquest, falling in love with the women who spurned him, or initially seemed too cool and indifferent, falling out of love again when their affection became genuine and committed. All that was over now and on some level Charlie had to know it. But it explained, perhaps, these imaginary little flirtations, his comical obsessions with recounting past seductions. *You've always been a fool*, she thought. *And now you're just an old fool.* But she squeezed his elbow, guiding him toward the double glass doors, toward the sunshine, and the open air of the atrium.

Near the center of the atrium, they found a sunny bench and settled themselves beside a bright bed of red begonias. The spring weather had lured others outdoors, too, and the little park-like space was populated with residents in walkers and wheelchairs, with patients and their attendant aides, but also with an unusual number of visitors, even for Sunday.

Under a green umbrella at one of the patio tables, a family of five had obviously exploited the weather for celebration. There was an open basket on the table, a litter of plates and napkins, and a small, half-demolished birthday cake on which remained a few burnt candles. A shriveled little woman, nearly bald and thin-shouldered, but with alert, glistening eyes, sat in a wheelchair beside the table. She was obviously the center of the gathering, the *recovering* resident, but it seemed quite clear from the solicitations of the others, their animated laughter and attention, and the tenderness with which they spoke to her, that this particular visitation was not an onerous Sunday chore.

A little girl of perhaps three or four, in a pink satin dress and charcoal sash, was pressing a tiny china teacup to her grandma's thin mouth. The child bounced and giggled each time the old lady sighed, rolled her eyes, and smacked her lips over the imaginary tea.

Abby watched in fascination and noticed that her brother, too, seemed transfixed by the little drama.

"We had a little girl." Charlie suddenly offered. "Once."

Abby frowned and turned a furtive sideways glance to take in her brother's face. He was still focused on the child in the pink dress, but his eyes were wet and glassy, his expression dreamy and faraway.

Of course," Abby said softly, placing her hand on his. "Ana! But we still have her, Charlie. We still have Ana."

Charlie shook off her hand roughly and began to rock his body back and forth on the bench.

"No!" he said. "Not her! I don't mean Ana. I mean the other one."

The other one? What *did* he mean? Was it possible that he had resurrected the memory of Ana's pregnancy? That he actually recalled that the child had been a girl? That somehow, after all this time, some prickling conscience had awakened?

"The *other* one?" Abby repeated.

Her own heart was hammering unreasonably and she looked around the atrium, trying to assess the location of nurses or uniformed orderlies who might come to her aid. Beside her Charlie had begun to rock faster. He was clearly agitated. He wanted something, some kind of acknowledgment from her, and there was a chance, a slim one, of real connection here. But there was also the risk. In all likelihood this was not what it seemed. Her own thoughts, Ana's call last night, were leading her assumptions. There was probably nothing to this at all. And she'd promised herself that there'd be no confrontations today.

"I'm not sure I understand you, dear," she began gently. "You'll have to explain . . . "

Abruptly Charlie stood up. He flourished his cane first in the direction of the little family under the umbrella and then turned to point it at her.

"Mother!" he shouted, "I'm not a fool! You've always taken me for a fool. I was a coward, but I'm not a fool. And you see, don't you, what it's got you. You see, don't you, what you've done!"

Abby gasped. Charlie's face was apoplectic with anger and for a moment she thought he might actually strike her with the cane. But suddenly his expression changed. The anger drained away and a look of abject horror replaced it. He looked down at himself and Abby followed his gaze. Across the center of his neatly creased dress slacks, a dark circle was spreading.

There was one sharp little whimper and then he was off, planting the cane far ahead of him on the walk, rowing his body after it in long, dangerous strides, plowing rudely between the young couple who had just opened the atrium doors. By the time she could react, mumble a quick apology on her brother's behalf, re-enter the building, and turn to look down the long corridor, Charlie was already disappearing into his room, dragging the door closed behind him.

Abby walked slowly to the nurse's station, waiting until Mattie Grayson finished labeling the last of a row of pill cups on a medication tray. Mattie looked up.

"Hi, Mrs. Stiles," Mattie said. "Everything OK?"

"Hello, Mattie," Abby said. "But, actually, no. My brother's had another accident. He'll need some help with cleaning himself up."

"Oh, well," Mattie said casually. "Don't you worry. I'll get an orderly. We'll fix him right up."

"Thanks," Abby said, casting one more quick glance toward Charlie's closed door before turning away and beginning the walk back toward the Center's entrance.

She was not sure about what had really happened. About what had actually transpired between herself and her only brother on a duty Sunday which she had determined would be light, pleasant, and without confrontation. But somehow the experience had undermined all the easy assumptions she'd become comfortable with since Mother's death and Charlie's accident.

She had always believed—in fact, she'd been certain—that both Mother and Charlie had escaped all the consequences of their actions. That neither of them had ever felt any responsibility for what had become of Maria or for Ana's lifelong struggles. After two short days of delirium, their mother had died peacefully in her bed, her funeral the largest the town had ever seen. Charlie's accident had seemed awful at first. But ironically it had become the very thing to seal him away. His crumbling mind would never have to come to terms with any of the past.

This Abby had always believed. She wasn't so certain now. She didn't know what had really happened with Charlie today. She could never know for sure what surreal worlds he inhabited. Or what faces might float up in a person's dying fever.

One thing, though, was certain. If Charlie had escaped the torments of guilt, he was also deprived of joy. In another hour and a half, she'd be home. Gordon would be waiting for her, one of his odd little Sunday suppers already assembled. But wherever Charlie was, he was all alone.

Chapter XXVI.

Richie had offered to drive her. "I'll wait in the car," he'd said. "You just take your time. But I'll be there when you're done."

Abby had made a similar offer.

"I don't think you should go there alone," she'd said. "You don't know these people, Ana. How they'll treat you. It could be pretty rough."

Ana had declined both offers, knowing full well that she might regret her decision. It could be delicate, this meeting. Antagonistic, perhaps. And ultimately disappointing. One couldn't really know what to expect when meeting the couple who had reared your child.

She knew that once, long ago now, these people must have given her a good deal of thought. In the first years, after the birth, she had felt an intense psychic connection to them. She had almost felt them wondering about her, imagining her, even as she wondered about them. She knew that her child had been adopted. It was one of the promises made by the Sisters. Her baby would go to a good Christian family. A loving home. Her daughter would grow up normally, happily, without the stigma of sin and shame.

She had spent her life concocting narratives about the people who had fulfilled that promise. She had made up pictures and stories, changing the pictures and the stories over the years as her own circumstances had made a new twist, a different narrative, more appealing. She had obsessed about these people, and, in the beginning, they had surely thought about her.

But time had passed. A lot of time. Long ago now they would

have vanquished her, letting the very fact of her fall away from their minds. Until only a few days ago she would have become irrelevant to them. Were it not for her own state of mind she could almost pity them this shock.

Her own state of mind, though, did not allow for much charity. While Richie had made the arrangements, through a series of telephone calls that had spanned eight days, she had not managed even a single night of decent sleep and eaten almost nothing. Her nerves lately had been a jangled mess and there had been few times in her life when she had felt a more desperate need for emotional support. But she had turned down both Richie's and Abby's offers. This was something she needed to do alone.

The place where they lived, the midtown neighborhood not ten miles from her own house and only five from the university campus, was not new to her. She had been here before, for small faculty gatherings, and most recently, she seemed to remember, for some type of shower. Somebody's wife or daughter or niece was marrying or having a baby, doing something that required gifts and finger sandwiches and insultingly silly games. She recalled it as another of those occasions when the gnawing had been especially intense.

It was a nice area, though, of modest three and four bedroom homes, most of them built twenty or thirty years ago. Atlanta's urban sprawl in the last decades and the neighborhood's proximity to a major university had made the area highly desirable. Most of these residents had done very well on their real estate investments here. These neighborhoods had acquired a reputation for solid respectability and nothing stayed on the market very long.

She already knew the general area, but lately she had become especially familiar with the particular streets of this particular neighborhood. Once Richie had given her the address she had wanted to see the place, and for the last week she had taken to driving here every evening after work, the thought of it drawing her like a powerful magnet, even when she hadn't planned to come again. Even when she'd just promised Richie that she was on the way home.

The Bartons lived on Meacham Park. Number 1334. And she knew this street best of all. She knew the houses, the deep front lawns, the idiosyncrasies of yard ornaments and shrubbery and flowerbeds. She'd driven round enough at this time of day even to know the paperboy's route, and which houses took the evening edition of the *Atlanta Journal*.

It was different now, she reminded herself. The trees would not have been so big then. The neighbors, of course, were not necessarily the same. But these were the streets, the yards, where her daughter had grown up. These were the very sidewalks where she'd roller skated, the lawns where she'd learned to somersault and cartwheel, the driveways where she'd jump roped with friends. This was where she had grown from baby to toddler, from child to adolescent. That door, right there, could be where her first date had called for her.

Right here in Atlanta, Ana. Do you believe it? All the time. And from everything that I can find out, they're nice folks. Salt of the earth types. Solid. Been living in the same house, it seems, for better than twenty years.

Twenty years then. *Better* than twenty years, Richie had said. That meant that her daughter's entire life had been spent here. The infant that Ana had inspected, swaddled in the poorly crocheted yellow blanket, around whose small neck she had hung the little Coptic cross—the baby she had know for only a few minutes—had been growing up, blossoming, *living* only a few miles away.

Her name was *Emily*, Richie had said. A pretty name. Not the name she might have chosen, but a pretty name just the same. For years she had tracked her baby's growth in the most secret place in her thoughts. She had privately acknowledged each successive birthday, noted the time for transitions to kindergarten, first grade, middle and high school. She'd passed every Christmas for more than two decades in a familiar, irremediable melancholy, and had a particularly hard time in the sixteenth year. But she had never dared to think of a name.

Today she had started out too early, driven around the block twice, sat in the parked car now for quite a while. Their appointment wasn't until 4:00 and it wouldn't do to be early. But being late was probably worse. She started the car, eased it forward a few yards, and cut the engine again. Bad idea. She'd be visible now from a window of 1334. But it was time anyway. Or close enough. Without risking another check on her reflection in the mirror, she opened the car door, swung herself out to the curb, and walked deliberately down the sidewalk to the house.

On the front porch of number 1334 she rang the bell and immediately heard footsteps and muffled voices just beyond the door. The door opened at once and she saw them both, a middle-aged couple, the man in front, the woman standing behind, a little to the side of him. The man was tall, silver-haired at the temples, and handsome in a dignified, statesmanlike way. *She* seemed attractive, too. A well-coifed strawberry blonde. But that was all. The man blocked her, or else she hid.

"Hello," Ana said. "Are you Mr. Barton?"

"Yes," he said. "I'm Roger Barton. You must be Ana. We were expecting you."

"*Well, hardly*," the woman behind him said, her voice only a low guttural murmur, but not quite low enough.

"Charlotte! Don't be rude," he said with a little chuckle, half-turning to put an arm around the woman's shoulders and to draw her forward.

"Please! Come in. This is my wife, Charlotte. You'll have to forgive her. This has been a little disturbing for her. Well, for both of us actually."

"Of course," Ana said. "It was good of you to see me."

Inside the foyer, Roger Barton offered his hand and Ana shook it. Charlotte Barton did not extend her own hand, but she did give Ana a quick, tight-lipped smile, and surprisingly was the one to speak next.

"Let's go in here, shall we?" she said, turning to lead them down the short hall that divided the living and dining room and led to a wood-paneled family den.

It was a comfortable room, cozy with bookshelves, a coffered ceiling, and a tall brick fireplace, its mantel laden with framed photographs. The house was not large. In the trim, affluent neighborhood that Ana had almost memorized, this one seemed one of the smaller houses. But the care that had been lavished on this home had been evident even at the curb, and now inside she saw the same harmony and attention to detail, the same studied good taste and subdued elegance.

From everything I can find out, Ana, they're nice, respectable folks. He's an engineer, or was. Been in middle management for the last ten years or so. She's been a housewife, mostly, although there was a little stint running a dress shop. The girl, her name is Emily, is an only child. I tell you Ana, it's not bad. They seem like nice people. Really! And they have a lovely home.

"You have a lovely home," Ana said.

"Well, thank you," Barton said warmly. "It's all Charlotte's doing. She's the decorator, you know. But we've been very comfortable here."

"Please," he continued, "Have a seat." He motioned to a pair of cranberry wingchairs banking the sofa and Ana moved to one of them, sitting down, too close, to the edge of the seat.

"Would you care for coffee?" Charlotte Barton asked. "Perhaps a cocktail? Roger can make anything."

"Oh, no," Ana said. "Thank you."

Had she answered too quickly? It was a mistake, maybe, not to take something she could hold in her hands. She edged back slightly in the chair.

The Bartons stood for a moment, hovering, and then they both sat down themselves, almost as one, and very close together on the big floral couch. Ana saw their hands find each other's, intertwine, and come to rest on Roger Barton's khaki knee. They reminded her a little of Gordon and Abby. The old gnawing sensation stirred again.

"It was very good of you to see me," Ana said. She had already said that, hadn't she? But they were only staring.

Barton smiled at her, gave a deferent little nod, and cleared his throat. The sound, businesslike, somehow signaled the end of their preliminary courtesies.

"Well," he said, "your friend was very persistent. He's been searching for your child a long time it seems?"

"Yes," Ana said, "he has. At least ten years or so. I came into an inheritance about then. My grandmother's will. I hired Richie then, and we began looking. In earnest."

Their faces still held polite half smiles.

"Richie tried everything at first," Ana continued. "He talked to everyone who would talk to him. We even ran newspaper ads. But all the adoption records, you know, are sealed. He didn't really get anywhere. And eventually we gave up. Or at least I did. So this, finding you, was the last thing I expected. It was a surprise."

Barton's brows lifted slightly and he gave another little chuckle.

"I can imagine," he said. "Emily is twenty-three now. And we're not sure . . . well, you can appreciate . . . we can't help thinking there's been a mistake."

A mistake? Yes, there had been mistakes. Errors and false leads. Dead ends. But this wasn't a mistake. She just knew it wasn't.

"We were working with a private agency," he continued. "A Catholic agency. We were told that it was, well, that this was a welfare case. We were given to understand that Emily's biological mother was a very young girl. Without means. In trouble."

Ana's hand jerked in her lap, but she fought the temptation to bring it to her mouth.

"Ah," she said. "Yes. I suppose that would be the expectation. And I was certainly young. Sixteen, actually. Two weeks from my seventeenth birthday."

The couple stared back at her. On the husband's face there was an expression of polite, interested curiosity. The wife's was blank and unreadable.

"But it wasn't a welfare case," Ana went on. "I lived with my grandmother, you see. She had raised me after my mother . . . after she . . . anyway, no. My grandmother had *means*. It wasn't that."

Her voice had become high and jittery, unfamiliar even to her own ears. The Bartons waited. As yet she hadn't really explained anything.

"It was a small town, you know. It would have been scandalous." She paused. "You remember, don't you? The way it was. Back then?"

Now the couple exchanged a quick side look. They were both in their late forties or early fifties. Maybe ten years older than Ana herself. Somewhere in their experience there had been a girl like she had been. They knew, or had heard of, a girl, or a woman, who had found herself in such a predicament. They would remember how it was.

"But you just gave her away!" Charlotte Barton exclaimed suddenly, startling Ana, and her husband, too, it seemed, with the intensity of her accusation.

Ana lowered her eyes involuntarily, caught her own reaction, immediately lifted her gaze.

"Yes," she said steadily. "I did. I've spent my life regretting it. But I was very young. And confused. And my grandmother was a very strong woman."

"You're a Catholic then?" Charlotte asked, her voice gentler this time.

"No. I'm not. My mother was, apparently. But that's something I didn't even know when I was growing up. My grandmother was religious. Devout, I suppose you would say. But, no. Not Catholic. She didn't hold Catholics in very high regard, I'm afraid. I assumed that was why . . . why she never came. Why she didn't visit me those months I was in the Home. But she made all the arrangements. My grandmother arranged everything."

Now Charlotte Barton leaned forward.

"And the boy?" she said. "Your baby's father?"

Ana felt her pulse jump and a flush of heat ignite the surface of her cheeks and throat. She had tried to anticipate the strains of this meeting. The subjects and uncomfortable questions it would engender. She had even practiced a little with Richie, each of them trying to guess what the Bartons would want to know, where they might challenge or doubt her. They would be interested, surely, in their adoptive child's biological parents. Both of them. And they had the right to know. She had given that right to them by appearing on their doorstep. They were entitled to their questions. But she realized now that she was not really prepared for this particular question at all and she felt strangely assaulted in their asking it.

A flash of memory, less visual than sensual, sprang into her consciousness. For an instant she was there again, *with* him, in the lower bunk of the lake cabin, their bodies still damp from the moonlight swim, her own skin cool but slightly tacky as it stuttered against his, slid and pulled away, touched again. They had stolen this night, lied about their plans and slipped away from the others at the church barbecue. She had expected to get caught. Her grandmother in all likelihood would find out and there'd be hell to pay. But time was running out for them. The summer was slipping away and there were only a few days remaining now before Billy left for boot camp. They'd felt they *had* to be alone. Really alone, and like this. Just once at least, and whatever the consequences.

For an instant only she was there again. She could hear his whispering, smell his damp hair and warm breath, and feel the pulsing urgency. For the space of a heartbeat she recalled it all—that first sweet terror of consuming desire.

But this she could not tell them. This, she presumed, was not what they wanted to know. And yet there was really nothing else to tell them about her child's father. There had been nothing else to add, those many years ago, to her grandmother's inquisition. She had loved him. Or she had merely wanted him, confusing animal lust with love. It really didn't matter. Her adult life had been cautious and colorless. In her thirty-nine years there had been a few other lovers. One short, sad marriage. But there had only, ever, been that one evening of passionate abandon. A single experience with what humans called "bliss." Even to talk about it seemed sacrilege.

"Dead," she said flatly. "Vietnam. He never even knew I was pregnant."

In spite of everything she had promised herself she saw now that there was real danger of losing her composure. If she were to cry now, to break down in front of them, they would take her tears for remorse, or guilt. They would misunderstand completely. There had certainly been error. Perhaps even sin. But for all the difference that evening had made in her life she had never been able to wish it undone.

Roger Barton was now looking at her with genuine sympathy, but on the couch beside him, his wife frowned and began slowly shaking her head.

"I'm sorry," she said, "but I just don't see how you can do this! How you can just waltz in here and say you're Emily's mother! She's a grown woman now. This would be a terrible shock. And there's no proof, really! She might not be the one.

There were lots of other babies that came out of that place."

Again Ana felt her heart race in her chest. It had never occurred to her that her daughter might not even know that she was adopted. Somehow this colored everything. And yet it changed nothing. She took her time about replying.

"Yes," she said. "There were other babies. Lots of them. But this time Richie found someone who was there that night. The nurse who came from the hospital to pick my baby up. Who carried her in the ambulance to the hospital. It was unusual, you see, to pick up a baby. It had happened before, apparently. Sometimes it happened. But it was unusual, and this woman remembers it."

Charlotte Barton's face now changed, relaxing and opening up, as though now she was genuinely intrigued. Ana saw the change and took it for encouragement. She picked up speed, her words beginning to tumble out.

"And the weather that night!" she went on. "There was this terrible storm. She remembered all of that. Even the yellow blanket my baby was wrapped in. And the little necklace! I'd put this little gold cross around her neck, you see? And this woman remembered that. And she remembered, later, giving those things to the social worker and to the parents who came to get the baby. To these people who had adopted her."

From the couch now Charlotte Barton let out a sharp little cry and Ana looked up to see her own astonishment mirrored in Roger Barton's face, too. They both watched as his wife dropped her face into her hands. They saw her shoulders being to heave. Ana rose to her feet and took a step forward, but Roger Barton held up a hand to her, in request, or warning. He half stood, produced a handkerchief from a hip pocket and pressed it against his wife's hands.

For a moment Ana only stood awkwardly in the center of the room, but it seemed indecent to simply stand there looming over them and in another second she turned her back to them and took a few steps away, moving across the room toward the big fireplace and its gallery of pictures.

There was the usual assortment of family scenes on the long mantel, a few formal sepia portraits mixed among candid color photos of happy, smiling faces. They were the conventional images of family life, the trophy portraits of middle-class affluence. She skimmed the array of these without focus until one picture caught her eye and stopped her breath.

The picture was a young girl, dressed in white, a bouquet of flowers held high under her chin. It was Emily, of course. Ana recognized the face. She recognized the delicately chiseled nose and mouth, the curly nimbus of gold hair, the impish twinkle in the green eyes. It was a familiar face, but her recollection of it came not from her own memory, but from the China box. It was the face of Maria Petrova.

Her hand trembled as she reached out, lifted the frame from the mantel and pulled it to her. She stared at it a long moment before turning to face her hosts. On the couch now Roger Barton's arm circled his wife's shoulders. His head leaned against hers, and his expression was clouded with concern. But Charlotte Barton seemed to have recovered herself. She sniffed, dabbed at her nose with the handkerchief, and looked up.

"This," Ana said, holding out the picture. "This is Emily."

Charlotte drew in a long breath, rose to her feet, and came to stand beside Ana. She looked down at the picture in Ana's hands and smiled.

"Yes," she said. "That's Emily. At the Standard Club. After her graduation. We made quite a celebration of it. All of Emily's friends, and ours. It was a wonderful night! And Emily looked so lovely."

"Yes," Ana breathed, "Lovely."

For a moment they were connected there, each of them holding to the frame of the photograph. But then, in unison, they lifted their gazes and turned, their eyes meeting and holding, each of them suddenly conscious of their Solomaic tableau.

Charlotte Barton was the one to relinquish her grasp, to release the portrait to Ana's hand only, and to take a small step backward.

"What do you want?" she asked wearily. "What do want us to do?"

Ana heard the weariness, and the fear, in her voice, and for the first time she saw herself as they must see her. A hectoring bully. An intruder. An invader with a weapon that could destroy their lives.

"I don't know," Ana said softly. "I guess I don't know. I mean, how do you manage a thing like this? I don't really know what's most important here. I'm not a . . . ."

Parent? There was the crux of it, wasn't it? The reason her own claim on Emily Barton was nothing compared to theirs.

For an instant Charlotte's eyes flashed in triumph, but Ana reached out, gently touching her on the arm, waiting until the flare had subsided.

"*Charlotte*," she said, pleadingly, half-turning so that it would be clear that she was addressing both of them. "*Charlotte*," she said again. "*Roger*. I know this is hard on you. I'm not even going to tell you that I know how you feel. I don't know. How could I know? But please! Try to understand. You've got to. I've been looking for her for a long time. For *such* a long time."

And for the first time today her voice broke, so that her last words, *a long time*, sounded a fractured, pleading croak.

The frustration, the guilt, the confusion welled up, and she saw all of them trapped in a complex and delicate web that none of them had made. Maybe the Bartons didn't know what was called for here, either. But they were merely protecting what was precious to her also, and these people could not be her enemies.

"Look," she began again, speaking as slowly and deliberately as she could manage. "I won't force myself on you. If you decide not to tell Emily the truth, I'll understand. It will be very hard for me. Hard, after all this time! But I can see that you've given her a good life. At least I know that now. I'll leave it up to you. The two of you decide. *You decide!* Decide for all of us."

And then she was done. All of the tension of the last nine days had simply evaporated.

There was one more moment of frozen silence and then their faces—Charlotte's first, then his—seemed to crumble, the steely defensiveness that she had seen all evening, melting into confusion, or relief.

There was no good reason for them to trust her. Or for her to believe in them. And she had not realized, until the moment of speaking, that she could offer such a bargain. But she saw now that she could. These were good people. *Salt of the earth*, as Richie had said, whatever that might mean.

There would still be some small talk. An awkward exchange of calling cards. But in a few minutes more they would all be standing again in the foyer.

"Thank you," Roger Barton said warmly, extending his hand again at the door. "We appreciate it. We'll be in touch."

"Yes," said Ana, "we'll be in touch."

She could feel their eyes on her as she descended the steps, but she felt no heat or heaviness from their watching. On the contrary, a remarkable lightness had come on her and it seemed that her feet barely registered the tactile pressure of lawn and pavement in her path to the car.

The tears that had she had suppressed all this long day were really threatening now. But they could wait. She would make them wait. For the first time in her life she really understood what people meant when they talked about "a good cry." Oh, God, she wanted it! The good cry. She wanted, she craved, its release and catharsis. But it would wait now until she got home. She hoped that Richie would be up for it.

Chapter XXVII.

At her station in the front of the university's language laboratory, Ana roused herself out of her brooding daydream, passed the back of a forearm over her eyes, and reached across to the console to switch off the French exercise tape. The lesson had been a first semester drill on the indefinite articles, but she'd heard no student responses for at least forty-five minutes and for the last quarter hour her own earphones had been draped ineffectually around her neck.

It was a not a good time for what the education theorists called "maximum utilization" of the foreign language lab. For one thing, it was late in the day. After five o'clock was much too late for most students of an urban university to be hanging around campus. It was too late in the day, but also too early in the term. The academic semester had only just started. Even the poorest students were still weeks away from worrying about flunking their French classes.

She removed her headset completely now and stretched her neck, lifting her chin to look up at the high, small windows of the Humanities Building. The light that filtered through them had already taken on the weak, yellowish tint of autumn.

September! Had it really been that long? She and Richie had managed more than four whole months now. Four whole months of behaving like civilized adults. This had to be a record for them. And something, this time, seemed different.

He was really working on it, she knew. And her own skin, she'd noticed, had grown a lot thicker, too. It was not clear whether Richie had changed more, or she had, but many of his odd little bohemian habits seemed to bother her less these days, and he was making lots of small accommodations for her own need for structure. There'd been an easiness to it this time that had escaped them before. This time, on the big stuff, they were meeting in the middle. And they were learning to let the small stuff slide.

Ana smiled to herself. Maybe the difference was that they'd had a witness this time. In Giselle. But the cat had certainly been a neutral arbiter. She offered the same occasional affection, and occasionally displayed the same magnificent indifference, to Richie that she did to Ana herself. The cat seemed to love, or be bored by, each of them in equal measure, and this had amused them, drawing them together in a new, familial way. They'd even had a half-serious conversation about getting a dog, too. Another about putting up a live tree at Christmas. They'd discussed a mountain vacation at semester break. This time they seemed to have crossed some threshold of permanence. They were actually making plans—projecting themselves into a shared future that was stretching, at least in their talk, into months, even years.

All of that was probably over now. At least since this morning, when he'd started up again, about the Bartons.

It had seemed an ambush almost, with both of them about to leave for work and not enough time for a reasoned discussion. Richie had just poured himself a glass of orange juice and put the carton back on the fridge's second shelf instead of where it belonged on the door.

"Do you want to know what I think?" He had asked. His voice had been uncharacteristically combative. Almost belligerent. Not like Richie at all.

She hadn't answered him right away. His tone alone made her wary. But it was also the kind of wide-open question that he especially liked. A detective's question. The classic fishing expedition. By now she knew that delaying her answer meant he'd have to get more specific. She'd kept silent, not wanting to give away unnecessary ground.

"I don't think you *want* to hear from the Bartons again," Richie had finally offered. "I think that's why you made them that stupid promise. You actually *hope* that they haven't told Emily anything."

"Richie! How can you say that? Why would I have *looked* for her all those years? Why would I pay *you* to look for her?"

"Oh, you wanted to find her all right! Because you wanted to know what kind of life she'd had. To expiate your guilt."

Ana flinched. What Richie said was true enough. He knew more than anybody, perhaps more even than Abby, about the guilt that she'd lived with all these years. So, why was he doing this?

"Well, sure," she said finally, grudgingly. "Of course I did. I've always wanted to know that. I did! I needed to know that she'd been safe. And healthy. And yeah, OK, *normal*. But for God's sake, Richie, what's wrong with that?"

"Nothing," he said. "Except that maybe it stops there. Maybe you did want to find *her*. But you didn't want her to find you!"

"What? What are you talking about? What are you saying?"

"I'm saying that you're scared."

"Scared? Of what?"

"I don't know of what. Maybe that she won't like you. Maybe you won't like her! But you need to deal with it, Ana. Otherwise, what's the point? Why did we go through all of this? What did it mean? What was it about?"

For a long moment they faced one another and she saw that this, again, was one of those tipping points—one of those starkly clarifying moments when one, or both, of them might decide that it was all simply too much. That they were too different. They'd waited too late. They were simply not willing, or capable, of making the necessary adjustments—whatever behavioral or philosophical sacrifices that this plural thing—a *pair*, a committed *couple*—required of them.

Their eyes remained locked and Ana knew that they both felt the weight of the moment. Richie spoke first.

"You need to call them again, Ana," he said, softly, almost apologetically, but then suddenly, with more energy, "I'll call them for you!"

"NO!" she had shouted. And she had shouted too loudly. She had seen him flinch, and the flare of surprise, and hurt, come to his eyes.

"I've got to go," she said. "We'll talk about it later."

"Sure," he had said. "Later."

He had accepted her light goodbye kiss, even taken a few steps after her as she swept up her things and walked out, but she could still see him now, leaning slack against the doorframe, his face dark with confusion, and defeat. She knew that expression. She had seen it before.

Ana sighed, jogged her stack of ungraded papers, and began pushing them into her briefcase. She stood up, checking to be sure she was leaving the station tidy for the morning before heading for the door. She was halfway down the center aisle when a sound, from somewhere at the far end of the last row of study carrels, froze her steps. The sound had definitely been human. A low moan or a sigh, but she could not see its source and she was suddenly aware of the eerie emptiness of the lab, perhaps of the whole building.

Her heart had begun pounding and she considered a sprint to the door, but in another moment a dark head lifted above the partitions. It was Liza Hendrix, one of her senior students, cupping a yawn with her hand.

Ana relaxed, annoyed with herself over the little fright, but still surprised by Liza's presence. Liza was a good student. Not just conscientious, but almost tenacious. She approached every assignment as though it were critical, and was self-ruthless about mistakes. That intensity made her a joy, and a challenge, to teach. But it also put her classmates off, and Ana knew she wasn't well-liked. Liza was a curious girl. But she was the last person in the world who needed help with articles. And the last person in the world Ana would have expected to be sleeping in the language lab.

Liza!" she gasped, "I thought everyone was gone! Goodness, dear, I could have locked you in!"

"Oh, sorry, Miss Atwood," Liza returned, and then corrected herself immediately with a nervous giggle. "I mean, *Je suis désolé, docteur Atwood. Je m'en excuse.* I'm sorry. Really. I didn't think of that. I was just waiting for the hour to be up. "

Now Liza rounded the corner, stuffing a spiral notebook into her bulging book bag, trailing a dark sweater behind her.

"I was hoping to speak to you," she said. "Do you have a minute?"

Ana hesitated. She really wanted to get home. To find that Richie was still there. Or to find the note he'd left her. She needed to check the closet. And to ponder, again, if this was another stage in their cycle, or really the end this time.

"Well," she answered finally. "I've got to go back to my office for a minute anyway. You can walk with me, I suppose."

"*Merci,* Liza said gratefully, "*merci beaucoup.*"

Liza waited while Ana locked the Language Lab door and together they walked to the stairwell where they descended two flights to the seventh floor. Most of the University's foreign language faculty had their offices on this floor, but the halls now were silent, most of the doors closed and locked. The French Department was locked up, too, at this hour, but Liza stood by silently while Ana fished for her key. Inside the department's reception area she waited again for a stop at the bank of cubby-hole mailboxes where Ana retrieved a mimeographed bulletin, a student paper, and two pink telephone call message slips from her box.

Near the center of the department's long interior hall she unlocked her own office door and motioned for Liza to go in. As yet the girl had offered nothing by way of explanation.

"What is it, Liza?" Ana asked, "Are you having trouble with

a translation?"

"No," Liza said. "It's about the trip." She drew in a long breath. "I guess . . . well, *I know*. I'm not going to be able to make it."

"Not make it?" Ana echoed. The news was terribly disappointing. Students like Liza were the reason she undertook the trip to France every two years. And she knew that Liza had been looking forward to it, as far back as sophomore year. They'd spoken of it at least a dozen times.

"I don't have it," Liza said glumly. "I don't have the money."

"The money?"Ana repeated. This, too, was something of a surprise. She knew that Liza's family wasn't well off. Liza studied here by virtue of a small scholarship she'd won in high school and the regular student aid. She'd had a little trouble, at least once that Ana knew of, procuring textbooks by the beginning of class, but she'd managed it. And Liza had a part-time job. She waitressed at the steak house on the north end of campus. Ana and Richie went there often. They sat in Liza's section. And tipped generously.

"But you turned in the deposit," Ana protested. "And all of your reservations are already booked with the group!"

"I know," Liza said. "I know. And I did! I *had* the money. *I had it!*" She stopped, dropping her gaze to the bundle of backpack and wadded sweater resting on her lap.

"Or almost," she said, softer this time. "I'd definitely have had enough by the end of the month."

When she looked up again her expression had become hard and defiant.

"I had it," she said again. "But Ralph, my stepfather. He found it. Or he made my mother tell him where it was. She knew. Anyway, it's gone."

Ana sighed. So that was it. The explanation for Liza's visit today, and probably for so much more

"Oh, Liza," she said. "I'm so sorry. I know you were really

looking forward to Paris."

"Thanks," Liza said, shrugging her shoulders. "But that's the deal."

Across the desk Liza's eyes met her own directly and Ana saw that she wasn't seeking sympathy. It was something else she wanted.

She leaned forward now, her brow furrowed, but her expression the familiar one that Ana knew. That intense, pugnacious scholar who would never settle for less than a full, and completely satisfying, answer.

"But is it really all gone?" Liza asked. "I mean, really?" I know they said it was non-refundable. The deposit, I mean. But is there any way I can get it back? There must be something you can do. *Anything?"*

Ana frowned. She had been teaching a long time. Ten years almost, if you included assistantships. There wasn't much she hadn't run up against and few cons she couldn't see through. Every semester, a fender bender, a household pet, a younger sibling, or occasionally a more imaginative and outlandish accident, created an existential emergency for some student who had missed a test or a deadline. Every semester, grandmothers died by the score, and their funerals interfered with the syllabus. She couldn't offer to pay for Liza's trip to France. There were always students with financial hardships, both acute and chronic. And there were always students who would happily take advantage of a teacher's sympathy, the slight weakness or willingness to break, or bend, the rules. And yet this seemed different. Because Liza was different.

Ana thought a moment. Maybe there was another way.

"Well," she began hesitantly, "Maybe we can work something out. How's your typing?"

"My typing?" Liza said. "Not great." But she cocked her head quizzically. "Maybe not all that bad either. I took a course in high school. And of course we've got to type for papers. I'm not sure.

Maybe I'm pretty good."

"Well, I have a need for a typist. Not just a typist, but someone like you who can read my handwriting. You'll need to translate a little French where there are gaps. It's pretty basic, for the most part."

"Well, sure," Liza said, her voice still cautious, her expression still skeptical. "I guess I can do that. I'll borrow a typewriter. I'll set it up in the kitchen. When Ralph isn't home I can . . ."

"No!" Ana interrupted. "That won't do."

Her reaction, she saw immediately, had been too reflexive. She had startled Liza, in exactly the same way she had startled Richie this morning. This was a pattern and there was no denying it. An image of the smiling Greta, the smile not really disdainful, but certainly self-satisfied, floated into her consciousness.

"I'm sorry," Ana said, by way of apology for her outburst. "It's just that this job . . . this particular manuscript, is very important to me. I hope you understand. It's just that I can't risk losing it. I can't let it out of my possession."

She waited a moment, allowing Liza to absorb her words.

"If you're interested," she continued, "you'll have to do it here, in the office. Or possibly at my home?"

Liza's face, which only a moment ago had looked shocked and stricken, seemed to melt into amazement.

"At your house? You mean, your place?" The idea seemed genuinely appealing.

"Well, sure," she said. "I guess. No. I mean, sure! I don't see why not."

"All right, then," Ana said. "We'll make an arrangement. If you'll type up this manuscript for me, if you'll make me a couple of copies, and bind them, and get them to me by the 25th, I'll pay for the balance of the trip. Maybe you've got time to scrape together a little spending money? You won't need much. Just for souvenirs and things?"

"Wow!" Liza said, genuinely enthusiastic now. "Sure! I can do that. Cool! It's a deal. When would you want me to start?"

When they had finished their arrangements, and when Liza had finally scrambled to her feet, bubbling, *merci, merci, merci* as she bounced out of the door, fairly running back down the department's corridor, Ana leaned slightly back in her desk chair and exhaled a satisfied sigh.

Yes. This would probably work. There was really no one better qualified than Liza Hendrix to undertake the relatively simple, but delicate, job of converting the handwritten diary of Maria Petrova into text. It was a task Ana had postponed, or avoided, for years. But there was a need now, or at least there *could* be a need, to have a readable copy of her mother's journal. A copy that someone else might someday want to read.

She began collecting her things, pushing aside the student papers and the stack of pink telephone messages that could wait for tomorrow. She had already stood, and was reaching to switch off her office light when the telephone on her desk rang, startling her with its overloud sound, a signal that the call was coming from outside the university switchboard. *Richie,* she thought, turning round again, rushing to pick up the black receiver.

"Yes?" she answered, "Hello?"

"Dr. Atwood?" the voice inquired. "Is this Dr. Ana Atwood?" The voice seemed familiar, yet she couldn't quite place it.

"Yes," Ana replied, lowering herself again to the desk chair. "This is Ana Atwood."

"Ana," the voice said. "This is Charlotte Barton."

"Oh," Ana said, "Yes! How are you?"

"I'm fine," Charlotte said. "At least I am now. I know you must be very disappointed in us. Taking so long to get in touch."

"No," Ana lied. "I thought I'd hear from you. Eventually."

She had not meant to sound sarcastic, but there it was, and the long pause on the other end acknowledged it.

"Yes, well," Charlotte said after a moment, "we had to work

it out, you know. I mean, I did. I did! It was always me, really. Not Roger. But I kept putting it off, you see. And then Emily got older and it just seemed too late."

Again there was a silence, but this time it was on Ana's part. There seemed to be something she should offer here, but she didn't know what it might be.

"I wanted to call you myself," Charlotte went on. "And let you know. To tell the truth, maybe I needed to call first to make sure we'd go through with it. But we're going to do it. We're telling her tonight. We're going to tell her that she was adopted."

"Oh," said Ana, and again more seem called for, but she could not manage another syllable.

"We don't have any idea, really, how it will go with Emily," Charlotte said. "It's going to be a shock. She's very bright, you know. But she's headstrong. Intense. *Feisty*, Roger calls her."

"Is she?" Ana said, the sudden wonderment of the placid, solemn-faced infant having become *feisty* producing a peculiar shiver between her shoulder blades, a sensation that was simultaneously sweet and painful.

"You were kind to us, Ana. Allowing us the time. Leaving it in our hands. And we feel that we have to do that, too. With Emily."

"I see," said Ana, though she wasn't sure that she did see. She couldn't anticipate where this was going, but in her stomach there was a sinking feeling. Do *what*, too?

"Leave it up to her," Charlotte supplied.

Now Ana felt disappointment, and the awful sense that this unexpected call was really bringing her bad news, not good.

"We'll give her your name, of course. The card you left with us. We expect that she'll contact you. At least we think so."

"Well . . . thank you," Ana said slowly, her response drawing out as comprehension settled in. Charlotte Barton was making no promises. The purpose, perhaps, of her call, was to make exactly that point. And she wasn't offering up Emily's own address or phone number.

"Thank you," Ana said again. "That's very good of you. Of both of you. And it was kind of you to call."

"Well, all right then, "Charlotte said brightly. "I guess that's it. Maybe we'll see you again?"

"Yes," Ana said, "I'd like that. I would."

The connection ended and she returned the receiver to its cradle, continuing for some moments to stare at it as though it might yet emit some communication that she had missed. Overhead the fluorescent lights evinced an insect-like hum, loud in the empty office, and again she became aware of her extreme isolation, here on the seventh floor, and well after dark now.

She reached again for the telephone, hurriedly jabbing the sequence for her home telephone number into the buttons, enduring the protracted agony of waiting for the ringtone to start on the other end.

"*Please*, Richie," she whispered into the receiver, "Please, please, please. Just *be* there!"

She pressed the receiver hard against her ear, listening as the line now rang twice, three, four, times. This last inert hour of a normally ordinary day, usually an unreactive, throwaway time of no particular consequence, had worked a peculiar alchemy, leaving her with a miraculous crystallized focus. She knew what she wanted to do. She knew what she wanted.

But her call was going unanswered. She swallowed hard, was reaching with a leaden arm to return the phone to its cradle, when a voice, breathless, overloud, and wonderfully familiar, came through the receiver.

"Hello!" he said, and in the background there was a clatter of objects falling to the floor.

"Richie! You're home!"

"Home?" he said. "Yeah, I'm home. It's after six. Where else would I be?"

"Oh, nowhere," Ana said. 'Nowhere else in the world."

Part IV.

Emily's Doll

Chapter XXVIII.

I was twenty-three years old when I discovered that I didn't know who I was. When I learned that I really didn't know very much at all about myself. Or at least that much of what I thought I knew had been seriously misrepresented.

Like many only children, I'm sure, I had wondered about it from time to time. The only child wonders. But if she is lucky—and I was *very* lucky—her singularity will not obsess her. She will wonder, but not much more. I recall, only once, asking my parents about it directly. My Dad's answer was succinct, and memorable. *"You don't improve on perfection, kiddo!"* he'd said, and the answer satisfied me. The only child, if she is lucky, doesn't obsess.

I had absorbed, while growing up, something of the adult conventional wisdom about only children. The assumption that they must be either terribly lonely or spoiled brats, but either way, the objects of pity. As though "onliness" were a disease, an incurable condition that shouldn't be wished on anyone. My own friends, though, didn't see it that way. On the contrary, they seemed envious of my solitary status and always wanted to be at my house where pilfering younger siblings and bossy, superior older ones didn't have to be reckoned with. I didn't feel myself an object of pity. I was never really a loner. My childhood was not characterized by loneliness.

If growing up as the only child of doting and devoted parents had done me any injury at all, it was to make me too complacent, too incurious. As the self-satisfied center of our small, safe universe, I was not much for questions. I felt different from my parents. Especially in my teenage years. But what child, and especially what adolescent, hasn't had that feeling?

I'd wondered, a little, about my onliness. But I'd never considered the possibility that I might have been adopted. I didn't actually suspect that my parents weren't my parents. I had no idea that my biological father had died in a history book war or that my biological mother had come here from another continent. At twenty-three, I wasn't expecting that kind of news. When it came, I wouldn't take it well.

On the day that that I learned I was not who I thought I was I was actually worrying about much bigger things. Mom had called me that afternoon. *Would I stop by the house tonight?* She was strangely insistent that it be this evening. And that I should come around seven. And that I shouldn't bring Blake with me.

Mom wouldn't tell me more, which was annoying, but her request was a problem for other reasons. I was already late with my second round of edits for my publisher, and her assistant was leaving me snippy little messages on my answering machine. This would be the third book, the last I'd contracted for, in my three-part series for young adult readers. The first two books had been decently reviewed and sales had been adequate. Good enough, my agent had let slip, to "barely cover the publisher's nut." But they hadn't exactly made me a household name.

I didn't really know how I'd gotten here. How my grand literary aspirations had resulted in work that I wasn't exactly ashamed of, but that I wasn't particularly proud of either. In my MFA program—small, but prestigious, and historically the incubator for more than one writer who'd gone on to bloom after the budding, I had actually been the fair-haired child. I'd been the one of whom adjectives like "original" and "promising," were whispered in faculty lounges. But I hadn't lived up to anyone's expectations. Once outside the ivory tower, I'd choked on the un-rarifed air.

Still. I needed to keep my head down. To get this thing finished and get free of my obligation. I had my own novel in mind. Not a story line maybe. Not fully conceived characters. But I was definitely thinking about getting started.

Yet here was Mom's request, and that odd, creepy tone in her voice, and frankly, when you're twenty-three, your mother announcing that *there's something your father and I need to talk to you about* is just scary. It scared me.

My mother is not ordinarily an alarmist. Not usually. Oh sure, she could go ballistic over the small shit. Like in fifth grade when they'd sent home the note about the head lice. Like in junior high when my sleepover guests had broken into the liquor cabinet. She could be a little histrionic sometimes. But in real emergencies, I mean *real* ones, Mom was always the rock. If Mom's voice had that *stay calm, don't anybody panic* quality to it, something was terribly wrong.

I thought of Dad immediately. Something was wrong with Dad. There had been a late diagnosis of a degenerative disease. My Dad had a fast-moving, inoperable cancer. It was probably serious and for the first time in my relatively charmed life I was about to face cruel existential realities.

On the way to the old neighborhood, I have already projected. I can already see him in the hospital, in his web of tubes and wires, growing weaker by the day. I can see the deathbed vigil and then the Dickensian huddle by the grave, all of the mourners in black, our forms scarcely visible through the fog. I am already preparing myself.

It is almost dark when I arrive, and from the moment I enter the house my premonitions seem justified. The first thing I notice is that the house has the Lysol-and-O'Cedar smell of serious cleaning. The second thing is that mother, for crying out loud, is wearing a business suit and high heels. And more than that, they're both nervous. Their eyes skitter away from mine when I look at them and there's a stiff formality in their words and gestures.

They invite me to sit down in the family room—another

anomaly, in that all of our family discussions, good, bad, and indifferent, have been conducted at the kitchen table. But I follow them into the family room where, on the coffee table, there is a nice little plate of cheeses and pickles, olives and crackers. I still don't know what the hell is going on, but now I change my mind about the nature of the catastrophe. It seems preposterous, but maybe one of them has had an affair? Could they be getting a divorce? Maybe they've blown all their money on some embarrassing speculative investment and they've called me here to tell me, gently, that they're penniless. I still don't know what this is about, but I'm enormously relieved. Mom wouldn't put out hors d'oeuvres to announce that Daddy has cancer.

Mom starts talking first, and she begins in the best James Michener tradition. At a point much too far back in time. She starts out by telling me a lot of stuff about how she and Daddy met, in 1965, in California. How they fell desperately in love and knew immediately, from Day One, that they were meant for each other. Most of this I've heard before. There was a period in my childhood that some version of the "Mommy and me and baby makes three" story was my favorite bedtime fare, but the novelty had worn off and tonight Mom is embellishing. Some of the details are new to me and rather embarrassingly personal.

I did everything to get pregnant. We went to a lot of doctors.

There's a lot of information, but they haven't coordinated their efforts and I'm not seeing the big picture. Dad chimes in now and again to add his own tidbits.

The company really wanted me in Atlanta. A good career move. We were attracted to the Southern lifestyle.

It's a rambling mess what they're doing, but eventually they get the facts out, at least the big ones, and then it's all apologetics.

We'd just moved here.

Nobody really knew us.

There were conflicting views, back then.

Not a lot of agreement on what to do.

We had every assurance of privacy.
We never wanted anyone to treat you different.
We always felt like it was nobody else's business.
You really looked like Charlotte! Everybody said so.

When at last they stop talking, it's because they've simply run out of excuses. For thirty minutes, I've sat here, a mute, immovable object in a reeling, tumbling universe, and now they just shut up. Data delivered. Mission accomplished.

I clear my throat. Not because I need to, but because it seems the most dramatic thing.

In the last few minutes my heart has begun pounding. An oceanic roar has filled my ears and a flash fire of heat, which began some time ago in my belly, has now ascended to my face. It seems to burn hottest, just now, in my jaw, where my upper and lower teeth have welded into a solid granite whole. Even my earlobes feel radioactive.

My parents—who, apparently, are *not* my parents—are now looking at me like love-starved puppies. Their faces are pathetically needy, and yet still relieved. With their exposition delivered, they've done all they can. They are belly up, vulnerable, but trusting. They know me, they think. For them, nothing has changed.

I take my time. My voice is firm, unquavering, but dripping with sarcasm when I finally speak.

"So!" I say brightly. "*So!* Let me see if I can condense this. If I'm hearing you correctly, you're trying to tell me that I'm not really your daughter. You're saying that you always *meant* to tell me this, but, for various reasons, you just never got around to it. If I'm following the two of you, you seem to be telling me, in a nutshell, that my whole life, *my entire life,* has been a lie!"

I've handled that much fairly well. I've managed to control my voice, to keep my hands locked in my lap so that they won't see how I'm shaking. I am not so controlled as I continue.

"Wait!" I say. "I've left something out, haven't I? You also mentioned this very nice person. This very pleasant person, who turns out to be my *real* mother. And she's recently stopped by the house for tea and crumpets. And you think . . . you think it might be a good idea, *a good idea*, for me to meet her!"

My parents—who apparently are not my parents—stare back at me, blanched and wide-eyed. They have obviously discussed some possible scenarios for this moment, but I sense that I have somehow surpassed their expectations. It is one of the things I do. Secretly I pride myself on my saber wit. On the ease with which I can shock them with sarcasm, even profanity when I need to, to make the important point. It's too easy, really. One of the reasons that I've always felt different from them. It is quite possibly a generational phenomenon. But at this moment, I think not. They are aliens, these people, completely incapable of understanding irony. They cannot possibly comprehend this most essential of betrayals.

"Emily. . . " my father begins, but to her credit, Mom stops him. She has put a hand over his and I see the veins rise, an indication that the touch is not merely casual.

"Leave her alone," my mother says. "She's angry. I don't blame her. It's a lot to take in. She'll have to think it through."

And then my mother-who-is-not-my-mother stands up from the couch. She gives a little tug at the side seams of her skirt, passes a hand over her belly, and inhales.

"But Emily," she says, and her tone already is of her old self. It is the tone of the Brownie Troop leader, the P.T.A. president, the confidant matriarch. "There's one thing I want you to understand. Your father was always in favor of telling you. If that's what's going to bother you, you'll have to blame me. I was the one who kept putting it off. In my mind you were our baby. You still are."

"I'm going to bed," she says then, and "Roger, are you coming?"

My father, who is not my father, who is sitting now, head down, his hands clasped between spread knees, looks up at his retreating spouse. Wearily he stands, casting me one sheepish glance and shrugging his shoulders. He is a bear of a man, my father, but my mother has always been able to hold against him, and this is not his finest moment.

"Emily," she says. "Lock the door behind you on your way out."

And then my parents, who are not my parents, walk casually across the family room and disappear into the short hallway that leads to the marital bedchamber.

There is a peculiar buzzing noise in my head as I watch them go and for a long time I just sit there on the couch, listening to the hum of silence in the house and the eerie hisses and whispery pops of the dying fire in the grate of the fireplace. There is still a fury in me that needs release, but they have abandoned me now and there is no one to take it out on. I feel the frustration of the impotent child, the desire to scream, to kick, or to break something.

I should go home, I think. I should just go home. But I haven't processed these events yet. And in no way am I ready to take my news home to Blake. He'll behave, probably, as if I'm only announcing a new pothole at the end of the block. Why the hell, I wonder, do opposites attract? And how in the world does Blake figure into this? What kind of deranged transference has made me angry at him, too?

Eventually I stand up. In some reenactment of those adolescent date nights, when things had gone poorly, or I just didn't know how I felt about the evening, I wander into the kitchen, open the refrigerator, and stare into its soft, surreal light.

The fridge's contents, now that I'm gone and my parents are devolving to their original selves, are strange and unappealing. There are none of those little Jell-O parfaits, magically suspending banana slices in their gelatinous jeweled interiors.

There are purple grapes, but not the green seedless ones I prefer. No string cheese. No ice cream bars in the freezer. The only attraction at all in the refrigerator is a large bottle of white wine, lying on its side, almost full, and plugged with one of my mother's Murano glass wine stoppers, one of the set of six, and *please put it back in the case, would you?*

I take the bottle out, unplug it, reach into the side cabinet for one of the everyday wine glasses, and fill the glass almost to the brim.

I walk down the hall to the door of my old bedroom, reach around the corner for the light switch, and illumine my old digs. I have been away from home for years now, but my bedroom is still a shrine to my teenage self. It is still decorated in its last incarnation—the pink peppermint stripe motif that had replaced the lavender décor of middle school, which had replaced the grade school zoo theme with its giant wall stencils of pandas and monkeys and elephants. There are pictures in the family album testifying to the fact that, even earlier, my bedroom had once been done in a buttery yellow with ball fringe curtains, a Jenny Lind crib, and a changing table. I don't remember that one. This is my room.

Beyond the bed, the bookcase, and the nightstand which still holds my pink Princess telephone, the only other furniture in the room is the white French provincial writing desk, set in the center of the room's double windows, from which I could see the backyard, the tops of trees, and the ever-changing inspiration of sky and cloud.

I walk across the room, pull out the desk chair and sit down in my old place, resting my wine glass on the blurry purple spot where I'd once left my pencil-sharpened Crayola shavings a little too long on a summer's day. This is my desk. The place where I wrote my first poem, my first feature for the school newspaper, the short stories, a few of them decent, that a handful of university lit mags had seen fit to publish. It is the place where I'd struggled with the application to my MFA program, and the last place, maybe, where I'd still been blinded by the light.

On the big cork bulletin board beside the window, there is a jumbled chaos of souvenirs, mementos, and childish nonsense. There are little thumb-tacked scraps of lined notebook paper, school paper headlines, buttons, ribbons, tickets and snapshots. It's not a coherent scheme. My method of preserving these memories has been sedimentary, piling layer on layer, the grade school memorabilia mostly buried under junior high's, senior year a sprinkled icing of wallet-sized yearbook photos of friends in cap and gown. But there, sticking out just beyond a concert ticket, my eye lasers in to a single snapshot. It is a square, crinkled Polaroid of me and my California cousins—Randy and Kate—taken at that brief stop we made at the birthday party for Dad's Uncle Roderick, turning ninety years old that year of the family reunion.

I move closer and look hard into the faces of my California cousins. I actually do remember them. Vaguely. I had been envious of their suntans, but I hadn't enjoyed their games, and especially not their dog, who had followed us everywhere, in love with the scent of my crotch.

After the reunion, Mom and Dad had taken me to Disney World, making that weekend, not the reunion, the mind-sticking highlight of that summer. But the brief exposure to Dad's family had given me something. The new knowledge that our little nuclear family was part of a bigger one. That I had "relatives" like everyone else, though mine lived on the west coast.

Except they didn't. My California cousins were not my cousins. The packages and the graduation checks, the birthday and Christmas cards that I had received for years had come from suckers. From folks that Clara and Roger Barton had knowingly deceived. It must have been easy for them, play-acting from such a distance. *We had just moved here and really didn't know anyone.*

I squeeze my eyes shut on Randy and Kate and stand up, moving to the bed. I lie down, relaxing into the feel of the pillow and mattress, and in seconds my eyes feel heavy. I could easily drift off here, falling asleep in my childhood room, dreaming the dreams of innocence. I could do that. In the morning, Mom and Dad would first discover that my car was still in the drive, and eventually they would open the door, seeing me in my old bed. They would assume then that I'd forgiven them. They would think that our little rough patch had been weathered and they would exchange a look, squeeze each other's hands, close the door softly before tiptoeing away. That could happen. I could let it. But I won't.

Wearily I haul myself up. I smooth the bedspread so that it bears no sign of my weakness, retrieve my wineglass, flip the light off in my old bedroom, and grab up my handbag in passing through the family room. In the kitchen, I drop the almost empty wine bottle into the trash without returning the glass wine stopper to its case.

I slam the door, loudly, when I leave. I don't lock it behind me.

Chapter XXIX.

It is not so late when I leave the old neighborhood. It is still well before midnight, and ordinarily there'd be time to catch up with Blake before he goes to sleep. But Blake has an early flight to San Francisco tomorrow. A career-critical four-day meeting that has been his focus for weeks. I know how Blake will take my news. He'll be infuriatingly calm. Sensible. Rational. But I know, too, that he'll let me talk. Ultimately, he'll sympathize. He'll hold me if I cry. But I can't do that to him. It's much too late to drop this big new sack of existential garbage at the feet of my beloved. As selfish as I am, as self-absorbed as I feel at the moment, I just can't do that to him. I know what this meeting means to him. We can't get into this tonight.

Besides, I'm not ready to go home. I'm not ready, suddenly, for anything, because I don't know anymore who I am. Or exactly what I should be ready for. I'm different now. Changed. But I don't know how exactly.

There is one thing that I do know. That achy, bittersweet sadness that I had felt in my childhood bedroom, that almost comic nostalgia that I'd indulged over my new loss of innocence, has left me completely now. I feel nothing but anger. A dangerous anger that makes me conscious of my foot on the accelerator. *Careful, Emily*, I tell myself. *Calm down. Take it easy.*

For a while I just drive, letting the one-way streets, the serendipitous green lights, direct my route. In a few minutes I'm in Buckhead, a posh residential and business district, but also the area with Atlanta's densest concentration of bars and clubs. Buckhead is a Mecca for young, professional singles and on weekends it can look like Mardi Gras here. This is Wednesday, not the weekend, and late, I think, for clubbing, but the streets are heavy with traffic. Groups and couples laugh and talk on the sidewalks. Music blares through the open doors of bars.

Ahead of me a dark sedan begins to pull out of a spot at the end of a block. I pull up, stake my claim, and with only a little maneuvering, I'm in. I turn off the ignition, leaving the key where it is. I'll just sit here a bit. Let some time pass so that Blake can finish packing and get to bed. So that when I get home he'll be asleep and out of harm's way.

I've parked in front of a place called *Cassidy's*. It's one of the district's older establishments, not so glossy as some of the others, but also not as pricey, and its location makes it a good place to launch, or wind down, an evening in Buckhead. I've been here a few times. Not lately. Blake and I don't do Buckhead much anymore. Since we moved in together we go out much less. We're pretty domestic lately, entertaining at home when we want company. I haven't decided yet whether that's a good thing or not. It may have something to do with why we haven't set a date. It may not mean a damn thing.

But I do remember Cassidy's. It's a very narrow structure inside. Two staircases. One that leads to a small quiet area upstairs with corduroy couches and marble-topped cocktail tables. I remember that we had martinis up there, and that the service was a little slow. The basement level I recall, too, because that's where the restrooms are. It was cold down there. Maybe because it was winter? But the décor was cold, too. Concrete walls. Battleship gray. They call it *The Cellar*, and there's an Improv group that performs down there sometimes. I've never seen them, but I've read about them in *Creative Loafing*. They're supposed to be pretty good.

Casey's main floor, though, is just a bar. There are a few tables at the street, practically in the window, but mostly it's just a long, black granite bar where you can drink and watch the passing parade.

I'm thinking now about going in and I lean into the rear view mirror to check my condition. The neon tubes of the Cassidy's scripted sign illumine the car's interior with a yellow-green glow. It's an unflattering light and I look a little greenish myself in it, but that's not what I notice in the mirror.

At the top of my neck, just right of my jaw line and thus invisible in most photographs if I turn my head just so, is a rather large brown mole. It's not a hideous thing. Not raised or dangerous-looking. Daddy called it his "beauty spot" and the phrase, I suppose, insulated me from self-consciousness. At twelve, when I was taken to a dermatologist for an especially bad case of poison ivy, I recall the doctor passing a finger over it, lingering there only a moment before moving on. There's another one, very like it, on my left shoulder blade. I have a couple more, smaller ones, on the inside of one thigh.

It occurs to me now that neither of my parents have brown moles. My father has a light sprinkling of freckles all over his body, and like my mother, is susceptible to sun burn. My own skin isn't especially dark. Not even olive, I don't think you'd say. But I can tan, it seems, in an underground vault. Yet until now, this moment, I have never even wondered about these highly heritable characteristics. About my skin color or brown moles. About naturally curly hair.

I lift my hands above the steering wheel. What else is here? How many clues to my otherness have I missed, or denied? I turn my hands in the eerie neon glow and a memory comes immediately. I remember that time on family vacation in Hilton Head when Mom and I had gone together for a manicure. The little Asian manicurist had remarked that day on how different our hands were—mine and Mom's.

My mother's hands, she observed, were sturdy and "work strong," while mine were quite small and "much more lazy." Mom's fingernails are rather flat, actually. Not spatulate, but flattish. And her cuticles are conspicuously tough. My own nails are arched, thin, the cuticles almost nonexistent. It amused the little manicurist, who lifted my hand, placing it alongside my mother's for comparison, to observe that our hands—her own and mine—looked far more similar than did mine and my own mother's.

Was she nervous, I wonder? Did Mom flinch at the pointed comparison of our very different hands? How did they manage it, all those years? Whenever Irma said I was the "spitting image" of Daddy, or the countless times that someone remarked on some habit or trait, even a food preference that I "got" from one of them?

The anger wells up again, and my hands tremble like a palsied old woman's. I am just so mad! So deeply, justifiably, indignant. Not just at their deception, but with how easily I've been deceived.

There's a burst of talk and laughter on the sidewalk outside the car. The little group coming out of Cassidy's seems so happy and carefree. I jerk my keys out of the ignition and grab up my coat and handbag. I'll have a glass of wine, give Blake a little more time, and see if I can get a better grip on myself before I drive home.

Inside the door I scope the narrow room, head for an empty spot at the back where the bar turns the corner. The barstools here are very tall. I'm not. But I've perfected the little jump, the quick swivel, and the technique of crossing my legs to the side that short girls learn early on. The fellow on the stool next to me has watched the maneuver, and taken it, apparently, as deliberately provocative. In the mirror behind the bar I watch him stare at my legs until the bartender blocks my view.

"What'll it be?" the bartender asks.

"Wine," I say. "Chardonnay. Just the house."

"Done," he says, dropping a cocktail napkin in front of me before he pivots, like a dancer, and glides away.

"You're not going to try a comet? They're actually pretty good."

It's the man next to me speaking, the admirer of short legs.

"Sorry?" I say.

"A comet!" he says. The drink special."

He points to a hand lettered poster at the end of the bar. *Halley's Comet Cosmo,* it reads. *$1.00. This month only!*

"Oh, I see. But, no. Thanks. I think I'll just stick with the wine."

"It's tomorrow, you know. The Perihelion. The point in the orbit when it's closest to the sun."

It's the word, new to me, seductive in its sound, the metaphorical possibilities, that causes me to turn slightly on the barstool, to look at him directly instead of in the mirror.

"The *perihelion*," I say, testing it, making it mine. "No, I didn't know that. I read something about it in the Sunday magazine a few weeks ago. That history of Halley's Comet piece. But I didn't realize it was coming up. Or over, I guess you'd say."

He chuckles.

"Yep. It swings around about every seventy five years or so. Eleven and a half million kilometers, round trip. Some people have actually seen it twice in a lifetime."

"And you? Have you seen it?

"I have!" he says triumphantly. "I have a pretty good telescope. But you don't really need one. If you drive out of town a bit, if it's clear, and if you take you a good pair of binoculars, anybody can see it."

"Well, "I say, "You're quite the comet expert."

"Not an expert, he says. "Just an amateur. My wife says I'm obsessed. But it's just lately that I've been interested. Since I knew it was coming. The timing seemed so . . . what is the word? Auspicious! That's it!"

I'm not following this anymore, and regretting, a little, that I've encouraged him. But suddenly he beams a smile and stands up. He digs into a back pocket and produces a color photo. Of a scrunch-faced newborn.

"My daughter," he says. "Born yesterday at Northside. Seven pounds, four ounces. And you'll never guess what we've named her."

"She's beautiful," I say, taking the corner of the picture in my hand. "But let me guess. It wouldn't be Halley by any chance?"

We erupt into laughter together. It's been sudden, explosive, and a little loud, and it's attracted attention down the long bar. In another moment he's passing his picture down, grinning ear-to-ear, accepting congratulations and handshakes and slaps on the back.

At some point another glass of wine has appeared in front of me and I sip it while we chat, a little about astronomy still, but mostly now about the new baby, and the changes that will come. He's a really decent guy, and it's been interesting, but all at once I know that I need to get out of here. I feel suddenly feverish, surreal, and wish fervently that I'd skipped that second glass of wine. *Wasn't it only two?* But I'd forgotten that first one at Mom and Dad's. And I'd eaten nothing since noon.

I call for my check, but he waves me off.

"This is mine," he says. "It was great talking to you. After they threw me out of the hospital, I just wasn't ready to go home by myself. And I was dying to show that picture to someone."

"Thank you," I say, "and congratulations again."

"Enjoy that little girl!" I sing out as I push into the street.

In the car again I realize that we had not even introduced ourselves. I feel sad, somehow, at leaving him, and grateful that our exchange had distracted me for a bit from my own problems. The anger has receded, but I feel blurry, somehow out of focus. It will take concentration to make my way back uptown and to get the car parked at a not too rakish angle in our numbered spot.

Once in the apartment I go directly up to bed, removing only my shoes and skirt before slipping in next to Blake. He is sleeping soundly, his breath coming in an easy, regular rhythm. In the kitchen I'd passed his suit bag by the door, his briefcase on the kitchen desk with the airline ticket on top, and I congratulate myself again for sparing him. But I don't feel especially saintly. I just feel lonely. My head hurts like hell.

I know that I won't sleep, and yet somehow I do, in fitful stretches that drag me down into a hot, cloying darkness, and then buoy me up into a shallow half-consciousness where I feel cold and shivery. The pattern repeats all night, the light in the room becoming less inky with each cycle, until morning really does come and I open my eyes to see Blake leaning over me.

He is costumed in executive persona. The starched white dress shirt, the suit and tie. I want to tell him how beautiful he looks. I want to tell him to have a good trip and to wish him luck on the proposal. But the scent of his aftershave assaults me, turning my stomach and threatening nausea.

"You're hot, "he says, dropping a light kiss on my forehead. "I'll turn the furnace down on my way out."

He did that, I guess. It will be days before I'm lucid enough to think about anything as quotidian as the setting on the thermostat.

There is something about illness that concentrates the mind. Not as much, perhaps, as Samuel Johnson's contemplation of being hanged in a fortnight, but it will do. Especially if you are sick enough. And if you've just managed to let your fiancée go off for four days. And if you've just lost your parents.

At some point after Blake's departure, minutes perhaps, but maybe hours, it becomes clear to me that I'm not merely nursing a hangover. I'm sick. Or getting sick. And I will have to manage it on my own—a feat, it occurs to me, that I've never even had to try.

The first challenge is the headache. Something has filled my skull with concrete and I must move slowly and gingerly to balance its enormous weight. The walk to the bathroom, the motions involved in stripping the damp turtleneck sweater, the bra and half-slip that I've slept in, and in redressing myself in clean pajamas, all reverberate painfully in my head. There is aspirin in the kitchen, orange juice for the foul flora in my mouth, and I know that I should eat something. But once there I feel confused and stupidly dysfunctional. I want coffee, but brewing it seems too hard. The thought of eggs makes me nauseous. But I can make myself a little tray, dry toast and orange juice, and take it back to bed.

While I wait for the toaster I pour the juice and fill a cereal bowl with ice cubes. From the cabinet over the kitchen desk I retrieve the fever thermometer and the whole bottle of aspirin. The answering machine on the desk below blinks an insistent "3" and I push the button to retrieve the calls. The first call is from Carmen Striker, my agent's churlish little assistant. I allow her half a sentence, hear the warning about "seventeen days" before advancing to the second call, a friendly reminder from the newspaper that our home delivery subscription is about to expire. The third call is from Daddy.

"Hi, honey! Dad here. Just checking up on you. Your Mom's a little worried. Well, we both are, really. Honey, we don't want you to be mad with us. So . . . well . . . give us a call, hear? We love you."

As lousy as I feel I find myself laughing out loud at the quirky, characteristic "mad with" instead of "at," but also at the chipper, matter-of-fact tone of his voice.

Jesus, Dad! Are you serious? You don't want me to be mad with you? Why would I do that, Daddy? What could possibly make me mad?

Back in the bedroom I put my tray on Blake's nightstand and crawl back into bed on his side, cooler, and less rumpled than mine, and smelling sweetly, the aroma benign this time, of his body. I am overcome, instantly, with a helpless rush of love for this patient, long-suffering man. Our relationship, I see clearly now, has always been hopelessly one-sided. The only really decent thing I've ever done for him is to allow him to go away, leaving me sick, it seems, and newly an orphan.

I drink the juice, swallow some aspirin, and manage a few bites of toast, before all of it comes back, a spare half-second before I've charged to the toilet, but a half-second too late to get the seat up. My head has nearly exploded with the violence of my sprint and the retching, and for a moment I consider just slumping down, here on the cold bathroom tile, to wait for whatever comes next. But the purge has actually made me feel a little better. I make it back to bed, close my eyes, and surrender to real sleep.

There will be only one dream that stays with me. Only one impression that I can drag up from my fevered unconscious, or the one perhaps that buoys me up. My Mom and I are on a diving board. Both of us stand on a three-meter diving board, above a huge, blue-green glittering pool, around which an entire stadium of spectators are gathered. I can see them down there, like the audience in a circus poster, their bodies painted ovals of red and yellow and blue. They're watching, and waiting, for my dive.

I am wearing my old bathing suit. The stretchy, silky, navy blue one with the single diagonal white stripe that had been my swim team suit, the one garment that I couldn't seem to outgrow and took to summer camp, to Hilton Head, to everything, it seemed, that required a swimsuit. Mom, though, is wearing a business suit. She's up there, at the back of the diving board, in an aqua business suit and heels. She is wearing her pearl necklace and earrings.

The crowd is waiting for my dive. I can sense their expectation and the growing irritation of the judges, frowning up at me from their table on the apron. I'm taking too long. Something doesn't feel right. The board is too high, the water too far. I start to turn back, but mother is coming after me. I can hear her high heels step onto the gritty surface of the board and I know that I have to go. And so I do. I run, spring, lift my knee for the hurdle, bounce solid for the takeoff, and I'm in flight, my body executing the one and half twists perfectly, easily, and entering the water clean.

If the dream holds keys to fears I'm not in touch with, there is one level at least on which it is wholly transparent. My father has been the parent easiest to please. He was the one who took me as I was, who accepted me, complete with foible and failing. Daddy's love, his praise, never had to be earned or won. For him, the mere effort was success in its own right, and he celebrated "the good try" as though it were the trophy.

My mother, on the other hand, was easier to disappoint. She was not often outwardly critical, but there was always the sense that the report card B, the second place, was not quite good enough. It was she who encouraged me to take classes that put the GPA in jeopardy, to go to summer camps in Maine, to apply to colleges out of state. Was she just pushing me? Or was she pushing me away?

The telephone on the nightstand rings, but the phone is on my side, an impossible yard from where I lie in a sweat-drenched torpor. From the kitchen I hear my Dad's voice again, leaving another message. I can't make out his words, but I detect a little more anxiety in his voice this time. He is calling, I suspect, without my mother's knowledge. "Leave her alone," she'd said. "She'll have to work it through."

My teeth chatter over the thermometer, but I take my temperature. It registers, I think, 103. Is that dangerous, I wonder? Mom would know. But this is another little nugget of data she's never shared with me. With the last of the melted ice water in my bowl I take aspirin again, and again, within seconds, the nausea wells. Again I stagger to the bathroom, expelling this last time only a burning yellow bile and tiny pieces of something, tissue perhaps, maybe the lining of my stomach. My bladder plagues me, but I can't eliminate. I'm just so dry.

Liquids, I think. You need lots of liquids with a fever. But I'm not sure I can make it to the kitchen. Water is a liquid! I can drink from the bathroom sink. The water is cool and delicious, but the simple act of swallowing turns me around again to the toilet. Nothing is coming up anymore, but the heaving goes on.

On each trip back to the bed I feel myself a passenger on a giant cruise ship. My stateroom floor rolls with the ocean, the bed swinging back and forth before I finally capture it, heave myself in, wait for the seawater to stop sloshing in my head and the wave of dizziness to pass.

Through the fading light of afternoon, as the bedroom windows become opaque with night, I drift in and out of delirium. But the nausea has let go of me for now and I think that if I can just be still, if I can possibly get warm and stop this rattling in my bones, I can sleep.

A sepia newsreel of my childhood has begun to run in my head. It's my life, possibly, passing before my eyes. There has been footage of the big, red letter days. The birthday celebrations and family trips. But there are smaller incidents, too. Tiny, telling little things that I'd forgotten. The time that Dad had left his work in midday to come home and help me search for a lost kitten. The time, after being accepted into grad school, that I caught Mom crying over my kindergarten picture.

The telephone is ringing again, unless I'm imagining it, but I rouse myself, make the herculean effort to grab at it, tumbling the whole thing into the bed.

"Emily, is that you? Emily, are you there?"

It's my mother's voice, not Dad's. My throat closes, tears of relief scald, but I manage to speak.

"Mom," I whisper. "Mommy. I'm sick."

Chapter XXX.

There is something about illness that concentrates the mind. And my mind, once I emerged from my bout with influenza, was definitely concentrated, differently focused. The days of fever have burned away more than one of my cherished ideas.

Independence, for example, I now saw as a seriously over-rated virtue. Compared to connection, to sharing, to being tethered to friends and family—even, as it turns out, to a good nurse practitioner and a friendly local pharmacist, the idea of standing strong and alone has lost appeal. The valiant, solitary warrior was not my hero anymore. I could now see him puking over the toilet bowl, waylaid by a tiny enemy in his bloodstream, too small to be threatened by sword, or gun, or rhetoric.

I am clearer now about several things. Blake's marriage proposals, tendered so many times in the last two years that they'd become a running joke, have been translated into a date certain in April, and my parents and I are almost back to normal. My anger hasn't completely disappeared. I'm still a little "mad with them," as Daddy would say, but that anger has certainly been tempered. It's difficult to stay angry with someone who is giving you a sponge bath.

After five days of nursing me—Blake had been banished to our house—Mom had finally gone away, leaving my apartment cleaner than it had ever been, and disinfected from top to bottom. The loads of sheets had been washed and the bathroom sanitized. My refrigerator was stocked with gallons of chicken soup, but also with fruit and popsicles and Jell-O parfaits and that string cheese I like. Even my office had been organized, a charity I appreciated much less, but since she had also told Carmen Striker to back off, I found it in my heart to forgive her.

That last evening before Mom left, we had finally been able to talk a little. She had helped me to shower and to wash my hair. I was still weak, a little wobbly on my feet, but it seemed clear now that I would live. Comparatively speaking, I felt wonderful.

We took it slow and easy and did all right, really. I got to tell her how betrayed I felt. She got to apologize again, but again without offering much in the way of excuse or rationalization. She was adamant, again, that Daddy not be blamed. She didn't remember the manicurist in Hilton Head. She didn't seem to follow my epiphany over the brown moles.

But we did pretty well, actually, until the subject of Ana Atwood came up and our communication began to break down.

I don't want to talk about her. It's a bridge too far for me just yet. But Mom keeps pushing.

"Emily, I don't know what this has done to us. To our family. But especially to you. I can see that you're confused. But this woman. I feel for her. I really can't help it, can I? I mean, I was the one who got to raise you. I was the one who got to watch you grow. And she didn't."

"But Mom! She just gave me away!"

"I know. I was very judgmental in my thinking about that, too. In the beginning. I wanted to condemn her for giving you up. For whatever happened. But now that I've met her. Now that I know more . . ."

"But you don't! You don't really know who she is. Maybe she's a con artist. Someone who found out I was adopted and is going to scam us somehow!"

There's a change that comes into my mother's voice when she's had enough. When she's reasoned and cajoled all she's going to, and the patience has worn thin. It's a change in temperature more than anything else.

"Emily, she *is* your biological mother. She is. She's the one who conceived you. And carried you and delivered you. The truth is that I knew it the moment I saw her. Not because she resembles you so much. I don't know about your moles or the hair or anything. She doesn't really look like your mother. I always imagined your real mother looking like . . .oh, I don't know. . . exactly like you look, I guess. Exactly like you *are*. But Emily, I felt it. And I listened to her, too. And I know! I know because of what she said. About the place. And the timing. The details. And I know because of this."

She stands up, goes to her handbag, and extracts a tiny white envelope. She walks it over to me where I sit on the couch and turns its contents into my lap. It glistens in the plush fibers of my bathrobe. It's a little gold chain.

"What is this?" I ask, picking it up.

"It's a necklace. A cross. It was around your neck when we got you home. It's sweet, isn't it? I've always thought that it meant . . ."

Her voice breaks. For the first time in our entire evening, the first time since this whole thing started, my mother's composure is crumbling.

She drops down to sit on the sofa beside me.

"Oh, Emily, you can't imagine how thrilled we were. And how scared! We didn't know a thing about babies. I didn't have anyone to tell me things. But I always thought that little cross was a sign. Like a message, maybe, from this child's mother. She had faith. Of some kind. She must have! She had faith that her baby would be all right. And I had to have it, too. I had to believe that I wouldn't hurt you. That I could keep you safe. But mostly that I wouldn't teach you to be afraid. Just because I was. I didn't know what I was doing. I was just bluffing. Pushing my way through. And parenting is like that. It's *always* like that. And someday you'll see. But I didn't know that then. I didn't know anything then. I just had to have faith that I would be all right. So that *you* would be all right."

A mother-daughter cry can be risky. You don't really know who's comforting whom when both of you have dissolved into blubbering fools at once. But there are just times when it's the very thing. And this was one of those times.

I'm not sure how long it might otherwise have taken me to come to some peace with my new realities. The process of "thinking it through," as Mom had phrased it that first night, might easily have taken years. It may have taken the rest of my life. But my bout with the flu, the talk with Mom, and that cathartic mother-daughter cry, had so escalated my thinking process that by March I'm pretty far along. By the time that the apartment has returned to its normal controlled chaos, that our stock of groceries has been depleted, and that I have finally written an adequate ending to my adequate children's series, I've come round to thinking about Ana Atwood. I've come this far, after all. It would be cowardly not to finish the journey.

My curiosity, too, is becoming harder to manage. If Charlotte Barton is not really my mother, and not responsible for my thin, arched fingernails, my green eyes, the brown mole on my neck, then who is? If Roger Barton did not bequeath me this unruly, curly hair, then who did? If it's true, as Mom had seemed to think, that I don't much resemble my birth mother either, then who *do* I resemble? Little by little, day by day, I am evolving from the incurious, complacent "only" child, to the restless, inquisitive adopted one. Only Ana Atwood could possibly have my answers.

The little cross, and the linen calling card bearing my birth mother's name and address, have found a place on the mirrored jewelry tray on my dresser. With increasing frequency I have taken to picking up the card, reading the engraved lettering yet another time, before putting it back in its place. Until one day, without having planned to, without any conscious forethought at all, I don't put it back. I take it with me and head to the door.

The door is opened by a young woman, just a girl, much younger than I am.

"Ms. Atwood?" I say. "Ana Atwood?"

"No," she says. "But this is Doctor Atwood's residence." Her emphasis on the *doctor* is protective, defensive even. "Is she expecting you?"

"No," I say. "I took a chance on finding her in. I'm Emily Barton. I'm . . ."

From behind the girl I hear a gasp of surprise and the flurry of approaching footsteps.

"Yes!" a voice sings out. "Yes! I'm here!"

A woman now appears in the doorway, flushed and smiling, but the shock in her eyes is almost painful. I could have called ahead to prepare her. To ask, at least, if my visit would be convenient.

"Oh!" she says. "Emily! How wonderful. Please, come in. Come in!" The girl moves aside, but she doesn't go far.

This, then, is Ana Atwood. *Doctor* Ana Atwood. I am still wondering about the girl, but I step inside the small parquet foyer.

"Emily Barton," my hostess says. "This is Liza Hendrix. She's a student of mine. One of my very best. Liza has been doing some work for me. Some very *good* work, actually, and she's just delivered the end of it."

They both glance at the dining room table and at two blue stationery boxes that hold, I presume, the very good work.

"Hi," Liza says. "Nice to meet you. I've heard a lot about you."

"Really?" I say, accepting her hand. "Have you really?"

It's nothing, the girl's remark. An ordinary social grace. But for some reason it annoys me. How could this child know anything about me?

For a moment the three of us stand awkwardly in the small foyer, until Ana Atwood turns suddenly to the girl.

"Liza," she says, "Thank you so much! You've done a wonderful job. I couldn't be more pleased." She has opened the door again, and is gently escorting Liza Hendrix outside. "Come by my office next week. We'll talk about the trip."

On the stoop they exchange a few more words. The girl casts me one more glance, wounded, a little confused, before Ana Atwood has closed the door, turned, and the two of us are alone.

She looks at me—a long, top-to-bottom look that makes me nervous and takes me by surprise. I had come here to inspect her, barely considering that it might work both ways.

"Emily," she says dreamily. And again, "*Emily*." But then she gives her head a little shake and motions me toward the living room.

"Come," she says. "Sit down. I'm so glad you came. I wasn't sure you would."

I follow her gesture, moving into the living room, taking a seat in an armchair rather than on the sofa. I'm afraid she'll sit next to me. That maybe she'll want to touch me. I don't know if I want that.

It's a comfortable room. A lot like our own house, Mom and Dad's place now. It's smaller, maybe. Not so showcase *House Beautiful*. Mom has been redecorating all my life. But it's nice. Neat, except for a few stacks of books, little clusters of papers here and there, and on the end of the sofa, nearest me, an enormous yellow cat. She lifts it, lowers it to the carpet, and takes its place on the sofa.

"I wasn't sure you would come," she repeats, that dreamy quality still in her voice.

"I wasn't either," I say. "It's been kind of a . . . well, it's been a lot to absorb."

Now *that*, I think, is a masterpiece of understatement. But she nods, and smiles.

"Of course," she says. "It must have been a shock. I'd never thought that you might not know. That your parents had never told you. I suppose I should have. But I didn't."

"Dr. Atwood," I begin, but she interrupts immediately.

"*Please,*" she says. "Please call me Ana."

"All right," I say grudgingly. And then I test it. My question is arch and superior.

"Well, *Ana*, I've been wondering. Would it have mattered to you? Let's say that you knew. You knew that my parents had never told me. Would it have made any difference? Would you have come that night anyway?"

She hesitates only a moment, but she looks away before answering.

"Yes," she says. "I would have." And then, more softly, "Because I came as soon as I could."

She looks back at me again now, leans forward in her seat.

"And what about you, Emily? Do you wish I'd left it alone? Left all of you alone? Do you wish now that you didn't know?"

That, of course, is the question I'd been asking myself for weeks. I'm no closer to the answer.

"I don't know," I say. "I still don't know."

She smiles, gives another knowing little nod.

"You're not married," she says.

It's a statement more than a question and I wonder suddenly how much Mother has told her. The anger that I've come so far in vanquishing rises up again, but I provide her answer.

"No, not yet. In April it looks like."

"And he's a nice boy, your fiancé?"

I bristle at this, too. Blake is not a boy, and I'm not about to open up my personal life to this stranger.

"You're not married?" I ask, parrying her question with one of my own.

"No," she answers. "I was. Once. For a while."

"But you didn't have any children?"

There is the slightest little twitch in the corner of her mouth. I note it, but I'm not sure what it means.

"No," she says. "We tried. There were two miscarriages. I took them pretty hard. Punishment, I thought. From God. What I deserved for giving up my baby."

"But you don't now?" I ask. "I mean, you don't still think that?"

"I don't know," she says. "I'm not sure what I think. I'm old enough now to realize that sometimes we punish ourselves. God just gets the credit."

I hide my smile. It's going to be hard to dislike her. *Did I want to?* Surely I hadn't come here hoping that she'd be horrible? That she'd be dim and stupid or so morally repugnant that I'd be forced to dismiss her? To simply wipe her out of my mind and go back to business as usual. But this whole excursion, I see now, has been terribly premature. I haven't thought anything through. I had wanted to know what she looked like. Not who she is.

Even in my curiosity about her appearance I feel frustrated. This woman is tall, very athletic looking. I'm quite short—petite, as I prefer to think of it—and extremely small boned. I am green-eyed, less blonde than when I was younger, but Ana Atwood's eyes are brown, deep-socketed, almost sorrowful. Her hair is gray-flecked now, but it had certainly once been quite dark. It seems wavy, but not unmanageable. It's not like mine at all.

She is not an unattractive woman. Not really. But she's dressed rather plainly. Hardly any makeup. No jewelry to speak of. Just a watch, and not a very pretty one. It has a black leather band. She strikes me as someone almost wholly without vanity. Maybe someone past caring. She could be a religious, I think. One of those habitless nuns. But, no. Mom had said that she was a teacher.

"You're a teacher," I say.

"Yes," she says. "French."

"I never took French," I say, that same, slightly defiant tone in my voice. I can't seem to help myself.

"How old are you?" I say, "If you don't mind my asking."

It's horribly rude, my question. But she doesn't seem to mind.

"Thirty nine," she says.

I try not to look surprised, but in truth I'm staggered. I'd thought she would be older. A lot older. Maybe she doesn't actually look it. I'm not really sure. But my parents are in their fifties. It just feels wrong somehow.

"I'm twenty-three," I say, stupidly, and watch as another shadow, a quick flicker of pain passes across her face.

"Yes," she says. "I know."

I'm not sure that I really comprehend my injury to her, but I feel ashamed of it. This has been a mistake. I stand up now. I'm going. But she's on her feet, too, and suddenly in front of me, a hand on my elbow.

"Emily! What is it? You can't go yet. You mustn't! You only just got here. Please, tell me what I said."

"You didn't say anything. It's me. I don't mean to be so rude. But I shouldn't have come."

"Oh, darling, I don't mind. You're not rude. You're still angry. Of course you are. I can understand that."

She has my hand now, tugging us both back down to our seats in the corner of sofa and chair. I let her do it, let her move closer, her knees almost touching mine now, and I allow her to keep my hand, held warm in both of hers.

"You know," I say wearily, "that's what everyone says. They can *understand* that. My Mom and my Dad. Even Blake. Everybody! Everybody thinks they *understand*. But they don't. They can't! They can't possibly understand what it feels like to learn that you've been lied to like this."

"Oh, but I can!" she says. "I can imagine that."

I pull my hand back.

"Really? And how would that be?"

"Well, it wasn't the same, of course. I wasn't adopted. But my own mother left me when I was quite young. I had assumed all my life that she walked away because she didn't want us. That she didn't want my dad and me. But when I was about fifteen my Aunt Abby gave me my mother's diary."

She points now to the blue stationery boxes on the table.

"That diary," she continues, "told quite another story. The other side, you know. Most stories, I think, are like that. Two sides at least. Don't you?"

Her question feels patronizing. I'm not a student in one of her classes.

"Oh, at least two sides," I say. "Some might even have three!"

She flinches, again, at my sarcasm, but this time I feel less guilty.

"Look," I say. "I'm coming to terms with it. Whether or not you're really my mother, the cat's out of the bag. I've heard Mom's version. But I guess I'd like yours. I mean, what makes you so damn sure?"

"Oh, I'm sure," she says, and she actually laughs. "Here! Let me show you something."

She stands up, hurrying to an old mahogany secretary and opening a deep bottom drawer. It's an old thing, but beautiful, and rather out of place here in her simply furnished house. She extracts a box, another odd, old thing, heavily carved and exotic-looking. It seems sturdy, but she handles it carefully, reverentially, as though it and its contents are extraordinarily fragile.

From inside the box she takes something out, a picture, and brings it back to me. I take it in my hand, look down, and stare at my own face.

"Your grandmother," she says. "And my mother. Maria Sergievna Petrova."

This, I suppose, is what I came for, and yet it's entirely

unexpected. My heart pounds in my ears.

"I know," she says. "I had the same reaction. When I saw your graduation picture. On the mantel at your house."

This is not just my own face, but it could be my own figure, the waist small, but the torso short, the turn of the body to the camera exactly my favorite pose. The portrait is sepia, no color at all, but I know her eyes are green. And her hair, even on her wedding day, is a piled bundle of airy curls.

Ana is still talking. I'm not sure I've heard it all.

"I had promised your . . . I'd promised your *parents*, that I wouldn't interfere. I'm not completely positive that I could have kept that promise. But I meant to try. I had my translation of the diary typed. And I made copies, too, of a few pictures. What I told myself was that if I hadn't heard from them, from your parents, in a reasonable period of time, I would send them these things anyway. In case they changed their minds someday. Or in case you changed yours. I'm not sure. But at least it would be done. All I could do. At least you would know something about where you came from."

It stays with me, that phrase. *Where you came from.* I will leave Ana Atwood with a warm, a genuine, embrace, and with promises of my own that I'm not sure I can keep. But I will take that phrase home with me. Along with a few other odd things. A blue stationery box. And the portrait of Maria Petrova.

Chapter XXXI.

Each of us would come to the knowing in our own time and in our own way. For Richie and Ana it had been the nurse, old now, and hazy about months and years, but clear in her memory of that stormy night and the trip to the hospital with a newborn in a hand-crocheted yellow blanket.

Charlotte Barton had known, and known absolutely, when Ana had mentioned the little Coptic cross. The yellow blanket had succumbed, years ago, to age and hungry moths, but the little gold cross had been preserved, and Charlotte Barton knew.

Roger Barton would always say that he knew when his wife did. *Because* she did, and when he saw her heart breaking at their twenty-three-year old secret revealed.

For Blake it had been seeing the picture, the wedding portrait of my maternal grandmother, in a wedding gown made of parachute silk, an enormous bouquet of lilies held beneath her chin. He quite literally had tipped back on his heels when I'd first shown him her picture, and that had settled it for Blake.

I know, of course, what they all know. The objective evidence suggests that Ana Atwood had given birth to me twenty three years ago, on the 18th of May in The Florence Crittenden Home in Decatur, Georgia. We could confirm all this with science. There are tissue tests now with remarkable accuracy and newer ones, too, which can read genetic material. No one, I suppose, would object. But no one has suggested that we look to the science, and even that, probably, wouldn't quite have satisfied me.

There are none so blind, as the saying goes, and I wasn't ready to see. For someone who doesn't want to see the truth, who cannot open up to it, there isn't enough objective evidence in all the wide world.

Each of us would come to the knowing in our own time and in our own way. For me it would take the diary. My grandmother would have to convince me herself.

"Listen to this," I say to Blake. "Some of this is very funny!"

We're in bed early tonight. Blake lies half-buried in the pages of the evening newspaper. On the television set the local weatherman is droning on about highs and lows, but, as usual, I am propped on two pillows, reading from the manuscript copy of Maria Petrova's diary. I read an entry to Blake.

> *The Americans, when there is a little cough, say there is a "frog in the throat." The French, of course, have cats in the throat, but when I told Rowena this, and said that it was the same, she said, No, missy, it ain't, because "leastwise" a frog don't got no fleas.*

Blake laughs.

"That *is* funny. Sounds like she had her problems."

"Oh, she did!" I say. "But most of them weren't with the language. They were with the culture, I think. And with these people who didn't even seem to want her to fit it. There are places where she sounds so hopeful and determined. And then there are places where she's just so confused and struggling to understand. It's heartbreaking really. Especially when she's writing about the plans she had for Ana. All the dreams that didn't come true. Listen! Listen to this."

> *It will be so wonderful one day to go back to Shanghai. I plan that we will do it all together—Katya and Grieg, and Charlie and Ana and me. I don't expect that Madame Atwood will wish to go, but she would be welcome, too.*
>
> *Charlie mocks me when I speak of it. When I say we*

should take a steamer again, but that we mustn't book passage on a ship that stops everywhere. He tells me that I dream of pipes and that it will not likely happen while there is still so much trouble in China.

But even Charlie cannot know the future. I persist in it. One day we will all go, and Mama and Papa will see our Ana.

"Wow," Blake says, "That's pretty sad. But she never got to go back, did she? And Ana, you say, barely even remembers her."

"No, she has only a few memories. She learned all about this the same way that I am, by reading this diary. Her father's sister gave it to her and . . ."

"Her father's sister?"

"Yes. The aunt. Her name was Abby. She and Maria were close. She talks about her all through the diary. "

"You're not buying it, are you? It's not sinking in."

"What? What do you mean?"

"Well, listen to you. *Maria.* Her *father's* sister. *The aunt.*"

"Yeah? That's right."

"But you realize who these people are, don't you? That's your grandfather, isn't it? And this Abby. She'd be your great aunt, right? And this horrible woman you keep talking about. This Madame Atwood. That was your paternal great-grandmother, wasn't she? And Maria? Who was she?"

Blake is right, and the point he's making shakes me to the core.

I'd been reading the diary as though it were a novel, a piece of fiction. I'd fallen in love with the protagonist and the narrative voice. I'd become fascinated with her, and with all of the characters in her sad, tragic plot. But they had nothing to do with me.

My voice is small and thin when I finally answer him.

"It's sinking in," I say. "A little. I suppose I do know who they are. I'm just having a little trouble with it. With internalizing it, you know".

He puts his paper down, scoots up a little straighter in the bed.

"Even Ana? Is *she* sinking in?"

"Ana? What do you mean?"

"I mean you haven't even told your parents that you went to see her, Em. I mean, you want them to know, don't you?"

"Well, sure I do, it's just that …"

"Just what? That you're still trying to punish them? You still can't forgive them for spoiling you rotten? For giving you this great life, *on purpose*, instead of because some condom broke?"

"Stop it!" I laugh, "That's terrible!"

I grab up a section of his newspaper, try to swack at him with it, but he grabs my wrist, looks hard into my eyes. He's not laughing, and for the first time I realize that all of this has been pretty rough on Blake, too.

"Listen, Em. I don't really give a happy damn who your real parents are. I like Roger and Clara just fine, and as far as I'm concerned, they've done a decent job. Considering what they had to work with." He manages to give me one quick little grin before going on, his face clouding again.

"But honestly, Em, I mean, really! What's the big tragedy here? Where's the real injury?"

He's right again, of course. But this time I was already there. Or almost.

In my rational moments, and there were getting to be more and more of those lately, I had been asking myself exactly that question. What *had* they done to me? Nothing really, except for nursing me through colic and teething. For getting me through roseola and chickenpox and mumps. For seeing that I didn't die of tetanus when I stepped on that rusty piece of tin in the Wilson's tool shed, or from more pedestrian diseases like polio or whooping cough. For teaching me how to skate and ride a bike and swim. For coaching me in softball games and swim meets, a few hundred math tests and spelling bees, and the Graduate Record Exam. For hosting an endless stream of birthday and slumber parties and being generous and enthusiastic Santa Clauses, Easter bunnies, and tooth fairies. They'd fed me and clothed me, fought my battles and dried my tears, and never stopped believing that I was worth all that effort.

Sure, they'd lied. And I wouldn't ever really be completely OK with that. But there was a lot on the other side of the scale to balance that sin of omission.

Blake was right. I would have to give it up. But there was one more thing I had to do first.

In March, in Atlanta, the weather can be anything. The odds, even late in the month, of waking up to winter cold, to freezing rain, or even snow, are still pretty good, even though the daffodils have been coming up for weeks now and the azaleas and flowering cherry trees already think it's spring. Today, though, the weather is glorious. The worst winter of my life really seems over. The frozen inertia, the long, troubled darkness, even the lousy bout with flu, is receding into memory, and the thawing is well underway.

I haven't spoken to Ana Atwood since the day we met and by now I doubted that she expected to ever see me again. In retrospect I could see how hostile and rude I'd been to her. At least until she'd stunned me with the portrait of Maria Petrova. But I'm not exactly the same person who'd been here last time. I feel pretty confident that we can start over. I'm nervous, but not unhappy, to be standing on her little porch again, ringing her doorbell, anticipating her surprise.

I ring the bell and wait, ring again, and wait. I ring a third time. But no one answers the door. I turn away, surprised at how deep my disappointment is. I will have to steel myself for doing this again, on another day, and on one that might not be this beautiful.

I am back at the curb, my hand on the car door, when I take one more look back at her house. I notice the little wooden gate to the side yard. It's unlatched and standing half open. I retrace the sidewalk to the drive, follow the stepping stone path to the gate and on through into back yard. The yard is narrow, but very deep, with a tall hedge of some type at its far boundary. There are a few of the enormous mature hardwoods that distinguish these older, midtown neighborhoods from the piney suburbs, and beneath them there are azaleas, magenta and purple, already in full bloom, and a sprinkling of wild dogwoods, their white-green blossoms floating magically in the air .

I step through the gate and into the yard now and see that here, closest to the house, is a lovely English-style garden. It's a little winter-ragged now. There are a few hardy weeds in the untended borders, and vines, clinging to naked stakes, are dry and thready. But there's an extraordinary variety of plants in this small space, and it's easy to imagine the lush profusion that will be here in only a few weeks time.

I am taking it all in, enchanted, when I see her.

She is sitting in an old, high-backed wicker chair set on a small patio of terra cotta tiles. I expect that my approach will alert her, but she doesn't stir. In a few steps, I'm standing directly before her and I see then why she hasn't moved. She is sound asleep in her garden, her chin tilted upward to the sun as though she'd been drinking in its warmth before falling asleep. Her hands rest atop an open book in her lap.

I step closer, looking down at her, at her hands, and the book. It occurs to me suddenly that I want to know its title. All at once I feel almost frantic to know the kind of books she reads, the music she listens to, the things she likes and doesn't. The rising curiosity I have felt in the last weeks has just now, all at once, become a desperate hunger to know her, and I wonder if she has felt this all her life.

At her feet, the big yellow cat looks up at me suspiciously, swishing the tip of its tail. I'm an intruder here on her property and now a voyeur. I should speak, I think, or touch her gently on the shoulder, but I do neither. I merely stand and look at her, this stranger who is my mother.

She is much prettier than I had first thought her. She seems even younger. There are fine creases beside the eyes and a few unmistakable glints of silver in the dark hair, but her brow is very smooth and unlined. Her lips, slightly parted, are fuller, a copy, exactly, of the lost Katya's mouth. They are not so different from mine.

I don't know why it happens this way. I won't know where it came from—the impulse to make this gesture instead of another. But I am moved to give her something. And this is what I brought with me. This is what I have.

From my pocket I extract the slight chain—the proof as it were, of our connection. I lift it up and suspend it between us, watching for a moment as the tiny gold cross twirls slowly in the sunlight. I lower it then into the cup of her hands, letting its light chain cascade over her fingers.

She has closed her hand on it even before opening her eyes. I sense that even in sleep she knows what she holds in her hand.

When she opens her eyes, though she clinches it tightly, she looks only at me. She smiles. She rises. And for the second time in my life I'm held in my mother's arms.

Epilogue

Mise en Abyme

They were trinkets only, but lovely ones, and much admired among the Russian aristocracy. A set of the little wooden dolls had recently taken a bronze medal at the world's fair in Paris— that *Exposition Universelle* also distinguished by the supremacy of Russian wines, by Gustave Eiffel's marvelous tower, and a new invention they called the *telephone.*

Already the matryoshka dolls were being copied in several places in Russia to be shipped around the world. But those in the set given to Valentina Gubinova were originals, painted by the artist Maliutin himself and presented to Valentina on the birth of her first child, a girl they had named Olena.

Valentina would treasure them, allowing her children only rare glimpses of the little dolls, and when the time came to flee the Rose Palace, they were among the few of its treasures not left behind. When the time came for Olena herself to flee her homeland, they would accompany her. And, as impossible as it seems, when her own daughter, Maria, was forced to repeat the cruel pattern, she would carry them with her to a new continent.

There is only a little more that I know of the nesting dolls. Only a little more I can surmise of the astonishing chain of events that brought them to my hand. Maria, it would seem, did not share the same reverence for the little wooden dolls that her own mother and grandmother had held for them. They were toys, after all, and she had allowed her own child, the little Ana, to play with them on the Atwood family hearth. In making her great escape from the Atwood household, Maria had not bothered to take them with her. She seems never to have asked for their return.

What was I to make of this omission? Of this seeming disregard for objects, toys though they were, that had already been passed, hand to hand, by three generations of mothers to daughters?

In fleshing the bones of my story there were two paths for imagination to take. One of carelessness. One of prescience.

Maria chose to leave her diary. To entrust to Abby the record of her memories and the most personal and secret of her private thoughts. How momentous that decision would prove! How much difference it would make to all of us.

Without the diary, Ana would never have heard her mother's version of the events that had shaped her childhood. She might never have resurrected the memories of Russian fairy tales or of whirling in her mother's arms in the ballroom of the Rose Palace. She would surely not have fallen in love with French and found the work of her life, the passion also of Olena Petrov. She would never have discovered the meaning of the objects in the China box—the meaning especially of a tiny gold cross whose fragile chain would someday link us all together.

Had Maria not left her journal behind, our story would be quite different. My family album, there on the shelf, stuffed with the pictures of holiday reunions, would not attest to such miracles of love and forgiveness.

Some of its record, certainly, would still seem dull and conventional. The pictures of holiday decorations. The turkeys of many years in various stages of preparation. Table settings and candles, side dishes and desserts, sinks piled with pots and pans—all of it unremarkable.

But, had Maria not left her diary behind, there'd be no photo of Gordon, sitting with Daddy and Blake beneath the tree, frowning at the perplexing clutter of an unassembled stroller. I'd have no silly shots of Richie's beagle, taunting the cunning

Giselle. I'd have no picture of Abby, posing coquettishly beneath the mistletoe, with the handsome and gentle and outrageously funny Colonel Jack Krebs.

That single chiaroscuro portrait of Charles Atwood in profile, looking for all the world like the gentle aging patriarch of a large and happy clan, could not be in my album.

And best of all, most miraculous of all, there'd be no photos in that series that now spans a decade. There would be no pictures of me, smiling, between two mothers.

Perhaps Maria didn't forget the nesting dolls. Perhaps she left them as purposefully and deliberately as she left her diary. This is what I choose to believe. I like to think that that she left the nesting dolls for me. A bequest to the unborn grandchild who would someday wear her face. A tangible legacy that I can hold in my hand, knowing that my mother, my grandmother, my great-grandmother, held them also.

They are trinkets only, but lovely ones, and after nearly a century they are as new-looking and beautiful as when they were made. I value them, as Valentina did, and won't allow my little Jeremy more than the occasional glimpse of these little toys which would mean only play to him, but mean everything to me.

There are times, when I handle them, that I can feel Artic ice, the chill of fear and rush of panicked flight. I hear the boots of the advancing enemy and sense impending doom. At other times, when I'm thinking of Olena, they evoke only a gray sadness, a choking longing for what has been lost. When I think of Maria, though, they summon something else. Maria's doll, after all, begets Ana's, and Ana's begets mine, and the set, unbroken, is here in my hand. With thoughts of Maria, my little dolls can only emit hope, a stubborn penchant for the belief in happiness, or the belief, at least, that it can be willed, bequeathed, to others.

It may be that I make too much of Maria's intentions. Too much entirely of all of this. This much I'm sure of. We are all of us matryoshkas. All of us, whether we are aware of it or not, live our lives within, encased, and surrounded by the lives of others. We are born, we grow, we live and die within the chrysalis of what, and who, has come before. We are all of us nesting dolls. Nesting dolls all.